129

D1353140

THE LONG WEEKEND

THE LONG WEEKEND

Veronica Henry

WINDSOR
PARAGON

First published 2012
by Orion Books Ltd
This Large Print edition published 2013
by AudioGO Ltd
by arrangement with
The Orion Publishing Group Ltd

Hardcover   ISBN: 978 1 4713 3260 9
Softcover   ISBN: 978 1 4713 3261 6

British Library Cataloguing in Publication Data available

Printed and bound in Great Britain by
TJ International Limited

The Mill House
Mimsbury
New Year's Eve 1999

My darling, beautiful boys,

I know by the time you read this letter, you will be angry with me. But please, think beyond what you are feeling just now and try and understand why I chose to do this. I know you will think that I was the only one who had a choice in the matter, that I didn't give you any, and maybe this is true. Maybe I was selfish. Maybe I did it for me. But then I didn't want to have to make the choice in the first place. That's the cruel thing.

So. I hope you will forgive me, and remember me as I want to be remembered. Just as my last memory of each of you was as you should be—happy, laughing, carefree. Stay like that for ever, for me.

With all my love, every day and always,

Mummy xx

Prologue

Even now, after seven years, the smell of him after a night's sleep, the faint, sharp scent of his sweat mingled with Issey Miyake, makes her shimmer inside.

He has a full mouth and a broken nose—the story of how it was broken changes depending on how much he has drunk and who he is with—and his dark-brown curls are still pinned down by the bandanna he wears to tame them while he works. His lids flutter slightly in his sleep, hiding greeny-yellow eyes that sometimes burn orange. He turns, and the aftermath of half a bottle of grappa hits her, so raw it makes her eyes water. He needs to wind down, he tells her, after a night in the kitchen.

She doesn't buy that for a minute. He can do it with his eyes shut, cooking for a dining room full of people. It's like breathing to him. Second nature.

Excess, too, is in his nature. Which is partly what she loves about him. But partly the problem. He will sleep now till gone eleven. Whereas she'll get up in ten minutes' time. She always wakes before the alarm for fear that it might never go off. One of them has to be up. A hotel, after all, does not run itself, and the staff are only as good as the person pulling their strings.

And Claire Marlowe is great at string-pulling. She is the mistress of delegation, of discretion, of diplomacy, of multitasking.

Luca is good at cooking. And talking. And partying. And drinking. Which is why people want to eat in his restaurant and stay in his hotel.

Luca is a legend.

Living with a legend is exhausting, and Claire is

3

tired. The very marrow of her bones yearns for rest. But this is going to be the busiest weekend of the year so far. The forecast is wonderful: guaranteed sunshine and warmth. It's a chance for the population to kick back and relax. Unless they work in a pub or a bar or a garden centre.

Or a five-star townhouse hotel by the sea.

She flicks the alarm to 'off' before it squawks. She doesn't need it to tell her it's time to get up. She throws back the duvet. Beside her, Luca stirs. He reaches out an arm and curls it round her before she can roll out of bed. She feels his hand slide up and down her flank. Immediately her weary bones turn to liquid; she shuts her eyes for a moment.

You can't base a relationship on sex, she thinks. You can't live with someone and excuse the fact that they take you totally for granted, just because their very touch makes you want to die.

Can you?

Outside she can hear the sound of the dustcarts collecting the recycling. Crash after crash as a week's worth of empty bottles consumed by the residents of Fore Street disappears into the gaping yellow cavern. Bottles of milk, Merlot and mineral water shatter into shards with a satisfying smash. She feels sure the men make as much noise as they possibly can, although it is barely six. Wouldn't you, if it was your job to collect other people's rubbish?

She rolls out of Luca's grasp. She's not going to give him what he wants: her unconditional yielding warmth. She's not here for his convenience. If he wants sex, he can at least do her the honour of gaining full consciousness first. Not that she's not tempted. She can't think of a nicer way to begin the day, to kick-start her body into action.

4

It's sad, she thinks, that sex has become a bargaining tool, that she is punishing him by withholding it, even though he is probably unaware of his punishment because he is out for the count. She longs to go back to when they first met, when she gave herself freely and willingly without thinking twice.

But things have changed since then. Now they have responsibilities. Or rather, she has. Luca floats through on talent and charm alone, leaving Claire to balance the books.

That was the deal right from the start, of course. They were organic and synthetic. Yin and yang. His skill in the kitchen and her business brain combined to make the perfect team. But somewhere along the line the balance has been lost and has tipped in his favour. Claire is feeling resentful.

And there is nothing like resentment for destroying a relationship.

She goes over to the skylight in the corner of the room and stands on a chair to look out at the rooftops. They are there, the trio of seagull chicks, ugly and expectant. She has monitored their progress since the day they hatched. She feels a tug deep inside her whenever she looks at them, and she knows damn well what that is. But there's nothing she can do about it. She couldn't possibly fit a baby into her life right now.

Satisfied that the chicks are alive and well and haven't fallen off the roof in their attempt to fly the nest, which they should be doing any day now, she breathes in the salty early-morning air. She can almost smell the sun, although she can't see it yet from her vantage point. She imagines it bobbing up over the estuary with coy enthusiasm, ready to greet the visitors who will be flocking to Pennfleet in their hundreds over the weekend. They will fill the

5

narrow winding streets and spill out on to the quay, as perpetually greedy for sustenance as the gull chicks. They will feast on fish and chips and ice cream and proper Cornish pasties and white paper bags full of crumbly fudge, and the townspeople will be grateful for the merry ringing of tills, if not the litter they will leave behind.

Claire pads over to the shower. Their room is right up in the eaves, because the ceiling here is too low to be suitable for paying guests—even though Luca is six foot one and continually bashes his head on the beams. The plan was for them to buy a little place somewhere else in the town to escape to, but it has never materialised. They don't have time to look. They don't have any spare cash either. When they first moved to Pennfleet, Claire used to leaf longingly through the property pages during her coffee break, looking for a dear little whitewashed fisherman's cottage to call their own, but all their money has been ploughed back into the hotel. So here they are, up in the roof. It's a nice enough room, with wooden walls painted white and one of the big sleigh beds they have in the rest of the hotel, but there's not much room for 'stuff' and barely any wardrobe space. She can only just squeeze in the selection of navy blue and black and grey wrap dresses she wears for work. She can't remember the last time she wore any of her 'Claire' clothes, which are stored away in a vacuum-pack bag. She can't remember her last day off. Even if she's not front of house, she is squirrelled away in her office doing marketing plans, budgets, press releases ...

Her shower takes five minutes. Getting dressed takes another five. By quarter past six she is at the front desk, double-checking the staff rota, praying that no one will be tempted by the sun to throw a sickie.

6

They are almost fully booked this weekend. Seven rooms and the restaurant. She will, if she is lucky, get twelve hours' sleep over the next three days. She knows this is because she is a perfectionist, but that's why they have been so successful. Because she doesn't let anything slip.

That, and Luca's formidable reputation as a chef, which has been the subject of endless articles in the weekend supplements and magazines and foodie blogs. People are happy to make the three-hour train journey from London to Pennfleet for the weekend, just to taste the clever things he does with baby squid and borlotti beans and courgette flowers; his gelati are close to orgasmic—or so says an infamous food critic, who ordered five gallons of his honey, coffee and ricotta ice cream to keep in his own freezer. He's quite the cover boy, Luca, which makes him a minor celebrity on this stretch of coast, infamous and instantly recognisable, but no one ever recognises Claire. Sometimes she feels totally invisible.

Everyone comes to The Townhouse by the Sea for the Luca experience. But nobody realises that without Claire, he would be nothing. Nothing at all.

CHAPTER ONE

Bloody seagulls. And bloody Jeff. Why couldn't he put the rubbish in the bin properly? They'd told him time and again that the gulls would rip the bag to shreds if he just dumped it on the top of the bin, but he never listened. And sure enough, the bag had been eviscerated and its contents strewn over the five square foot of grass that passed as a front garden. The grass that no one ever mowed, so it had grown as high as it could then drooped with the effort. Angelica banged on the bathroom window, but the five gulls took no notice, lighting with glee on the remains of a Kentucky Fried Chicken bucket that someone must have brought back from a night out, though heaven knows where—Angelica was pretty sure there wasn't a KFC for fifty miles. That was the price you paid for living in Pennfleet. Pretty views, yes, but none of the things that were the lifeblood of your average twenty-one year old, like Topshop or Maccie D's or even a bloody cinema.

Mention Pennfleet to most people and they thought of a picturesque harbour filled with merrily bobbing boats and quaint narrow streets lined with even quainter cottages painted in ice-cream pastels. It was the subject of a thousand clichéd paintings, many of which hung for sale in its bars and cafés, hefty price tags swinging from their distressed wooden frames. The shops sold self-consciously stylish leisure wear—ditsy dresses, sloppy sweatshirts in dusty pinks and blues and patterned Wellingtons—bijou mugs with clever-clever slogans and hand-made jewellery, all at overinflated prices.

Families thundered through the streets in an orgy of excitement, revelling in the playground that was theirs for the summer, with little regard for the custodians, the locals who held it together over the long winter months and served them their cream teas and gin and tonics. Boden-on-Sea, they called it, and in the summer you couldn't move for men in khaki shorts and deck shoes, and fragrant yummy mummies in capri pants and Chanel sunglasses.

What most visitors to Pennfleet didn't know was that if they followed the road up past the museum and forked left, past the tiny fire station and then over the hill and right into Acland Avenue, they would find a grimy grid of uncared-for terraced houses totally out of keeping with the maritime idyll it overlooked. Here was the underbelly, the residents of Pennfleet who weren't blessed with a view of the verdant mouth of the river and the sea beyond and whose only hope of gainful employment was a season of backbreaking sheet-changing or toilet-cleaning, unless they were lucky enough to have a job at the pie factory on the nearby industrial estate on the way to St Austell.

And even the chance to change sheets and clean toilets was diminishing. The hotel and café and restaurant owners were doing a lot of their own dirty work to keep costs down, and many of the B&Bs had been converted into self-catering apartments. Times were hard, and although the word on the street was that people would be holidaying at home this summer thanks to the recession, bookings so far were down. Except at the high end, it seemed, which remained buoyant, with bookings ahead for the whole summer. And for that Angelica was grateful. She had started out as a chambermaid at The Townhouse by the Sea five years ago, at weekends and during the holidays. When she left school they offered her a full-time job as receptionist, and she'd grabbed the opportunity with both hands. Then, three weeks ago, they'd promoted her to assistant manager.

She picked up her suit from where she'd left it on the floor the evening before. The black linen skirt was crumpled; the jacket not so bad. She tried to smooth out the fabric but the creases were deeply engrained. She'd have to iron it. Claire would go ballistic if she was less than bandbox-fresh. The Townhouse by the Sea was all about style over practicality. Everything was high-maintenance, from the Egyptian cotton sheets to the glittering glass and chrome surfaces in the bathrooms that needed polishing with a soft cloth. No corners were cut.

At least as assistant manager she wouldn't have to do the backbreaking donkey work any more, unless they were really short-staffed. Angelica had been thrilled with her promotion, although the gloss had been taken off that thrill by the fact that her pay packet wasn't going to show much increase.

'Our margins are so tight at the moment,' Claire had explained, her eyes wide. 'But if the summer is a success, we can give you a bonus.'

And if it wasn't? Angelica knew only too well, having lived in Pennfleet all her life, that a dull, rainy summer could be the kiss of death to any seaside business. And she wasn't convinced that the Townhouse was going to get away for much longer with the rates they were charging. Luxury was all very well, but over two hundred quid a night? Unless it was a real scorcher, they'd be lucky if they

11

weren't bankrupt by the end of the summer.

Which would be devastating. Not least for her. For Angelica realised that she had landed on her feet. She loved every minute she spent in the hotel, and she was hungry to learn everything she could. Every job she'd had before had just been a means to an end, a way to get cash into her hand, but this was different. If she was going to be stuck round here for the rest of her life—and at the moment it looked that way—then the Townhouse was the place to be stuck.

It was certainly a marked contrast to her home surroundings. She looked around the bathroom with distaste. The pink suite was ancient and cracked, dirt settling into every nook and cranny. Jeff had fitted a rubber hose-style attachment to the taps so they could attempt to have a shower, but it wasn't long enough to be any use. Angelica hardly used the bathroom at home any more. She sneaked into the en suites at work instead, during her break, checking on the rota which ones were waiting to be cleaned. She loved the powerful stream of water from the showers, the blistering heat, the herbaceous rosemary scent of the complimentary shower gel, the thick white towels . . .

How wonderful it would be to live that life all the time. Because there were people who did, she knew that. Not everyone was trapped. Although at least the trap she was in wasn't of her own making. She thought of her friends, her naïve, foolish friends, who'd painted themselves into a corner by using the baby meal ticket. She scoffed at their supposed wiliness. How could saddling yourself with a kid work to your advantage? She'd seen the scuzzy flats they'd been given; knew the meagre amounts they

12

were handed to live on. That was no future.

Of course, technically speaking, she was free to walk away any time she liked. But how could she? It simply wasn't in her to be that selfish. A trait she hadn't inherited from her mother.

She looked at herself in the medicine cabinet that hung over the sink. Milk-white skin, eyes that made up for their smallness by being a brilliant blue, fine, silky black hair that hung to her shoulders with a blunt fringe, a wide mouth with a full bottom lip. She looked nothing special without make-up, which was useful for the day job, because she could blend into the background. But come the night, with black eyeliner and false eyelashes and red, red lipstick, Angelica could paint on a face that would never be forgotten. It was just a shame there was no one to appreciate it.

Well, except one person, and he was definitely out of bounds. So she didn't let herself dwell on him any longer than was necessary.

She grabbed her clothes and skittered down the stairs into the kitchen on long legs. She pulled the ironing board out from its resting place between the fridge and the wall, erecting it with a clatter and total disregard for the fact that Jeff was listening intently to the traffic report on the radio. He was a courier, so it was important for him to find out if the bank holiday jams had already begun.

'Pour us a cup of tea, Jeff,' she wheedled, plugging in the iron and twirling the dial up high. She wasn't going to tell him about the rubbish. If she admitted to noticing it, she would feel obliged to pick it all up, and then she would be late for work. Her mother would find out soon enough, when she deigned to drag herself out of bed.

13

She could have the argument. Trudy didn't have anything else to do, after all.

Jeff reached out an arm without blinking and poured the dark-brown dregs from a stainless-steel teapot into a mug, sloshed in milk from the carton, then held it out to her obligingly.

'Ta.' Angelica held the mug to her mouth, then grimaced as she realised the tea was lukewarm. 'Yuck—it's disgusting.'

'You know where the kettle is,' riposted Jeff.

She plonked the mug down on the side as the steam came out of the iron in an angry hiss.

'Go on. Make me a fresh one. You know you want to.'

He rolled his eyes and got up, lumbering over to the kettle. It turned her stomach just to look at him, his belly bulging under the Jack Daniel's T-shirt optimistically tucked into jeans and cinched with a belt displaying a hefty gilt eagle. Add to this his wispy grey ponytail and the goatee beard . . . Angelica shuddered, wondering just what it was that had attracted her mother to him.

Actually, she knew. It was because Jeff was kind. Plug-ugly and boring to the max, but a kind-hearted soul. He couldn't do enough for her mother—well, except actually get the rubbish into the bin—and for that Angelica was grateful, because it took the pressure off her. Anyway, Jeff might look like a skank and have dodgy dress sense, but he was a million times better than her mother's last boyfriend.

Angelica had never seen why she should have to cover up her modesty while she ironed. Unfortunately Jeff's predecessor had taken advantage of the fact that she was only wearing her

14

underwear to have an experimental grope, sliding his fingers into her knickers. Angelica had grabbed his wrist, slammed his hand down on the ironing board and shoved the iron on his palm. There was a hiss of burning flesh, followed by a roar of pain and rage. It had taken the bloke a few seconds to realise what had happened.

'You mad cow! I'll call the bloody police on you. That's assault, that is. Jesus!' He had run to the sink and turned on the cold tap. 'I'll sue you into the middle of next week.'

Angelica had watched him calmly.

'I think you'll find it was self-defence,' she replied.

Trudy had come down to find out what the rumpus was all about.

'You'll have to take me to the hospital!' He held out his injury for inspection. 'She put the iron on my bloody hand.'

'The hand you had in my knickers,' Angelica pointed out fairly. 'And stop moaning. It wasn't that hot; it was only on polyester.' It had been before she worked at the Townhouse, when she was serving at the pasty shop.

'You shouldn't be ironing in your underwear!' shouted her mother.

'It's my house too. I'll iron naked if I want,' Angelica shouted back.

The bloke had never been seen again, and Angelica's mother had sulked for weeks. Until she'd found Jeff at the country-and-western night she went to at the local pub, and dragged him home. He'd been part of the fixtures and fittings ever since. He brought a little bit of stability to the household, for when Trudy had a man she

15

was definitely calmer, which made things easier to handle.

Angelica stuck the iron back in its holder with a crash.

'Put it away for me, would you?' she asked as she left the room, knowing full well that he would.

'Oi—what about your tea?' he demanded, indignant.

'Haven't got time . . .'

She raced up the stairs, checking her watch.

She'd given Dill as long in bed as she could, but if she didn't get him up now, they would be late. She pushed open his bedroom door, her eyes seeking out the shape of his little body under the SpongeBob duvet, and stepped inside, avoiding the detritus on the floor—empty DVD cases, football cards, plastic mutants with hard edges that killed your feet if you stepped on them by accident.

He was still out for the count, his headphones clamped to his ears. She could hear the tinny treble of Jessie J on a loop. He always went to sleep with his iPod on. Angelica worried that it meant his brain never rested properly. She had read somewhere that children should sleep with the light off, and no stimulation. The health visitor had told her not to worry. Angelica didn't have a great deal of faith in the health visitor, however. All she seemed to want was a quiet life, just like Angelica's mother. Neither of them really had Dill's best interests at heart.

'Hey. Sleepyhead.'

She prodded him through the marshmallow of the duvet. His eyes opened. She pulled the headphones off him gently.

'Don't wanna get up,' he groaned, stretching

16

out, the top of his pyjamas riding up to expose his belly. At eight, he still had the plump cheeks and chubby fingers of a toddler. Her little brother. Well, half-brother—none of Angelica's siblings shared a father—but he never failed to make her heart squeeze.

'Come on. You've got half an hour. Get dressed and do your teeth.'

If it was up to their mother, Dill would still be in bed for another two hours. Trudy couldn't see how it mattered if he was late for school, given that he was never going to learn much anyway. What difference did a couple of hours here and there make? But Angelica believed in routine. Routine was important to Dill, whether he or anyone else liked it or not.

He rolled over, putting his arms over his head in protest. She bent down to tickle him, and he flailed around, eventually rolling off the bed in capitulation and landing with a plop at her feet, grinning up at her in delight.

Her heart melted, as it always did. She loved him. Which was lucky, because he needed her. If she ever left, she didn't hold out much hope for his future. Trudy wouldn't fight his corner; fight for him to have a place at the local school, fight for him to be treated like a normal kid. As Down's syndrome went, he wasn't severe. But he needed continuity, stability, nurturing, discipline. None of which Trudy was capable of. Her haphazard parenting style, her volatility and her periods of black gloom were the last thing Dill needed. Not that Trudy didn't love her son—of course she did— but she didn't seem able to make the sacrifices needed to ensure he thrived as best he could.

17

Angelica tried to give him what he needed. She was as good as a mother to him. She didn't resent it. How could she? Dill was the card she had been dealt, and she was never going to leave him as long as he needed her. And it wasn't *that* tough. She could work when she wanted; go out when she wanted, because the buck didn't stop with her. The others did their bit—even her two half-sisters, Kimberley and Faye. And Jeff. But Angelica was Dill's safety net. She noticed things before anyone else, and acted on them. Her mother was inclined to let things drift. Of course Dill would survive if he was left in Trudy's care, but Angelica wanted him to do more than survive. She wanted him to get everything he could out of life. She took him swimming and horse riding. She read to him; helped him with his homework. Took him to football practice. Gave him as much stimulation as time and money would allow.

He was her little mate.

Half an hour later, the pair of them walked out of the front door: Dill with his hair carefully gelled as he liked it, in his green school uniform, his Doctor Who rucksack on his back, and Angelica, her linen suit pristine and her hair immaculate. She walked him to the school gate and kissed him goodbye with the other mothers, while their own mother slept on in bed, oblivious.

It was the same every day.

* * *

Guests invariably gasped with delight when they walked into the Townhouse. A square five-storey building overlooking Pennfleet harbour, it had once

18

been the custom house. It had thick stone walls and large windows that filled it with a translucent light. Inside the feel was opulent, steering firmly away from maritime jollity—Pennfleet was already well served with nautical stripes. The walls were covered in pale-green wallpaper embossed with birds in golden cages. A Murano chandelier hung over the reception desk, throwing a rosy glow on to the chalkboard that bore the day's weather forecast and tide times; below that hung the keys to the eight rooms, attached to outsize leather fobs, impossible to lose. A small seating area housed a chaise longue covered in burnt-orange velvet and two distressed-leather club chairs; on a round table in the middle of the hall was a glass-lined crate filled with moss and stuffed with blowsy, fat ranunculus. The air smelled delicious: fresh coffee mingled with the scent from a large three-wick candle that burned cinnamon, ginger and cardamom.

The overall effect was both calming and stimulating. Guests felt as if they were walking into a little haven that was unique and special. Claire hated the descriptions 'quirky' and 'classic with a twist'—she found both overused—but she supposed the hotel was both, though she never once sacrificed style for eccentricity. Everything was just as it should be.

She ran her eye down the list of guests for the coming weekend. The three rooms on the third floor had been booked by a stag party. Two blokes in each. Normally Claire baulked at stag events, but the best man, Gus Andrews, had reassured her. 'We're coming down for some sailing. We just want a good dinner and some nice wine,' he told her. 'We won't leave the groom trussed up naked in reception, I promise you.' He sounded civilised and was happy to leave a hefty deposit, so Claire accepted the booking, crossing her fingers that he was true to his word.

Two of the rooms on the next floor were interconnected, and could be reserved for families with 'well-behaved children over ten'. These interconnecting rooms had been booked by a Mr Colin Turner, who wanted a double in one room and twin beds in the other—for his 'friend' and her daughter. Claire was immediately intrigued. 'Friend' always had connotations.

The smallest room, the one they fondly referred to on their website as 'the Broom Cupboard', had been booked by a Miss Laura Starling. And finally, the grand suite on the first floor, with its drawing room and balcony overlooking the harbour, was reserved for their most important guests, Mr Trevor Parfitt and his wife Monique. Claire's stomach churned slightly at the thought of their arrival.

Trevor and Monique always had the grand suite, because they had a twenty per cent stake in the Townhouse. Trevor had long been a fan of Luca, when he had been a chef in London. When he'd heard that Claire and Luca were planning to buy a hotel of their own, he had jumped at the chance to invest. The Parfitts visited regularly, coming down for long weekends to enjoy the fruits of their investment, and had even bought a boat—a shiny white gin palace that stuck out like a sore thumb in Pennfleet harbour.

And now, it turned out, the pair of them had had a brainwave. They wanted to open a hotel in London, and for Claire and Luca to go in with them. They had mooted the idea at their informal

20

AGM three weeks ago. Trevor had pitched it as 'The Townhouse in the City', and Claire had felt a prickle of irritation. The Townhouse name had been her idea. Now Trevor seemed keen to roll it out as a brand, and Claire couldn't help feeling that he had somehow hijacked her concept. She told herself that that was how he had become successful, which he undoubtedly was. Not many people had spare cash to invest in a new hotel these days.

Trevor was also keen for Monique to have as much input as possible, especially on the 'dekkor' front. Claire didn't need to see their house to know that Monique would go for a Jackie-Collins-meets-Versace-in-*Hello!*-magazine look, all marble and leopardskin and glitz, which wasn't Claire's style at all.

When she expressed her fears afterwards to Luca, he just laughed. 'You can handle her. Let her choose a bit of curtain fabric and some cushions.'

'She'll want more input than that!'

'Then make her work really hard. Run her ragged trotting round London for samples. She'll soon get bored.'

Claire looked doubtful. Monique was the sort of person who would get the bit firmly between her teeth and never let go.

'Just smile sweetly and pay lip service. Then we'll take the money and run. I promise you, Trevor will just let us get on with it. It's a vanity project.'

Claire wasn't convinced of the value of being involved in a vanity project, but Luca persisted.

'Trevor won't want it to fail. And Monique will get bored eventually. Then one day we'll be able to buy them out. Trust me, Claire.'

Claire couldn't help wondering if this was what

she and Luca really wanted. Yes, Luca's ultimate dream was to have his own place in London, but they were already overstretched. He seemed to think they could just leave The Townhouse by the Sea to fend for itself, in the capable hands of whoever they chose to delegate to. Claire knew it was not as simple as that. Who, for example, would cook? People came to eat Luca's food; it was his light touch and inspirational juggling of flavours they wanted to experience. They didn't want a substitute.

She decided she wasn't going to worry about it for the time being. There was a long way to go before the dream became a reality. Instead, she printed out the registration forms for the weekend's guests, and was just noting any special requests on a notepad when the front door opened and Angelica came in.

Angelica was Claire's lifeline. When she had first started, as a part-time chambermaid, Claire had recognised something in her, a hunger to learn, a quickness that she was convinced she could harness. When she heard Angelica was leaving school, she offered to train her up as the hotel receptionist. Angelica had been thrilled—she'd been on the verge of taking a job at a travel agent in Bodmin. Claire gave her two hundred pounds to go and have her pink-streaked hair dyed back to a normal colour, and to buy some respectable clothes. And she had to take her tongue ring out. Pink streaks and body piercings were acceptable in a chambermaid, but not front of house.

Angelica had reappeared the next Monday with a dark chestnut bob, dressed in a black linen skirt (it was a little on the short side, but Claire had to concede that probably wouldn't do any harm), a fitted white blouse (again, her black bra was clearly visible underneath, but the same conclusion applied), a boxy linen jacket and a pair of ballet flats. And now, three years later, she was almost—*almost*—fit to be left in charge of the hotel. She still had a tendency to be a little sharp-tongued, and Claire was working on rubbing off these rough edges before letting her loose, but she was proud of her protégée.

She was also very protective of her. She knew that all was not as it should be chez Angelica, that she took her responsibility to her little brother very seriously and that her mother Trudy was a bit of a loose cannon. Claire never pried, but she always noticed when Angelica was feeling the strain, and lent her as much support as she could. In the meantime, it gave her a warm glow to think that she'd provided an opportunity for a local girl, rather than some smugly ambitious trainee fresh from a university hotel-management course. And in a strange sort of way they had become quite close, despite the age gap. In quiet moments at the hotel they would gossip and chat and share confidences. And once or twice, in the depths of winter when the hotel had been almost empty, they had gone off to the big shopping centre in Bristol, like two naughty schoolgirls doing a bunk from double maths, coming back laden with shoeboxes and make-up samples and the sort of dresses they would never wear in Pennfleet, but that every girl needed in her wardrobe.

In return, Angelica never abused Claire's generosity or openness. During working hours they were a team, and they both knew better than to blur

23

the distinction between employer and employee. Becoming too close to someone who worked for you could be the kiss of death, Claire knew. She thought she'd managed to get the balance right.

'Hey,' she said. 'I hope you're ready for the weekend. It's going to be a long one.'

'The car park's already filling up,' Angelica told her. She picked up the guest list and made a face. 'Mr and Mrs Parfitt? Again? They were only down two weeks ago.'

'Well, we have to be extra specially nice to them this weekend.'

'We always are,' protested Angelica. 'I go out of my way not to slap his face when he pats my bottom.'

Claire laughed. It was true: Trevor Parfitt was of the old school, the type who really didn't think bottom-patting was offensive. He called his wife 'babe' without a hint of irony.

'Trevor's not going to change.'

'No,' said Angelica. 'But why do we need to be *extra* nice? The Parfitts always get treated like royalty when they come here.'

Claire hesitated. They hadn't told anyone about the possibility of a new hotel yet—rumours like that always unsettled staff—but if the deal did come off, she was going to be relying on Angelica more than ever. She decided to take her into her confidence.

'This is strictly between you and me,' she said, 'but Trevor and Monique might want us to open a hotel in London.'

Angelica's face clouded.

'You won't be leaving, will you?' she asked. 'Because I won't work here without you. You know that, don't you?'

'I didn't,' replied Claire lightly. 'But you don't need me.'

'I'm not working for anyone else.'

'I'm touched by your loyalty.' Claire smiled. 'Don't worry, I'm not leaving yet. And anyway, it might be good for you. We'd need someone to hold the fort here if it does go ahead.'

Angelica said nothing. Claire rather wished she hadn't mentioned the London hotel, but she didn't like secrets. In her experience, they were bad news. From the corner of her eye she saw the fisherman walk through to the dining room en route to the kitchen with today's catch—she'd better check it over and sign for it.

She picked up the phone and handed it to Angelica.

'Can you call Buddleia? We need a large bouquet for the Parfitts' room and a replacement for the flowers on the front table, as well as the usual.' Angelica nodded and took the receiver from her. 'And if you can bear it, take Luca a coffee and tell him to get up. We need all hands on deck this morning.'

Claire headed for the kitchen. She needed some super-strength coffee herself, and a bowl of their hand-made granola mixed with Greek yoghurt and berries. It was going to be a long day.

*   *   *

Angelica watched Claire go, a horrible sinking feeling in her stomach. She felt unsettled. A hotel in London? What was that going to mean?

Change, definitely. Angelica didn't like change. She wanted things to stay the same, for ever.

25

Except, of course, for the things she wanted to be different. But life didn't work like that. She knew that perfectly well. She took a deep breath, and told herself that nothing was definite. She didn't need to panic yet. Anything could happen. She dialled the number of the florist, running her eye down the list of other requests Claire had written out, making a mental note of the things that needed doing first. Angelica was nothing if not well trained.

CHAPTER TWO

There weren't many people who considered Colin Turner a foolish man. On the contrary, most people had an enormous amount of respect and admiration for him. He managed to be a success without inviting jealousy. After all, there was no denying that he was a grafter. He was always on site by six o'clock, dressed in his whites, ready to get his hands dirty. He looked after his workers, and was a most generous employer. Conditions at both the cake factory and his half-dozen cafés were exemplary. He didn't try and screw extra hours out of anyone, and the perks were legendary: hefty discounts, generous bonuses and an extravagant Christmas party at a local hotel, all drinks on the house. And he had reaped the rewards of his hard work. The sleek Jaguar he was driving as he pulled on to the M5 was testament to that.

He had only ever made one mistake in his life, he reflected as he glided over into the fast lane. But it was a big one. And his only crime had been to crave affection. Physical contact with someone who didn't

26

flinch. When had he become so repulsive? he'd wondered on that fateful day, nearly twelve years ago now.

Of course now he understood. Eventually the GP had diagnosed depression and prescribed a course of antidepressants for his wife, but by then it had been too late. How was Colin supposed to know that post-natal depression could still have a grip more than five years after a child had been born? He was a baker, not a psychiatrist. By then the nights of rejection had stacked up, leading to desperation. Which in turn had led him to act on impulse, something he rarely did.

It was the birth of his second child that was to blame. For years after Ryan was born, Alison was a no-go area. The birth itself had been traumatic—a protracted labour, forceps, an episiotomy; he wished he had insisted upon her having a Caesarean when the going had got tough, but the midwives had brainwashed her into a natural birth. And for what? Months of agony, and physiotherapy, and a total aversion to sex that no one had ever seen fit to discuss with her. Or him.

Which had ended up driving Colin into Karen Griffith's arms. Or rather, legs—for Karen didn't really do affection either. There were none of the hugs Colin was craving. No tender caresses or brow-smoothing. But she did do sex. When he realised the price, it was too late.

He wondered afterwards if he'd been set up from the start. Karen insisted that Chelsey was an accident, but how hard would it have been for her to work out how much he was worth, and then lay the time-honoured trap? For Colin wasn't one to shirk his responsibilities. He would never have

27

insisted upon an abortion. He was, despite his one-off infidelity, a gentleman.

And so now here he was, on his annual guilt trip. The visit he insisted upon, because Chelsey was, after all, his flesh and blood, and even if he couldn't admit her presence to the rest of the world, he could do her the courtesy of acknowledging it to her personally once a year.

He had plenty of excuses. He was always off to trade fairs, and on research trips, and at conferences, so Alison never queried yet another weekend away. But lying made him feel sick to his stomach. He knew plenty of men who were adept at it and lied to their wives all the time: about where they were, what they were up to; about money— where it had come from and where it went. He had seen them prevaricate, glibly, smoothly, not a trace of conscience. But Colin believed in total honesty. There was no point in being married to someone if you lied to them.

As far as his Chelsey weekends went, however, he had left himself with little choice but to be dishonest. Luckily, Alison had never suggested accompanying him on one of these trips. She had her own life: the gym, tennis, dog-training, charity lunches—endless lunches—and shopping trips to buy clothes for those lunches. Not that he begrudged her a penny that she spent. She worked hard, at keeping the house impeccable, looking after the children, looking after him, in fact.

Colin didn't consider himself sexist. He'd given enough women opportunities at work to defend himself against anyone making that accusation, and he would have been quite happy for Alison to pursue a career if she'd wanted one, but sometimes he couldn't help wondering if more women would be happier if they followed Alison's suit. It made for easy teamwork. Their roles were clearly defined. Their life ran like clockwork and their interests and timetables rarely clashed. In fact, apart from this one blip, it was a pretty perfect marriage.

He glanced at the clock on the dashboard. He was in plenty of time. He was due to pick Karen and Chelsey up at half ten, which meant they would probably reach the hotel just after lunch. He'd spotted an article about The Townhouse by the Sea in the *Sunday Times* travel section—it looked idyllic. He'd checked out Pennfleet on the Internet and thought it would be fun for Chelsey. They could go to the beach, take a boat out, and there were lots of pizza places and ice-cream parlours that he knew his own kids would have enjoyed, so why wouldn't she?

At the thought of his children, he felt guilt nip at his heart: Ryan, on his gap year, living it up in Oz; and Michelle, in her second year at uni in Warwick. He was incredibly proud of them. They'd achieved so much. That was largely down to Alison and the attention she'd lavished on them while they were growing up, painstakingly helping them with their homework, running them to extracurricular activities, encouraging them to do everything they wanted to do. Not that Colin hadn't been interested, but his working hours were brutal. He rarely got home before seven, and by then all the hard work had been done. He had, of course, paid for their education, and all the extras, and was funding Ryan's gap year, and over his dead body were either of his kids taking out a loan to pay for their tuition fees at university, so he had contributed in no small way, but it was Alison who'd put in the blood, sweat and tears that had led to their success. Not that he spoiled his kids financially. On the contrary, he'd taught them both the value of hard work. They'd had jobs with him in the holidays: Ryan had worked at the factory, and Michelle had waitressed in one or other of the cafés, so they understood what it was to have your own money. They were grafters, like him.

Now, he burst with pride when he thought about the pair of them, and it made him feel quite ill to think of them knowing his dirty secret. The secret he'd kept quiet for so long it had become a part of him, a piece of his heart that had turned as black as coal.

He came off the motorway and headed into the service station where he'd arranged to pick them up. He didn't want to turn up outside Karen's house in his car, so she was leaving hers here for the weekend—he would drop them back here on his way home. He felt his heart rate increase slightly. This was one of the danger areas, where he might be spotted. It wasn't beyond belief that someone he knew might have pulled in. He determined to get in and out as quickly as he could.

He peered over the rows of parked cars to the Costa Coffee. There they were, the two of them, sitting at an outside table. Karen, her dark hair scraped back into a high ponytail, her face fully made up but obscured by huge sunglasses, her heels high and her jeans tighter than tight, a camisole and a cropped pink suede jacket over the top. And next to her, Chelsey.

His heart turned over every time he saw her. She was only up to Karen's shoulder, but she must be a

30

stone heavier already. Small, plump, pale, worried, she had a pretty heart-shaped face with a perpetual frown. No eleven year old should look as if they had the weight of the world on their shoulders, thought Colin, but no doubt living with Karen would leave you in a constant state of anxiety. Chelsey seemed to have dressed in whatever was to hand: pink leggings, scruffy sheepskin boots and a yellow sequinned T-shirt that didn't quite cover her tummy—whether this was a fashion statement or whether it was simply too small, Colin couldn't be sure. Her hair was straggly and needed cutting. He knew Alison wouldn't have let Michelle out looking like that. Uncared for. His kids had always looked immaculate.

They hadn't noticed him yet. Karen was busy smoking a cigarette. Chelsey was eating a doughnut. He waited a moment, watching them. He didn't like anyone smoking or eating in his car, but he didn't want to come across as pernickety. He felt the metallic taste of guilt in his mouth, wondered if he could sneak into the service station for a drink to wash it away before they saw him, but no—that was too risky. As he watched, Karen handed Chelsey another doughnut from a bag. Chelsey took it wordlessly and bit into it.

Colin frowned. He might be a purveyor of cakes, biscuits, scones, bread and all things fattening, but there was no way that child needed a second doughnut. He headed the car towards them, attracting their attention with a merry little parp on the horn. Karen dropped her cigarette butt and ground it out with her heel. Chelsey crammed another bite of doughnut into her mouth and began hastily wiping away the sugar crumbs.

31

They crowded up to the car door.

'All right?' Karen bent in and brushed his cheek with hers. She smelt of Benson & Hedges, chewing gum and toxic vanilla perfume. 'Give your dad a kiss, Chels.' She grabbed Chelsey by the shoulder and pushed her towards Colin.

He gave her a peck on the cheek. She tasted of sugar.

'We're going to have a great weekend,' he told her. He jumped out of the car, picking up their bags to stow them in the boot. They'd packed enough for a week between them, but it didn't matter. There was plenty of room.

'I looked up the hotel on the net. It hasn't got a pool. Or a spa.' Karen wrenched the back door open and pushed Chelsey in, then stalked round to the passenger door. Colin looked at her as she settled into the front seat, pulling the seat belt across those boobs that had been his downfall.

'There's one up the road—you can borrow their facilities.'

'Why didn't you check us in there?'

'It didn't look as nice. This one's by the sea. Right on the water. We've got rooms with a view.'

Karen looked doubtful.

'How've you been, anyway?' he asked her.

'Nightmare. They've been laying people off at work and the rest of us have to cover for them with no extra money.' Karen pulled the passenger mirror down to check her make-up.

Colin looked in the rear-view mirror. Chelsey was staring out of the window.

'How about you, Chelsey? How's school?'

'Nightmare.' Karen repeated her favourite description. 'She's been picked on by some kids in

32

her class. They've been calling her fat.'

Colin felt himself go red. The trouble was, Chelsey *was* fat. And kids being kids were no doubt happy to point that out. But it hurt him, to think she was being teased.

'Does the teacher know you're being bullied, Chelsey?'

'Yeah, but she's not bothered.' Chelsey's tone was flat, matter of fact. 'She reckons they'll stop when they get bored.'

Little buggers. Colin felt the urge to go to Chelsey's school and seek them out, give them a good old-fashioned hiding. But he couldn't. The only thing he could do was make sure she had a wonderful weekend. A weekend to remember.

As he pulled back on to the motorway, the sun came out.

'Hey, hey, we're on our way,' he sang tunelessly.

Karen looked at him sideways and began prodding at the CD player.

'Have you got any Take That?' she demanded.

In the back seat, he could hear Chelsey rustling her hand in a bag of pick 'n' mix, and smelled the additive dust cloud that came out of it. He wanted to tell her to stop. Not because he cared about the mess, but for her own sake. But now probably wasn't the time to start. He was only a part-time father, after all. Very, very part-time.

*   *   *

Angelica used her elbow to push down the handle of Claire and Luca's room. Either Luca was still fast asleep or he was in the shower and hadn't heard her knock. She edged inside cautiously, holding the tray bearing his wake-up ristretto—it seemed to have become her job to get him up in the mornings. The room was in half-light—sun was streaming in through the tiny skylight, but the curtains were still drawn.

He was asleep. She could make out his figure in the bed. She breathed in, inhaling his scent, sharp, musky and masculine.

'Luca!' she called gently. He groaned and rolled over, rubbing his hands over his eyes. 'Claire says get up.'

'Tell her to fuck off.' His voice was husky with sleep.

'I've brought you coffee.'

She walked across the room and round to his side of the bed, standing over him. She kneed him in the side.

'Oi. Come on. You know we're busy today.'

He took his hand away from his eyes and stretched out an arm. She thought it was to take the coffee. She was about to pass it to him when she felt his warm fingers on her thigh, just under the hem of her skirt. The lightest touch. A gentle caress. Familiar, affectionate. Meaningless.

Was it?

'Just five more minutes. Please, Angelica. I'm knackered . . .'

Her heart was racing, stumbling over itself as he stroked her. How tempting it was to tumble on to the bed with him, roll under the duvet, feel those hands not just on her thigh but all over her body. Did he know what he was doing to her with that tiny, infinitesimal tease?

Of course he bloody did.

She put the coffee down on the bedside table

34

with trembling hands.

'Up to you, Luca. But I've always been told that working here was a team effort.'

And with that retort she left the room.

Outside the door, she leant against the wall. Her legs were shaking. She could barely stand. She gave a groan, shut her eyes and tilted her head back in despair.

Some days she could handle her obsession. And some days she couldn't. This was going to be a 'couldn't' day. Her skin was going to creep with it; her blood fizzing beneath the surface, buzzing like an overhead cable.

She didn't understand why she couldn't control it. She had tried to rationalise it so many times. Sometimes common sense prevailed and she could function like a normal human being. But sometimes it just washed over her, taking her breath away, sucking all reason from her, leaving her limp in its wake.

It wasn't even as if she liked him much.

She hated the way he took Claire for granted. She hated his cockiness. The way he made assumptions. The way he bullied people—not all the time, but when the pressure was on in the kitchen, Luca gave everyone short shrift. Yet there was something magnetic about him. He fascinated her. She wanted to know what made him tick. What he really felt. What his innermost hopes and fears were. He seemed to live in the moment, but surely he had regrets? Memories? Ambitions? Did he ever ask himself 'what if' . . .?

She asked herself that all the time.

Not that she would go near him. Not in a million years. She liked and respected Claire far too much for that. But at home, in the privacy of her own room, in the privacy of her own mind . . . that was a different matter. She could fantasise.

And she knew that Luca knew. He could smell it on her; see it in her eyes. That was why he taunted her. It was a game to him, the way he played her. Tested her, tempted her; made her believe that anything was possible.

She remembered a moment at the last staff Christmas party, which they held in January, when the silly season was over. She and Luca had met on the stairs. She had been two steps above him, which brought her to his eye level. And he had looked at her. Mocking, inviting.

'Angel. Angelic. Angelica,' he said, his voice low and teasing.

He leant forward. Their foreheads were touching. She would only need to move a millimetre for their lips to touch too. They stood there for a full five seconds, each waiting to see who would make the first move. Angelica's head was swimming. She wanted to reach up, grab his hair, pull him in to her and devour him. But she knew that once she had given in, there would be no return.

Instead, she reached up and put her index finger on his lips.

'Naughty,' she chided. 'Don't even think about it.'

He looked deep into her eyes, and she could feel her soul trying to tug itself free.

'Don't tell me you don't think about it.'

'Oh yes,' she replied. 'But I think about all sorts of thing I can't have.'

Out of the corner of her eye she could see Claire

36

making her way towards the stairs. She looked ravishing in a dark-red velvet dress, a Father Christmas hat at a jaunty angle on her curls, her high heels kicked off long ago.

'What are you two up to?' she laughed, hooking her arm around the newel post beneath them, a half-empty glass of champagne in her hand.

'Just giving the boss a Christmas kiss,' replied Angelica, and in full view of Claire she put a hand either side of Luca's head, pulled him in and kissed him. It was a pantomime kiss, a kiss for dramatic effect, an over-the-top office party gesture that no one could take offence at. Claire just giggled from the bottom of the stairs. Angelica wriggled past Luca and came down to join her. She could feel his eyes boring into her back as she headed for the steaming bowl of mulled wine for a top up.

Afterwards, as they all sat round in a circle opening their Secret Santa presents, Angelica caught Luca's eye. He held her gaze a moment too long; his meaning was unmistakable. She widened her eyes at him in innocence and turned away. She wasn't going to be his toy. She wasn't going to embark on a torrid, seedy affair with him. Hurried sex between shifts behind locked doors. She valued herself too highly for that. She valued her job even higher. And her relationship with Claire even higher than that. Claire was her idol, her mentor, her girl crush. The first person in her life who had shown faith in her. She wasn't going to sacrifice that for a tumble with Luca, no matter how much her body craved it.

Besides, Angelica had always been an all-or-nothing girl. If she couldn't have Luca to herself, she certainly didn't want to share him. Yet

37

still she tortured herself. To be honest, it was the only thing that kept her going; the only thing that stopped her going completely mad. Even though it was a kind of madness in itself.

Inside the room, she could hear the creak of the bed as Luca turned over. An image of his body sprang into her mind, for she knew he'd been naked under the duvet. She brushed herself down, ran her fingers through her hair and made for the stairs. Thank God it was going to be busy. She could think of nothing worse than sitting behind the reception desk burning with unrequited lust all day.

CHAPTER THREE

Laura Starling stood on the crowded concourse at Paddington, chewing her bottom lip. Her gaze flipped between the announcement board, waiting for the platform number to appear and trigger the surge of people towards the train bound for Penzance, and the escalator leading up from the Tube. Where was he? She knew perfectly well, of course. He would have his arm hooked round a pole in a carriage on the District Line, listening to his iPod, in his own little world, oblivious to the fact that she was about to explode with anxiety.

Dan always left things to the last possible moment. She, conversely, had been here for over half an hour, just in case. Just in case of what, she couldn't say, but she always liked to be on the safe side. Dan would, she knew, appear in the nick of time. He always did. In the six months she had known him, he had never actually let her down, but she was always convinced he wasn't going to turn up.

He just didn't have the worry gene. He was totally laid-back. The hideous possibilities that occurred to Laura every minute of the day weren't on his radar. When she ran a potential snag past him, he just shrugged and said, 'So what? What if that does happen? The world won't come to an end.' And the annoying thing was, he was right. But no matter how hard she tried, she couldn't train herself to think like him. Or get him to accommodate her fears and worries into his timetable. It was her problem. One of the things she was working on, that would make her the person she wanted to be.

This was despite Dan repeatedly telling her she was perfect as she was.

'Well, not perfect.' He qualified his statement. 'Because perfect would be dull beyond belief. And you're certainly not that.'

She looked at her watch, in case it told a time different from the station clock, but it didn't. She breathed in to calm herself. The air was filled with the scent of fried doughnuts and sweat. Anticipation hovered, for this was more than just the usual Friday commuter crowd. It was a bank holiday weekend and there were adventures afoot. The exodus from the city had already begun.

Here he was, at last. Loping across the concourse with his endless legs, a canvas rucksack on his shoulder. She knew all that would be in it would be a spare shirt and pants, his toothbrush and his camera. Her case, by contrast, was filled with an array of dresses, jeans, tops, make-up and shoes. In faded jeans and a plaid shirt, his hair messy, he looked like any other scruffy twenty-something boy, until you clocked his bone structure and those extraordinary eyes—a deep, soft grey, fringed with thick black lashes. Laura had seen girls visibly wilt when he turned to look at them, just as she had when they'd met at a mutual friend's party. The kindness in them was infinite. For Dan was, above all else, the kindest person she had ever met.

'Hey.' He ambled up with a grin and dropped a kiss on her head, just as the platform number appeared. She grabbed his sleeve.

'Come on,' she urged, picking up her overnight bag, heavier than she had intended, and checking her pocket again for their tickets so that they could slip through the barrier with no delay. She'd reserved their seats, her finger hesitating on the 'purchase' button for so long that she had to remind herself that even if she bought the tickets, they didn't have to go; that she could change her mind right up to the last minute.

They were swept along in the current of travellers, all trying to outrun each other, as if there was some elusive prize at the end of the platform. They hurried past the first-class carriages, all tauntingly empty, until they reached coach F.

'This is the one,' she told Dan, and jumped on board.

'Calm down,' he laughed. 'The train isn't going to drive off while we're getting on.'

He went to sling his rucksack in the luggage compartment, but she put out a hand.

'No,' she said. 'Put it in the overhead rack. I know people who've had their cases pinched.'

'No one would want my stuff. They'd be sorely disappointed.'

'What about your camera?'

He shrugged. 'Insured.'

Laura shook her head. How could he be so cavalier about the tools of his trade? Surely it would be a disaster if someone took it? She didn't pursue this line of thought, however, as he had bowed to her better judgement and was stuffing his rucksack on to the rack over their seat. He put out his hand for her bag too. A moment later they were in their seats, side by side.

Laura brought out two smoothies and two plastic tubs of breakfast muesli she'd bought in Marks & Spencer.

'I knew you wouldn't have had breakfast . . .'

'No,' admitted Dan happily, unscrewing the cap of one of the smoothies and gulping it down.

Laura pulled out the brochure she had sent off for. A small, tasteful A5 booklet, printed on cream cartridge paper. The cover showed a painting of the harbour at Pennfleet, executed in bright, splashy colours. 'Learn to draw or paint in a stunning and inspirational seaside setting. Royal Academician Tony Weston will unleash your creativity and give you the confidence to bring out your inner Monet or Picasso. An ideal birthday gift or simply treat yourself—the ultimate in "me" time.'

Inside was a list of Tony Weston's credentials, galleries he had exhibited at and more examples of his paintings. His photograph showed a man in his fifties sitting in front of an open French window that looked out on to the sea. He had cropped grey hair, fashionable black-rimmed glasses and a shirt with a round-necked collar—a typical ageing trendy media type, for his CV revealed that he had worked in advertising before retiring to Pennfleet.

41

Laura had analysed his features over and over again, but the picture was too lacking in detail for her to come to any conclusion. A static photograph was never an accurate representation of someone's physiognomy. You had to watch them talk, smile, frown, laugh to pin down any resemblance to another human.

For most of her life Laura had been cool about not having a father. It made her different from other kids at school, but that was something she relished rather than resented. She had a great relationship with her mother. It had always been just the two of them. Marina was like a mate, or a big sister. All her friends were green with envy that she had someone she could share her secrets with. And over the years Marina became a confidante to them too. Their little house was always bursting at the seams, full of music and laughter and gossip and home-made chocolate chip cookies. Marina had the answers to the knottiest of problems. She was unshockable. There was nothing you couldn't talk to her about.

Except one thing, and she made it clear that was a no-go area. She simply refused to be drawn on the identity of Laura's father. Laura had learnt to stop asking. By the age of thirteen, she had resigned herself to the fact that she was never going to know. She had been, to all intents and purposes, an immaculate conception.

At fifteen, she panicked, wondering perhaps if her mother had been raped. That would certainly explain Marina's reluctance to divulge the truth. One evening when Marina was in a calm and reflective mood, she'd plucked up the courage to ask. They were sitting out on the tiny terrace that served them as a garden. It was covered in brightly painted pots stuffed with flowers, and strung with fairy lights; they were sitting in the last of the sun, Marina with a glass of wine.

Laura fiddled with the edge of the pink linen tablecloth that was spread over the rickety wooden table Marina had picked up from a junk shop.

'Mum, just tell me one thing. Did he rape you? My father?'

Marina reached out and stroked her hair. The expression on her face could not be read.

'No, my darling. Absolutely not. I promise you.'

Laura nodded. She knew not to probe any further, but she had needed to put that possibility out of her mind. And she believed her. Marina's reassurance had come from the heart.

It wasn't until she met Dan that her curiosity was piqued again. He'd been intrigued by the fact that she didn't seem to want to know who her father was. He was never intrusive or judgemental, but it set her thinking about her father's identity. And then he had shown her a feature in a magazine he'd done the photos for. It was about men who had discovered late in life that they'd fathered children they never knew they had. To a man they revealed what a delight it was to find a new son or daughter, and how it had enriched their lives, even when they already had other legitimate children.

'I'm not saying you should look for him,' Dan said, 'but not one of these guys was upset or angry. Although obviously you'd need to be careful.'

Laura thought about it. She had always presumed her father didn't know of her existence, but she'd never really considered it from his point of view. Did her mother really have the right to

43

deny him knowledge of her existence, whoever he was? Maybe he hadn't gone on to have other children. Maybe he too would be delighted to know he had a daughter. Not to know you had a child was peculiar to men—it was an experience no woman could ever share. And so how could a woman really empathise?

It began to eat away at her. And she began to resent Marina for her arrogance. Surely every child had the right to know her father, and a father to know his daughter? But she knew, absolutely, that she would never be able to worm it out of her.

'I'll never get Mum to tell me,' she told Dan. 'I'll have to figure it out for myself.'

He promised to help her in any way he could. And to be there for her, whichever way it went. She began looking for clues in earnest. Rifling through Marina's drawers when she went round for Sunday lunch. Rummaging through cupboards, shoeboxes, empty suitcases, pulling up pieces of loose carpet. But there was never anything that gave even a hint. Surely if the relationship had had any meaning, which Laura felt it had, she would have kept some relic, some tiny memento? Her mother kept everything—ticket stubs, photos, postcards, programmes, souvenirs. She was a hoarder.

The only place she hadn't managed to look was the box file Marina kept her paperwork in—her passport and driving licence and chequebooks. It was kept firmly locked, and Laura had no idea where to find the key.

Dan laughed. 'Not a problem,' he said when she described the lock to him. And so one weekend, when they knew Marina was away, Laura and Dan sneaked into her house with the spare key, and Dan picked the lock of the box file.

'Where did you learn how to do that?' Laura demanded.

'Ask me no questions and I'll tell you no lies,' he told her, laughing. And she thought that was probably the moment when her feelings for him tipped from delicate and fragile embryonic love into something more profound. It was the first time in her life that she had felt protected by someone other than her mother. It made her feel warm inside.

Carefully and meticulously, Laura searched through the contents of the box file and found the clue she was looking for, amidst tax returns and bank statements. A tiny, perfect life drawing of what was clearly a teenage Marina. Carelessly impressionistic but brilliant, it brought to life her slight figure, her full breasts, and a lustrous sheet of black hair falling past her shoulders.

'Wow,' said Dan. 'Your mum's still stunning, but . . . wow.'

Laura, who was pretty but had suffered all her life from knowing she didn't have her mother's arresting aura, smiled wryly. Her boyfriends had often been dumbstruck when they met Marina. Dan had seemed unfazed up till now, but this drawing captured her raw beauty so perfectly that even he couldn't fail to express admiration.

She held the drawing with shaking fingers as she deciphered the scrawled signature in the right-hand corner.

'Tony Weston. I think it says Tony Weston.'

Dan scrutinised it and agreed.

'Probably a pretty common name.'

'Do you think this is my dad? This would have

been drawn just before she had me. She had all her hair cut off after I was born, she told me, because I kept pulling it.' Laura knew she was gabbling. This was the closest she had ever come to unveiling the secret. 'Do you think it's him?'

'Well,' said Dan. 'They were obviously quite close, judging by the way she's looking at him . . .'

The drawing was intimate, there was no denying that. Laura swallowed. Tony Weston might be her father. She couldn't take the picture with her, so she photocopied it, then put it back in the box file and snapped it shut again. She had found the one thing her mother had never wanted her to find. But why all the secrecy? Why didn't Marina want her to know who her father was?

It took Laura and Dan a while on the Internet to compile a shortlist of possibilities. Dan was right— Tony Weston was a common name. But in the end they narrowed it down, by a meticulous process of elimination and extensive research in the local library, until at last they had a prime suspect.

This particular Tony Weston had once been the head of art at St Benedict's School for Girls, in the town where her mother had grown up. The school Marina had attended. He had left there the year before Laura was born.

Laura found his website, advertising painting courses.

'His CV doesn't mention St Benedict's,' she pointed out to Dan.

'That smacks of guilt in itself. He must be hiding something. Why would you leave that out, unless you didn't want anyone to know?'

'Or you wanted to forget . . .'

They examined the evidence. Forensically, the

drawings on his website were similar in style to the sketch they had found—bold, impressionistic, exuberant.

'Do you think it's him?' Laura asked Dan.

'There's only one way to find out,' he replied. 'You'll have to go and see him. We'll go there for the weekend.' He scrolled down Tony Weston's website. 'Pennfleet looks like a nice enough place.'

And so Laura emailed Tony Weston and booked a weekend of private painting tuition, under a false name—Starling was too unusual; she didn't want to ring any alarm bells, so she called herself Emma Stubbs, after a childhood friend. She paid using one of Dan's cheques, explaining that the weekend was a birthday gift. Tony Weston would have no reason to suspect he was being hunted down.

And now here they were on the train, rattling past Staines, Slough, heading relentlessly west. She had no idea how she was going to play it, if she was going to reveal her identity, or how she would even know if she'd found the right person. Maybe she wouldn't have the courage to see it through.

When they reached Reading, she was tempted to jump off.

'I don't think I can go through with this,' she said to Dan. 'Let's get off and get the next train back to London.'

'Don't be silly,' he told her. 'We've already paid for our tickets and the hotel. It would be a waste. If you do bottle it, the worst that can happen is we spend the weekend in Pennfleet.'

Laura had to admit that she couldn't argue with his logic. And so the train rattled on, past Newbury, Hungerford, Pewsey. By the time they reached Castle Cary, the warmth of the carriage and the

47

sleeplessness of the night before had lulled her to sleep. There was no turning back now.

CHAPTER FOUR

Just before eleven, Claire heard the front door open and prayed it wasn't an arrival. She hated it when guests checked in early. The corridors were still busy with Henry the Hoover and lined with canvas bags of dirty linen, and there was nothing worse than the sight of a hotel room door agape and a stripped bed. There was nothing you could do about it—rooms had to be turned round—but she wished people would wait till after midday at least to turn up.

She looked up nevertheless, with her most welcoming smile. If their room wasn't ready, complimentary coffee and shortbread on the terrace usually mollified.

'I know it's too early to check in, but I wondered if I could leave my . . .'

The guest trailed off, dropping his battered leather Gladstone bag with a clatter. 'Claire?'

She dropped her pen with a matching clatter.

She'd dreamt of this moment for years. More years than she cared to remember; years that had seemed interminable as she struggled to get him out of her mind. And eventually, of course, in the fullness of time, the dream had faded, only sneaking back to catch her unawares every now and again, in her sleep, when she was at her most unguarded.

'Nick?' She got to her feet and they gazed at

48

each other across the desk. 'What are you . . .? Are you . . .?'

She felt completely at a loss for words. She indicated the computer helplessly.

'Checking in?' he filled in for her. 'Yeah . . . Um . . . Do you work here?'

'Actually, it's mine.' She gave a faltering smile. 'It's my hotel.' She paused. 'Me and my . . . partner's.'

She didn't say boyfriend.

'Wow.' Nick gazed at her.

Claire shook her head in disbelief.

'This is such a shock.'

'Tell me about it.' He smiled wryly. 'Gus will be mortified when he finds out.'

'Gus?' The name rang a bell.

There was a pause.

'Gus Andrews. My best man.' He pushed back his fringe. That fringe she herself had pushed back so many times. 'It's . . . my stag weekend.'

Of course. The six blokes on the third floor.

'You're getting married.'

It was a statement. It hung heavy between them, just as Angelica came in, dwarfed behind a huge sheaf of gladioli that had just been delivered from the florist. She plonked them on the reception desk, and looked between Claire and the new arrival.

'Is everything okay?' she asked. 'You look as if you've seen a ghost.'

A strange expression flickered over the man's face. Claire hurried back behind the desk and grabbed a key off the hook.

'Mr Barnes is a bit early, but luckily his room's ready—it wasn't used last night. If you could show him up . . .'

49

Angelica took the key and went to pick up the bag, but Nick demurred.

'No, it's okay. It's heavy. I'll—'

'I can manage.'

Angelica took the bag firmly. They had a strict policy of carrying guests' luggage. And not hovering for a tip.

The two of them were still staring at each other.

'Would you like to follow me?' Angelica asked, trying to break the spell.

'Um, sure,' said Nick, looking back at Claire. 'Maybe see you later? For a coffee?'

Claire managed a nod. Angelica moved off towards the stairs.

'The bar's just through there to your right, if you want a drink.' She began her introductory spiel. 'We'll be serving light snacks on the terrace at lunch. And if you'd like to reserve a table for dinner . . .'

'I think that's all been organised.' Nick followed her, allowing himself one glance back, but Claire was starting very intently at her computer screen.

Moments later, the hall was empty. Claire could hear Angelica chattering away up the stairs, her voice fading gradually as they went up another floor.

Married. Of course he was getting married. He was what—thirty-three? Two years older than she was. She looked down at her own left hand, bare, ringless, and imagined a slender finger with a sparkling diamond belonging to a shiny-haired blonde. She was astonished at how much it hurt.

Of all the hotels in all the world, Nick Barnes had to walk into hers.

Angelica unlocked the door to Room Seven and stood back to let the new arrival in. She surveyed him with approval: fairly typical Pennfleet summer fodder, in jeans and a sage-green cord jacket, everything expensive but subtly distressed and faded, his hair dirty blond and pushed back by a pair of tortoiseshell Ray-Bans. Posh, but without that way of looking right through you that some of the visitors seemed to have. He was distracted, but not rude.

Swiftly she pointed out the bathroom, the minibar, the heating control and the television remote. He seemed to be barely listening. He obviously couldn't wait for her to leave. She handed him the key with a welcoming smile.

'Just phone reception if there's anything you need.'

He thanked her, and Angelica slipped out of the room, closing the door behind her. She ran back down the stairs as quickly as she could, curiosity eating at her. She had never seen Claire look so rattled, and those two definitely had history.

Claire was behind the reception, wrestling the gladioli into a square vase and positioning it carefully on the desk. She was definitely still flustered, her cheeks pink. Angelica had never seen her fazed, not by the most difficult customer, not even by Luca at his most ornery. She always remained cool, serene, dignified.

'Are you okay?' asked Angelica.

'Yes.' Her voice was too careful to be convincing.

Angelica surveyed her. Claire took a deep breath to calm herself.

'I'm fine. Honestly.' Her eyes flicked to the clock. 'Actually, no. No, I'm not. Let's have a drink.'

'It's not even midday.'

'Who cares? It's a bank holiday weekend. There are no rules.' Claire tweaked the last flower defiantly and led the way through into the bar.

Astonished, Angelica followed her. This was totally out of character. Claire might occasionally succumb to a glass of wine at the end of a long day, but unlike Luca, alcohol wasn't her automatic solution to a problem. But here she was, determinedly pulling a bottle of house white from the fridge at half past eleven in the morning. Who *was* that guy? Angelica wondered.

The bar wasn't huge—there was enough room for a dozen people at the most to have pre- or post-dinner drinks; they didn't want to waste valuable dining space—and it was chicly stark in comparison to the more opulent reception area. The walls were white, adorned with bronze and silver casts of fish skeletons by Abigail Fallis, and the chairs were covered in slubby turquoise linen.

'If we sit here, we can see if anyone comes in.' Claire indicated the two chairs nearest reception. Angelica took a glass from her and sat down, not quite sure how to play this unusual turn of events. She took a tentative sip of wine; she wasn't a great drinker, and when she did, she favoured sugary alcopops. She shuddered slightly as the sharp tang of gooseberry hit her taste buds.

'So,' she ventured finally. 'Who was that?'

She knew she was prying. She didn't think there was much chance of Claire confiding in her. She wasn't the type to share her personal life.

'He's an old boyfriend.' Claire took a grateful

52

glug of Sauvignon Blanc. 'My first boyfriend. I haven't seen him for . . . twelve years?'

She didn't know why she was questioning the length of time. She knew exactly how long it had been.

Eleven years and five months.

The phone rang, breaking the moment. Claire looked irritated.

'Five minutes' peace and quiet. Is that too much to ask?'

Angelica stood up.

'I'll get it.'

Claire watched her go. She knew she shouldn't be doing this. There was so much to organise. Getting sloshed at this time in the morning really wasn't going to help her get through the day. She was usually so conscientious—it was counterintuitive, this behaviour. But shock did that to you, she supposed, as she raised the glass to her lips and took another shot of coolly delicious anaesthetic.

Eleven years, five months and twenty-seven days.

*   *   *

Nick Barnes stood in the middle of the room he had been shown to on the third floor. He barely noticed it, although normally he would have fully appreciated its understated luxury—the fat goose-down duvet, the chic supersized sisal carpeting, the Bose iPod dock. He dropped his bag at his feet and walked through into the bathroom for a pee, again hardly seeing the mother-of-pearl mosaic tiles and the range of Molton Brown accessories.

What bloody awful timing. This was absolutely the worst thing that could have happened, the eventuality he had dreamt about so many times. And how ironic that it should happen on his stag weekend. Someone up there was having a laugh. Not that Nick believed that there was someone up there. He had stopped believing anything like that a long, long time ago.

He checked his watch. The other guys would be here in a couple of hours. He'd wanted to make the journey down on his own; use the time to get his head together. Little realising that any togetherness he might have achieved would be blown to buggery. He kicked off his shoes and flopped down on one of the twin beds; the one nearest the window. He didn't even bother looking out at the incredible harbour view. He shivered, although it wasn't cold in the room.

He thought about Sophie. She would be on her way to Brighton. She and five of her girlfriends, booked into a hotel for a weekend of hen hedonism.

'I know it's really naff,' she'd told him. 'But the shops are great, and I've found a fantastic hotel. And we won't get up to anything too wild! Just cocktails and dancing and shopping and spa treatments.'

Sophie. The girl who was going to walk down the aisle and join him at the altar next Saturday, in St Mary's Church in Mimsbury, with the reception afterwards at his father's house, because although it defied convention, they had both agreed that a marquee on the lawn by the river at the Mill House was the ideal spot. Why pay for a swanky hotel when they had perfection on the doorstep? A hundred and forty guests, canapés, a string quartet, an exquisite buffet—neither of them could face the horror of a seating plan—and then dancing barefoot till midnight at the water's edge. They'd been planning it for months. This weekend was a much-needed break for both of them. Nick had been really looking forward to chilling with his mates, taking a boat out on the water, having a few beers, chewing the fat . . .

If he had any sense, he thought, lacing his hands behind his head as it sank into the pillow, he would walk now. Phone the others, plead a stomach bug. Go back to his father's, bury himself in work, or mowing the lawn, and try and forget that she had walked back into his life at the most inopportune moment possible.

He jumped off the bed and walked to the window. In the harbour, boats were riding the wavelets, tugging against their buoys like unbroken horses. A tiny ferry chugged across the water, taking passengers to the far shore, where another village, the mirror of Pennfleet, nestled amongst the trees. The sun threw its rays down on to the water, casting a fine coating of gold on to the blue. He should be filled with excitement and exhilaration, longing to get out on the water, to breathe in the ozone, luxuriate in the warmth. Instead he felt filled with fear.

Leave now, he told himself. You have nothing to gain from staying. You're just going to rake up pain and misery and regret. And ghosts. He felt for the car keys in his pocket, pulled his phone from the breast pocket of his jacket, scrolled through to find Gus's number. Gus would understand that something was wrong; he wouldn't give him a hard time. And the others could carry on as normal. Just because the groom wasn't there didn't mean they couldn't make a weekend of it.

His finger hovered over the number, pressed it. The phone rang for a while. Gus must be driving. He would have to leave a message. Maybe that would be easier.

'Hey, Nick.' His friend's voice came down the line. 'How's it going?'

Nick didn't reply immediately. He looked up at the ceiling, as if the answer might be written there. But it wasn't.

'Buddy?' Gus sounded concerned.

'Hey,' replied Nick. 'I just wondered what time you guys were going to arrive. This place is incredible. Get yourselves down here as quickly as you can.'

*   *   *

Angelica hung up the phone and came back into the bar.

'Just a booking for the restaurant tonight,' she told Claire, surprised to see that she had nearly finished her glass of wine. Even more when she reached out to top herself up.

'Don't worry,' Claire replied as she noticed Angelica's frown. 'I'm not on a mission. Just taking the edge off the shock.' She poured herself a more restrained inch and a half and cocked the bottle towards Angelica, who shook her head.

'One of us better stay sober.' She grinned as she sat down again. She wondered how to get back into the conversation; if Claire would still want to talk.

'So,' she tried. 'Did he dump you, that bloke?'

56

'You could say that.'

'Bastard.' Angelica knew from her mother men's capacity to hurt. Their selfish, treacherous ways.

'No,' Claire contradicted her. 'There were reasons. Good reasons.'

'What? Like he'd found someone else? *It's not you, it's me*; that sort of thing?' Angelica rolled her eyes. 'He looked very nice, but they are all the same, you know.'

Claire smothered a smile at Angelica's world-weary wisdom. It was a shame that she was quite so cynical so young. She supposed it was a defence mechanism; the protective armour of a girl who'd never known stability in her family life. She'd heard about her mother's string of men. She looked at her watch. It was twenty to twelve. People would start coming in for lunch any time soon. They only did bar snacks at lunchtime during the week— Fred and Loz, the two local boys whom Luca had trained up, were in the kitchen prepping—but it was Friday, a bank holiday weekend, and the sun was out. They would have a flock of spontaneous lunchers any moment.

Lunch, however, wasn't the problem in hand.

'I did something terrible,' she told Angelica.

'I can't imagine you doing anything terrible.'

Claire leant forward.

'I thought I was doing the right thing,' she said fiercely. 'At the time, I thought I was doing the right thing.'

'Of course you did!' Angelica reached out and stroked her arm, to reassure her. It was strange, to be comforting Claire. She'd never known her to need a moment's reassurance about anything.

'Shit.' Claire sat back and put her face in her

57

hands. 'Oh God, I'm sorry. You must think I'm mad.'

'No. Of course I don't.'

'I've thought about this happening so many times, but you never think it's really going to . . .'

'He seemed happy enough to see you.'

'That's the problem.' She glanced round her anxiously. 'Luca's not up yet?'

'Not yet. I did try waking him, but he's out for the count.'

'Good.'

They sat in silence, Claire alone with her thoughts, Angelica with her curiosity. Eventually Claire spoke.

'I'm not sure if I can handle this. But I'm going to have to.'

'Do you want to talk about it?'

'I don't know. I never have. Not even with Luca.' She paused. 'Especially not with Luca. I'm ashamed of what I did. I've lived with it all this time. But I was only nineteen.' She looked at Angelica, anguished. 'I had no idea how the world worked. I was burdened with the biggest secret imaginable and I couldn't share it with anyone.' She slumped down in her chair, exhausted by the memory. 'Eventually I did, of course. But by then it was too late.'

'Maybe what you did wasn't as bad as you think. Things often aren't. They just build up in your head and you end up feeling guilty.' Angelica had been made to feel bad about herself often enough in her short life to know that this was true. She'd come to the conclusion that guilt was a pointless emotion; that for every bad thing you did, people around you did worse. It had made life a lot easier once she'd worked that out.

Claire looked at her thoughtfully.

'I try not to think about it. It makes me feel sick, even now.'

Angelica leant forward.

'Tell me,' she urged. 'I'm not going to judge you. Honestly, I could tell you things about my life that would make your hair curl.'

Claire picked up the bottle and poured another inch.

'Oh God. I'm going to be drunk in charge of reception at this rate.'

'It's okay. It's fine. I'm here. I can deal with it.'

For a full ten seconds there was silence, except for the ticking of the clock on the wall and the shriek of seagulls.

'I didn't expect to fall in love,' Claire began. 'And it wasn't just with Nick. It was with his whole family. His life. His house. The whole thing. The whole Barnes package . . .'

CHAPTER FIVE

Claire was waiting for a train when she first met the Barnes brothers.

Her parents had dropped her at the station before tootling off in their brown Rover to their jobs at the Atomic Weapons Establishment in Aldermaston. Claire was never really clear what it was they did there. A lot of it was secret, but anything they discussed in front of her was certainly safe, as it meant nothing to her. She hadn't followed in their scientific footsteps. She was

59

doing English, art and economics at the college in Reading, and although they had never said so, she felt they weren't terribly impressed.

She was taking the train to college. They appeared on the other side of the track by the level crossing, just as the barriers went down and the lights began to flash. She saw the three of them look at each other conspiratorially and run for it. Idiots! They tore across the track, jostling and laughing, before jumping on to the platform. Claire saw a tangle of tousled hair, jeans and perfect teeth as the fast train to London tore past the station.

Her heart was thumping in her chest. She held her portfolio in front of her like a shield as she strode up to them.

'Have you any idea how dangerous that is?' she demanded.

They all turned to look at her, their expressions polite but puzzled.

'I know you think it's hilarious, but what if you got hit? How do you think the driver would feel?' She could feel her voice rise with indignation.

'Hey, look—we've been running across that track since we were . . .' The tallest held his hand out to indicate the height of a small child.

'I don't care. Have you ever seen someone hit by a train?'

The three of them looked at each other, and shook their heads.

'Well I have, and it's not pretty.' She hadn't, but she wanted to get her point across.

'Everyone does it,' said one of them.

For some reason Claire felt tears stinging her eyes.

'You're total idiots,' she told them. 'You

obviously don't have a thought for anyone else, do you? All you care about is how much of a laugh you're having. You deserve to get squashed.'

She spun on her heel and walked off. She could hear the three of them conferring behind her, whispering, laughing. She felt a hand on her shoulder and whirled round, furious.

'Don't take the piss.'

'I wasn't going to. You're totally right. And our mother would be livid if she knew what we'd done. It's one of her rules. One of her only rules.'

By her estimation, this must be the middle brother. Maybe a couple of years older than her? Certainly old enough to know better. He was wearing faded jeans and a striped shirt under a baggy jumper, and Converse sneakers. His hair was dirty blond, the fringe falling into his eyes, which were twinkling at her. Brown eyes, with long lashes. Thoughtful eyes, she decided, and realised she had been totally disarmed.

The little local train pulled in, insignificant by comparison to the 125 that had sped past earlier. He took her by the elbow.

'Come and sit with us,' he pleaded. 'We want to prove that we're not prats. Not really.'

It was the last thing she wanted to do. She wanted to sit as far away from them as possible, plug herself into her music, think about her project. But they were completely and utterly impossible to resist. They herded her into the carriage; sat her by the window. Her assailant was Nick, the middle brother and nineteen, just as she had guessed. Felix was the oldest at twenty-one; seventeen-year-old Shrimp, still at school, was so-called because he was nearly six foot four. They hit her with a barrage of questions. When had she moved to Mimsbury? And why? What was she doing there? Who did she know?

She laughed.

'What is this? The Spanish Inquisition?'

'The Mimsbury Inquisition. We need to know.'

'Okay. I moved here with my mum and dad three weeks ago. They work at Aldermaston. I'm at the college, doing A-levels. And I don't know anyone yet—though I've just started working at the Mimsbury Arms. Waitressing.'

The three of them looked at each other.

'Well,' said Nick. 'You better come to our party on Saturday. Actually, it's our parents' party, but we're allowed to ask friends.'

'Party?' Claire panicked inwardly. She thought she could imagine the sort of parties they had. Girls with long, glossy hair in taffeta dresses. Men in dinner jackets. The thought made her stomach curdle.

'Don't look so frightened,' laughed Nick. 'It's not a posh do. Just come as you are—that's the rule. We live at the Mill House.'

He said it as if she would know exactly which house he meant.

'I don't know what I'm doing on Saturday. I'll probably be working.'

'Well, come afterwards.' These boys were clearly not used to taking no for an answer. 'Things never get going till eleven o'clock anyway.'

Claire decided it was easier to agree to come than to carry on protesting. They were the sort of people who would probably forget they had even invited her once she was out of their sight.

'Well, thank you,' she said. 'I'd love to come.'

Of course she had no intention of going. Charming though they appeared, Claire didn't think the Barnes boys were her sort of thing at all. She would have nothing in common with them whatsoever.

Yet when they got off at Newbury and hugged her goodbye, she watched them ramble off down the platform together and felt a strange warm feeling in the pit of her stomach. And then Nick turned round and looked at her, held up his hand to wave, and the warmth diffused further, spreading up towards her heart.

'See you Saturday,' he shouted.

He was so not her type. He was posh, privileged, educated, rich, glamorous . . .

Kind, fun, thoughtful.

Sexy.

She was disconcerted to find the warmth spreading downwards too.

*   *   *

Saturday arrived, of course, unashamedly glorious, the perfect English summer's day. Phil, the landlord of the Mimsbury Arms, had called to ask Claire to come in—the pub was going to be rammed; he needed all hands on deck. She was more than happy to oblige. It meant she didn't actually have to make a decision about whether to attend the party. The decision had been made for her.

Nevertheless, as the afternoon drew on, she decided to leave home early and take the scenic route into work by cutting across the field at the back of the house and approaching the pub from the other direction, following the river.

She pretended that this was to give herself some exercise, but deep down she knew it was curiosity. She found herself intrigued. She wanted a closer look at the house the Barnes boys lived in. She had a feeling that their world and hers were miles apart, but she wanted to make quite sure.

The house her parents had rented in Mimsbury was fairly nondescript, which took some doing, as the little village was famously picturesque. It was mostly made up of cottages in mellow red brick and flint, but the council had obviously got lax at some point in the mid-seventies and allowed a small close of boxes to be built just on the outskirts, as dreary and anonymous as you could wish, which of course suited Claire's parents down to the ground. They managed to find the most unprepossessing house in the village, with its metal windows, mean patch of garden and larch-lap fencing. On the other hand, it was more attractive than the semi they had lived in on the main road through Isleworth, though that wasn't saying much.

Claire had lived a totally urban existence until now. From the age of twelve she'd been a latch-key kid, making her way to and from school by bus, travelling further afield by train at the weekends, buying herself food from the One Stop shop if her parents were late home. Moving to the country made her feel listless, lacking in tension. She found that the fresh air and the sunshine and the quiet and the sound of birdsong rather than aeroplanes flying overhead took some getting used to. And not having to worry about traffic was strange. She was grateful for the job at the pub, which gave a momentum to weekends she had no idea how to fill. She'd met a few people at college, but she

64

didn't know them well enough yet to agree to meet up. She was essentially quite shy, and not keen on change, so serving food at the local seemed the perfect way to fill the void until she got herself a social life.

Her encounter with the Barnes brothers had taken her by surprise. Instinct told her to run a mile from their privileged insouciance, yet there had been a warmth in them that spoke to her. And so she found herself leaving early for work, taking a diversion, irresistibly drawn to see just where it was they came from. It was a balmy evening as she crossed the field, the long grass slapping at her bare legs, then wandered through the lanes to the east of the village, passing slumbering cats and sweet-scented hanging baskets—in Mimsbury, you were undoubtedly judged on your horticultural ability. Only the occasional car passed by, at a sedate speed. Isleworth would have been frantic with Saturday traffic at this time—the boom of bass and pipping horns, the smell of exhaust fumes entwining with the stench of frying food from the takeaways gearing up for their busiest night. As she took the left fork past the station and followed the river, she felt the tug of anticipation in the pit of her stomach. She knew from consulting the OS map her parents had bought that the Mill House was just around the corner.

Nothing could have prepared her for the fairy tale she found as she rounded the bend. The Mill House was built of brick that had softened to a mellow dusty coral. With a profusion of wonky half-hipped roofs, and run through with bleached oak timber beams, it sprawled behind the ebullient river Pease, a wooden bridge connecting it to the real world. At its side the mill wheel turned, determined and relentless, whilst behind it languished an acre of softly lush lawn studded with weeping willows. Outside were parked a silver Range Rover, a sporty Golf and a small van with smart black livery that proclaimed 'Melchior Barnes—Wine Merchants'.

The scene took Claire's breath away. It was hard to believe that mere mortals actually lived there. What was particularly charming was that it wasn't preserved in self-conscious pristine perfection, which you might have expected from the jewel in Mimsbury's crown. It was clear on not especially close inspection that it was a family house, and the chaos of their life was evident to anyone who cared to look. The smell of cooking and the sound of laughter and music floated out of the open windows: the party preparations were clearly in full flow. Claire could see a man battling to put up a green linen gazebo in the garden. He must be the boys' father. Even from here, he looked too posh, too well bred, to be staff.

She felt like some Dickensian urchin pressing her nose up against a window into a better world. Before anyone could see her staring, she slipped away, wondering why on earth she had done this to herself. Yes, they'd extended a disingenuous invitation to a party, but she knew wild horses wouldn't drag her there, and they wouldn't miss her. She was taunting herself.

She hurried away, anxious to put as much distance between herself and the Mill House as possible. She headed back along the main road towards the centre of the village, her shoes coated in dust, perspiring slightly from the heat of the

66

early-evening sun. It would be boiling in the kitchen at the pub. And it would be crowded—people would be crammed into the garden, hoping to eke out the last hour of sunshine over a drink. Oh well, at least she'd be busy, not left alone with her thoughts.

At last the Mimsbury Arms came into view, perched on the other side of the road, a handsome coaching inn painted a soft cream. She darted inside, greeting Mel, the landlord's wife, with relief and more effusiveness than she usually managed. Mel she could handle. Mel was salt of the earth, the proverbial busty barmaid, Mimsbury born and bred. She had no airs and graces. She was no threat.

Nevertheless, as they stacked the shelves with bottles and filled the ice buckets, she found herself asking, as casually as she could, about Nick and his brothers.

'The infamous Barnes boys?' Mel's eyes widened. 'Where did you meet them, then?'

Her tone indicated that she was surprised Claire had come into contact with them.

'At the train station. I had a go at them for running across the tracks when the barrier was down.'

Mel grinned. 'How did they take that?'

'Actually, I felt a bit like the nanny, telling them off like that. But they were all over me afterwards.'

Mel nodded knowingly. 'They're lovely boys, all three of them. They just get a bit high-spirited sometimes. When their mum was ill, they were positively feral, but they've calmed down a lot since. Grown up, I suppose.'

'What was the matter with her?'

'The Big C. It was terrible.' Mel started

67

unloading the glass washer. 'They spent loads of time in here while Isobel was having her treatment,' she continued. 'Gerald, their dad, is a bit useless. A total charmer, but he didn't have a clue how to look after them. He used to bring them in here for their dinner every night. Or just send them over with fifty quid. More money than sense. He should have got a woman in to look after them all.' She went a bit misty-eyed. 'I'd have done it.'

'They live in the Mill House, right?'

Mel sighed. 'Wouldn't you just die to live in a place like that? It's my dream house. It's not going to happen, though. None of them would look at me.'

'Or me,' laughed Claire in collusion, and Mel didn't contradict her, thereby confirming her suspicions. The Barnes brothers were out of her league. As she laid out fresh towelling cloths on the bar, she felt relief. She wasn't going to have to subject herself to the inevitable humiliation after all.

*   *   *

By quarter to eleven she was done in. She was rushed off her feet serving breaded scampi, steak and ale pie and chips, and black forest gateau, for the restaurant was extremely popular on a Saturday night, and they managed to squeeze in three sittings. By eleven o'clock every table was cleared, and Phil told her to go to the bar for half a lager—waitress's perks. All Claire wanted to do was to go home and crawl into the bath, to get the smell of cooking out of her hair and skin, but it was rude and unsociable not to take him up on his offer. She had just perched

68

at the bar and asked for a splash of lime in her lager when she felt a tap on her shoulder.

It was Nick. Nick, looking dishevelled in a white shirt with the collar turned up and the cuffs undone, and tight black jeans. Her mouth went dry.

'I knew you wouldn't come of your own accord,' he grinned. 'So I've had strict instructions not to leave until I've dragged you kicking and screaming.'

Claire shook her head.

'No way. I can't come dressed like this.' She indicated the polyester shirt and black skirt that was the pub uniform.

Nick held up a bag, triumphantly.

'We knew you'd say that, so we raided Mum's wardrobe. You're about the same size.'

He pulled out a dress—a red silk shift, totally plain but beautifully cut.

'I need a bath. My hair's . . .'

She held her hands up to her head in mock despair.

He reached behind and pulled out the scrunchie that was holding back her curls, and ruffled his fingers through them till her hair fell to her shoulders.

'It's great. What's the problem?'

Claire searched for another excuse.

'I've got no make-up.'

Nick whistled to get Mel's attention.

'Mel—can Claire borrow some make-up?'

Mel came over, eyeing the pair of them with relish. She could sense gossip brewing. She grinned at Claire as she rummaged in the handbag she kept behind the bar and pulled out a bag bulging with Boots special offers.

Claire stood for a moment, the dress in one

69

hand, Mel's make-up in the other. She had run out of excuses.

'Go on,' said Nick. 'Go into the bog and change. I'm not leaving without you. And don't get any ideas about jumping out of the window.'

Moments later Claire stared at herself helplessly in the mirror. What on earth was she supposed to do to make herself presentable? She wasn't a vain creature, but every girl faced with an invitation such as this would want to look her best.

She rarely wore make-up; she didn't see the point in drawing attention to herself. She thought she was ordinary at best, and would have been surprised to discover that, in fact, she had the sort of natural beauty that crept up on people. It was only when they'd known her for a while that it occurred to them that she was utterly ravishing. She was completely unaware of the phenomenon, as people tended not to mention their discovery. Instead, she was hypercritical; she considered her features unassuming, and rarely did anything to enhance her looks. Yet her face was a perfect oval, with a high forehead from which her dark-brown hair sprang wild and untamed to her shoulders. Her eyebrows arched over blue-green eyes with a dark rim around the iris. Her skin was pale, smothered in freckles, and her mouth, with its full, pale-pink lips, curled up in a smile like a cat. She was skinny, but she hid her figure under jeans and baggy beaded tops and an old army parka. The whole effect screamed 'don't look at me'.

Tonight, however, she felt the need for artifice. And although Mel's colours were all wrong and too harsh for her, she rooted through the bag with shaky fingers, applying the contents in a haphazard

70

fashion. Then she hurled off her uniform and slipped into the dress Nick had given her. The silk was slippery under her fingers, and as she pulled it over her head, she breathed in the perfume Nick's mother must have had on the last time she wore it, something hauntingly floral. She battled with the zip for a few moments, and as it closed, the dress moulded itself to her, sweeping over the curve of her breasts, in at her narrow waist then out again over her hips.

As she bundled her own clothes into the bag Nick had brought the dress in, she realised she had nothing at all to put on her feet. She couldn't wear the shoes she'd worn to work. They were flat and black with clumpy soles. She'd just have to go barefoot, she decided.

She fluffed up her hair, breathed in, and plucked up the courage to look in the mirror. The dress fitted perfectly. The neckline was low; the hem fell just above her knees. It emphasised her tiny waist and her not inconsiderable cleavage. Her cloud of hair fell wild down her back. Her eyes were ringed with kohl and her lashes were thick and long with mascara. Lipstick had transformed her mouth into a red pout. She felt a little fizz in her stomach. This was why people dressed up. For the thrill of being someone else. She grinned at herself, and a minx grinned back.

She came back into the bar barefoot. Nick's jaw dropped when he saw her.

'Bloody hell,' was all he could manage.

Behind him, Mel gave her a triumphant thumbs-up of approval.

'Come on then,' said Claire. 'Let's party.'

Because of her bare feet, they walked over the verges, retracing the journey she had made earlier, although she made no mention of it. She didn't want to admit to her interest, like some weird stalker. As they walked, Nick filled her in on his family. He and his older brother, Felix, worked for their father in the family business.

'Dad's a wine merchant. He says the business is his legacy to us, though to be honest, Felix isn't really interested. He's finally going up to Cambridge to do law in October, because it turns out he's a bit of a brainbox. Mum and Dad don't know how it could have happened, because they haven't got a qualification between them. Dad says he's just a professional pisshead, and Mum . . .' He paused for a moment. 'Mum's just Mum. She's never been interested in a career. She says she's never met a happy career woman.'

'How very . . . post-feminist of her.'

Nick looked sideways, not sure if Claire was winding him up.

'She's probably right,' Claire added hastily. 'I'm not sure that my mother's happy. And her work is the only thing that matters to her.'

'What does she do, then?'

'She's a scientist. A physicist. I have no idea what she *actually* does. I didn't get her brains, or Dad's. I think I'm a bit of a disappointment to them.'

'That's sad.'

Claire shrugged.

'I'm used to it. They're not horrible or anything.'

'No . . .'

'Just . . . not very interested.'

'That's cruel, to have kids and not take an interest in them.' He stopped and turned to look at her. 'How could anyone not be interested in you?'

Claire felt her heart start to melt, just a little, like an ice cream that's being eaten too slowly.

'They *care*. Of *course* they care. But they just don't understand art or poetry or music . . . any of the stuff I like.'

Nick made a face. 'They sound . . .'

'Boring?' Claire laughed. 'They enjoy a lively debate on quantum physics.'

'And do you?'

'Um . . . no. I gave up science as soon as I could. Which didn't thrill them, but as Dad said, you can lead a girl to science but you can't make her think.'

'Wow.' Nick looked disgusted. 'You'd better not introduce me.'

'It's okay. They let me go my own way. It's cool.'

'But . . . lonely. You seem lonely.'

Claire bristled. She realised she painted a blacker picture of her life than it really was.

'I'm not. Honestly. They do love me. And I love them.'

'Good.'

'And if I seem lonely, it's because I've left all my mates behind. I don't know anyone here.'

They'd arrived outside the house. It was lit up from the inside, loud music spilling out on to the road. Claire stopped, suddenly overcome with nerves.

Nick took her hand.

'Hey. It's okay. After tonight, you'll have more friends than you know what to do with.'

Claire's mouth felt dry. This had been a really bad idea. Given half a chance, she'd turn tail and run barefoot up the road back to her mum and dad right now. Flop on the sofa, flip on the ancient telly, make them a cup of tea, raid the biscuit tin . . .

'Come on.'

He could sense her disquiet, but he wasn't going to give her the chance to bolt. She screwed up every last drop of courage as he led her over the bridge. The river swirled underneath, dark and cool and dangerous. She could hear the mill wheel turning, scudding through the water. He pushed open the front door, led her through a hall that could comfortably have accommodated her own lounge with room to spare, and then into the kitchen.

It was mayhem. Unashamed mayhem. There must have been thirty people, all talking, laughing, drinking. A girl in a short swishy black skirt and long black boots stood on the kitchen table, dancing an improvised flamenco to the sound of Spanish guitar on the sound system, flicking her hair back and forth provocatively. A Rubenesque woman sat in a huge armchair dandling a baby—he paddled his feet in the air, seemingly oblivious to the noise and the hour. A birdcage hung over the table, and in it an orange canary sang along to itself. A set of folding glass doors at the back opened out into the garden, where lanterns led the way to the river's edge. More people were spilling out of the doors, laughing, drinking, dancing on the terrace.

And in the middle of it all was the most beautiful woman Claire had ever seen. Tiny, fragile, with a white-blonde pixie crop, wearing an ice-blue dress and an armful of silver bracelets, she flitted from one guest to the next. Nick took Claire's hand, pulled her towards the woman.

'This is my mother,' he said, grabbing a glass of

74

champagne from a tray on the side and handing it to her. 'Mum, this is Claire, who I told you about. Claire, this is Isobel.'

The woman turned, and Claire was met with a pair of eyes that exactly matched the ice blue of her dress. But they weren't cold. They were the colour of the sun dancing on a fjord—bright and clear and shining. Isobel held out her arms and wrapped them around Claire's neck, hugging her to her. Claire wasn't used to effusive body contact. Her parents never hugged her. Usually she would stiffen given such familiarity, but Isobel was so warm, she just melted into her embrace, breathing in the scent of crushed violets. The smell of the dress she herself was wearing.

'Nick tells me you tore the boys off a strip for running across the level crossing?' Her voice was surprisingly deep for such a fragile creature; a Marianne Faithfull drawl.

Claire felt her cheeks redden. Was Isobel one of those protective mothers who didn't like other people disciplining her offspring?

'It's dangerous.'

'It certainly is. And I've told them often enough. Good for you.' She flicked her eyes to the ceiling in a minimal gesture of fond exasperation. 'Honestly, do you think they'll ever grow up?'

Claire could tell that, despite her plea, Isobel thought her sons were pretty much perfect as they were. And indeed they were. You couldn't fail to be charmed. Gangly Shrimp, slight Felix, and the relatively solid Nick, as close as the Three Musketeers but individuals in their own right. Already she could see that Felix was the thinker, Shrimp the joker and Nick the mediator, the roles clearly defined between them.

She realised that Isobel was still looking at her, still had her arms wrapped round her neck.

'Nick said you were gorgeous.'

Claire started. No one had ever called her that before.

'He's right. You *are* gorgeous.' Isobel stroked a finger down Claire's cheek as if to confirm that she was a living, breathing human, then nodded in approval before sliding off and going to greet the next guest. People still seemed to be arriving, even though it was almost midnight. Nick had disappeared, swept off into the crowd now that he had made his introductions. Suddenly self-conscious, both from Isobel's attention and because of the fact that she was now standing on her own and knew no one, Claire took a greedy gulp from her glass of champagne. She wasn't equipped for this party. Not at all. She thought perhaps she'd been brought along as a novelty. A curiosity for them all to gawp at. They seemed the type of people to have low boredom thresholds.

She wondered if she could just slink away. No one would notice if she trickled out of the front door. She could put the dress back through the letter box tomorrow . . .

And then she felt a pair of arms slide themselves around her waist from behind, and a warm mouth burrowing itself in her hair, and the world around her fell away. She knew without looking that it was Nick. He crossed his hands over her tummy and it turned over and over, like an exuberant toddler who has just learnt to somersault.

'Come and dance,' he said.

Ricky Martin was on the sound system, 'Livin' la

Vida Loca', and everyone had hit the floor.

'I don't dance.'

'Don't be silly. Everyone can dance.'

'I didn't say I couldn't. I said I didn't.'

But he was leading her through the crowded kitchen, disregarding her protests, which were by now interspersed with laughter, until he found a space, and then he put one hand on her waist and held her hand with the other. Claire forgot that dancing made her feel clumsy and self-conscious and moved with him, twirling like a ballerina on top of a jewellery box. Ricky Martin faded into 'Smooth' by Santana, a slower pace, and Nick pulled her in close.

'Tell me something about yourself that you've never told anyone before,' he said.

She put her head to one side, considering the challenge.

'I love spiders,' she replied.

'You'll like this house, then,' he told her. 'It's full of them. Big, fat, hairy ones.'

'My favourite sort.'

'You are funny.'

'What about you?' she said. 'Tell me something about you.'

He looked at her. Her tummy flipped again.

'I believe in love at first sight.'

She took a breath.

'Of course,' she replied. 'Who doesn't?'

'I didn't until Tuesday.' The import of this statement hung between them. 'I want to kiss you.'

He stopped dancing and looked at her. There were bodies all around them, spinning, gyrating, arms and hair flailing, but in the centre of the vortex it felt still. Claire wondered fleetingly if he did this all the time, brought home some random pretty girl and kissed her in full view of everyone. Then she tipped back her head and a sensation of blissful warmth washed over her from head to toe as their lips met. Their arms became more tightly wound around each other, as if they were each trying to pull the other inside them.

If she'd known that falling in love was going to be this easy, she would never have been afraid. If she'd known it was going to be this wonderful, she definitely wouldn't have waited so long. Although perhaps it wouldn't have been the same with someone else . . . How would she know? She had nothing to compare it to.

On the other side of the room, Isobel watched. And smiled. Then turned away. And if anyone had looked closely, they would have seen pain in her face, just for a fleeting moment, before she picked up her glass and made her way outside.

*　　　*　　　*

By two o'clock that morning, Claire realised that Nick was right. She had made more friends than she knew what to do with. Far from being intimidating, the Barneses and their friends were charming. They made her feel interesting. Made her feel beautiful—many of the men had commandeered her for a dance, and she'd felt like the belle of the ball. And whilst they were admiring of her, none of them was groping or lecherous. They treated her with respect. As she danced to 'Jumpin' Jack Flash' with Gerald, Nick's father, she reflected that she'd never had such a wonderful time in her life, never allowed herself to let her hair down. She'd always judged 'posh' people, assumed them to be obsessed with avoiding tax and using the right knife and fork and killing defenceless animals.

As the song ended, Gerald led her away from the dance floor with the utmost chivalry and gave her yet another glass of champagne to cool herself down. Her head was starting to spin with all she had drunk, and she put out a hand to steady herself.

'Hey.' Nick was at her side, concerned. 'Come on. Let's take you to bed. You look done in.'

She felt slightly alarmed as he led her out of the kitchen, through the hall and up the meandering staircase. What did he mean? Had he just assumed she was going to stay the night? Did he think he had some right over her? Was she going to have to fight him off? Just because she'd accepted his hospitality, had she entered into some unspoken agreement? *Droit de seigneur*—she remembered that from history . . .

She braced herself as they reached the bedroom door, but as Nick put his hand on the handle, he turned to her with such a kind smile, a smile that reached right inside and reassured her, that she didn't care what happened. She trusted him, implicitly. She felt entirely safe in his hands.

She followed him in. It was an attic room, long and low-ceilinged, with dormer windows and wooden floors. Snug and cosy, with built-in cupboards at one end, almost like a ship's cabin. It was a riot of blokiness, a weird mixture of boy meets man; Ralph Lauren meets *The Beano*. Old school photos jostled for position with posters of Kylie and Elizabeth Hurley. The dressing table was covered in bottles of expensive aftershave, cans of deodorant and jars of hair gel. An ancient teddy sat in a chair, gazing at the surroundings solemnly. There were piles and piles of CDs, some of them in wooden wine crates that were stacked up against one wall next to an elaborate sound system. A huge corkboard was covered in invitations, postcards, concert tickets and silly photos of Nick and his mates—a collage of a life that was so different to hers, as she spotted formally engraved requests to attend eighteenth birthday parties, and pictures of the family on the slopes in Val d'Isère. She had never been to a black-tie party or skiing; nor was she likely to go, yet it was as normal as breathing to Nick. For a moment she wished she had insisted on going home. Nerves overtook her again. This wasn't her world.

'You can have my bed,' said Nick cheerfully. 'Mrs B changes the sheets on a Friday, so you've only got one day of my mucky sweat to contend with.'

He plumped up the pillow and shook out the duvet—navy blue-and-white stripes. Claire could imagine Isobel choosing his bed linen with care. She couldn't imagine her mother buying sheets at all. She had no idea where anything in the house had come from. Her mother never went shopping.

'I won't look,' he said, turning away. 'I've got a spare duvet and pillows in the cupboard. I'll sleep on the floor.'

When he turned back with his arms full of bedding, Claire was standing by the bed, naked in the moonlight.

'Share with me,' she said. 'Keep me warm.'

And so, in his single bed, with 'Nightswimming' by REM playing softly in the background, she gave herself to the first man she had ever fallen in love with.

The first man. And the last.

*   *   *

Claire found herself in a brand-new world. Sometimes she asked herself why. Why had she been chosen? She was so unlike all the other girls in the Barnes circle—the Tashes and Hatties and Millies. Nick could have had any one of them. He had charm, money, background, confidence, the big house—all the attributes that entitled him to one of these long-haired, long-legged creatures with their affected drawls, their Pony Club confidence, their assumption that the world owed them a wealthy husband.

Maybe it was because she didn't make that assumption. Nick just shushed her when she asked what he saw in her, then pointed out that she made him see the world differently.

'I love my friends, but they are all tossers,' he admitted to her one day as they lay in bed. 'They don't give a thought to anyone else. But you do. You make me think.'

'Oh right, so I'm your social conscience?' Claire wasn't sure this was a compliment.

'There's other things.' Nick ran a hand up her thigh and nuzzled her shoulder. 'Like the fact that you fuck like a wild thing. All those other girls just lie there until it's over, thinking of England.'

Claire gave an indignant gasp, pretend-fighting him off, but it was in vain and eventually she gave herself up to him, laughing. She could never get enough. They were joined at the hip from that first night, she and Nick. Soulmates sounded like such

81

a cliché, but she really did feel as if they shared a spirit, an understanding, even though they were so very different. It transformed her from a girl into a woman. Life suddenly made perfect sense. It had meaning.

And, thankfully, the rest of the family took to her. She wasn't made to feel like a black sheep, like some commoner who wasn't good enough. Felix and Shrimp treated her like a sister, teasing her but also protecting her: one of them would always give her a lift if she needed it and Nick wasn't available; they made her cups of tea, lent her their big fleecy sweatshirts when she was cold, and their favourite CDs so she could play them in her Walkman on the way to college.

And Gerald, who adored female company, was delighted to have another woman about the place. With his dark soulful eyes and thick hair that was just starting to grey, he had the air of a devil-may-care roué, and he played up to the role. He was an incorrigible flirt, with a battery of outrageous remarks, and was rarely to be found without a drink in one hand and a cigarette in the other. But Claire soon worked out that it was just an act, that he was all talk, and was utterly devoted to Isobel.

When Claire revealed that she had subsisted most of her life on offerings from Fray Bentos, Crosse & Blackwell and Heinz, Gerald took it upon himself to educate her. Gerald was obsessed with food and wine, and didn't understand why the whole world didn't feel the same. Having a keen student meant he could run riot with his culinary expertise. He fed her plump olives coated in fine herbs, and fat, juicy *boquerones*, and Venezuelan dark chocolate. Soft, oozing Vacherin and piquant Dolcelatte. He made her crab linguine and Irish soda bread and coq au vin. Claire was gratifyingly appreciative, while the rest of the family rolled their eyes. They had been brought up with Gerald's passion, learnt that he needed praise like a small child for each of his offerings, but her relish was genuine.

And if food was a revelation, wine was an epiphany. She discovered—or rather Gerald did—that she had an extraordinarily refined palate. He loved nothing better than to open a bottle of something new for her and ask her for tasting notes. Since she hadn't been brought up drinking wine, she was a total novice, and her reaction was always unaffected. 'Play-Doh?' she would suggest, and Gerald would bark with delighted laughter.

She found the family business fascinating. Melchior Barnes (there was no Melchior—Gerald had simply rather liked the name when he set up the company fifteen years ago) was housed in a canal-side warehouse in Sandleford, a nearby town made up of genteel antique shops, delicatessens and boutiques. They supplied wine to restaurants and hotels, as well as discerning individuals. They also imported the finest Cuban cigars. Gerald was the sales director and spent his life schmoozing clients old and new, luring them to tastings and urging them to be ever more experimental in their choice of wine. Felix and Nick dealt with the practicalities—the ordering, the storage, the delivery.

'What we really need, though,' said Gerald one day, staring at Claire, 'is a marketing director. We should be sponsoring events, getting our name out there, going to wedding fairs, setting up a wine club . . .'

'You don't mean me?' she said.

'Why not? It would be perfect for you. You're creative, imaginative. You love wine. You're far more organised than any of us.'

'I haven't even finished my A-levels yet. I can't be a director.'

Gerald did the habitual Barnes wave of the hand, which summarily dismissed any fears.

'You'll be finished by June. You can start in the summer.'

Something inside Claire urged caution. It really did smack of having all her eggs in one basket. So much of her life was already taken up with the Barnes family. For a moment she felt slightly smothered.

'Surely you need someone with experience?'

Gerald flapped her objection away.

'I can train you up. How hard can it be? You're smart. You get what we're about. Learn on the job.'

Claire looked sceptical.

'Can I think about it?'

'Of course. I don't want to railroad you into anything.'

But that was the trouble with the Barnes family. They did railroad you into things, without you even noticing. You got swept along by their enthusiasm, their infectious *joie de vivre*, and before you knew it, they had you exactly where they wanted you.

Isobel shared the family trait. Claire knew that boyfriends' mothers could be tricky and jealous and manipulative, but nothing could be further from the truth in Isobel's case. She welcomed Claire with open arms, becoming a combination of sister, best friend and mum. And subtly and tactfully, she masterminded Claire's transformation from drab student to siren, encouraging her to develop her own style, luring her into shops she would never have dreamt of going into, urging her to try things she would never normally try.

'Of course you can wear a dress that short. You're only seventeen and you've got amazing legs.'

'Go for the pink. Grey's so drab. Pink makes you look an absolute angel.'

'Have two. If you like it, have two.'

Of course, it helped that quite often Isobel was picking up the tab. Not that Claire expected her to—she was happy to pay her own way from what she was earning at the pub—but Isobel was embarrassingly generous, and seemed to get as much of a thrill out of buying for someone else as she did for herself. Until now, Claire's uniform had been jeans, but in Isobel's world jeans were for gardening. It wasn't that she was overly dressy, but she loved beautiful clothes, pretty things, looking nice, and she was quite determined that Claire should be the same. And Claire found that she enjoyed this new, more feminine version of herself. Superficial it might be, but it made her feel good to walk into a room and be greeted enthusiastically, be showered with compliments.

This was what having a proper mother felt like, thought Claire. It wasn't that her own mother didn't love her, of course she did, but she never took any real interest in her, or wanted to spend time with her. Whenever Claire was at home, she felt like A. N. Other member of the household, an independent being who came and went regardless of what everyone else was up to. There was usually food in the cupboard or the fridge, but the meals they had were still mostly out of a packet or a tin or the freezer section. Claire tried to cook some of the dishes she'd picked up from Gerald, but her parents were politely uninterested. There was no enthusiasm. So she spent less and less time with them, and sometimes she thought that perhaps they were relieved to have her off their hands.

Isobel insisted on asking her parents to supper, and Claire couldn't think of any way of getting out of it that didn't make her seem rude or cruel. It was excruciating, watching her drab, passive mother and father in the riot of the Barnes kitchen, trying to make polite conversation about whether they were going to the open-air concert at Highclere Castle (no), where they were going on holiday (nowhere), and were they joining in the open garden scheme in August (not a chance). Claire squirmed with embarrassment at her mother's shapeless blue cardigan and drawstring trousers; her father's supermarket trainers. Both Isobel and Gerald battled valiantly; plied them with delicious food and delicious wine that was totally wasted on them. Claire knew that the Meursault was heading for thirty quid a bottle, and it might as well have been Blue Nun as far as her parents were concerned. For a moment she hated them for their introspection and their lack of social skills, and then she hated herself for feeling that way. They were her parents, after all, and they had never been unkind, and it was hardly their fault that they weren't like Isobel and Gerald.

She knew she'd changed, and she wondered if they had noticed. Claire suddenly felt visible. Alive and sparkling and visible, having done her best to keep herself unnoticed for most of her life. And with this new lease of life came confidence. She felt like a someone, and not a nobody. And if, perhaps, she feared that without the Barnes she would go back to being a nobody, she never vocalised it.

*   *   *

By the time her A-levels were nearly over, Claire knew that working for Melchior Barnes was her destiny. She hadn't found an alternative that offered a life anything like as challenging or exciting. And so it was decided that after her exams she would take up the post of marketing director. Her future was mapped out. She knew that before long she and Nick would get married. They'd even, one idle afternoon, decided on their children's names. Tabitha for a girl; Archie for a boy.

But fate, it seemed, had other plans for all of them.

*   *   *

One afternoon Claire finished college early and headed straight to the Mill House. She knew Nick wouldn't be home yet, but she had learnt to treat the place as her own. She would make herself a cup of tea, read a book in the garden for an hour or so, then go up to his bedroom to wait for him.

Isobel was at the kitchen table. She looked up as Claire came in, but she didn't smile. Claire stopped in the middle of the room. Isobel always smiled.

'What is it?' she asked, feeling cold dread claw its way up her spine.

Isobel didn't reply. There was a terrible stillness to her. She pressed her lips together, and Claire could see they were trembling. She stepped forward. Whatever was wrong with Isobel, it wasn't an accident, or something that involved another member of the family. It was something private; something personal.

'Isobel?' She bent down towards her and slid an arm round her shoulder. The older woman felt fragile, her shoulders bony under her cashmere sweater. She sighed and rested her head against Claire, and a tangible weariness emanated from her.

'I couldn't beat the bastard,' she said. 'I just couldn't fucking beat the bastard.'

Claire frowned. Isobel rarely swore. She sat down in the chair next to her, took her hands in hers, rubbed her thumbs over the backs of them in the hope of giving some comfort.

'What bastard?' she asked. 'Who?'

Isobel's eyes sought hers. Her gaze was piercing, the bright blue made even brighter by unshed tears.

'You're absolutely not to tell the boys. Or Gerald. I trust you, Claire. They won't be able to cope. They couldn't last time. I can't put them through it again. This is my battle . . .'

'Of course I won't tell them.' Claire felt a black cloud on the horizon. It loomed, menacing, threatening to engulf them all.

'I don't know if Nick told you . . . I had cancer about four years ago.'

Claire frowned.

'He has told me, yes. But he's never really talked about it.'

'No. Well, it was a pretty awful time. And

none of us handled it terribly well. I was very ill, obviously, and Gerald just . . . fell apart, and the boys ran amok.' She breathed in, as if to compose herself. 'I had surgery, and the dreaded chemo, and it was grim, grim, grim. I genuinely did just want to roll over and die. And I think they all thought I was going to. You hear such amazing stories of families pulling together and being brave in the face of illness, but it nearly destroyed us.' Isobel put her hands on the table, as if to give herself support. 'Eventually I came through it, but it took me at least another year to regain my strength. I knew my hair would never be the same again.' She ruffled her blonde pixie crop ruefully. 'I used to have a golden mane that Barbie would kill for. Maybe it was nature's way of telling me I was too long in the tooth for big hair.'

'It suits you like that.'

Isobel just rolled her eyes.

'Hair isn't really the issue here.' She paused. Claire shivered. The cloud was pressing in. 'I've known something wasn't right for the past few months. I've been an ostrich about it. Because I can't go through it all again. And the boys can't. And Gerald absolutely can't.' She looked up. 'I went to my consultant last week. He sent me for a scan. I had the results today.'

She didn't need to tell Claire any more.

'Oh, Isobel . . .'

She half stood to go and hug her, but Isobel put her hands up.

'Please. Don't. I'll go to pieces. And they'll all be back in a minute. I've got to keep it together.'

She was tightening her fists into little balls, squeezing at the pain.

89

'I'm really sorry. I shouldn't have told you. But I only heard this afternoon. And I want you to promise me, absolutely promise me, that you won't say a word. I've got to find my own way to deal with this and I don't want any of them to know. They're all that matters to me and I don't want them to suffer any more than they need to.'

'But they'll want to know. They'll want to help. You can't go through this on your own.'

Isobel gave her a penetrating look.

'Yes I can. That's what I'm choosing to do. I'm appealing to you, as someone who loves Nick, and hopefully the rest of us, to be my ally. And sometimes my alibi. I'm going to need you to be both.'

Claire's stomach felt as if it was full of oily black diesel. She had no idea how to handle a situation like this. Her life had been so dull, so ordinary: until now she had never experienced drama or crisis. She adored Isobel, almost as much as she adored Nick. She had been so kind to her, so generous, so loving—almost, although she never said anything so corny, treated her like the daughter she had never had. So Claire owed her support.

'Of course. I'll do whatever you want. And I won't say a word.' She hoped she could talk her round eventually. Isobel was obviously still in shock from the news. Given time, she would see that this was not the way to deal with what had happened.

'Thank you.' Isobel grabbed her hands and squeezed them tight. 'It's very important. I'm going to deal with this. This is my problem . . .'

'But surely they'll know? Surely they'll notice?'

Isobel didn't answer. She looked away.

'They mustn't know. You must promise.'

Her tone was flat. And final.

Claire swallowed.

'Okay. I promise . . .'

The enormity of what she'd done overwhelmed her. How on earth was she going to keep her word?

CHAPTER SIX

A single tear trickled down Claire's cheek as she reached this part of her tale. She'd given Angelica a garbled précis of the story, but the memory was almost as painful as the day it had happened. Surely it should have faded, after all this time? She wiped away the tear before any more could come, although she could feel them queuing up. She couldn't lose it, not in public. Not in front of Angelica, who was looking aghast. And no wonder. She had never shared so much as a moment of weakness with her.

Until now. Claire, who had carried the burden of what had happened with her for twelve long years, was about to crumble. Guilt, regret, anger, grief— they all threatened to spill out of her.

'It's okay,' said Angelica, anxious. 'It's okay to be upset.'

Claire leant back in her chair and looked up at the ceiling.

'I know,' she said in a tight voice. 'It's just . . . I haven't thought about it for so long. And Nick turning up like that . . .'

She was interrupted by the sound of footsteps thundering down the stairs. Moments later, Luca appeared on the bottom flight, jumping the last three steps and bounding through the reception, as eager and leggy as a wolfhound ready for its morning walk. Luca, who could go from unconscious and supine to upright and alert in seconds, was ready for the day ahead.

He stood before them, smiling broadly. He was in a long-sleeved T-shirt and cargo pants, his mop of dark hair still wet from the shower. 'Hey, girls. What's going on?' he asked, bemused, raking one hand through his damp curls and tucking his T-shirt in with the other. Angelica gulped at the sight of his flat brown stomach.

'Nothing,' lied Claire. Not very well.

'You don't usually sit around quaffing Oyster Bay.'

'I'm sorry. It's my fault.' Angelica decided that Claire was rubbish at dissembling and was going to give herself away. 'Claire was just giving me some advice.'

'Oh.'

'Nothing major. Just a row with my stepdad. Same old, same old.' Angelica knew that the first rule of lying was not to give too much detail.

Luca turned to Claire, his lack of interest in Angelica's personal life obvious.

'Do we know what time Trevor and Monique are getting here?'

'Not till the evening, I don't think. I've booked them in for dinner.'

'I know. We're eating with them.'

'We are?'

'Eight-thirty.'

Claire sighed. 'This really isn't the best weekend for a major business meeting.'

'Tough.' Luca was crisp. 'You know what Trevor's like. He's the money man. If he wants to talk about business, then we drop everything.'

'And what about all our other guests? We're fully booked except for one room.'

'We can handle it. The guys in the kitchen know they've got to pull their weight if I need to take some time out. We're covered for staff.'

'I can stay till whenever, if you need me,' Angelica offered.

'Thanks, Angelica. You're a star.' Angelica knew that Claire's accompanying smile signified more than just gratitude for the offer. She'd got her out of a hole.

But with an awful inevitability, the hole was opening up again. Behind Luca, Angelica could see Nick coming down the stairs. As could Claire, who jumped up with a false hostessy smile.

'Nick,' she said, her voice high with tension. 'Come and meet Luca. He's going to be in charge of your stag dinner tomorrow. Luca, this is Nick. You won't believe the coincidence. I had no idea he was the groom. He's an old friend. We go back a long way.'

'Really.' Luca's tone was dry. He smiled, but it didn't reach his eyes, then held out his hand as an afterthought. Nick took it, the epitome of well-bred charm.

'It's a wonderful place you've got here.'

'It is,' agreed Luca. 'It is indeed.'

His eyes flicked from the empty bottle to Claire to Nick.

He knows, thought Angelica. *He knows this guy is a threat.* It was basic instinct, she supposed. Any minute now he'd be cocking his leg and peeing all over the furniture.

Nick smiled round at the three of them, sensing

93

awkwardness. Angelica thought she detected Claire giving him the slightest shake of her head, to warn him not to give anything away.

'I thought I'd go and check out the town, before the others arrive,' he managed eventually. 'They've not long left London, so they'll be a while yet.'

Claire nodded. 'Good idea. We'll look after them when they get here, don't worry.' She cleared her throat. 'The delicatessen does a good pasty.'

Luca smirked. Angelica felt queasy with tension. Nick shoved his hands in his jacket pockets.

'Well, I'll see you later, I guess.'

As he walked out of the door, three pairs of eyes followed him, but nothing was said.

'Well, this won't get the baby a new bonnet,' Claire spoke finally.

Luca raised an eyebrow.

'No, indeed.'

Angelica gathered up the empty glasses. And the by now empty bottle.

'It was only half full,' Claire told Luca.

'You don't have to explain. It's important, to have good staff relations.' He turned to Angelica. 'Let us know if you need any time out to get over your trauma.' You could have iced a cake with the sweet mockery in his voice.

Luca sauntered off towards the kitchen. Claire couldn't quite meet Angelica's eye. She realised she had told her too much. The shock and the wine had loosened her tongue.

'Shit,' she said.

'What are you going to do?' asked Angelica, dying to hear more.

'I've got no choice,' replied Claire. 'Keep calm and carry on.'

94

And she walked over to reception without a backward glance.

*   *   *

Luca always felt relaxed in his kitchen, even if no one else did. He had designed it exactly as he wanted it. He knew every switch, every appliance, every flame. He could have cooked a meal in here blindfold. He loved every square inch of its stainless-steel perfection. His knives were murderously sharp; his pans heavy and solid. His fridges were at the optimum temperature. His private collection of tools was kept in a big drawer, and woe betide anyone who borrowed so much as a measuring spoon. His rules were not made to be broken; they were made to be followed to the letter. Anyone who bucked the system wouldn't last the day. His two loyal sous-chefs, Fred and Loz, had learnt the hard way how to handle him, and had now earned his respect. Sure, they might have an easier life at one of the other hotels or restaurants in the area, but the food they produced would be nowhere near as good. Luca set the pace, and they were happy to keep up. They knew that if they screwed up one day and suffered his wrath, they would be triumphant the next and be heaped with praise. And now, he trusted them enough to let them do lunches without his supervision. They were prepping them now: a selection of light dishes to be served in the bar or on the terrace. Today's delights included a crab salad, a chunky rabbit terrine and lobster ravioli.

'Hey, boss!' Fred looked up from coaxing silken sheets of pasta out of the machine. Loz brought him over a caffè ristretto without being asked. They could already sense that Luca was feeling uptight. He wore his emotions so clearly on his face. Something had rattled him, so the two boys knew to keep their heads low and their output high.

. This was usually the part of the day Luca loved best, when he came into the kitchen to see what his suppliers had bought and began to put together the evening's menu. But today something wasn't right. He sensed a shift in Claire that he didn't like, and he suspected it was something to do with the man she had introduced him to. Claire wasn't very forthcoming about her past; she never had been. She said it was irrelevant and unspeakably dull, but Luca knew that a woman of her depth, her passion and her wisdom must have done some living.

Was this stag more than just an old friend? Something inside Luca told him he was. But he was going to play it cool for now. He'd learnt to curb his temper over the past few years. If Claire had taught him anything, it was that overreaction didn't get you anywhere. He was going to bide his time and make sure of the facts before he made his move, if any move was necessary.

He gulped down his coffee, reminding himself that, after all, the bloke was getting married next week. Maybe Claire just felt awkward at someone from her past appearing unannounced. She was very private.

So why had she hit the bottle? He'd never seen her do that before, not even when that couple had done a bunk without paying after staying a week and running up a massive bill. He certainly hadn't bought Angelica's cover story. Angelica was a tough nut. She was like him. A survivor. She didn't need Claire's bloody reassurance over a row with her

96

stepdad. Girls like Angelica ate stepfathers for breakfast.

He put the tiny cup in the dishwasher. He wasn't going to let the situation rattle him. This weekend was an important one. He didn't want to mess things up in front of Trevor and Monique. He was desperate for his own place in London; desperate to make a real name for himself. Sure, he had a great reputation, but Pennfleet was off the map. This was the next step, and a big one, and the last thing he wanted was for his investor to get cold feet. They had to come across as a team. A great team. Which they were. They absolutely were.

Luca liked to tell people he had learnt to cook in borstal, which was bullshit. Not that he hadn't been to borstal—he had; when he was seventeen, for stealing a car—but actually he'd learnt to cook when his mother dragged him to live with one of her lovers in the south of France. He had spent the whole summer in the kitchen of the village restaurant, learning at the feet of the irascible patron, and had emerged as accomplished a cook as any Michelin-starred chef. This was a typical interlude in Luca's life. His past was a patchwork splatter-gun portfolio of über-glamorous and harrowing, as he and his mother lurched from squalor to splendour, depending on her moods and who she was squiring. The little boy had trailed in her wake, one day playing with his toy cars on the terrace of a hotel in Cap Ferrat, the next shivering in a bedsit in Hammersmith. It had turned him into a complicated person. He was by turn arrogant and self-deprecating. Ebullient and withdrawn. Super-confident and needy. Addictive and controlled. Energised and exhausted. Gradually, over the past few years, Claire had learnt to predict his moods, had spotted the behaviour patterns and learnt how to deal with them. And taught him how to deal with them too, by and large. He was a much better person, he reflected, than the animal he'd been when they met.

Which was why he had been able to walk away from what he recognised as a situation, and was now calmly observing the fish tray.

Plump coral-coloured scallops—they could be pan-fried with some chorizo. A big net of navy-blue mussels—he would do something Thai, with coconut and chilli and coriander, to make a change from the usual moules marinière. Hot-pink crabs held out their claws in supplication—sorry, mate, he thought; it's a tian for you, with slivers of pink grapefruit. The sea bass wouldn't need any messing about with; he would just bake it in a thick crust of Cornish salt and serve it with some braised fennel. He picked through the assortment of mixed fish, checking for quality, but the fishmonger never let him down, never slipped in anything less than fresh. All that would go into the huge cast-iron pot that was already simmering on the gas burner, a rich mix of garlic and onions and tomatoes for his signature fish stew—he wasn't pretentious enough to call it bouillabaisse.

His menu was short, fluid, spontaneous. It included some old favourites, and he usually experimented with something new, but it entirely depended on what his suppliers brought him and how he was feeling. He ran his hands over the skin on a slab of pork belly—he would roast it until the fat was crispy and delicious, then serve it with a rhubarb compote. He could see the pink and green

98

stalks in the vegetable box. He squeezed some plump pears, visualising them in a toffee sauce with a frangipani crumble topping.

His last inspection was the bread basket. He didn't have time to bake the bread as well, and they couldn't afford to employ someone to do it at the moment, so he outsourced the breadmaking to a woman who had done location catering and had retired to Pennfleet. He frowned. The walnut rolls looked overdone. He prodded one suspiciously. Too hard; too dark. He ripped it open, tasted, grimaced.

'Fred!' he roared, as he snapped a parmesan shortbread straw in half, nodding in approval at its texture. 'Tell whatsername to bring me another batch of walnut rolls. These are no good.' He lobbed them across the room into the bin. 'And I've got some extra special guests tonight. I need to cook them an amazing meal. I want you to get your thinking caps on. Come up with a menu.' His eyes twinkled. 'Fifty quid to the winner.'

He was impulsively generous too.

He pulled a freshly laundered green bandanna out of a drawer, rolled it up and tied it round his curls.

'Okay,' he said. 'Let's go.'

*   *   *

At reception, Claire picked up a pile of envelopes.

'Angelica . . . I'm just popping out to the post office. I need to get these brochures in the mail today.'

Angelica looked at her. Claire never went to the post office. 'No problem. I'll be here.'

99

'Thanks.' Claire put the envelopes in her bag and headed for the door.

Outside, on the front step, flanked by two pristine bay trees, she looked to her left and then to her right. Pennfleet was tiny. There were only a few places Nick could possibly be. To the left there were a few shops, and then the road meandered towards the yacht club; he was unlikely to have gone that way. She turned right, raking her eyes from side to side as she hurried along the street, searching among the heads for his familiar dirty-blond hair. The sun was out; the town was filling up, people ambling along slowly. They were alarmed by her haste, which seemed out of place. They were all in holiday mode, in no rush to get anywhere, and her urgency jarred. It was the sort of behaviour that belonged in the rush hour, on the Tube, not at the start of a sunny weekend.

As she passed each shop she gave a perfunctory look inside to see if he might be browsing. The bakery, dispensing freshly made sandwiches and sticky cakes. The tiny bookshop, which made a precarious living out of blockbusters, crime novels and local maps and guides. A high-end gift shop that sold things nobody needed but that they somehow suddenly wanted when they were on holiday. Not Nick's cup of tea. An antique shop—she peered into its murky depths, through the coronation china and art deco lamps and lace tablecloths, but he wasn't there. The deli, where she'd recommended he get a pasty—there were plenty of people queuing up, but not him. The White Lion? She didn't think he'd venture in there, it wasn't his scene. She'd try in there later if she had no luck, but she didn't want to waste time. A card shop, the tea rooms—nope. She nipped inside the newsagent's in case he'd gone in to buy a paper or a Kit Kat . . .

He loved Kit Kats. They often used to share one, lying on his bed. She remembered the snap of each finger, the way just a little sprinkle of chocolate would always end up on the sheets, the way they would feed each other. And afterwards, chocolate kisses.

He wasn't in there either.

She had nearly reached the end of the street. Her next plan was to cut through to the quay behind the shops and walk back until she reached the hotel. As she turned the corner, the brilliance of the sun on the sea dazzled her for a second. She held up an arm to shade her eyes from the light, scanning the people leaning on the wrought-iron railings. The view never ceased to gladden her heart, but today she wasn't interested.

She realised that people were staring at her, and that she must be looking a bit wild-eyed. She didn't want to draw attention to herself, so she slowed to a walk. There were even more people here, licking ice creams, tossing the crusts of their pasties to the seagulls, who were revelling in the increase in available rations. She searched through them: young families with small children; retired couples; no teenagers, as presumably they hadn't yet been released from school. A coachload of pensioners in a cluster, on a day trip, anxious not to lose each other. The tables at the back of the White Lion were crammed; the harried waitress was scurrying about with endless baskets of scampi. It reminded her that the terrace would be filling up with diners; that she should be back at work by now; that the afternoon's guests would be arriving.

She wrapped her arms around herself and headed back towards the Townhouse. She'd been mad to come out. What would she say to Nick anyway? And what would Luca think if he knew she was missing?

And then she saw him. Leaning on the iron railing at the end of the quay, looking down at the water lapping against the grey brick of the wall. She would know the back of his neck anywhere, the way the fine blonde hairs gathered into a point at the nape. The hollow where his hairline ended and his spine began.

She was twelve steps away. Then seven.

'Nick.'

He turned.

She walked towards him slowly, then flew the last couple of yards. He pulled her into his arms.

He smelled the same. Of Persil and Must de Cartier and . . . Nick. Oh God, if she hadn't smelled him, she might have been able to survive, but she felt as if she was coming home. The same feeling she had dreamt of so many times. He mustn't kiss her. He was squeezing her. Was it the hug of a long-lost friend, or something more?

'I don't know what we're supposed to do,' she told him, her voice tight with tears. 'I don't know what to think.'

He stroked the hair back from her face tenderly. 'Where did you go?' he asked. 'Where did you go? I looked and looked for you, but you disappeared off the face of the earth . . .'

'You said you didn't want to see me again.' Her voice was muffled; her mouth pressed up against the comfort of his chest.

'I didn't mean it, Claire.' There was a crack in his voice. 'Of course I didn't mean it.'

She looked up at him. There was no point in trying to stop the tears. So what if someone she knew saw them?

'How was I supposed to know?' she whispered. 'After everything that happened, how was I supposed to know you didn't mean it?'

'We were kids, Claire. And there was so much shit going on . . . I couldn't make sense of any of it.' He buried his face in her hair for a moment, breathing her in. She smelled the same. It was as if the twelve years between had never happened. 'I still can't,' he told her.

They held each other in silence for a moment. People swarmed round them, oblivious to their predicament. How could they unfold their intervening lifetimes here, in public?

'We can't do this here,' he murmured.

'I know. And I've got to go back to the hotel,' she replied. 'Everyone will be arriving.'

It seemed strange, to talk about what was happening in the here and now, when they were both preoccupied with the past.

'It might be better if I went,' said Nick.

'No!' She heard the hysteria in her voice. She tried to calm herself. 'No. We're both grown-ups now. There's no need to spoil all your plans.' She held on to his hands. 'This doesn't change anything. It just means that we can make our peace with each other, after all this time. A reconciliation, so we can get on with our lives.'

She didn't want him to leave. She didn't want him out of her sight. But she had to play it cool. If it looked as if she was investing too much in this appalling coincidence, Nick might turn tail. Men didn't deal with the unexpected very well.

She gave him another reassuring smile, the perfect impersonation of a calm, reasonable woman.

'Your mates will be gutted.'

'Yes,' agreed Nick. 'They arranged it for me as a surprise. They're all guys I know through work. They'd think it was weird if I just left.'

'Are Shrimp and Felix coming?' Claire's heart thumped at the thought of Nick's brothers too. More memories walking back into her life.

'No. They couldn't make it. We're supposed to be going out on the razz on Thursday. Only the Mimsbury Arms...'

She could imagine it. Mel behind the bar; the three brothers intent on drinking it dry. She managed a smile.

'Anyway, Luca's going to do you an amazing meal for tomorrow night, and you can't miss that. Let's not make more of this than what it is. A... happy coincidence. Which will allow us to put our ghosts to bed.'

'Sure.' Nick was nodding in agreement. 'No, you're right. No big deal. Just a bit of a mind-fuck for a minute there.' He let go of her and stepped back.

'Maybe we can have a drink. When the hotel's not too busy...' She was stepping away. Out of the past, back into the present.

'Of course. That would be great. And I'd like to get to know Luca.'

She nodded, then held up her hand in a farewell gesture.

'See you later.'

He held up his hand too, mirroring her.
'See you.'
He watched her go.
Okay, Mum, he thought. *What do I do now?*

*   *   *

'Doesn't this hotel even have its own car park?' Karen was sounding querulous. The winding lanes that made up the last part of the journey had made her feel sick, and she was desperate for a cigarette as Colin steered the Jaguar carefully past the bollards and into the public car park.

'You know what these tiny seaside towns are like. Parking's at a premium.'

'That's why we should have gone to Torquay again.' She liked the Palace. It had all the facilities she wanted.

Colin didn't rise to the bait.

'A change is as good as a rest. And I thought we could hire a boat.'

'Well, you can count me out.' Karen wasn't getting in a boat for anyone.

'It would be fun, wouldn't it?' Colin looked at Chelsey, who smiled at him.

'Yeah.'

Colin surveyed the car park. It was already full to bursting.

'There's nowhere. It's rammed.' The voice of doom came from the passenger seat.

'Then we'll wait.' Colin let the engine idle. 'Someone's bound to leave any minute. And we're in no hurry.'

Karen sighed. She picked up her bag and opened the car door.

'I'm going to have a fag.'

'No problem.'

Colin watched her get out and go and stand by the ticket machine, rummaging in her bag for her cigarettes and lighter. As she lit up, she spotted a car leaving and waved at him, frantically pointing, urging him to commandeer it. But there was somebody around the other side who had been waiting longer than him, so he indicated that they should take it.

Karen snatched the door open.

'For God's sake—quick!'

'They were here first,' Colin pointed out reasonably.

'But you're nearer.'

'Karen—just calm down, will you? Finish your cigarette. We'll get a space.'

Karen shut the door with a clunk and walked back to her post, crossing her arms.

Colin looked at Chelsey, who gave a little shrug.

'She's like that the whole time,' she told him.

Colin smiled at her. She was a sweet kid. Not at all like her mother. Stolid, patient. Like him, maybe. She'd definitely inherited his metabolism. He'd never had much of a figure, being only five foot six, and the nature of his business meant that the extra pounds slipped on gleefully when he wasn't looking, and no amount of pumping iron in the home gym he'd installed in his conservatory seemed to have any effect.

Karen, conversely, seemed thinner than ever. Except for her boobs, which were suspiciously round and high. With her straightened hair, her blingy jewellery and her too-tight clothes, she turned Colin's stomach slightly. What he had once found so attractive now repelled him. She obviously worked hard to keep the years at bay—her forehead had the smooth rigidity of one addicted to cosmetic jabs—but she looked totally out of place in the Pennfleet car park. He shuddered slightly in distaste.

Three cars up, a Volvo started backing out of its space. Colin put the car into gear.

'There you are,' he said cheerfully. 'Perfect. Good things come to those who wait.'

*   *   *

As she headed back to the Townhouse, Claire realised that she hadn't posted her letters, her alibi, so she dashed into the post office and hastily bought some stamps. It seemed like a lifetime, but she'd only been fifteen minutes. As she pushed the brochures into the box outside, she glanced in the window of the boutique next door. There was a dress on the mannequin. It was a halter-neck with a full skirt, royal blue, printed with vintage seaside postcards.

She could hear a voice in her head: *Darling—it's absolutely you. You must have it. Go on.*

She froze in the middle of the street. The tiny hairs on the back of her neck rippled. She told herself not to be ridiculous. People couldn't talk to you from the other side. Yet still she couldn't drag her eyes away. Somehow the dress represented the girl she had once been. She had to have it.

After all, when was the last time she had bought something frivolous? Something she loved? Just for the hell of it?

She marched into the shop and found the

107

assistant.

'The dress in the window. Do you have it in a twelve?'

'Would you like to try it on?'

'No. I'll just take it. I'm sure it'll be fine. But I'm in a hurry . . .'

'No problem.'

The assistant hurried to a nearby rack and pulled out the right size, then took it to the desk as Claire found her credit card.

'Is it for something special?'

Claire didn't know. She just felt as if she should have it. As if the dress was somehow going to make a difference to what happened next.

'I don't know exactly,' she said. 'I just love it.'

'That's absolutely the best reason to buy a dress.' The assistant wrapped it in tissue and slid it into a bag. 'In fact, the only reason.'

*   *   *

When she got back to the hotel, the place was in chaos. There were several people in the bar waiting to be served, so she put down her shopping and hurried over, offering apologies. Within moments she had flourished a bottle of wine from the fridge and settled three of them at a table, and ushered another couple through to the dining room into the hands of Cherry, the daytime waitress. Angelica was behind the reception desk, looking harassed, checking in a stocky man and a young girl. A woman loitered nearby, looking bored, dressed for a nightclub rather than a weekend by the sea. Claire remembered the 'friend' Mr Turner had mentioned when booking. As Ben, the young boy they employed at weekends to help with luggage, led the strange little party towards the staircase, Claire thought that perhaps she wasn't the only person with a complicated life.

'Luca's on the warpath,' Angelica hissed as Claire slid back behind the reception desk. 'Where have you been?'

'Yes.' Luca appeared behind them as if by magic. 'Where?'

Claire threw back her shoulders. She didn't need to be interrogated.

'I went to the post office,' she declared. 'And I bought a dress. What's the problem?'

Luca looked at the bag she was holding aloft as proof.

'Shopping. You've been shopping. When it's been chaos in here.'

'Not chaos. We're managing,' Angelica contradicted him.

'I just thought it would be good to have something new to wear for dinner with Trevor and Monique. You know how dressed up she always is. I thought I'd make the effort.' Genius. She was a genius. She pulled the dress out of the bag and held it up.

Luca nodded his approval. He didn't look entirely mollified, though. Instead, he dropped into the leather office chair behind the reception desk and swivelled it from side to side, his long legs stretched in front of him.

'So,' he said pleasantly, 'tell me about whatsisname. Your long-lost friend.'

There was no point in Claire pretending she didn't know who he meant. That would indicate guilt immediately.

'Nick? His parents had the biggest house in the village when I was growing up. I used to hang out there for a while. With him and his brothers.' She swallowed on her equivocation. 'We lost touch when his mum died.' She flashed a disingenuous smile. 'I hope you're going to do him proud for his stag dinner. My reputation in Mimsbury depends on it.'

'I always thought you couldn't wait to get away from there?'

'I couldn't, but I'd still like to be well thought of.'

'Typical middle-class insecurity.'

Claire thumped him playfully. 'Who are you calling middle class?' She put on a mock south London accent. 'I'm from Isleworf, remember?'

Luca grinned.

'Don't worry. I'll make sure he has a stag night he'll never forget.'

He sat still for a moment, looking between the two girls, then stood and headed off back towards the kitchen. Claire blew her cheeks out in relief. It had been a huge effort keeping the banter light, but that was the best way of keeping Luca off the scent.

Next to her, Angelica's eyes were like saucers.

'Don't say anything,' said Claire. 'Don't ask any questions. I've already told you too much.'

'So she did die? His mother?'

'Of course she died. She had grade four cancer.'

'Grade four? What does that mean?'

Claire sighed.

'Let's put it this way. There is no grade five.'

*　　*　　*

She was echoing Isobel's own words.

110

After finding her in the kitchen that day, Claire had continued to be her confidante, though she still didn't understand why Isobel wanted to keep her illness quiet. Of course the boys and Gerald would be upset, but surely they needed to know?

Isobel was adamant.

'I'm trying to protect them, darling. Can't you see? Them knowing won't help at all. It's what made it so hard before. And now that Nick and Felix are working for Gerald, it's even more important to keep them in the dark. I can't risk the business falling apart. I know it looks as if we've got pots of money, but it's all a bit precarious financially. Melchior Barnes needs to keep afloat. If Gerald's worrying about me, he'll take his eye off the ball. He nearly went under last time—he lost several big contracts. Screwed up loads of deliveries. It was nearly a year before he got the business back on its feet. What's the point of risking it all if they don't need to know?'

And so Claire came to the conclusion that if Isobel was brave enough to face her illness alone, she had to respect that, and that she had no right to reveal the truth. She became very protective of her, and did everything she could to help. She saw that Isobel tired easily, and she took over the shopping and the cleaning as discreetly as she could.

As summer slid into autumn, Isobel grew thinner and paler. The family couldn't fail to notice. Gerald was beside himself, nagging her to go to the doctor.

Claire became anxious. 'You have to tell him. It's obvious there's something wrong.'

She watched, aghast, as Isobel lied glibly to the family as they sat round the dinner table.

'I've had the results back. I've got a stupid bloody

virus. They gave it a name—I can't remember it; something unpronounceable—but the doctor says it's not uncommon for people who've had chemo to be more susceptible. Something to do with my stupid immune system. I've just got to rest a lot. And he recommended a holiday. Sunshine.'

'So . . . it hasn't come back? They've checked?' Claire could see the anxiety on Gerald's face.

'Of course they've checked. It's the first thing they checked for.' Isobel's smile was dazzlingly convincing. 'Anyway, I've phoned Sally in Lanzarote. She says I can go over there in the New Year and stay for as long as I like.'

'Go now!' urged Gerald. 'Get your strength up in time for Christmas.'

'No,' said Isobel. 'I'd rather get Christmas out of the way. And anyway, I can't miss New Year's Eve. The party of the century?' She smiled round at them all. They'd been planning it for months— the celebration of all celebrations to mark the end of 1999. 'Then I can start the new millennium with a treat.'

Everyone seemed happy with that. Except Claire, who had a growing sense of unease. Surely, she thought, Isobel should be having some sort of treatment to keep her illness at bay?

'What are they actually doing?' she asked her one day.

Isobel looked her straight in the eye. 'Nothing,' she replied. 'There's nothing they can do. I'll have pain relief towards the end. Palliative treatment. But this is it.'

Claire frowned. 'It? What do you mean, it?'

'I'm dying, darling. Four months if I'm lucky.'

Claire sat down, shaken. She hadn't realised

she'd been colluding in Isobel's eventual death. Of course, with cancer that was always a possibility, but she'd thought they were just covering up the treatment. Now she realised how stupid she had been. There was no treatment.

Isobel held Claire's hands over the kitchen table. The table where the family had had so many happy meals together.

'Listen to me, Claire,' she said. 'I'm going away on New Year's Day. If I make it to then, that is. I'm going to a hospice. And I don't want anyone to know. I don't want anyone to watch me suffer. As far as they know, I'm going to Lanzarote to stay with my old schoolfriend Sally for a few weeks to convalesce.'

Claire shook her head.

'You can't do this.'

'So what's the alternative?' Isobel's voice was harsh. 'I tell them, and spoil our last Christmas, then lie upstairs rotting from the inside while they try and keep everything together and wait for me to die. Watch me racked with pain—because it's going to bloody hurt; I've been through it often enough with the nurse. That's not what I want for Gerald and the boys. Weeks of not knowing when the end is actually going to come. Why would I want to put them through that, Claire? Why?'

She smashed her fist on the table, and winced with the pain. Tears came into her eyes. Isobel rarely cried, but she did now, sobs racking her tiny body.

'You have to understand why I'm doing this. I don't want their last image of me to be some hideous skeletal cadaver who doesn't know who they are. I want to go out on a high. We're going to have the biggest party on New Year's Eve, the party to end all parties, and that will be it. I want to remember them happy. And I want them to remember me as *me*. Do you understand?'

Claire had never felt fear like it. Isobel was such a force, but death was an even greater one. And try as she might, she could find no argument to convince Isobel that her plan was wrong. How could you persuade someone that their nearest and dearest would want to see them suffer right up to the bitter end? Of course they wouldn't.

'When you're a mum,' Isobel told her, 'you'll understand.'

'I understand now,' said Claire. 'I think.'

'You're going to have to be their rock,' Isobel went on. 'You're going to have to be their me. I know you can do it. They all love you to bits.'

'So what will happen?' Claire could barely ask. 'How will they find out?'

'The hospice will contact them. Tell them I've slipped away in my sleep. Even if I go out screaming in agony.'

Claire put her head on the table and covered it with her arms.

'I can't bear it,' she sobbed.

'Tell me the alternative.' Isobel had gathered her composure now. She was resolute. She was the strong one. 'You tell me a better way, and I'll consider it. Bearing in mind that one thing's for sure—I'm going to die.'

But try as she might, Claire couldn't think of an alternative. There was a warped logic to what Isobel was saying. And as she was the one who was dying, Claire had to respect her wishes.

What she didn't know then was if Nick would

ever forgive her. If he ever found out.

CHAPTER SEVEN

'This isn't like our usual suite at the Palace. There's no lounge.'

Karen stood in the middle of her room, scowling. Colin suppressed his irritation. It was the nicest hotel room he'd seen in a long time, but then after years of five-star opulence he was beginning to appreciate character and understated good taste over showy luxury. Not Karen, though. She needed to be hit over the head with the trappings. This was far too subtle for her.

'They didn't have a lounge available,' he told her. 'But look at the view. Isn't it fantastic?' He walked over to the window and threw it open, breathing in the wonderful fresh air.

Karen ignored him, heaving her imitation Louis Vuitton on to the bed.

'Chelsey?' Colin turned to his daughter. 'Come and look. You can see right out to the sea.'

Chelsey came over, and the two of them leant out. To the right, the estuary opened up on to a wide expanse of ocean that you couldn't see from ground level, miles and miles of billowing turquoise infinity.

Karen flipped open her suitcase and started rifling through her clothes. She'd brought enough for a week. Women always over-packed, in Colin's experience, but he wasn't sure how sequinned leggings and a leopardskin dress were quite going to fit into the surroundings. And by the looks of it,

115

she hadn't brought any sensible shoes, so his idea of walking the coast path was probably a non-starter.

'Fuck,' she said. 'I forgot my straighteners. I left them on the side at home.'

'Doesn't matter. We're on holiday. At the seaside.' Colin adopted a cheery sing-song tone that he knew would do nothing to avert the crisis.

Karen shot him a withering look and slammed the lid of her case down.

'I bet there isn't a decent hairdresser in this godforsaken place.'

Chelsey slunk away and sat on the corner of the bed looking miserable.

Colin turned away from the window. He couldn't suppress his annoyance any longer.

'Are you going to spoil the whole weekend?' he asked. 'Only I was hoping—'

Karen stepped back from the bed, throwing her hands in the air in a defensive gesture.

'I'm sorry,' she said. 'I know I'm being a mardy cow. I'm just stressed about work, that's all. It's been really tough.'

She tried to smile, and Colin realised that her stress was genuine; that she really was sorry.

'Why don't we order up some tea?' he suggested. But Karen wasn't going to let it drop.

'They're laying people off left, right and centre. Everyone else is doing double the workload. And you can't moan in case it's you next. The customers are complaining because the place isn't run like it should be. They're all leaving and joining the gym on the other side of town, because they don't cut corners. And you can't blame them.'

She was getting tearful. Colin could empathise with her plight. It was happening all over the country. He was proud that he ran a tight ship and hadn't let anyone go yet. He had a certain amount of natural wastage and he had relied on that to cut his staff numbers down. So far, so good, and he went out of his way to assure his workforce that he would endeavour to keep them in their jobs as long as he could. He wasn't one to sacrifice people for profit, which was one of the reasons for his success. He got the best working for him because they knew he was a good boss. A philanthropist, he would have been called once.

He couldn't, however, assure Karen that her job was safe, because he suspected it very likely wasn't.

'Look,' he said kindly, 'let's talk about it over dinner, when we can have a nice glass of wine and put the world to rights.' He turned to Chelsey, who was still sitting on the bed looking miserably down at her lap. 'Come on. Let's take a walk down to the harbour while your mum freshens up and gets your stuff unpacked.'

Chelsey looked relieved and jumped up eagerly. Colin suddenly wanted to get away from Karen's stifling scent, and her even more stifling mood. Maybe he should have booked the Palace instead? But no—he'd chosen Pennfleet for Chelsey. This weekend was supposed to be about her, after all, not her mother.

*   *   *

Just after four o'clock, Trevor and Monique Parfitt came in through the door of the Townhouse, reeking of money.

Actually, they reeked of Gucci—Envy for her, Guilty for him, which they had bought jointly the

117

last time they were in Harrods. But the fact that they weren't short of a bob or two was screamingly obvious. And the fact that they didn't want anyone to miss that fact was screamingly obvious too.

They were both deeply tanned. Trevor was tall, shaven-headed and built like the proverbial. He was wearing a black trouser suit with a white silk T-shirt underneath that clung to his overworked pectorals. He wore suede loafers with no socks; a thick gold chain nestled round his neck and the predictable Rolex was on his wrist. His wife Monique was a diminutive size eight beside him, dressed in a white trouser suit with nothing underneath, showing off an impressive décolletage. Her four-inch heels and bouffant mane of platinum white brought her up to about five foot three. She was immaculate, but the overall impression was spoilt slightly by the fact that she was chewing gum.

They both wore sunglasses perched on their heads, Prada for him, outsize Chanel for her.

'Mr and Mrs Parfitt,' gushed Angelica, moving out from behind the reception desk with a smile to shake their hands.

'Angelica, babe,' Trevor beamed. 'You're looking as gorgeous as ever.'

'Thank you. And you both look very well.'

'We'll be all the better for a weekend here. Now, tell me, has Luca sorted valet parking for this place yet? Only I've left the Merc outside on the double yellows.'

'Well, I'm afraid we haven't,' said Angelica. 'But if you wait a moment, I'll get Ben to bring your cases in . . .'

She waved at Ben, who surged forward on her signal.

118

'. . . then I'll see if I can find someone to park it.'

'It's all right,' said Mrs Parfitt. 'Trevor will do it. I told him, this isn't that sort of a hotel. He should know by now.'

Trevor shrugged. 'You know what a perfectionist I am. And if I've told Luca once—if we want five stars, we need valet parking. People expect service.'

Angelica nodded in agreement. 'If you could just wait two seconds I'll tell Claire you're here. You'll be all right outside for a minute while you unload.'

Angelica disappeared into the back office, where Claire was doing the wages for the weekend staff.

'Trevor and Monique have arrived,' she whispered. 'You should see the diamonds on her.' She circled her thumb and forefinger and put them by her ear. 'They can't be real, but I bet they are.'

Claire stood up. She looked weary, thought Angelica. Obviously the strain of the unexpected arrival was getting to her.

'Thanks,' she said, and walked out into the reception area with a welcoming smile.

'Trevor. Monique.' She held out her hand to be shaken, but Trevor wasn't having any formality. He grabbed her in a big bear hug.

'Claire. Babe. I can't tell you how excited we are. And you've organised the weather for us.'

'Well, we try to please,' gasped Claire, wriggling out from his grasp and going to air-kiss Monique. 'Has Angelica arranged for your luggage to be brought in?'

'Ben's just bringing it,' Angelica told her.

Claire turned to see Ben struggling in with an enormous pair of matching suitcases.

Trevor held out his key fob and a twenty-pound note. 'Here you go, mate. You can park it for me.

It's insured for anyone. And don't forget to put the roof up.'

Ben looked at the keys in horror. 'Um . . . actually, I can't drive. I'm only sixteen.'

'I'll do it.' Angelica stepped forward and held out her hand.

'Do I trust a woman with my motor? It's top of the range, you know.' Trevor twinkled at her, dangling the keys just out of reach.

Angelica's eyes widened slightly.

Monique smiled fondly. 'He doesn't mean it, love. It's just his way.'

'Of course I don't. My Monique's a better driver than I am any day of the week. She's got patience.'

Trevor dropped the keys into Angelica's outstretched palm just as Luca came through the bar with a wide smile.

'Trevor! Monique.'

In the flurry of overexcited greetings, hand-shaking and kissing, Angelica slipped away unnoticed.

*   *   *

The car was parked on the pavement, a Mercedes SL convertible in gleaming cherry red that made her mouth water. She opened the driver's door and slid inside. It smelled delicious, of leather and newness, even if the seatbelt did reek of Trevor's aftershave. She nestled into the butterscotch hide with glee, enjoying the luxurious way it moulded itself around her bottom, then ran her hand over the sleek dashboard, admiring the layout, the high-tech state-of-the-art instruments, the steering wheel.

She put the keys into the ignition and looked

around her for a moment, trying to recall Jeff's instructions.

What she hadn't told Trevor Parfitt was that she hadn't actually passed her driving test. She'd had a few lessons, and been out for some practice with Jeff in his van. He was incredibly patient with her, bless him. There was no wincing or hysteria, just a measured calmness combined with meticulous instruction. He had been a driving instructor in a former life, and had told her she was a very competent driver, a natural, so Angelica felt quite confident that she could handle the Merc.

Moments later, the engine was purring. She flicked the indicator, slid the car into first and pulled away from the pavement, driving carefully up the high street towards the car park, enjoying the envious and admiring glances of passers-by. She was oozing with excitement, the thrill of it all. The glamour, the power, the naughtiness. She pressed the play button on the sound system and Elton John burst out—it wouldn't have been her choice, but it didn't matter. The music swirled round her, the bass reverberating through her body.

She suppressed the urge to scream with excitement. She was smiling from ear to ear. The entrance to the car park appeared on her right. She started to slow down, disappointed that her adventure was going to come to such an abrupt end, then met the eye of a man who was giving her a look of pure envy.

What the hell? she thought. When was she going to get the chance to sit at the wheel of a car like this again? She was going to take it for a spin. She'd say she had to wait ages for a parking space. She pulled away smoothly, and made her way up the hill and out of the town.

She could drive for ever like this. Leave Pennfleet behind. How long would it be before they caught up with her? The road stretched out invitingly in front of her, hugging the coast. She put her foot down and felt the power of the car surge beneath her.

This was it. This was the life she longed for. Freedom. Luxury. Fast cars.

She felt her hair stream out behind her and let out a whoop of pure joy. She knew she was being irresponsible, but she didn't care. She was responsible every other day of her life.

She came to a halt on the brow of a hill, pulling over into a lay-by that looked out over the sea. A white speedboat was cutting through the waves in the far distance. Angelica could imagine the exhilaration the passengers were feeling, like the exhilaration she'd just felt. Then her heart sank. Who was she trying to kid? A jet-set lifestyle was totally out of reach. She had to accept it. She stroked the tan leather of the steering wheel, wondering about the Parfitts, and where they had got their money, and whether Monique had married Trevor because of it. It was the obvious route to wealth and luxury for an attractive woman, she thought.

She flipped the driver's mirror down. She had the wherewithal to attract a man like Trevor, she knew she did. She'd seen men look at her hungrily. She held her hair up behind her head, narrowed her eyes, glimpsing herself sideways through almost closed lashes, pouting. How hard could it be?

Yet in her heart of hearts she knew it wasn't a route she wanted to take. Come the day, she would marry for love, she thought, and a shadowy image of Luca hovered on the edge of her consciousness. She batted it away, reminding herself that she was lucky: she lived in a town most people would give their eye teeth to live in; she had a job she loved, working with people she admired . . .

A solitary cloud scudded in front of the sun, and she shivered. She needed to get back before anyone wondered where she was. She struggled to turn the car around, flustered and confused now that the adrenalin was gone. Back to reality, she thought, and for a moment she wished she hadn't allowed herself to flirt with something that was so out of reach. She turned the music down and drove the car back down the hill, soberly, sombrely, suddenly afraid that she was going to prang it or cock up the parking. Her heart rate subsided as she drove back in through the familiar outskirts of the town, and she couldn't help hoping that her mother would catch a glimpse of her gliding past.

Maybe one day, she thought. Maybe one day.

*   *   *

Laura had set her phone alarm in anticipation—she was worried they would both fall asleep and wake up in Penzance—and it burbled at her five minutes outside Pennfleet. She woke to find her head on Dan's shoulder. He smiled down at her, and she sat up, confused, not quite remembering where they were, or why. Then she leapt up and starting pulling down her luggage.

'Hey,' said Dan. 'Calm down. We're not even at the station yet.'

'I know,' said Laura, already edging her way

towards the carriage doors. 'I know I'm a neurotic freak, but that's just the way I am.'

Dan pulled his rucksack down and followed her. As they stood by the doors, waiting for the train to slow, he wrapped his arms around her. Laura leant back into him, grateful that he had come with her. She would have hated arriving in a strange place on her own.

The train ground to a halt and Dan opened the door on to the platform. The station at Pennfleet was entirely unprepossessing. Grey, rundown, with iron railings and overgrown grass sprouting through the Tarmac, a million miles from the jolly seaside scene they'd been expecting.

They went to find a taxi. There were two on the rank, one driver idly chatting to the other through the window in the afternoon sun, and they stood for a moment waiting for them to finish, until Dan ran out of patience and emitted a pointed whistle.

'The Townhouse by the Sea, please,' Laura told the driver.

'Ooh, posh,' he remarked, and she wondered if he was going to surreptitiously jack up his meter, thinking they could afford to pay over the odds. She didn't usually indulge in expensive boutique hotels, but the whole prospect of the weekend was so scary, so intimidating, that she wanted to be in comfortable surroundings, and the Townhouse had looked so perfect. She didn't want them to be stuck in some dreary bed and breakfast with orange-and-brown carpets and a bed you didn't want to get into in case the sheets weren't fresh.

The taxi spun out of the car park. As she settled back in her seat, Laura thought about how they could be making their way up to Camden this

124

evening with their friends, for cocktails in the last of the sun and then clubbing, their usual Friday-night ritual, finishing with delicious kebabs and fiery harissa on the way home. This whole trip was going to be a waste of time and money.

'You ready?' asked the driver as they approached a bend. 'This is the view of a lifetime. You wait.'

Dan and Laura both sat up expectantly as they rounded the corner. Then Laura gasped in delight, for there in front of them was an expanse of glittering sea, and the little town of Pennfleet perched on the harbourside, nonchalant with perfection.

'Wow,' said Dan.

The driver grinned.

'Never fails to get a reaction,' he replied. 'You'd have to be dead not to think that was something special.'

*   *   *

'Haven't you seen it already?'

'Loads of times. But it's my favourite.'

Colin looked down at the DVD Chelsey had handed him. *Tangled*. His heart creaked just a little bit.

He and Karen had argued earlier about whether Chelsey should join them for dinner. Colin was all for it. He'd always enjoyed having his children at the dinner table; from an early age he and Alison had let them eat with them in restaurants. He thought it taught them how to behave properly, and what was the point of having them if you couldn't make the most of their company? Karen, however, had other ideas.

125

'You don't want to have dinner with the boring grown-ups, do you, Chels?'

Colin could see Chelsey was used to being fed lines like this, and that she was programmed how to answer.

'No—I'll be fine here.'

'She can have room service. And she's got the telly.'

Colin suspected it was better not to rock the boat. And in a way, Karen was right. They definitely needed to have a chat without Chelsey around. He had a few things to say, for a start. But to salve his conscience he had brought her down to the newsagent to choose a DVD to watch.

'Why don't you have two?' he suggested now.

She hesitated. 'Really?'

'Of course.'

She studied the rows of DVDs again. Colin thought that if it was Michelle, he would buy her a bag of sweets to go with it, but the last thing Chelsey needed was another input of calories. What should he do? There was a bowl of fresh fruit in the hotel room, but it would seem miserly to suggest that. He wanted to spoil her this weekend. He believed wholeheartedly in spoiling children.

He sighed and picked up a bag of Minstrels. One more packet wasn't going to make a difference at this stage. He'd talk to Karen about Chelsey's eating habits over dinner. Though he suspected his entreaties would fall on deaf ears.

Chelsey had chosen another DVD and proffered it awkwardly. He thought about the kids' playroom at home, the huge wide-screen TV and the rows and rows of DVDs, almost more than there were on display here. The room was empty for most of

126

the year now, eerily silent. He missed them both so much. He knew Alison did too.

He held up the Minstrels.

'Do you like these? They're my favourite.'

Chelsey nodded, and he walked over to the till. He looked at the cigarettes behind the counter, and felt an urge that he hadn't felt since he'd given up fifteen years ago. It was Karen smoking around him that had given him the craving. He wasn't going to succumb. Instead, he picked up a packet of Orbit.

'Anything else you want?' he asked Chelsey, and she shook her head.

He felt his heart melt a little bit more. Didn't she realise he would give her anything she wanted? Anything.

*　　　　*　　　　*

Angelica returned from her joyride looking as if butter wouldn't melt. She put the keys of the Mercedes in the reception drawer, ready to return to the Parfitts, and turned to smile at the young couple who were about to check in.

She felt a tug at her heart. The girl wasn't much older than she was, and they seemed so sweet, the pair of them. The boyfriend was holding a flowery overnight bag without a hint of embarrassment, as well as his own rucksack, and had his other arm around the girl's shoulders.

'We're booked in for the weekend,' the girl told her. 'In the name of Starling? Just two nights.'

'You wouldn't think it was just two nights,' observed her boyfriend with a grin. 'Given the amount of stuff you've packed.'

He received a nudge in the ribs for his cheek.

127

'You have to be prepared,' said the girl. 'Don't you?' She turned to Angelica for support.

'Oh yes,' agreed Angelica. 'Who knows what the weather's going to be like? Or what might happen.'

She called their reservation up on the computer screen and saw that they were booked into the Broom Cupboard, the tiniest room in the hotel. It was sweet, but really only suitable for a person on their own: even though there was just enough room for a double bed, it was pretty cramped.

On impulse, Angelica checked her watch. It was late afternoon, and unlikely that anyone else was going to book in for the weekend at this stage.

She leant forward, her eyes twinkling.

'Listen. We've got one of our bigger rooms still available,' she told them confidentially. 'I'm going to move you into that one at no extra cost.' She flashed them a grin. 'Don't tell anyone.'

'Wow!' The girl looked delighted. 'Thank you very much.'

Her boyfriend nodded his appreciation. 'Cool,' he said, and he was. Very cool indeed, thought Angelica, entranced by the deep grey of his eyes and hoping the girl knew just how lucky she was.

Having given them their key, Angelica watched the two of them follow Ben up the stairs. She felt a little glow in her heart that she'd been able to do them a kindness. Then she wondered if she would ever turn up to a hotel like the Townhouse with a man she loved and find herself upgraded. She couldn't imagine how it would feel. She amended the room reservation on the computer, the glow of her generosity fading somewhat, but hoping that her gesture was good karma and that the same might happen to her some day, somewhere.

128

Minutes later, Laura bounced into the middle of the king-size sleigh bed, piled high with cushions.

'I don't believe it. We got an upgrade!' She hugged a cushion to her and looked around the room, her eyes wide with delight. 'Oh my God, it's just so gorgeous.'

The room was painted in pale coral and deep cream. Curtains with a starfish motif hung to the floor. There was a huge silver beanbag by the window. A blown-up print of Enid Blyton's *Five Go Down to the Sea* was framed and hung over the bed, while on the wall facing the window three paintings by Pandora Mond glittered their metallic pewters and blues.

Dan put his iPod into the iPod dock. Moments later, the lush, swirling chords of his favourite new band filled the room.

By now, Laura had bounced into the bathroom. She came out brandishing a bottle of bath oil.

'Look! Molton Brown. Tons of it. I'm going to have the deepest bath ever.' She took off the lid and gave an appreciative sniff.

Dan found a silver biscuit barrel. It was stuffed with home-made shortbread.

'This is going to be a good weekend,' he mused, pulling out a piece and biting into it with relish. He held one out to Laura.

She shook her head, walking over to the window. The room was at the side of the hotel, but if you craned your neck, you could see the sea. To the right, the little town of Pennfleet unfolded itself, an inviting maze of narrow streets. As she looked, she remembered why they were here. Not for a romantic weekend away at all. She cast her eyes over the houses clinging to the side of the hill, wondering which one of them belonged to the man who might—or might not—be her father.

Dan came up behind her and put his arms round her. She melted into his clasp. Thank goodness for Dan. She would, she knew, never have made it this far without him. Whatever happened, she would still have him at the end of the weekend.

*   *   *

Monique walked across the living area of the grand suite and threw open the door of the tiny balcony that looked out over the harbour. A gust of salty air blew into the room, and she breathed in, shutting her eyes in the warmth of the sun.

'Magic,' said Trevor.

Monique smiled and scanned the boats tugging against their moorings in the breeze.

'There she is.' She pointed to a large white motorboat. Trevor came and stood behind her, smiling proudly. *The Blonde Bombshell.* Monique's fortieth birthday present, which he'd given her more than ten years ago now. He'd had it built to an exacting specification, visiting the boatyard every week to make sure everything was as he wanted it, down to the last white leather cushion. He knew he'd driven the boatbuilders mad, but he didn't care. It was his money, his wife's present, and he wanted it to be perfect.

He remembered her face the day he had given it to her. Her eyes had been alive with surprise and delight as they launched it into the harbour at

130

Lymington. She'd smashed the bottle of champagne on to the boat's side with glee. And it had given the two of them more pleasure than they could have imagined.

But where once there had been laughter, now there was darkness. Still Monique's eyes sought a glimpse of that shadowy figure who was never going to be there. There was nothing he could do for her, his beloved wife. It tore him apart, to know he was powerless to bring an end to her agony. And so he piled upon her distraction after distraction, in the vain hope that one day she would stop hoping.

Trevor himself had stopped hoping long ago.

This weekend, however, he felt sure was going to be a turning point. Opening a London hotel had been his brainwave, and he was delighted that Monique had leapt upon the idea with enthusiasm. Surely that would occupy her mind, stop her brooding; stop her restless search? He just had to pray that Claire and Luca would agree to come on board. He trusted them, and their vision, and he didn't want to have to find someone else to mastermind the project for him. Despite his bluff geniality, Trevor didn't take many people into his confidence. The Parfitts didn't let anyone come too close these days.

They'd become very good at pretending. Anyone who met them would think they hadn't a care in the world; that they lived life to the full. And yes, on the surface, they had a dream existence. Despite everything, Trevor's financial success had gone from strength to strength, and they never stinted themselves.

It never ceased to crucify him that he couldn't buy Monique the one thing she wanted though. He would have done anything to have that smile back again. The one that reached her eyes. Instead of the slightly blank gaze that wasn't helped by the antidepressants, though he knew they made it just a little bit easier for her to get through the day. And people were prescribed them for a lot less. For nothing, it seemed.

He watched in silent despair as she walked over to her handbag. For the millionth time she pulled out the phone she kept in there, checked it for a message; held it up to verify there was a signal. There wasn't always in Pennfleet—satellite coverage could be sketchy—but today there must have been, for she nodded to herself in satisfaction and dropped the phone back in her bag.

There wasn't a message. There never would be. Trevor knew that, but Monique wouldn't give up hope.

She walked back over to the window and looked out again. The sea breeze ruffled her hair. She looked so young, so vulnerable, and he felt that terrible lump in his chest, the lump that reminded him how helpless he was. He swallowed it down.

'Shall we go for a little stroll before dinner?'

She smiled over at him and nodded.

'Yeah, let's go down to the harbour. Get some sea air. Work up an appetite.'

Sometimes he thought it would be easier to bear if she wasn't so brave.

CHAPTER EIGHT

Claire loved early evening in the hotel the best. Between five and six, when the sun slanted in through the windows, it had a sort of sleepiness combined with a sense of expectation. As the kitchen launched into preparation and the barman filled his ice bucket and laid out bowls of olives, guests retired to their rooms, relaxing on their beds for a quick power nap, or watching the news, or putting on make-up over sun-kissed skin, or making lazy holiday love.

Claire used this time to make sure everything was perfect, ensuring that the newspapers were put away, the flowers hadn't wilted, the bathrooms were up to scratch. Of course she employed staff to do all these things, but it didn't hurt to double-check and make sure her high standards were being met. Mitch the barman would often bring her a sample of his latest cocktail to try, and if she was lucky, she would spend ten minutes sitting at a table on the terrace relishing the delicious smells coming from the kitchen.

By quarter past six, the respite would be over. Passers-by would start drifting in to see if they could nab a last-minute table, local regulars would pop in for their habitual early-evening drink, and the bar would start filling up with guests coming down for dinner.

And with the glorious bank holiday weather forecast this weekend, the hotel was filling up even more quickly than usual. The restaurant was fully booked, and Claire had already turned away several disappointed holidaymakers.

In the bar, she could see Nick's stag party. They were an eligible bunch by anyone's standards—all early thirties, all confident and successful but not showy. Claire was fairly sure they would stick to their promise not to get rowdy, but it was plain they were up for a good time. They weren't eating at the Townhouse tonight; they were saving that for their celebratory dinner tomorrow night. Instead they had booked supper at a pub a couple of miles up the river that Luca had recommended.

Claire brought over a plate of complimentary canapés for them to try—Stilton and chutney rarebits, rosemary drop scones with goat's cheese, and crab cakes with chilli and lime mayonnaise, all done in miniature but the flavours robust and gutsy.

One of them stood up to greet her.

'Hi—I'm Gus. The best man? I think we spoke on the phone.' He introduced the rest of the party to her quickly, a predictable roll call of Wills and Jamies and Tobys. Then he noticed Claire eyeing up the mojitos lined up on the table in front of them. 'Don't worry—this isn't going to get out of hand. It's just an ice-breaker.'

With his curly brown hair and freckles, Gus didn't even look old enough to be served alcohol. Claire wondered if Nick had hinted anything to him about his relationship with her. She smiled reassuringly.

'You are allowed to have fun,' she told him. 'Just . . . no vomiting or nudity. Preferably.'

'No nude vomiting,' Gus promised her solemnly. 'We're just waiting for the groom. He's having a shower.'

'One more week of freedom,' said one of the

134

others. 'Poor bugger.'

'Oh, come on,' said Gus, chiding him. 'Sophie's a doll. They're going to be the perfect couple.'

Everyone laughed.

Except Claire. An image suddenly came into her head of the little church at Mimsbury, of Nick standing at the altar with Gus as the congregation watched a beautiful bride walk down the aisle, and Nick turning to look at her adoringly.

She put down the plate of canapés hastily.

'Enjoy these on the house,' she managed, and walked away from the table, knowing they would find her abrupt departure strange. But she couldn't hear any more. As quickly as she could, she bolted into the cloakroom that served the dining room and locked herself into a cubicle. Then she put the loo seat down and sat on it, resting her whirling head in her hands.

*   *   *

The weeks after Isobel revealed the final part of her plan to Claire were terrible. She found the strain of pretending that everything was normal almost unbearable, while Isobel seemed able to carry on as if nothing was wrong.

From time to time Nick wondered why it was that Claire seemed so withdrawn and tired.

'Is it Dad?' he asked. 'Is he driving you too hard at work? I know he expects a lot of people, but you only need to tell him if it's too much. He doesn't know he's doing it.'

Claire didn't know what to say. She loved working at Melchior Barnes. She didn't find it stressful at all. But it was easier to blame that pressure than to tell Nick the truth, although several times she came close. Then she would remember that it was nearly Christmas. She couldn't ruin Isobel's last Christmas, she told herself.

And all the while she prayed and hoped for some miracle, some reprieve. Of course there was none, and before she knew it, Christmas Day had arrived. She woke with a sore throat, a muzzy head and a heavy heart, but dragged herself out of bed for her parents' sake. She knew they had been concerned about her recently, and she didn't want to spoil Christmas morning for them, especially as she was going over to the Mill House after lunch.

They sat in the kitchen in their dressing gowns, eating bacon sandwiches and drinking Nescafé. It was a million miles away from the scene Claire knew would be unfolding at the Mill House— there would be smoked salmon and scrambled egg, champagne, carols from King's College, Cambridge on the CD player, real coffee, a properly laid breakfast table—but for the first time since she had met the Barneses, she longed to stay at home all day. She felt safe with her parents, who, despite all their shortcomings, would never have forced her into the situation she was in. If they knew of her pact with Isobel, they would be horrified. They wouldn't understand at all. Her parents never pretended. It just wasn't in them. Perhaps this denoted a lack of imagination, but at least you knew where you were with them. Always.

Claire was incredibly touched by their present— they gave her a very generous cheque to redecorate her bedroom.

'There's no point in us doing it,' her mum told

136

her. 'We wouldn't have a clue what you wanted. But we want you to make the room your own. We haven't done much to the place since we moved in.'

'I'll give you a hand with the painting,' her father went on. 'We could have it walloped out in a weekend.'

The numbers on the cheque went all blurry when she looked at them, especially when she remembered all the times she had felt resentful at how little care her parents seemed to give to their surroundings in comparison to Gerald and Isobel.

She was due to go over to the Mill House at three o'clock, but her heart was filled with dread at the prospect. How could she sit there amongst the baubles and glitter, knowing this was very probably Isobel's last Christmas with her family, while they carried on with the festivities oblivious?

She wouldn't go, she decided. She had the beginnings of a cold. It wouldn't be fair to spread her germs. She called and left a message on the Mill House answerphone to say she wasn't well, but the Barneses were having none of it. They phoned her three times to see where she was—they were waiting for her to come over and open her presents before lunch, which they always had in the late afternoon. At half past four, Nick came and knocked on the door.

'What on earth's the matter?' he demanded. 'It's just a cold. No one minds. Come on. A couple of glasses of bubbly and you won't feel a thing. Bring your parents too, if you're worried about leaving them.'

'It's not that,' sniffed Claire.

'Then what? Come on. Mum's done you a stocking.'

And despite her protests, Claire found herself route-marched back to the drawing room at the Mill House, where Gerald poured her a glass of champagne and Isobel handed her a red velvet stocking filled with enticing packages. 'I never get to buy girl things,' she said. 'I'm sick to death of buying aftershave and socks and things with batteries. Don't get excited—it's full of rubbish really.'

Claire was totally overwhelmed. Ten minutes later she was surrounded by shreds of silver gossamer paper and more presents than she knew what to do with: a beaded purse, sheepskin slippers (the floors at the Mill House were freezing in winter), lacy tights, a Jilly Cooper paperback, a bottle of Romance by Ralph Lauren ...

'And this is from me,' said Gerald. It was her very own Riedel wine-tasting glass. He jumped up to open a bottle, hiding the label from her and pouring her an inch of burgundy.

'Tell me what you think of that,' he commanded.

Claire burst into tears. 'I'm sorry,' she managed to blub. 'I don't feel awfully well ...'

She fled the room, locking herself in the downstairs loo. She had to get it together, for Isobel's sake. Isobel was behaving as if nothing in the world was the matter. How on earth did she find the strength, Claire wondered, knowing this was the last Christmas she would spend with her husband and her beloved boys?

Even in the loo, Claire couldn't escape Isobel's presence. The room summed her up so perfectly. It was painted a deep dusty Jaipur pink. An ancient chandelier hung from the ceiling, the droplets sparkling and spinning. The towels were thick and soft; the soap a thick creamy brick scented with lavender. She thought of her own parents' downstairs loo. Sterile, empty. A ratty old towel that was rarely taken away to be washed. A cracked piece of supermarket soap, the lines engrained with dirt. The only sign that anyone had given any thought to decoration was an outdated calendar from the Lake District. She had no idea where it had come from. Her parents never went on holiday. Suddenly she wished she was back with them. The kitchen at home this morning had seemed so safe.

She put the lid down on the loo seat, sat down and rested her head against the wall. On the opposite wall was a photo collage, of the kind so beloved by the English middle classes. She had seen several at the houses of Nick's friends. It was a perfect timeline of the Barneses' life. Fat, happy babies rolling on rugs. Three tow-haired children frolicking in the garden. Cricket matches. Skiing holidays. Parties. And always amongst them, Isobel. Beautiful, smiling, full of life and love, her eyes alive with the joy her family gave her.

Claire had never seen her own mother look like that. Carefree. Besotted. Generous of spirit. Her mother never let go. Never gave any indication that people really mattered to her.

A hard lump rose in her throat as she wondered if she would sacrifice her own mother for Isobel. It would certainly cause less grief. If you could quantify grief. She pushed the thought away, hating herself for even having it, because she knew it was selfish. Because if it was her mother who was dying, she would at least have a chance of happiness with Nick. She and her father would be sad, of course, but...

She didn't want to think about it. It just wasn't fair, to compare the effects of one person's death with those of another, as if anyone was more important than anyone else just because they happened to have more children, or appeared more loving. And anyway, she knew her mother loved her. She just didn't have Isobel's flamboyance.

After five minutes, Nick knocked on the loo door.

'Claire? Are you okay?'

She edged her way out. 'Sorry. I don't know what the matter is. Christmas always freaks me out a bit.'

'And you feel guilty.' Nick looked at her knowingly.

Claire stared back at him. Did he know something? How could he know something?

'About what?' she stammered.

'About not being with your parents, of course.'

Claire rubbed her hands over her face. Her head was pounding. She shouldn't have had so much champagne, but at the Mill House your glass just refilled itself. She thought for a moment she was going to keel over.

Nick grabbed her.

'Maybe you should lie down.'

'Nick,' she blurted. 'I can't . . . I can't bear it any more.'

'What?'

She had to tell him. The burden was too enormous. She couldn't keep it to herself a moment longer.

At that moment Isobel came out of the drawing room into the hallway.

'Claire, darling—you look ghastly. Come with me. You need a Lemsip with honey and a double

140

dose of vitamin C. Nick, we need some more logs on the fire. Would you?'

And before either of them knew it, Claire had been whisked off to the kitchen, where Isobel made her the prescribed Lemsip.

'I can't do this.' Claire was desperate.

'You have to.' Isobel drizzled manuka honey from a spoon into the cup. 'This is how it should be,' she told Claire firmly. 'We're all having a lovely time. A Christmas to remember. What would be the point of blowing it all apart?'

Claire took the steaming mug.

'How can you be so . . .?'

Cheerful. Glamorous. Unaffected. Buoyant. Carefree.

But Isobel's answering smile was bleak.

'Inside,' she told Claire, 'I'm an absolute mess. But I'll have all the time in the world to fall apart when the moment comes.'

New Year's Day. Claire felt sick when she thought about it. In the meantime, she had to step up to the plate. She had to match Isobel's dauntless spirit. She drank the Lemsip, had another glass of champagne, and pasted on a smile. That night she held on to Nick in bed as tightly as she could, drenched in sweat and dread. She was going to lose him. She could feel it coming.

By New Year's Eve, she was still streaming with cold. All day she helped with preparations for the party. She could barely look Isobel in the eye, or any of the rest of the family. Luckily she had her cold to blame for her deflated mood. She put on the thigh-skimming black lace dress Isobel had bought her, and the stretchy knee-length boots, and the chandelier earrings.

141

'You look . . . incredible,' said Nick.

She managed a wan smile. 'You look amazing too.' She turned away before he could see the tears in her eyes. The boys were wearing black tie; they all looked devastatingly handsome. She couldn't bear to think how proud Isobel would feel of them all.

She managed to get through the evening somehow. There were so many people, and she kept herself busy by topping up drinks and passing round canapés. As the hands crept towards midnight and the excitement of the millennium grew, she crept into the kitchen—everyone was crowding round the clock in the hall. Prince's '1999' was playing at full blast as the mood reached fever pitch.

Claire curled herself up in the squashy armchair by the Aga. She felt almost as if Isobel had offloaded all her guilt and grief on to her, and she was carrying it round like a surrogate mother incubating a big ball of pain that was just going to grow and grow and grow. Of course, Isobel must be suffering, but it was Claire who was going to have to deal with the aftermath. Claire who would be left with the fallout, mopping up everyone else's pain and anguish. The pain and anguish that Isobel was so deftly avoiding.

She could hear the countdown to midnight. The uproarious bellow of a roomful of people moved by the momentousness of the occasion, the dawn of a new millennium. All the optimism of a fresh year, but a thousandfold. The future was bright for them all. The slate clean. The year 2000—a chance to start again and make a difference.

She should get up and go and join them. Nick

142

would be looking for her. He would want to kiss her on the stroke of midnight. It should have been a perfect moment for the two of them, young and in love. But she couldn't kiss him with the burden of the secret she carried.

She couldn't stay in hiding either.

She opened the kitchen door and stepped into the hallway. It was crammed with guests, all watching the minute hand of the grandfather clock as it jerked to join the hour, both pointing vertically to twelve. As midnight struck, a mighty cheer rose. There was the sound of champagne corks popping, party blowers hooting, a rousing drunken chorus of 'Auld Lang Syne' as people hunted for their loved ones and embraced them and streams of party-popper ribbons flew into the air.

She could see Isobel across the room. She had lost so much weight, she looked like a twelve-year-old girl. But she was beautiful nonetheless, in a silver sequinned dress. She looked as if she was having the time of her life, partying as though she hadn't a care in the world, though Claire knew she'd spent most of the afternoon asleep to give herself the energy to get through the evening. She watched as Isobel pulled Gerald to her and kissed him, the deep kiss of a couple who meant the world to each other. Then she looked for her sons through the fray, grabbing Felix and hugging him tight, reaching out for Shrimp's hand and drawing him towards her, all the while looking for Nick, who was looking for Claire.

She was standing in the cloakroom doorway as he grabbed her.

'Where've you been?'

He scooped her up, pulling her into his arms and

143

off her feet, kissing her as if his very life depended on it. She shut her eyes for a moment, wishing this was real, wishing their future could be the happy one they surely deserved. When she opened them, Isobel was next to her, waiting patiently for the chance to wish her son a happy New Year, and Claire stepped aside and watched as they hugged, mother and son.

And then Isobel turned to her and slid her arms around her neck, and she breathed in the smell of crushed violets.

'This is how it should be,' Isobel was whispering urgently into her ear. 'This is just how it should be, Claire. Thank you.'

She felt Isobel's lips on her cheek, dry and warm. She wanted to push her away, scream at her; scream the truth to everyone. She didn't want to be the keeper of the secret any more. In one moment, she could share it with the entire party, spread the burden amongst the guests and be free of its malignant grip.

Yet that wouldn't change what was going to happen. It wasn't going to halt the dreadful disease and grant Isobel a reprieve. And in that moment Claire realised that Isobel was right. It was about damage limitation. What good would knowing the truth bring to this houseful of joyous guests, who were dancing and singing and carousing and celebrating the dawn of a new era? What right did she have to deprive Gerald, and Felix and Shrimp and Nick, of an untainted memory of this historic moment?

Nick was looking down at her. He took her face in his hands.

'You're crying,' he teased her. 'You soppy thing.'

144

She hadn't realised that her eyes were brimming with tears. She didn't reply. She couldn't. She looked at the clock.

One minute past midnight, and it was already the worst year of her life.

On New Year's Day, she had stayed in bed, shivering under the covers, using a hangover combined with her cold as an excuse. She couldn't bear to watch Isobel saying goodbye to Gerald and the boys, hugging them for the last time as the taxi waited outside, supposedly to take her to the airport but in reality taking her to the hospice. Instead, she had curled up in a ball under the duvet, trying to block out the awful image of Isobel's last wave to her family as she drove away to die . . .

*   *   *

Now, staring at the limestone floor of the cloakroom, Claire felt sick at the memory. All the guilt and the horror had been stirred up again. But they were nothing compared to one overriding realisation.

She had thought herself healed. She had thought herself happy with Luca. She thought she'd moved on and left the memories behind her. But it was as if the intervening years had never happened. Her feelings were as strong as they ever had been. She leant her head against the wall in despair.

She was still in love with Nick.

And he was about to get married.

She had to go and find him. She had to tell him he couldn't stay here. Either that, or she would have to leave the hotel for the duration of the weekend, but short of feigning appendicitis, that just wasn't possible. No, Nick would have to make his apologies and make himself scarce. Then she would be able to deal with the weekend; with Luca and Monique and Trevor. Tonight's meeting was vitally important, but with Nick under her roof, she couldn't concentrate, couldn't operate, couldn't converse. She needed to be on top of her game. She and Luca needed to come across as a team.

She came out of the cubicle and ran the cold tap in the sink for a moment, splashing water on to her face in the hope that it might clear her thoughts. She looked in the mirror. Her face was blank. It showed no evidence of the secrets she was hiding. She dried her face and smoothed back her hair, then left the cloakroom, walking steadily through the bar back to the reception area.

'Hold the fort for me for a few minutes, would you?' she said to Angelica.

Angelica looked up, scenting trouble.

'Are you okay?' she asked.

For a moment Claire felt tempted to confide in her again. There was something refreshingly non-judgemental about Angelica. But there wasn't time.

'I just need to go through some notes for tonight's meeting,' she told her, knowing how unconvincing she sounded.

Angelica nodded, not taken in for a second.

'If you want to talk . . .' she offered.

Claire nodded, with a tight smile.

'Thanks,' she replied, 'but I'm fine.'

She ran up the stairs two at a time. She found Nick's room and tapped on the door. The rest of the stags would be kept well oiled by Mitch; Luca would be busy prepping in the kitchen with Fred and Loz. She had just enough time to talk him

146

round.

He answered the door wet from the shower, a towel round his waist and a question in his eyes.

She ran her eyes over his body, so familiar even after all this time. There was a little more definition to his shoulders, a little more breadth to his chest. She remembered how he felt without even having to touch him. Her mouth went dry.

'Hey,' he said. 'What's up?'

'I can't do this,' she said, and felt hot tears well up. 'You have to go . . . I'm sorry. I can't deal with it.'

Nick stood there for a moment, saying nothing.

'I know,' he said eventually. 'I should have gone straight away.' He wrapped the towel more tightly round himself and stepped back. 'I'll pack my stuff. Tell the guys there's a crisis at work or something . . .'

But he didn't move. They stood staring at each other. Claire felt foolish; like a hysterical teenager laying down terms and conditions. Surely at her age she should be able to deal with this graciously. She was ruining what should be the happiest time of Nick's life because she could only think about herself. She needed to grow up. Apart from anything, the stag weekend was going to be good business. If she drove Nick away, the rest of them might disband; tomorrow night's dinner might be cancelled. They could ill afford to lose that money. And it wouldn't look good in front of Trevor and Monique.

'I'm sorry,' she said. 'It's just . . .'

What was she supposed to say? How could she explain to him how she felt? That the feelings were just as raw as they had been the day they had last

147

seen each other? That all she wanted to do was touch him? That she was insanely jealous?

'Difficult,' she managed finally. The word sounded so insufficient.

'I know.' He looked at her. Didn't move.

Claire managed a smile. She shouldn't have come up here. She should have let it lie and carried on regardless. She took a deep breath; drew herself up. She could do this. Banishing Nick would turn his appearance into a bigger deal than it should be. A classic case of making a mountain out of a molehill. Claire had always prided herself on not being a drama queen.

'Ignore me.' She gave a self-deprecating laugh. 'Of course you don't have to go. I don't want to spoil things for you. You'd better get dressed. Your friends have got a bit of a head start down there.'

She turned to go.

'Claire!' She felt his hand on her shoulder. She turned back. He took her by the arm, still holding on to his towel with the other hand.

If he hadn't touched her, she would have been okay. She would have gone back downstairs, charmed her guests, prepared for dinner. But in one fluid movement she found herself in his arms, the two of them moving back into the room, the door closing, his towel falling to the floor.

She pressed her lips frenziedly against his damp skin. They fell on to one of the single beds as he pushed up her dress. There was no refinement. There was no protest, either. Nothing could stop them. No conscience, no fear of being caught, no self-preservation, no guilt.

It was madness. It was destiny. It was wrong. It was so right. If the world stopped after this, it

148

wouldn't matter.

It was as if they had never been apart. His hair felt the same as it slipped through her fingers. His chest was broader, his arms stronger, but she would have known him anywhere. Her hip bones fitted against his as they had always done. He belonged inside her. She could feel herself losing herself in him, that moment when she felt weightless, as if she was all spirit and no substance.

She felt tears on her face and then realised that they were his. Their hearts were pounding arrhythmically; their breathing gradually slowed and synchronised.

'Oh,' said Claire softly, and there were a million different emotions in just that one word. Awe, surprise, trepidation, appreciation, anguish. Nick peeled himself away from her and lay beside her. Their hands found each other and their fingers entwined. What now? They only had seconds to decide. It wouldn't be long before one of the other stags barged into the room, or someone began to look for Claire.

'I'm going back on Sunday night,' said Nick. 'If you want to come with me, I'll cancel the wedding.'

Claire didn't reply. There wasn't anything to discuss. They each knew exactly what they had to lose and to gain. She rolled off the bed and picked up her clothes. Her limbs disappeared into the garments as quickly as they had been peeled off only minutes ago. She stood over him, gathering her hair back up into its clip. Her throat felt tight with longing, even though her heart hadn't yet subsided to its normal rate from their coupling.

He sat up and went to take her in his arms again, but she put out her hand to stop him.

149

'Don't.' Her voice was low. A warning.

She smoothed down her clothes, looked at him. She lifted her shoulders in a shrug of uncertainty.

'We already know there isn't always a happy ending,' she told him.

He looked at her.

'Is that a no?'

'I don't know . . .'

She bent over him, took his face in her hands and kissed him.

'I have to go.'

'It's okay. I understand.' He stared out of the window for a moment. 'Do you want me to leave? Would it be easier if I left?'

She hesitated. It would be so much easier.

'No,' she answered.

'It's up to you. To decide what to do. Because I've already made my decision.'

She nodded.

'I know.'

Two seconds later she had crossed the room and walked out of the door. It shut with a click.

* * *

Angelica was behind the reception desk having a fight with the printer, trying to print out the evening's menus, when she felt a pair of warm hands on her waist.

She turned round with a yelp and found herself looking straight into Luca's eyes.

'You shouldn't do that to people!'

'I couldn't resist.' He gave her a grin.

She held up the crumpled bits of paper.

'Bloody printer chewed everything up again.'

Luca took the paper off her and chucked it in the bin. 'We'll get a new one.' His eyes flickered around. 'Where's Claire?'

Angelica tensed. She was pretty certain Claire had been banking on Luca staying in the kitchen for a while.

'I think she's gone up to change,' she told him.

'I was going to do the same thing myself.' Luca took off his bandanna. 'I've got Fred and Loz on the case. Big evening for us tonight.'

Angelica thought quickly. What if Claire was still embroiled with the stag bloke?

'Luca . . .' she began, just as he was about to walk off.

He turned.

'Yeah?'

'Claire . . . told me what might be happening. About the London hotel. With the Parfitts.'

'Did she?' Luca frowned.

Maybe she shouldn't have told him that. But what the hell—it was better than him catching Claire doing something she shouldn't be.

'I just wondered . . . what it would mean. For here. For . . . well, for me, actually.'

Luca walked back towards her. He was so close. He looked at her with a concerned smile.

'You're not worried, are you?'

Angelica nodded. Her heart was thumping. Whether it was fear on Claire's behalf or because of Luca's presence, she couldn't be sure. He was putting a hand on her shoulder.

'Claire and I value you extremely highly. If anything comes of this venture—which I hope it will—then whatever decisions we make will be done in consultation with you. You're a very important member of our team.'

'Thank you.'

'We're not just going to abandon ship. Claire and I will probably take it in turns to stay down here, while the other one is up in London.'

She met his gaze. His expression was deadpan, but his meaning was perfectly clear.

'Oh,' she said, and managed a dimpled smirk. Anything to keep his attention on her and stop him going upstairs. She shouldn't be encouraging him. It was totally inappropriate. And it was only fuelling her ridiculous fantasy crush. Everything inside Angelica told her Luca was bad news. She would only be a toy to him. She would only get hurt.

'Although thinking about it,' he continued, 'there may well be an opportunity for you in London. We're going to need a team we can trust. And I don't suppose you want to be stuck in Pennfleet for the rest of your life?'

Angelica realised it hadn't occurred to her for a moment that they might need her in London. But of course, it was a possibility. She'd been loyal and faithful and a hard worker. She had promise. Why wouldn't they utilise her in their new venture?

London, she thought. The idea made her throat tight with longing. She imagined herself with a little apartment, maybe sharing with some other staff from the hotel. She saw herself trip-trapping along a London street, swinging a carrier bag from a top department store. A solvent, single girl-about-town.

Her and Luca in a cocktail bar.

Dream on, Angelica, she told herself. Where exactly did Dill fit into this picture? Don't even go there.

'Well,' she said. 'Fingers crossed that the deal

comes off, then.'

'Indeed.'

He was holding her gaze. She didn't know what to do next. Angelica was usually a cool customer, but Luca always made her feel flustered and unsure of herself.

Thankfully, Claire came down the stairs before she could think of a response.

'I thought you were dressing for dinner,' said Luca.

'No.' Claire looked puzzled, then caught Angelica's eye. 'Well, yes—but you know how it is. I got waylaid.'

Luca nodded.

'Yep,' he said. 'I know exactly how it is. I got waylaid myself.'

He flashed Angelica one last wicked smile before turning back to Claire.

'We should go and get ready. I've booked the table for half eight, but we need to chat things through. Make sure we're both singing from the same song sheet.'

Claire nodded. 'Why don't you go first? Have a shower. I'll have a bath after you.'

Luca loped across the hall and up the stairs. Angelica and Claire watched him go, then looked at each other.

Neither of them said anything. It was all too complicated.

*   *   *

Nick lay on the bed, listening to the silence of the room.

He should get up. He should get dressed. He

should bound downstairs and buy the next round; get drunk with his friends. But he felt poleaxed. As incapable of movement or decision as he had been the day of his mother's death. As the day he had realised that Claire had betrayed him.

Of course they'd all believed Isobel's cover story: that she was going to Lanzarote to recuperate from her virus. She was entirely convincing. And of course they didn't find it strange that they didn't hear from her much—Sally's villa in Lanzarote didn't have a phone, she told them. She'd called twice, sounding distant, blaming the bad line in the phone box in Teguise. They soon found out she'd phoned from the hospice, from the bed she was dying in, when the nurse had called them three weeks into January to say she had passed away.

They were devastated, the four of them. Utterly bewildered and shell-shocked, none of them able to come to terms with what Isobel had done. Gerald was bereft, incapable of making a decision, and the three boys tried to pull together and organise things. It was Claire who'd been their saving grace. Claire who kept the house running, dealt with the undertaker, liaised with the vicar. She was a tower of strength to them. She knew instinctively the right thing to do about everything, and she was there for them twenty-four hours a day, holding them, hugging them, cooking for them, turning visitors away or letting them in, depending on who they were. She arranged flowers, hymns, orders of service, announcements. She made casseroles and forced them to eat. She marched Gerald to the doctor and got him pills to help him sleep. She spoke to Shrimp's housemaster, contacted the major clients at Melchior Barnes to put them in the

154

picture, got in touch with the solicitor.

Nick clung to her warmth at night. He felt adrift, furious with himself for not knowing what to do and how to behave, unable to communicate with his father, all of them locked into their grief so deeply that they couldn't function. He just couldn't imagine life without Isobel. Her absence had already halted the momentum in the house. She was their anchor. Without her they were directionless, none of them strong enough to take charge. Thank God, at least, for Claire. He felt guilty that they were leaning on her so heavily, but she seemed to cope, even though the cold that she'd had at Christmas had gone on to her chest and she couldn't get rid of it. They all needed her. She had stepped into Isobel's shoes so valiantly, without question.

And then, three days before the funeral, he realised why.

They were in the kitchen, having a debate about something trivial—whether to have music on when people came back to the house afterwards—and Claire said, 'Yes, she wanted music.'

Nick looked at her. 'She *wanted* music?'

'Yes,' replied Claire.

'Surely you mean "would have wanted"?'

There was a pause. A long, long pause before Claire gave a little laugh and said, 'Yes. Would have wanted.'

And in that moment, Nick realised that Claire had known all along. That she had been in on the subterfuge. She'd been groomed for this role. She was prepared. She knew exactly what Isobel wanted. She'd been primed to look after them.

He stood up from the table, shaking.

'You knew.'

Claire couldn't look at him. 'Knew what?'

'You knew where Mum was.' He took a step towards her. 'Admit it, Claire. She got you onside, didn't she? You were her bloody accomplice. I can see it now. That's exactly how Mum worked . . .'

The tears streaming down Claire's face told him all he needed to know.

'Get out,' he told her. 'Get out of this house and don't get any ideas about coming to the funeral. You've betrayed me, and Dad . . . all of us. How could you?'

'She made me promise,' sobbed Claire. 'And maybe she was right. What good would knowing have done? It wouldn't have stopped her dying.'

Nick could hear his father coming in through the front door.

'Tell that to Dad,' he told Claire. 'Stand there and justify what you've done. See if he agrees.'

Claire stared at him, appalled. Then she picked up her bag. She turned to him.

'I did it because I loved her. I love all of you. And because I thought it was the right thing.'

And before he could stop her, she ran out through the French windows and across the lawn. As Gerald walked into the kitchen, he could see her disappearing over the bridge and out of sight.

'Where's Claire going?' he asked.

Nick couldn't reply. He sat down at the table, put his head on his arms and cried his heart out. He couldn't believe what the girl he adored had done to him and his family. He never wanted to see her again as long as he lived.

*　　　*　　　*

156

On the surface, the funeral was as dignified and beautiful as Isobel had been. But underneath, the truth was as ugly as the cancer that had taken her away. Gerald, Shrimp, Felix and Nick kept it together for the ceremony, but the shock of Claire's deceit only compounded their grief. For Nick had to tell the others the truth, to explain Claire's absence. The four of them didn't really have time to take the implications on board, or examine the rights and wrongs, before the solicitor presented them each with a letter from Isobel.

They were written by hand, in the familiar turquoise ink she used for thank-you notes and invitations, her writing full of extravagant loops and greek 'e's and 'a's, and were identical in their wording:

My darling, beautiful boys,

I know by the time you read this letter, you will be angry with me. But please, think beyond what you are feeling just now and try and understand why I chose to do this. I know you will think that I was the only one who had a choice in the matter, that I didn't give you any, and maybe this is true. Maybe I was selfish. Maybe I did it for me. But then I didn't want to have to make the choice in the first place. That's the cruel thing.

So. I hope you will forgive me, and remember me as I want to be remembered. Just as my last memory of each of you was as you should be—happy, laughing, carefree. Stay like that for ever, for me.

With all my love, every day and always,

Mummy xx

Nick's, however, had a separate PS.

Darling Nick,

Please don't hold Claire accountable for being my ally. I needed someone very much, and she was very brave to respect my wishes. I know how difficult it was for her, but please know from me that she did the right thing. She loves you very much, as much as I did, and I know that your heart will always be safe in her hands.

Mummy

He lay on his bed, staring at the words. He realised now that he couldn't bear to lose the two people he loved most in the world at the same time. The grief of losing his mother had cancelled out his grief at the loss of Claire, but at least he could get her back.

He knew how cajoling his mother could be. How she could twist you round her little finger. He imagined those bright-blue eyes reeling Claire in, that husky voice dripping with honeyed persuasion, the emotional blackmail.

He suddenly felt a surge of anger towards Isobel. What right did she have to jeopardise his relationship with Claire? She would have known that Nick would be furious, would find her actions untenable.

He crumpled up the letter and threw it across

the room, then rolled off his bed, grabbed his Converses, and ran for the door, along the corridor, down the stairs and out of the front door. He flew over the bridge and along the lane, jumping the fence that led to the field that was the short cut to Claire's house.

He arrived, breathless, at her front door. Her parents' anonymous Rover was parked in the drive. There was no knocker, no bell, as if they had no need for one because they never had any visitors. He rapped on the glass, scanning the front of the house, trying to remember which was her window. He'd only been up to her bedroom once, when she went to find a cardigan.

Her father answered.

'Hello?' He looked at Nick warily.

'I wondered . . . if Claire was in. I need to speak to her.' He smiled, as if to prove he wasn't a madman, even though he knew he probably looked like one, breathing heavily, perspiring.

'I'm sorry, but she's not here.'

'Do you know what time she'll be back?'

Mr Marlowe frowned slightly. 'I'm afraid I've no idea.'

'Is she working? Will she be back later on?'

'I'm afraid . . .' Her father trailed off, as if he was reluctant to be the bearer of bad news. Nick's heart lurched. There could have been an accident. Of course there could, and he wouldn't have known about it. 'I'm afraid she's gone away. And we don't know when she'll be back.'

'You mean . . . like on holiday?'

'No.' His expression was solemn. Almost emotionless. 'She's gone abroad.'

'Where?' Nick tasted metallic fear. He hadn't

foreseen this eventuality. Claire didn't strike him as a traveller, an adventurer, someone who would fling a few things into a bag and grab her passport. Then be gone.

'I'm sorry. She's asked us not to tell anyone.' Mr Marlowe looked at him hard. Nick felt as if he was judging him. He wondered how much Claire had said to her parents. She usually told them nothing about her life, but after the way he had treated her, maybe she had taken them into her confidence. Who else would she have had to turn to?

He appraised Mr Marlowe, wondering how much he knew.

'It's rather urgent. I've got something I need to tell her.'

'Well,' said Mr Marlowe, 'I'm afraid it will have to wait.'

How dare this man, who had shown his daughter no love or interest to speak of, stand there and judge him?

'If Claire wants to get in touch with you, she will. In the meantime, I think you should respect her privacy. Please don't call again.'

And with that, he shut the door.

Nick had no idea what to do next. There was no point in ringing the mobile phone he had given her for Christmas—she had left it on the table in the kitchen when she'd fled the Mill House.

In the next few days, he tried everywhere else he could think of to find out where Claire had gone. He went to her old college and hung around outside the art block, approaching people who might have been in the year below and asking if they knew her or had heard from her, but all he got was strange looks, until eventually a teacher came over and warned him that he would be escorted off the premises.

He went to the pub. Claire still worked there sometimes on a Saturday when they were busy. He thought that surely she would have given them a forwarding address, or some sort of explanation that would give him a clue.

But Mel had no inkling either. She sat him down and gave him a lager and blackcurrant, as if he was still fifteen.

'She just told us she wasn't coming back. She didn't even come in and pick up the rest of her wages. She said to give them to her parents. She wouldn't tell me where she was going.'

Nick buried his head in his arms on the bar top. Mel enveloped him in a hug.

'Oh you poor chick,' she said. 'It's unbearable for the two of you. For *all* of you. Life's so bloody unfair.'

'Not as unfair as death,' Nick mumbled into his jumper sleeve.

'It's all right to cry,' Mel told him, and he turned, sobbing, burying his face in her barmaid's bosom that smelt of Obsession, and she was so kind, and although she wasn't anything like his mother, it made him miss Isobel so badly he could barely breathe. They never cried at home, the four of them, because once they started they would probably never stop. He cried for over an hour, and Mel held him and stroked him and murmured comforting nonsense in his ear, rocking him like a baby.

Afterwards, he walked back home, slunk up to his bedroom, bathed his eyes over and over again

161

to try and hide the redness. Then he lay on his bed and stared up at the ceiling, wondering how to find someone who didn't want to be found. All he could do was hope and pray that somehow she would feel his love and come back to him. That she would get to wherever she was going and decide it was the wrong decision.

She hadn't come back.

He had spent the next few years grieving. For his mother and his lover, and the terrible turn of events that had taken away from him everything he held dear. Eventually the pain had faded, although it never disappeared completely, and he had edged himself back to a normal existence, going out with his mates, having the fun he deserved. And of course there were girls—lovely girls who helped him heal.

And in time, there was Sophie, with whom he had fallen gently in love. Not a passionate, all-consuming love, but an easy, companionable love that he knew felt right, and that he could maintain. He told her the story one night, because you couldn't decide to share the rest of your life with someone and not let them know the real you, and she had been so kind and understanding. She had held him tight and told him that it was all going to be okay, that they could be happy, that she wanted to make him forget and give him a reason to look forward.

Until today, he'd thought Sophie was the answer. He'd been looking forward to her becoming his wife, the prospect of starting a family, which they'd talked about. But now that Claire had walked back into his life, all that had changed.

And his mates were sitting downstairs, waiting

to give him a send-off. He'd have to go down and pretend everything was hunky-dory. Until he knew what Claire was going to decide, he had to keep his options open.

He rolled reluctantly off the bed and pulled on the jeans and shirt that were waiting for him. He couldn't let his mates down. They were determined to make it a weekend to remember.

It was certainly shaping up to be that so far.

*   *   *

As soon as Luca came out of the shower, Claire slipped into the bathroom, locked the door and ran a deep bath, scrubbing away the evidence of her encounter.

She didn't feel guilty. She felt shaken. All the emotion of the last time she had seen Nick came flooding back. She could remember that afternoon as if it was yesterday. She had fled from the Mill House, over the bridge, and run all the way home without stopping, flinging open the front door and running up the stairs to her room, where she had fallen on to her bed and wept. Her distress had been so audible, so tangible, so overwhelming that even her parents couldn't fail to notice.

In fact, if there had been one good thing to come out of the tragedy, it was that her relationship with her parents had deepened almost overnight. They had come to her room, concerned, and wormed the whole story out of her.

Her father was magnificently furious. Not with Claire; not in the least. But with Isobel, and the rest of the Barnes family, and himself, and Claire's mother, for letting the situation become so irretrievably awful.

'What the hell was the woman thinking?' he thundered to his wife. 'Letting Claire take the burden? She must have been a monster. A selfish, uncaring monster.'

'She wasn't a monster,' sobbed Claire. 'She loved them all too much.'

'Yes, but now she's gone, and you're paying the price.'

'It's our fault,' said her mother. 'Claire should have felt she could turn to us, and she didn't.'

Claire didn't deny this. At no point had it ever occurred to her to draw her parents into the intrigue. Now she realised that by putting up a pretence of being able to cope, they had genuinely thought she was getting on with her life, and was happy. They had all co-existed in their own little worlds, oblivious to each other's needs, never scratching beneath the surface of what they chose to present to each other.

Now that the truth was out, however, her parents became stalwarts. They were a tower of strength to Claire, protective and loving and concerned. They talked the whole episode through with her, stressed that she should not feel guilty, that she had been put in an untenable situation. She couldn't believe how understanding and kind they were. Why had she never trusted them before? She felt ashamed that she had treated them so shabbily, turning her back on them for her glitzy new life with the Barnes.

Meanwhile, the cold that had started on Christmas Day was still lingering and had made its way down to Claire's chest, developing into a racking cough that she couldn't seem to get rid of.

The trauma of Nick's discovery only made it worse. That night, Claire developed a raging fever. By midnight, she could barely breathe. At one o'clock her parents called an ambulance.

For five days she was dangerously ill with double pneumonia. It was touch and go as to whether she would survive. Eventually she started to respond to the antibiotics. It was another week before she was allowed out of hospital, pale and barely able to stand.

When she was back home, in the safety of the kitchen, she asked her father if Nick had been to see her at all.

'No,' said her father. 'No, he hasn't. We haven't heard a word.'

Claire lay on the sofa, mute with grief. He didn't want to know. He really didn't want to know. If there had been any chance of him forgiving her, he would have been to see her by now.

No way did she have the strength or the courage to go back to the Mill House and put forward her side of the story. It wouldn't just be Nick she would have to face. It would be Gerald and Felix and Shrimp too. She had betrayed them all.

'You should go and stay with Annie, in California,' suggested her mother. 'You need some sunshine. And Annie will be a tonic. I'll get on to her straight away.'

Annie was her mother's sister, the complete antithesis of her and fifteen years younger. She lived in Sausalito with her architect husband and two young children, and had a California-dream lifestyle.

Claire lay on the sofa and thought about it. It was the only answer. She had no job: she could hardly go back to Melchior Barnes. And the thought of getting far, far away from the nightmare was too enticing for words. She'd always been fond of Annie, who was as hyper and enthusiastic as her mother was understated.

'Do you think she'd have me?' she asked. 'And what about the air fare?'

'Of course she'll have you,' replied her mother, who was already on the phone.

'And don't worry about the fare,' said her father. 'Don't worry about anything. We've got enough put aside to tide you over, for as long as it takes.'

Annie was thrilled at the thought of a visitor. She'd been toying with the idea of starting up a new business making silver jewellery, and had considered hiring a nanny for her two children. She suggested that Claire take on the role for six months, while she tested the water to see if her business was viable. After that they could all reassess, but in the meantime it seemed to solve everyone's problems.

If she couldn't heal herself in Sausalito, Claire realised as soon as she arrived, there was no hope for her. The house was stunning: a waterside haven overlooking the Golden Gate Bridge filled with light, and she threw herself into the relaxed Californian lifestyle. She slotted straight into the family, because of course she *was* family. The children were easy and biddable, and life adopted a gentle rhythm: walks along the park trails, cycle rides, messing about in the boat the family kept moored in the bustling harbour. It was a million miles from Mimsbury. And if, occasionally, she felt tempted to scrawl a postcard to Nick, she managed to pull herself back from the brink just in time.

As she relived those warm, healing days, Luca banged on the door, dragging her back to the present.

'Have you fallen down the plughole?'

'Two minutes!' Claire shouted in reply.

She had to get dressed, paint on a face and gear herself up for dinner with Trevor and Monique. The last thing she felt like doing was discussing a bold new venture. But she had no choice.

She slipped into the dress she'd bought earlier and let Luca do up her zip.

'You look fabulous,' he said, kissing her neck, and she fought off the urge to push him away.

*   *   *

'Do you think this is stalkerish?' Laura looked down at the email she had printed out, giving directions to Tony Weston's house.

'Immensely stalkerish.' Dan looked at her, amused. 'But sometimes stalkerish is okay.' He paused. 'I drove past your flat three times before I asked you out.'

'No way!' She looked at him in astonishment.

He nodded. 'Sometimes you just need to do the research. Get a feel for how things are.'

She frowned at him, half laughing. 'What did you see, when you drove past?'

Dan laughed. 'Bugger all. Just . . . your flat. You have a weird neighbour, though, who goes to the shop in her pyjamas.'

'No,' said Laura. 'Those are her clothes.' She laughed when he looked disconcerted. 'That's crazy, trendy Hoxton for you.'

Dan hit his head as if he had forgotten

something. 'Of course.'

Laura squinted along the terrace.

'I think it's that one. Clarence House.' She didn't point, just tilted her head discreetly towards it. She didn't want anyone noticing them and thinking their behaviour odd.

Clarence House was in the middle of a row of Victorian villas, positioned high on a steep bank to give them a view over the houses opposite, which backed directly on to the harbour. The villas were in various stages of dilapidation and renovation. Some were tired-looking; some had been given a state-of-the-art makeover, with black decking and balconies made of glass and stainless steel. Clarence House fell somewhere between the two: it retained its original features, but had been thoughtfully tweaked to bring it into the twenty-first century. The terrace at the front was crammed with pots brimming with geraniums and busy Lizzies. Rustic wooden furniture had been washed with a pale lavender paint. Moroccan lanterns were dotted amidst the pots, and an antique triptych mirror leant against the wall of the house, reflecting the sea in its glass.

With a thump of her heart, Laura realised that it reminded her of home.

'What do you think?' she asked Dan.

'It's a fantastic house. It must have a stunning view.'

'No, I mean do you think it could be my dad's?'

Dan put an arm around her. 'Laura, you can't guess by looking at his plant pots. You won't know until you ask him.'

'What if I bottle it?'

Dan sighed. 'Let's forget about it for this

168

evening. Let's go back to the hotel and have a drink. Enjoy the weather. I don't want you stressing about this.'

'Sorry. I know I'm being a complete pain.'

'You're not. This is a huge deal for you. But there's no point in speculating.' He put his hands around her face and kissed her on the nose. 'There's going to be loads to talk about tomorrow. So let's just have fun tonight.' He took her hand and drew her back down the road towards the hotel. She had to run to keep up with his stride, but she knew he was right.

They came to a gap in the houses where a little wall overlooked the harbour. The evening sun was an impossible orange; the water played with the light it threw, tossing sparks of gold and silver around the bay.

'Stand there,' Dan commanded, and pulled out a tiny camera from his pocket, the one he used for snaps.

Laura leant back against the warmth of the wall, smiling. The sea breeze tossed strands of her hair around her face, and she tried to smooth them down.

'No. Leave them. It's fine. Windswept is good.'

Afterwards, she looked at the pictures of herself on the screen. That's me, she thought, the day before I meet the man who might be my father. How will I look tomorrow?

CHAPTER NINE

Colin was not enjoying his dinner.

It was a shame. One of the reasons he had chosen the Townhouse was because he thought the menu looked wonderful. But Karen made it very obvious that it wasn't her idea of good food. She didn't like fish, for a start, and as that was a speciality, it narrowed her options considerably. In the end she went for pâté and steak, while Colin ordered mussels, which came in a big, steaming pan. She looked at him in disgust as he scooped up the shells and devoured them.

'I don't know how you can eat those things.'

Someone else turning their nose up at what you were eating invariably spoiled your pleasure.

Plus Alison had phoned just before they had come down to dinner. She didn't usually phone while he was away. She said she hated the idea of bothering him with trivialities while he was in the middle of something. But tonight she'd needed to double-check a date with him urgently, and when he reassured her that he wasn't in the middle of business, she had chatted away to him about her day—a bit of village gossip, Ryan had sent through some photos, the agricultural contractor had finally come to trim the hedges . . . By the time they said goodbye, Colin wished he was at home, about to sit down to a quiet supper with his wife, instead of what he suspected would be a far from quiet dinner with his ex-mistress.

Karen had drunk far too much too quickly. She didn't want wine—she didn't drink the stuff—so

Colin had chosen a bottle of white for himself while Karen stuck to vodka and soda.

'It's got the least calories,' she told him. She was neurotic about her weight. She was on her fifth double nevertheless, and he decided he'd better broach the subject before she got too lairy.

'We need to talk about Chelsey.'

'Yes.' She banged her glass down on the table. 'We do.'

'She doesn't seem very happy.'

'She's not.' Karen signalled to the waiter to bring her another drink. 'I told you, she's being bullied at school.'

'Do you think it's because of her weight?'

Karen shrugged. 'Probably. But what can you do?'

'A lot, actually. You could start by not feeding her so much junk.'

'What?' Karen's indignation was almost comical.

'She does seem to eat an awful lot of rubbish.'

'Says the man who's made a million out of flogging biscuits and cakes.'

'I didn't force-feed them to my children. I made sure they had a sensible, balanced diet.'

He knew he was straying on to dangerous ground, but you had to be forceful with Karen. Subtlety didn't work.

'No you didn't.' Her eyes were narrowing dangerously. 'Your wife did. She was the one who cooked for them, and did all the shopping. It's bloody easy to be perfect parents when there's two of you.'

Her voice was rising. Colin put his hand up.

'Okay. I'm sorry. I know it's hard.'

'Yes. It is.'

171

Colin looked at her. A few drinks had made her appear the worse for wear, and he realised that up close the years had not been kind to her. The tanning didn't help, or the smoking, and he thought she probably hit the bottle quite a bit, because her eyes were rather bloodshot. He told himself he was being harsh—maybe she was just tired. But he didn't think her lifestyle was doing her any favours. Or maybe it was just that she tried so hard to give the illusion of youth, when she should just give in gracefully.

He thought about Alison, who had if anything improved with age. Once she had got her bounce back, she had kept herself trim, and liked to look nice. She'd found her style—nothing wild, but she always looked groomed. She was probably ten years older than Karen, but looked younger. Although he thought Karen would probably sneer at Alison's dress sense; would think her a frump.

None of these musings were going to solve the problem in hand.

'Is there anything I can do to help? With Chelsey.'

'Actually, yes, there is.' Karen leant down into her huge handbag and pulled out a white A4 envelope. 'I'm working all the hours God sends. The gym want me to do lates nearly every night. I don't get home till ten. I can't turn them down because anyone who doesn't cooperate gets sacked. So I'm constantly having to farm Chelsey out. Or get someone in.'

'I can see that's tough.'

She pulled out the contents of the envelope and slid it across the table to him. It was a prospectus. A glossy prospectus for a private school.

The very school his own kids had gone to. The one Ryan had just left.

She was looking at him, judging his reaction. He deliberately kept his expression deadpan. Across the table he could smell her perfume. It reeked of bitter almonds. Cyanide, he thought. His toes curled up in his shoes.

'Thing is, if she went here, she could board some of the time.' She raked her ghastly square-tipped nails through her hair. 'She never sees me as it is. At least this way she's got company, and they can monitor her homework.'

'What about Chelsey? What does she think?'

Karen blinked.

'I haven't told her yet. I didn't want to get her hopes up.'

'Do you really think this is the answer? Sending her to a private school, when she's already being bullied? This place will be full of skinny girls with more money than sense. Trust me, I know. Michelle had a hard time at one point, till she learnt how to handle them.'

Karen looked sulky.

'I'm just trying to do what's best for her.'

'What's best for Chelsey?'

His implication was obvious. That her decision was a selfish one.

'It was good enough for your kids, wasn't it? But maybe Chelsey doesn't rank as highly as they do.'

She might as well have picked up her steak knife and plunged it into his guts.

'I can't put this through the books, Karen. Four grand a term. Twelve grand a year. That's the same again as I pay you now.'

'So . . . your illegitimate daughter's not worth the

173

money, is that what you're saying?'

'No.'

'It's only the same amount as . . . a family holiday to the Maldives.'

He shouldn't have told her about that.

'I'm not quibbling because of the money— though it would be difficult. I'm concerned because I don't think this is what Chelsey needs at the moment. I think she needs stability. And attention. Not to be thrown into an alien environment that will undoubtedly unsettle her.'

He broke into a bread roll with unnecessary force. Karen nodded at him solemnly, as if in agreement.

'Really?' she asked him, then picked up her drink, dangling the glass casually, and leant back in her chair. 'You obviously don't think I'm fit to judge what's best for our daughter. Even though I'm the one who looks after her.'

'I didn't say that. I'm just . . . giving you my opinion.'

'Well I think we need to get a few things cleared up before we make any further decisions about *our* daughter.'

She leant across the table.

'I was there for you, Colin, when you were having a hard time. When your marriage was on the rocks and you needed someone to turn to. I listened to you, and I was there for you, and I never asked anything of you. And then suddenly it was "Sorry, Karen, I can't do this any more, Alison needs me", and you were gone. And I just had to accept that you were out of my life. I didn't kick off, or make a fuss, or turn into a bunny-boiler. I knew the deal. And then I found out I was expecting Chelsey . . .'

She was gripping her glass so tightly Colin thought she might break it. He put out a hand to touch hers.

'Hey, it's okay.'

She snatched it away and shot him a look. He saw the pain in her eyes. Not venom, which was what he'd expected, but pain.

'I could have done what other people do. I could have made an appointment, got rid of her, but I didn't think that was right. I know what you think, that I saw her as a meal ticket, that I thought "Hooray! Blank cheque"—'

'I never thought that.'

'Bullshit.'

She stared at him again and he couldn't meet her eye. Of course he had thought that, time and again.

She leant forward over her plate. He could see her cleavage, the breasts that had transfixed him all those years ago, the breasts that had lured him into the trap.

'I loved you, you know that? I used to dream that your marriage would collapse. That one day you would turn to me and say that we could be together. But I never put any pressure on you. You don't do that to married men. It's the law.'

Colin could feel himself breaking into a sweat. This was a total revelation; after all their years of meeting up, he had never known she felt like this. He looked around to see if anyone could hear their conversation. The tables were quite well spaced, but there was no doubt any eavesdropper would find this exchange completely compelling.

'Listen to me!' Karen grabbed his attention back. 'I never stopped dreaming, all the while I was pregnant. It was what kept me going. I imagined

175

everything. The little cottage with the roses over the door. You and me choosing her name. Days out at the seaside with a bucket and spade. Stuff like . . .' She waved her hand around to indicate the surroundings. 'This. You, me and her.'

Colin could see that she was perilously close to tears.

'I knew that dream wasn't going to come true when you didn't come and see me in the hospital. Because how could you, what with your wonderful family that you didn't want to jeopardise?'

Colin remembered the day. He was with Alison, Michelle and Ryan, having Sunday lunch with friends in their new conservatory. The lamb had stuck in his throat, knowing that five miles down the road his secret had just come into the world. He'd been to see Karen and the baby at home as soon as was decently possible, given her a generous cheque to buy everything she needed, sorted out the monthly payment.

'It's been bloody tough, you know? Yes, you've been generous and done your financial *duty*.' She spat the word out like an oath. 'But who was there when all the decisions had to be made? Who was there when she had chickenpox and I had to go to work? Who do I have to turn to when she's being bullied? Who do I rely on now, when the pressure is on at work and if I don't play ball I'll be the next one for the chop? Because your *contribution*—' again she spat out the word '—doesn't cover all of it, you know.'

Her voice was rising.

'Karen, please. Calm down. We can talk this through.'

'I don't think there's anything to talk about

176

really.' Karen picked her napkin off her lap, crumpled it and put it on the table next to her plate. 'I've done my best for her, but I can't cope. I don't mind telling you, I'm on antidepressants to keep me going. Just like your wife was once. Sound familiar?'

She stood up and leant over him.

'I'm exhausted, Colin. I'm right on the edge. I can't cope any more.'

She was nearly shouting. People were starting to look.

'Karen.' Colin stood up and put a steadying hand on her shoulder. She threw it off.

'Don't touch me. And don't patronise me. I know exactly what you think. I can see it in your eyes when you look at me. *What was I thinking of?* Well, I've done my best to bring up your child, but to be quite honest, I don't know that she's safe with me any more.'

She indicated the prospectus, which was still lying on the table.

'I thought this was going to be the solution. I thought it would help me through a rough patch. But you made it pretty clear what you think. That I'm trying to pull a fast one. Get something for nothing.'

'I promise you. I didn't think that.' Colin kept his voice low, but he was desperate to calm her down.

'Yes you did.' She was adamant. She picked up her bag. 'I'm going for a cigarette.'

He watched her go. The high heels, the too-tight cropped trousers, the slinky off-the-shoulder top, her hair extensions swishing, her bag clamped to her side. He could see everyone else watching her too. Her body language was shouting all the way across the room, and her heels clacked loudly over the hum of conversation.

Colin stayed sitting at the table. He wasn't going to rush after her. Trying to placate a woman in that state of hysteria was asking for trouble. He'd let her calm down.

He looked down at his plate, still pristine and untouched, the slices of belly pork in a perfect fan. His appetite had gone. He picked up his wine and drank deep, then topped it up from the bottle in the cooler at the side of the table.

He picked up the prospectus and tried to digest what she'd told him. That she'd always been in love with him. That she'd hoped for something more. He had never got an inkling of that from her. She had always seemed so self-sufficient.

He thought back to when they'd first met. In what he called the Dark Ages, when Alison had shut down and gone in on herself. He'd taken to going to the gym, to work off the stress and keep his weight down, because it was too tempting to comfort-eat and drink when things were tough at home. He'd tried to get Alison to come too; to get her to shift some of the weight she hated, but she refused. She wouldn't leave the children, even though his mum had offered to sit while the pair of them went out.

So he had gone on his own. Karen was always there, part of the fixtures and fittings, one of the beauty therapists in the salon attached to the gym. When she wasn't working, she worked out, and he admired her figure from his stance on the treadmill or the rowing machine. They exchanged pleasantries at the water cooler or by the free weights. Pleasantries that morphed into mild flirting over the months, as Colin became fitter and his confidence grew. And when the gym had a Christmas party, he had gone, because he had sponsored one of the raffle prizes—a free cake every week for a year, which amused him highly given that most people were desperately trying to work off the calories they consumed.

They spent the evening drinking cheap, sickly cocktails and chatting. Then dancing—Colin liked a bop, and he didn't get much chance to strut his stuff on the dance floor these days. And when Karen had asked him back for coffee at the end of the night, to her flat just down the road, it had been so easy to say yes. So easy when she'd peeled off her dress in her lounge and stood in front of him in a basque and stockings and those trademark high heels. She'd put on 'Sexual Healing' by Marvin Gaye, and danced for him, totally unselfconscious. In his sex-starved state—it had been more than two years—he felt as if he had died and gone to heaven.

She was beautiful then. He defended himself now for his weakness. He'd have had to be made of steel to refuse.

No, he told himself. It was no good trying to make excuses. He'd been despicably weak. Given in to his basest instincts without a thought for either Alison or, it seemed now, Karen. It was men like him who gave his sex a bad name. Men like him who had their brains in their trousers.

The affair hadn't lasted all that long. Six months at the most. Sneaky sessions after the gym. Or sometimes in the morning before he went to work, because she worked shifts and started late, so he would swing by and she would answer the door, wearing one of the astonishingly short and sheer

179

nightdresses she favoured. So far removed from the buttoned-up pyjamas that Alison had taken to wearing, to protect herself from any possible advances. Advances that he'd long since given up making.

He never flattered himself that Karen got all that much out of their relationship at the time. He thought she probably enjoyed the flowers he sent her, and the kudos of sleeping with the man with the flashiest car in the gym car park. He'd bought himself a Porsche for his thirty-fifth birthday; drove it round with the roof down and the music up. He'd stopped that once he turned forty. He didn't want to look like a prat.

He ended it when Alison had finally gone for help, when her depression had been diagnosed at last and she started the medication that helped her get her head over the parapet, until gradually the woman he had fallen in love with had re-emerged. And their relationship had become ever stronger, blossoming as their children blossomed, only marred, for him, by his annual excursion with Karen and Chelsey.

He looked at his watch. Karen had been some time. He wondered if he ought to go and look for her. The waiter came over.

'Is everything all right, sir?'

Colin looked down at their untouched plates, embarrassed.

'Um—just give us a little longer. It's all great. Thank you.'

The waiter nodded and melted away, trained not to make his guests feel awkward in any way.

Ten minutes. How long did it take to smoke a cigarette? Maybe she'd had two? She couldn't go long without nicotine; maybe she was stockpiling. Or maybe she'd gone to the loo.

Colin waited another three minutes before making up his mind to go and look for her. They needed to decide what to do about their food— eat it or have it taken away. He certainly couldn't face his now. He got up, and walked as casually as he could through the dining room. One or two guests glanced at him as he passed, and he thought he detected a trace of sympathy in their smiles. He nodded back, giving nothing away.

He walked into the reception area and out of the front door where he thought she was probably lurking on the pavement, sucking in the life force that her cigarettes seemed to supply. But there was no sign of her. Just the usual tourists ambling along the street, on their way to dinner or the pub.

Disquiet gnawing at his empty belly, he went back inside and approached the reception desk.

'Um . . . I wondered if you'd seen my . . .' He didn't know what to call her. 'My dining partner,' he finished lamely. 'Tall, thin, long hair?

The girl behind the desk looked concerned.

'Sparkly top and skinny jeans? She just got a taxi.'

Colin swallowed.

'A taxi? Do you know where to?'

'I've no idea, I'm afraid. She's only been gone about . . . five minutes?'

Five minutes? It would take him ten to get up to the bedroom, find his car keys, run to the car park. And he still wouldn't know what direction to head in. The station, probably . . . but even then he couldn't leave Chelsey in her room while he went off in pursuit.

181

'Do you know what firm it was? If they'd be able to tell me where she went?'

The girl shrugged. 'I don't know if they'll tell me, but I can try . . .'

She picked up the phone as his mobile went off in his pocket. A text. The sweat that had gathered round his collar trickled down his neck.

'No, it's fine. Don't worry.'

He walked back outside and stood on the pavement. Took his phone out of his pocket and pressed the message icon.

It's your turn now. I've done my best but I can't do any more. It's up to you or you can call the social services. They'd find her a nice foster place.

He shut down the message, put his phone back in his pocket and looked up at the night sky.

To his surprise, he felt completely calm.

*   *   *

As Luca led the Parfitts through the dining room, the other guests couldn't help but follow his progress. The women took in his perfect arse and the freshly washed curls that were wilder than ever; the men noted the air of authority that seemed in total contradiction to his black skinny jeans and Gitane-blue shirt with the tails hanging out. He radiated a rock-star glamour that left the women weak and the men envious.

Behind him, Claire's eyes looked to the right and left to make sure that everything was perfect. The restaurant was at peak capacity, all the tables full, yet the staff had everything under control.

She loved the dining room. It had taken such a long time to get it right. They didn't want it twee or cluttered, or too stark. Nor did they want to detract from the stunning view that it looked out on to. The walls were painted a gun-metal grey that reflected the soft light from the pewter wall lanterns and the candles. The floor was a light polished oak, chunky wide boards that showed up the knots and imperfections. The upholstered chairs—they had spent months searching for the right ones; it was so important to be comfortable whilst eating— were covered in dark-grey stripes with either coral, turquoise or plum, the only splashes of colour in a neutral palette.

Written on one wall, in spidery black writing, was John Masefield's poem 'Sea Fever'. Claire had been worried when they commissioned it that it was a cliché, but the look of pleasure on diners' faces as they read it was undeniable.

I must down to the seas again, to the lonely sea
 and the sky,
And all I ask is a tall ship and a star to steer her
 by,
And the wheel's kick and the wind's song and
 the white sail's shaking,
And a grey mist on the sea's face, and a grey
 dawn breaking.

I must down to the seas again, for the call of the
 running tide
Is a wild call and a clear call that may not be
 denied;
And all I ask is a windy day with the white
 clouds flying,
And the flung spray and the blown spume, and
 the sea-gulls crying.

183

I must down to the seas again, to the vagrant
gypsy life,
To the gull's way and the whale's way where the
wind's like a whetted knife;
And all I ask is a merry yarn from a laughing
fellow-rover
And quiet sleep and a sweet dream when the
long trick's over.

It was so evocative; so reminiscent of Pennfleet. It was all the decoration the room needed.

As Claire sat down at the table with Trevor and Monique—the best table in the room, by the French windows that led out on to the terrace, although it was too chilly to have them open this late in the evening—her stomach was churning. She had no idea how she was going to get through the meal.

'This is fabulous,' said Trevor, taking the seat opposite her. 'Fabulous as ever. I have to say, Claire, Monique and I eat out a lot—a *lot*—and we still haven't found anywhere to beat this place. It's welcoming, it's stylish, everything's just right. And that's not easy to do—I know that.'

'Gordon Ramsay,' said Monique. 'He always gets it right.'

'Well, yeah, but you're talking in a different league there, Monique.'

'That's not to say we can't emulate his standards,' Luca pointed out, pulling out Monica's chair. 'Aim high.'

Trevor cocked a finger at him.

'I like your style. Aim high is right.'

Claire smothered a smile—Luca being

184

oleaginous was always amusing, because it didn't come naturally to him.

'I think what we're trying to say,' Trevor went on, 'is we're very proud to be a part of the Townhouse.' He was distracted by the arrival of the waiter with a bottle of champagne. 'Perfect timing!' he crowed. 'And Taittinger. Our favourite. How did you know?'

Claire gave a coy little shrug, not liking to say that she'd simply gone into their account to see what they had ordered on their last visit. For a man of the world, Trevor seemed easily flattered. Another waiter came out of the kitchen with a silver platter smothered in ice, on which were perched two dozen of the finest, plumpest rock oysters. He put it down on the table with a flourish.

Monique looked alarmed.

'I'm not sure about oysters,' she said.

'You absolutely have to have one,' insisted Luca. 'It's the food of the gods. Fresh out of the sea today. It doesn't get better than this, Monique.'

Claire watched fondly as he selected an oyster, held it to his lips, and tipped his head back as he swallowed. Then he chose one for Monique and held it out to her.

'Go on,' he urged. 'You simply can't die without having tried an oyster. It's the ultimate taste of the sea.'

Monique simpered and took it from him. With Luca in such a seductively persuasive mood, Claire thought she would have eaten the shell if he'd told her to.

The table watched as Monique followed Luca's example. She gave a little shudder, then looked pleasantly surprised.

'My goodness,' she said. 'It's quite nice.'

'Well, here goes then,' said Trevor, reaching out a huge paw and grabbing one. 'In for a penny.'

He slugged it back and nodded appreciatively.

'Bit like the time I nearly drowned in Yarmouth when I was a kid,' he said. 'But not bad.'

'Come on, Claire,' urged Luca. 'You love oysters.'

Claire stared down at the platter. She could think of nothing she felt less like eating. But it was vital to this meeting to be seen to be toeing the party line. She picked one up, thinking of Nick with his friends in the pub further down the river, wondering what he was thinking.

What was she going to say to him? What was she going to decide?

She picked up an oyster and threw it back, gagging on the salt, the unwanted substance in her mouth.

'Delicious,' she smiled, and Luca smiled back.

*   *   *

Colin crept into the bedroom, where Chelsey was lying on her bed. She was fast asleep, the television still blaring, the colours flashing across her body. Around her were empty wrappers, from the Minstrels he'd bought her, but also from other sweets she'd obviously had stashed in her bag.

Colin stood and watched her, as he had stood and watched his other children sleeping so many times. It was one of the best things about being a parent, he thought, being able to watch your kids without them knowing, wondering about their dreams, relishing the rise and fall of their chests as they breathed. A wonderful feeling of love and protectiveness washed over him.

She was his daughter, he thought. It was his duty to love and protect her, to make sure she had the best. How he was going to do that, he didn't know. Not yet. But he wasn't going to let her down. He wasn't going to let her feel that she was a burden any longer.

He wasn't sure what to do or where to sleep. He didn't want her to panic if she woke up and saw Karen wasn't there, but he didn't feel quite right about getting into Karen's bed. In the end, he decided to sleep in the armchair.

He crept around the room, clearing up the mess, turning off the television, switching on a standard lamp and turning off the main light. Then he took the mohair blanket off the end of Karen's bed and settled himself into the chair by the television. He needed to sleep. He needed all his energy to deal with tomorrow, and the decisions it was going to bring. And as well as the decisions, he had to make sure that Chelsey had a wonderful day—the day she deserved.

*   *   *

The oysters were devoured; the table were onto their second bottle of Taittinger. As the waiter brought over tiny earthenware dishes of asparagus baked in tarragon custard, Monique produced a Mulberry document wallet and pulled out three sets of house details.

'I've had every agent in London on to it,' she said. 'I've been to view seventeen different properties. And I've narrowed it down to three.

Trevor and I have our favourite, but it's got to the point where we need your input.' She laid the details out on the table for the four of them to analyse.

'Thing is,' said Trevor, 'we need to act fast. If I don't reinvest some of my profits quickly, I'm going to get walloped for a pretty hefty tax bill this year. Ideally we need an offer in and completion lined up for the end of the summer.'

Claire picked up one of the sets of details, her heart thumping. Things were moving too quickly.

'Surely we need a business plan?' she asked. 'I mean, I'd like to see some concrete figures before we go any further. A hotel in London is going to cost a whole lot more than setting up this place, for a start.'

Trevor waved away her concern.

'We've had the calculator smoking all week,' he assured her. 'And don't worry: we wouldn't go into something like this without doing the maths. We're very confident. And I want to stress that your investment would be yourselves, rather than your money. You don't need to make any financial commitment at this stage.'

Monique pulled out a sheaf of documents, one for Claire and one for Luca, neatly ring-bound.

'The number-crunching is all here.' She smiled. 'We're not expecting you to sign on the dotted line straight away, obviously. It's far too big a decision. Come up to London; have a look round. Tell us what you think.'

Claire felt uneasy. The Parfitts seemed a bit glib, almost naïve—as if they thought that opening a hotel was just a question of choosing a building and sticking a chef in. There were all sorts of things to be taken into consideration. Who were their potential clients? Tourists, business people? How upscale were they going to go? Was the restaurant more important than the hotel? A million questions flew through her mind, not least whether the Parfitts could be trusted. They had been wonderful sleeping partners, with their twenty per cent investment in The Townhouse by the Sea, but would the balance of power shift with this new venture? She couldn't help thinking it would. And charming and generous though they were on the surface, the Parfitts hadn't got as rich as they were just by being nice. Which was why she was suspicious that they made it sound so easy. What was the catch? Were they just trying to pump her and Luca for ideas, which they would then incorporate into their business plan without cutting them in? She leafed through the figures, wondering if they were being taken for a ride.

Strangely, Luca, who was naturally suspicious, didn't seem to share any of her reservations. Claire knew he was hungry for this, but she was surprised at his overt enthusiasm. He was usually a much cooler customer.

'Let's do it this week,' he suggested. 'We'll be quiet again after the bank holiday, before the season proper kicks in. We could come up on Tuesday. Stay a couple of nights. The hotel can look after itself for a day or two.'

'But how's it going to work long term?' asked Claire. 'We can't run this place *and* set up somewhere new in London.'

'Of course we can,' said Luca. 'We've got to think big, Claire, if we're going to move on. Lots of chefs do it. Rick Stein, Mitch Tonks. Jamie Oliver, for heaven's sake.'

'Lots of chefs also go bankrupt,' she pointed out. 'Historically, overstretching yourself is a classic mistake.'

'The biggest mistake,' said Trevor, 'is not having a wealthy backer with deep pockets. I admire your caution. It's one of the reasons I want to invest in you both. You're not reckless. I've kept a close eye on the way you run this place.' Claire's eyebrows went up at this; she didn't like to feel as if they had been spied on, even if Trevor did own a slice of the hotel. 'But you've also got the magic. And it's your magic I want.'

Monique leant in to Claire. 'What do we have to do to persuade you?' She gave her most alluring smile. 'We're not fools. We know we can't do it without you. Well, we could, I suppose. Let's put it another way. We don't *want* to do it without you.'

Trevor chuckled. 'And we are used to getting what we want. Whatever it takes.'

Claire looked at her plate. This was a nightmare. She was being railroaded. The situation would have made her feel uncomfortable even without the added complication of a big, fat skeleton in her cupboard. What would she be thinking about this proposition, she wondered, if Nick hadn't wandered back into her life this morning?

She picked up one of the sets of details. A perfect Georgian house, on the edge of Soho. She could see it in her mind's eye. A dozen bedrooms, a buzzy restaurant, a hip cocktail bar . . .

She could feel Luca's foot pressing down on hers. She didn't look up. She knew his eyes would be boring into her, asking what the hell she was playing at, dragging her feet. She would have to feign enthusiasm. After all, it wouldn't mean a contractual obligation.

She managed a smile.

'This one looks perfect,' she observed.

Monique leant forward. 'That's my favourite! Of course, it's also the most expensive. But you know what they say . . .'

Monique, Trevor and Luca chorused together.

'Location, location, location.'

Claire looked round at them all. Under any other circumstances she would be fizzing with excitement. This was, after all, everything she and Luca had ever dreamt of. They had started out together with the intention of making their mark. Trevor and Monique were the key to making that dream come true.

But which of her dreams did she want to pursue now?

Trevor was pulling out his BlackBerry.

'Okay, guys,' he said. 'I'm going to email my assistant and ask her to book you in somewhere really nice for Tuesday. And I'll send a car to bring you up. I'm not taking no for an answer.'

His thumbs skittered over the tiny keyboard. Claire imagined his assistant, out somewhere on a Friday night, rolling her eyes when she got the email. Trevor was the sort of person who expected twenty-four-hour dedication from his employees.

Which was why she was wary. Although he was being charming, Claire knew that his charm evolved from pure self-interest. Working with the Parfitts would be tough. Though that wasn't to say they shouldn't do it.

'There's no harm in looking, I suppose,' she ventured finally.

191

'Fantastic!' Monique looked delighted.

'That's not a yes,' Claire warned. 'We're only looking.'

'When you see it, you'll love it.' Monique seemed confident.

Claire smiled. 'We'll see.'

Luca put his hand over Claire's.

'The reason I love Claire,' he told Trevor and Monique, 'is because she's cautious. Not like me. I'm impulsive. Claire's my voice of reason. My sounding board. It's why we make such a great team.'

'I know,' Trevor replied. 'It's the same for me and Monique. Yin and yang. And the four of us together—we're going to take over the world.'

And with a triumphant smile he pressed Send.

*   *   *

Walking home from her shift at the end of the evening, Angelica could hear the row before she got to the top of her road.

Well, her mother's half of the row. Trudy was screeching at the top of her lungs. Jeff, Angelica knew, would be sitting on the settee, placid and calm, his hairy tummy peeping out from under his T-shirt. It was anybody's guess what would have set Trudy off. It didn't take much. She was so angry. All the time. With everything and everybody.

Angelica sighed. She didn't need this. She'd spent all evening going over and over what Luca had said. Thinking about London and whether it could ever be a possibility. Whether he had really meant it, or if he had just been playing her. Imagining what her life could be like. And

192

wondering how on earth she could make the opportunity work, given her circumstances. Maybe she could do two nights in London and the rest of the time in Pennfleet? That way she wouldn't be totally abandoning Dill, but she would have a taste of another life; something for herself. She felt cheered by the thought of this compromise as she turned in to the gate, just as Jeff came out of the front door, his van keys in his hand.

'I can't take any more,' he said. 'That's it. I'm off.'

'You can't go,' replied Angelica. 'We need you.'

'She called me an impotent, minging slob.'

Angelica winced. She had no idea about the first slur, but the second was harsh. Jeff was no looker, but it was unkind to go for the jugular about his appearance. Besides, her mother was no beauty queen, not any more, nor a paragon of virtue in the hygiene stakes.

'She's a bitch. Don't listen to her.'

'I've done everything in my power to make her happy. But I've come to the conclusion that she doesn't want to be happy.'

Jeff looked utterly deflated, but adamant. Angelica couldn't blame him, but she still didn't want him to go. Her mother without a man in the house was ten times worse. Trudy couldn't operate without male approval.

Suddenly the upstairs window opened and a bin bag came hurtling out. Angelica and Jeff grabbed each other and ran to safety, standing under the lamplight as Trudy leant out of the window.

'Take your fucking shitty clothes with you and don't bother coming back.'

She slammed the window shut.

Jeff and Angelica looked at each other.

'She's mad. You know that,' Angelica told him.

'Er . . . yeah. I was coming to that conclusion.' Jeff walked slowly over to the bag and picked it up. 'Will you lot be all right?'

Angelica shrugged. 'We'll have to be.'

'You should keep her off the sauce.'

'How?' Angelica sighed. 'I don't know what it is she wants.'

'Neither does she,' said Jeff.

'The only time she's okay,' said Angelica, 'is when she's up the duff. But that's not the answer. Anyway, she's too old.'

'You've got my mobile.' Jeff put out an awkward hand and patted Angelica's shoulder. 'Call me if you need me. It's not a problem.'

'You were too good for her, you know that?'

Jeff looked at the ground. 'I know I'm not George Clooney, and I don't bring in a fortune, but I loved her, you know?'

Angelica's heart filled with pity. Poor Jeff had squandered too much of his life on her mother.

'Don't waste your time a minute longer, Jeff. She's an ungrateful cow. A mad, ungrateful cow.'

From inside the house, music started up at full blast. The walls shook. Bloody Fleetwood Mac. Her mother thought she was Stevie Nicks. Angelica couldn't count the number of times she'd seen her do 'Dreams' at a karaoke night.

Jeff blew out his cheeks and scratched his head.

'Where are you going to go?' Angelica asked.

'My mum's. At least I know where I am with her.' He looked down. 'I feel bad about Dill. I was supposed to be taking him to the football.'

Angelica glanced away, because she thought

she might cry. Jeff was brilliant with Dill. He quite often took him off on little excursions. It eased the pressure a bit. But she couldn't expect him to carry on, not now that Trudy had kicked him out.

'Dill will be okay,' she assured him. 'He's got me.'

She held out her arms to give Jeff a hug, holding her breath so she didn't have to breathe in the smell of slightly stale sweat masked with cheap aftershave. Then she watched as he ambled off down the hill to find his van and go to his mother's in St Austell.

He had a kind heart, did Jeff, and that counted for a lot. But deep down Angelica understood her mother's frustration. Bastardness was so much more attractive than kindness. Look at her, for God's sake. Pining over Luca, patently a card-carrying bastard and all the more alluring for it.

But then where was her Jeff? wondered Angelica. Some kindly soul whose *raison d'être* was to make sure she was happy. Maybe if she had a Jeff, she wouldn't be so besotted.

She'd watched Luca go into the dining room with Claire and the Parfitts this evening. She would have given her right arm to be in Claire's place—to be plotting and planning with them. And she could tell by Claire's face that she wished she was anywhere else in the world.

Funny, thought Angelica, how we always want what we can't have.

She braced herself and went in to find her mother.

The scene was predictable. The lounge was a tip. Dill, along with Kimberley and Faye, her half-sisters, had obviously eaten dinner in front of the telly and just left their plates. Someone had bought a tub of popcorn, and half of it was trodden into the maroon carpet. The leather sofa, which had been bought on four years' interest-free credit and had once had pride of place, was scratched and scuffed and split open, the stuffing poking out. There was a half-empty bottle of pop with the lid off, several plastic beakers dotted about, and two very telling empty bottles of cheap wine from the garage.

Trudy was in the middle of the room, swaying her hips to the music, her long, blonde hair wild with split ends around her shoulders, her make-up smudged. She was smoking a cigarette while she sang along and gesticulated, totally caught up in the music, her face taut with concentration.

'Go your own waaaaaay,' she sang tunelessly, pointing her fag at Angelica accusingly before raising her arms skywards and waving them around.

She was completely pissed. As she looked at her hopeless, feckless, useless mother, Angelica realised that any dream she might have had of making her possible new life a reality had definitely been extinguished now.

'Why do you have to ruin anything that's ever good about our lives?' she shouted. 'Why is it always about you?'

Trudy looked at her blankly. There was no point in shouting. She was too far gone.

Angelica left the room, hot with fury. She looked up to see Dill at the top of the stairs. His Super Mario pyjamas were halfway up his legs and barely covered his stomach. She would have to get the train to Exeter when she could; get him some new stuff from Primark. He was growing so fast.

'Can't sleep,' he complained, grumpy with drowsiness.

She ran up the stairs. 'Come on. Let's get you back into bed.'

She snuggled in beside him, pulling the cover over their heads to drown out the music. His breathing was soon heavy next to her as he fell back to sleep. She held him tight to her. This was love, she thought. This was what mattered. How could she ever have thought about leaving him?

CHAPTER TEN

It was just gone midnight, and gradually doors were closing and lights were being turned out in the hotel. In the height of summer, Pennfleet might still be lively at this time, but it was too early in the season for raucousness and revelry. Even the stags had gone to bed, knowing they had to be up for a day's sailing first thing in the morning: they all knew from experience that hangovers and sea were bad bedfellows, and they were saving up the real celebration for the next night. A gentle quiet descended on the building as the night wrapped its softness around the walls.

In the room at the top, Luca was lying on the bed in his boxer shorts, his arms behind his head. His body looked lean and chiselled in the lamplight; his eyes were dark with wine.

'Come here,' he said, holding out an arm.

Claire hesitated in the doorway of the bathroom, pulling her kimono more tightly around her.

She would have to feign illness. There was no alternative. There was no way she could have sex with Luca tonight. He would be expecting it, and usually she relished the chance to make love after an evening spent together. So often he was locked in the kitchen until late, and by the time he got to bed she was asleep. On any other occasion she would have wallowed in the luxury of his undivided attention.

There was no point in waiting for him to drift off. After sex, yes, he'd be out like a light. But in the meantime, he wouldn't rest until he was satisfied.

'What an amazing evening,' he said. 'I think we're going to nail it, Claire. We're on our way. Can you believe it? A London hotel.'

'We haven't said yes yet,' she replied, padding towards the bed. 'There's a lot to think about.'

'Yeah, but it's a no-brainer, isn't it? They put up the money; we put in the time. We're never going to get that opportunity again.'

Claire hesitated. She didn't want to put all her objections forward now. She was tired, and confused, and didn't know what she really thought. If she started picking holes in the project, Luca wouldn't let it rest. And she needed the chance to think. The sooner Luca was asleep, the better.

So she just smiled. 'We are lucky.'

'It's got me thinking about something else,' said Luca. 'Something I've been thinking about for a while.'

'What?' Claire sat on the edge of the bed tentatively, affecting an expression of interest, wondering when she should start mentioning that she felt a bit off colour. She could blame the oysters.

198

He gazed up at her, a smile playing on his lips.

'Marry me, Claire.'

If she didn't feel sick before, she did now.

'What?' She felt her face go pale. 'You are joking.'

A dark shadow flickered across Luca's face. 'That wasn't really the reaction I was hoping for.'

She laughed, a nervous, playing-for-time laugh.

'I'm just . . . surprised. I didn't think you were the marrying kind.'

'Neither did I.' He rolled closer to her, looked into her eyes, stroking the inside of her thigh under the silky fabric of her kimono. By now she would usually be melting. 'But you know—maybe you've made me grow up. You've helped me realise my dreams, Claire. It means a lot to me. *You* mean a lot to me. I want to recognise that. And what better way of doing it?'

Claire had no idea how to react. If he'd said this to her just twenty-four hours before, she would have been weeping with joy, accepting his proposal with fervour. Now she felt dread in the pit of her stomach. How the hell was she going to get out of this? Luca wasn't the sort of person who would take kindly to the refusal of a proposal of marriage.

He rolled away from her and stood up. Claire panicked. She didn't want to start an argument.

'I'm sorry. I didn't mean to sound ungrateful. I'm just shocked . . .'

She broke off. He was rummaging in his bedside drawer, looking over at her with a smile. He found what he was looking for and held it aloft.

It was a box. A small box that could only contain one thing. She felt an icy-cold shiver pass over her body as he walked back round the bed and sat beside her.

'If you don't like it, or it doesn't fit, we can change it.'

This couldn't be happening. Luca wasn't this sort of person. Never in her wildest dreams had Claire envisaged this moment. Yet she watched as he opened the box and pulled out a ring, holding it reverently between thumb and forefinger as he reached for her left hand and put the box back on the bedside table.

He looked at her, his eyes feverish with excitement.

'I want us to get married, Claire.' Before she could protest, he slid the ring on to her finger. 'I want us to get married here. On the terrace. As soon as we can. I want us to go into this new venture as man and wife.'

She looked down. The ring was perfect. A love knot of brown diamonds: unusual, discreet, elegant. She couldn't have chosen better herself.

She swallowed. Her mouth was as dry as dust.

He was gazing at her.

'Claire?'

She felt a wild desire to burst out laughing. This was a combination of her dreams and her nightmares come true. How could she say no? She couldn't. Not without revealing what had happened between her and Nick. An image of their recent lovemaking slid into her mind, crash-cutting with a vision of herself dressed up in white on the terrace, her past, present and future spinning round and round.

'I don't know what to say . . .' she managed. The ring was burning on her finger, the hot metal digging into her flesh.

'Yes! That's all you have to say! Yes.'

He grabbed her, held her tight, looking into her eyes.

'Yes . . .' she managed. What else could she say? Luca was wrapped up in the romance of his gesture—he wouldn't take no for an answer. He took her in his arms and kissed her, in a frenzy of passion she had hitherto only dreamt of. They fell back on to the bed.

No, thought Claire. Please, this couldn't be happening. He was kissing her neck, pulling at the tie on her kimono. As he pushed the slippery silk aside, she tried desperately to think of how to take evasive action. He pulled her on top of him, running his hands over her, stroking her breasts.

There was only one solution. She pushed his hands away.

'Now, now!' she said playfully, holding up an admonishing finger. 'Don't touch. Just lie there, and keep your hands to yourself.'

She gave him a wicked smile, keeping eye contact, and he smiled back as he realised her intention. He wasn't going to refuse. She sat astride him, running her fingers over her breasts, her hair tumbling over her shoulders. As he watched, his eyes glazed over with lustful appreciation.

She leant over and snaked her way down his chest, kissing and licking, teasing him with her tongue and her hair, until she reached his cock. She took him gently in her mouth and he gave a groan. She'd got him. Tenderly, expertly, she circled her tongue around him, moved her lips up and down, until she got the desired result. He held her hands tightly as he came, his body tensing for a full ten seconds until he fell back, seemingly exhausted, his

201

breathing deep.

Moments later, he drifted off into sleep. Claire looked down at him, unable to resist tracing her fingers over his stomach, his chest, his shoulders. She always felt compelled to touch him. Yet his beauty was no longer enough, not even when combined with the energy and vitality he brought to her life; the edge. She longed for something sweeter, mellower, deeper.

She rolled off him and lay on her back, staring at the ceiling. Then she held her hand up in front of her and gazed at the ring. It glittered in the half-light. For a moment she was entranced.

It was everything she could have wished for.

*   *   *

Trevor Parfitt had never been a praying man, even after everything he had been through. But as he stood on the balcony of his bedroom and looked out at the stars spattering the inky blue of the sky, he wondered if perhaps he was wrong; if perhaps there was a higher being out there whose help he could invoke after all.

No deal had ever been so important to him. And he'd done a fair few in his time. It wasn't as if this was even a profitable venture—in fact, he would bank on losing a fair bit of money, at least in the beginning. His own secret business plan, the one he hadn't shown anyone else, showed a significant loss for at least three years, because Trevor was a realist. Anyone opening a hotel in the current climate had to expect to take a hit until they could guarantee some customer loyalty and repeat business.

No, the reason this new hotel meant so much to him was because it mattered so much to Monique.

He looked over at the bed, at his sleeping wife. She was out for the count, and would be until nine o'clock tomorrow, thanks to the pills. There was no way she would sleep without them. He had put his foot down, after years of her pacing the floor, gazing out of the window, smoking cigarettes (which he'd finally got her to stop). He'd sent her to the doctor. He didn't want her tranquillised, but she had to sleep. She'd drive herself insane otherwise.

Tonight at dinner she had sparkled and shimmered, just like his old Monique. Tomorrow she would charm and cajole. She was still the perfect hostess. She could turn it on and off like a tap. Only he knew the truth. She was like a ghost; a ghost who could bring herself back from the dead at will, for as long as it mattered, only to take off the mask and shrivel back to her cadaverous self as soon as the attention was off her.

He shivered as a cloud glided in front of the moon and the water below turned black. He walked over to the minibar and pulled out a miniature of brandy. As the fiery liquor hit his throat, he thought about Luca and Claire. He was pretty sure Luca had taken the bait. He would make a lousy poker player, thought Trevor, who had taught himself to read people very well over the years.

No, it was Claire who was the weak link. Claire who had reservations. Claire who needed to be worked on. There was something holding her back. Trevor wasn't sure yet what it was. He needed to get her on her own; gain her trust in order to allay her fears.

And maybe, just maybe, taking her into his

confidence was the way to do it. He looked over to the Provençal sleigh bed, piled high with bedding and pillows and cushions that were as soft as a cloud, where Monique lay as still as Sleeping Beauty. She hated anyone knowing their business. Of course, close friends from the time knew, but anyone they met now, through either business or pleasure, was kept from the truth, and that included Luca and Claire. It wasn't relevant, argued Monique. There was no reason for people to know. Trevor had always respected her wishes—anything to help her cope—but now he felt the time was right to let Claire into the secret. Monique need never know.

*   *   *

In a room two floors above, Nick sighed and looked at his watch. One thirty-eight. He should have been long asleep by now, but it wasn't going to happen. He threw back his duvet, got out of bed and stood by the window, watching as the moon slid shyly out from behind a cloud, like a girl appearing from behind a changing room curtain. He thought about leaning out of the window and having a cigarette. It wouldn't, he knew from experience, set the smoke alarm off. But somehow he didn't want to break the rules in Claire's hotel. Maybe he'd go outside, take a walk in the fresh air and clear his head. He'd drunk a fair bit tonight, though not a ridiculous amount by stag-weekend standards. Nevertheless, the melancholy that a surfeit of cocktails, wine and tequila shots often brought was settling in. Melancholy, disconcertion and paranoia.

In the bed next to his, Gus turned, then sat up.

Bugger, thought Nick. He wanted to be alone with his thoughts.

'What's up, mate?'

'Can't sleep.'

'You're not getting cold feet?'

It was a jovial question. Nick didn't reply. It wasn't a question of cold feet. It was far more complicated than that.

He looked over at Gus, who was staring at him quizzically. He and Gus had been firm friends for five years. Okay, so they didn't have the history of someone you'd grown up with, someone you'd been to school with, but they'd done a few business deals together that had required a certain trust. He was pretty certain he could take him into his confidence.

If Felix or Shrimp was here, they might know what to do. They knew the story, after all. But he wasn't seeing them till Thursday, and he couldn't call either of them at this time of night, out of the blue.

'I don't know what to do, Gus.'

'Hey.' Gus swung his legs out of bed. 'Last-minute nerves. You'd be weird if you didn't have them. It's a pretty big step.'

'It's not last-minute nerves.'

The tone of Nick's voice made Gus frown. 'Then what?'

'The girl who owns this hotel? Claire?'

'The pretty one? With the . . .' Gus indicated lots of hair with his hands. 'You haven't got a crush, surely?'

'She was . . . my girlfriend. I was going out with her when my mum died. We broke up. It was all pretty messy.'

'Uh-huh,' Gus nodded, pretty sure there was more to come.

Nick looked at him, anguished.

'She was the love of my life. What can I say? And here she is. A week before I'm due to get married, she walks back into my life.'

Gus flopped back on to the bed with a groan.

'Don't say it's made you have second thoughts.'

'Of course it has!' Nick turned away from the window and started pacing the room. 'She's never been out of my thoughts, Gus. Even now, twelve years later. I think about her hourly. About where she is, what she's doing, who she's with. And now I know . . .'

'Well, okay. So now you know. She's well and happy. She's got a pretty hot boyfriend . . . partner . . . whatever. And now you can move on. Put it to bed.'

'It's not as easy as that.'

Nick came and sat on his bed so that he was facing Gus.

'I've told her . . . she's got the weekend to decide. If she wants to come away with me, I'll cancel the wedding.'

'You can't do that, Nick!' Under any other circumstances, the indignation on Gus's face would have been comical. 'You cannot do that. What about Sophie? No way can you do that to her . . .'

'Why not?' Nick stared at his friend. 'Surely it's better than marrying her when I'm in love with someone else?'

Gus looked scandalised. Nick wished he hadn't told him. After all, he wasn't going to say anything Nick didn't already know. Gus's input would only add to his dilemma.

'But you love Sophie!' Gus insisted. 'You can't just stop loving someone, just like that.'

'Yes, but there's love, isn't there? And then there's . . .' Nick trailed off, not sure what to say without sounding like an idiot. '*Love*. With a capital L.'

Gus stood up and walked over to the minibar, pulling open the fridge door and peering inside until he found two miniature bottles of Jack Daniel's. He twisted off the lids, handed one to Nick, and knocked his own back almost in one.

'Over a hundred guests.' He spoke finally. 'Everything's arranged. A new flat, for God's sake. You're supposed to be moving into a new flat . . .'

'We haven't exchanged. It's not too late to pull out.'

Gus stood with the bottle two inches from his mouth, too outraged to drink.

'You're serious, aren't you? You really have thought this through.'

'Have you any idea what it's like when someone you love disappears from your life? Vanishes completely, overnight. You wonder every day for the rest of your life what has happened. You don't just say *oh well* and forget it. It taints everything. It . . . haunts you. There hasn't been a day when Claire hasn't been the first person I think of when I get up . . .'

'Shit,' said Gus. 'This is bad.'

He chucked the empty miniature in the bin.

'So what does she think?'

'I don't know,' replied Nick miserably.

'You must have some idea. You must . . . know if she was pleased to see you or not. I mean, was she . . . polite? Or does she feel the same? Did you fall

207

into each other's arms?'

'Well, no, not in front of everyone. But . . .'

Nick decided it was better not to confess too much more.

'What?'

'Nothing.'

'Come on. You can't give me half the story.'

Nick chewed the inside of his cheek and looked out of the window.

'She came up here before dinner. It was pretty obvious she felt the same.'

'By pretty obvious, you mean . . .?' Gus peered at him, eager for further clues. When Nick wouldn't look him in the eye, the penny dropped. 'Oh my God. You shagged her.'

'Don't say shagged.'

'Jesus, Nick. You're a week away from your wedding day. This is not good.' Gus looked as distressed as any best man might be on hearing such news. 'So what's your plan?'

'I'm waiting for her to decide. We haven't had a chance to talk about it properly.'

'No—only long enough to get your leg over.'

Nick looked exasperated. Gus held up his hands.

'Sorry, but I can't help thinking that this is some kind of eleventh-hour fantasy shag—'

Suddenly Gus found Nick grabbing the front of his T-shirt, twisting the fabric and holding his fist at his throat.

'It's not a fantasy shag, okay?' growled Nick. 'She's the love of my life.'

Gus fixed him with a glare, and removed Nick's hands, putting his own on Nick's shoulders instead.

'No,' he said. 'Repeat after me. She *was* the love of your life. *Sophie* is the love of your life. Sophie,

208

who is on her hen night right now. Sophie, who loves and adores you. Sophie, who is going to be at your side on Saturday, saying *I will* . . .' He released Nick, moved away, started looking for his clothes in the chaos. 'We should leave right now. I'm taking you with me.'

He grabbed his jeans and started putting them on.

'Don't be an idiot. Neither of us can drive for a start. We're well over the limit.'

Gus stopped, letting his jeans fall to his ankles. 'I've just realised. This is totally my fault. I chose this place.' He put his hands to his head in semi-drunken despair.

'It's fate,' said Nick.

'Bollocks,' said Gus. 'It's a pain in the arse, is what it is.'

Nick sat back down on the bed.

'So what do I do?'

Gus kicked his jeans away.

'You're in love with the idea of being in love. You've been swept up by the romance of it. Get a grip, Nick.'

Nick looked at the floor. If only he could. If only he could talk to Claire, talk things through with her. About the past. The present. Their future.

But Luca didn't look like the sort of guy who would take kindly to his girlfriend's ex knocking on the door in the middle of the night for a heart-to-heart. And he couldn't screw things up for Claire. After all, if she didn't feel the same as he did, she had a life to get on with. And Nick loved her enough not to burn her bridges.

If she wanted him, she'd come.

CHAPTER ELEVEN

Claire woke even earlier than usual the next morning, just after dawn. She knew there was no point trying to get back to sleep, so she pulled on her sloppiest clothes and went down to the kitchen to make herself a latte with a double shot of espresso to offset the fact that she felt light-headed from tossing and turning all night. And before Luca got any ideas about sleepy early-morning sex . . .

She stood on the terrace with her coffee, dressed in leggings and a baggy sweatshirt, shivering in the damp morning air. An eerie mist hung over the harbour, but high above it, the sun was nudging its way through. In another half-hour it would have won the battle and the mist would reluctantly evaporate, revealing the boats and the village on the far shore. It was going to be glorious.

She pulled out a chair and sat down, putting her bare feet up on the wooden railings and curling her fingers around her mug. The only signs of life so far were the seagulls, though it wouldn't be long before the first of the fishermen set sail. She looked round at the terrace, the most perfectly positioned vantage point in Pennfleet, with its view out to sea and back down the river, the lushness of the trees on the opposite bank softening the view and making it even more magical.

There was no doubt about it. It was the perfect venue for a wedding reception—they'd had a few here already. They would put up a huge canopy sail over the terrace. The railings would be entwined with greenery and cream flowers and swathes of organza. They would have a jazz trio playing Billie Holiday; a long table groaning with *plateaux de fruits de mer* and a towering pavlova instead of a wedding cake, studded with plump fresh raspberries and drizzled with white chocolate. She couldn't pretend she hadn't planned it all out in her mind's eye in the past: all girls fantasised about their perfect wedding, didn't they, even if they didn't admit to it? She had never imagined that hers would become an eventuality.

Or that come the day it would be the last thing she wanted . . .

She twisted the ring on her finger. How could she get out of wearing it? She couldn't say it didn't fit, that she was afraid it might fall off, because it fitted perfectly. She took it off and rolled it between her fingers. She could drop it. She could drop it on the decking and it would roll between the cracks and fall—plop!—into the water underneath. She could feign distress. It would be easy enough.

As the early-morning sun finally broke through, it caught the pinky-brown of the diamonds. She would never have guessed that Luca had such perfect taste in engagement rings. When had he bought it? she wondered. When had he made the trip to a jeweller, pored over the selection he had to offer until finally choosing this one? How long had he been planning a proposal? She had seen no sign of it coming. He hadn't so much as hinted.

Luca, who always kept her on his toes. Luca, who she had never entirely trusted, because he was clearly a rogue, though that was what had attracted her.

Everyone had warned her off him. Men and women alike. Everyone adored him, because he was great company, the original party animal, but they were all too clear about his shortcomings. He was described variously as a player, a wolf in wolf's clothing, as being only interested in himself. A pisshead and a philanderer. A loose cannon. Bloody impossible. A nightmare.

'He'll chew you up and spit you out and you'll never get over it,' warned a girl who had known him a long time. Claire just smiled. She'd got over much worse than maltreatment by a jack-the-lad who thought he was God's gift. If anything, it made the challenge more enticing. She'd gone ahead and done the classic good-girl thing, of thinking she could tame the bad boy.

And my God, she realised with a lurch to her stomach as she slid the ring back on to her finger, it looked as if she had.

*   *   *

The phone on his bedside table chirruped to tell Nick he had a text.

He lay there for a moment, not wanting to look at it. He knew who it would be from.

Eventually he stretched out an arm and picked up the phone.

Hey! How's the head? Not too bad here. We're going to have a massive breakfast then hit the shops. Have a lovely day xxxx

He didn't know what to reply. He could ignore it and plead lack of signal. But that seemed mean somehow. His thumbs raced over the keyboard.

Heads not too bad here either. Looking forward to a day on the water. Love to all the girls and have fun x

He imagined them, the six of them, sitting round

the table at their hotel, revelling in the decadent sin of a full English despite knowing they would have to get into their various frocks the following Saturday. Sophie would be immaculate, her blonde hair freshly washed and falling to her shoulders. She'd be in jeans and a twinset, bright-eyed and ready for the day ahead, everything organised down to the last cappuccino. Sophie never left anything to chance. Not that she was boring, but she liked to have a plan. She believed that that way you got the most out of life. She would have emailed the other girls a detailed itinerary of the weekend; they were used to her exacting ways and seemed to love her all the more for it. And they would all, Nick knew, have the greatest fun. Sophie would have researched everything thoroughly—the hotel, the restaurants, the spa, the bars—booked the best tables, made sure that all their requirements were met. It was, after all, merely an extension of her job in event management: they had met when Nick had supplied the wine and champagne for a Gold Cup day she had organised in a wealthy client's garden. Nick remembered it all too clearly, seeing her wrapping yellow organza around the poles in the marquee, her T-shirt riding up to expose her midriff as she reached up . . .

He couldn't think about her. He put his pillow over his head to try and block out the memory. But there she was, turning to him, charming him with her easy manner, directing him to the place where she wanted the wine stored . . . then laughing with mortified apology when she realised that he was the sales director, not the delivery boy. They'd been short-staffed that day. She'd insisted on taking him to the pub over the road for a drink to apologise.

Eight months later they were engaged.

Did he love her? Yes, absolutely he loved her. He loved her dauntless enthusiasm, her unflappability, her certainty. The way she always looked perfect. The way she got what she wanted without coming across as a princess. He knew his life with her would be ordered: not rigid in any way, but pleasantly calm, with no unexpected upheaval or drama. He'd been looking forward to marrying her, making a home with her, starting a family.

There was, though, something missing. He had never had the urge to bury his face in Sophie's neck and breathe in the very essence of her. His lips didn't tingle with electricity when he brushed them over her skin. She didn't appear in his dreams, a shadowy figure just out of his reach.

He didn't want to die in her arms.

Every time he thought about Sophie, she was overshadowed by Claire. Every time he thought about the wedding next Saturday, it was Claire's face he saw as he turned to look at his bride at the altar. Claire whose very essence was filling his head, his heart and his soul.

He'd come to accept, subconsciously, that you probably only got that feeling with another person once in your life. And he'd also come to accept that perhaps life would be easier with a person who didn't make you feel that way. There would be less passion, certainly, but how much easier to manage your life, your career, your family with someone whom you loved and respected, but who didn't haunt your every waking hour.

Like Claire had. He'd wondered, over the years, if he had built her up into a fantasy figure simply because he couldn't have her. But now he had seen her, now he had touched her again, he knew that wasn't true. The magic, the chemistry, the longing, the *rightness* of Claire was still there. Sophie would never arouse those feelings in him.

And if Claire decided that being together wasn't the right thing to do, could he then go ahead and marry another woman knowing that his heart belonged to someone else?

In the meantime, he had the rest of his stag weekend to struggle through. The six of them were due to be getting a boat for the day. It was anchors aweigh at ten o'clock—they needed to be up, dressed and fed by then. He looked at his watch. Seven o'clock. The dining room should be open any minute. But he couldn't face going down to breakfast in case he saw her. He decided to ring room service.

In his experience, the world always looked a better place after a big, fat bacon sandwich.

*   *   *

Dan and Laura were the first people down to breakfast on Saturday morning. They took a table near the windows so they could look at the view.

Dan was in seventh heaven. He ordered up a full English breakfast, stretched luxuriously and cracked open the Saturday *Independent* with a sigh of pleasure.

'God, it's great not to be hotfooting to some random church in the bloody Cotswolds,' he observed, taking a swig of delicious coffee. He quite often did weddings on a Saturday—more for friends and friends of friends than officially, but because he offered a good rate and didn't mess

215

about or do endless permutations of relatives and bride's friends, he had become quite popular.

Laura sipped at a glass of fresh pink grapefruit juice, a pot of Earl Grey tea in front of her. She'd ordered mushrooms on granary toast, even though she wasn't hungry. She wished she didn't feel so stomach-churningly nervous. After all, this was the first time she and Dan had been away. The first time she'd been to a hotel like this with *anyone*.

Holidays with Marina had always been chaotic camping trips with other single mums and hordes of children, or a rented cottage; there had never been enough money for hotels. She'd been away on conferences with work, to impersonal, faceless chain hotels. But never to somewhere as exquisite as this.

Suddenly she thought about cancelling the whole madcap plan. The pressure was spoiling what should be a lovely, romantic weekend. She had been awake since dawn going over and over the wisdom of what she was doing and debating the likelihood of a happy outcome. She was trying not to burden Dan too much with it all. She didn't want him to get sick of her anxiety. She didn't want to become a bore.

Still, she couldn't help wondering what Tony Weston was doing: whether he was still in bed or if he was an early riser; if he'd already been to the shop for the paper. She wondered what he read. Did he get the *Independent,* or the *Times,* or perhaps the *Guardian*? Was he leafing through it now? Or was he preparing for her arrival, laying out paper, pencils, brushes, tubes of paint? Was he wondering what she would be like, his weekend student? What was he picturing? A middle-aged woman looking for a new lease of life? An exhausted mother indulging in a weekend of 'me' time?

Probably not, she reflected as the waitress brought her breakfast, the long-lost daughter he never knew he had.

She picked up her fork and speared a mushroom, plump with melted butter.

'What are you going to do today?' she asked Dan.

He peered at her over the top of his paper.

'Don't you worry about me,' he replied. 'I'll be perfectly happy.' He nodded to the view outside. 'I could just sit here all day and watch the harbour, to be honest.'

Laura followed his gaze. She could easily send Tony Weston a cancellation email. She could spend all day with Dan.

But then she'd never know.

*   *   *

When Chelsey woke, just after eight, Colin had already woken and crept back into his bedroom to shower and dress. He found her standing by the window, the curtains drawn back, staring out at the sea.

'Hey. Good morning. You slept well.'

She turned to him with a smile. She looked so much younger than her eleven years, in her Hello Kitty pyjamas, her pale-brown hair with its centre parting messy from bed.

'Where's Mum?' she asked. 'Is she up already? She never gets up before midday on a Saturday.'

Her eyes strayed enquiringly towards the

217

interconnecting door. Shit, thought Colin. She thinks Karen spent the night in my bed. He came into the room, marshalling his thoughts, knowing he had to be careful.

'Your mum had to go,' he told her. 'There was a problem at the gym, they called her in, so she's gone home.'

Chelsey frowned. 'Is that what she told you?' she asked.

'Yes,' lied Colin, because he couldn't think of a better reason.

Chelsey looked at him. Her little face was troubled.

'What's the matter?'

'She can't have gone to the gym.'

'Why not?'

'She'll kill me if I tell you.'

Colin hated to see his daughter's distress, but he needed to know the source of it.

'No she won't.' He put an arm round her. 'She won't, because I won't tell her you told me. What is it, Chelsey?'

Eventually, reluctantly, she told him.

'She was fired from the gym a few months ago. She hasn't been there for ages. I wasn't supposed to say anything.'

'I see.' Colin digested this information, rapidly putting it into context, taking in all the implications. No wonder Karen had been so on edge. He sat down on the end of Chelsey's bed. 'Well,' he carried on carefully. 'She probably needs a bit of time on her own, to think about what she's going to do.'

Chelsey put her hand to her hair and started twirling a strand around her finger. A nervous habit, Colin thought.

218

'Is there something else?' he asked. 'You can trust me, Chelsey. Honestly. I understand your mum gets cross with you, so I won't let you get into trouble.'

This, he realised, was the start of their relationship proper. From now on, he was going to have to gain her trust, if they were going to get through this.

'I expect she's going to Hot Legs,' she said finally. 'She works there sometimes.'

Colin felt a chill. Hot Legs.

He knew about it, of course. Who didn't? The infamous 'gentlemen's club' on the edge of the Chinese quarter in town—although there was nothing gentlemanly about it, in his opinion. It was open twenty-four hours, with non-stop dancing girls. He had never been there, although he'd heard stories of the scantily clad beauties who performed at your table in front of you for twenty pounds. The thought made him queasy. He didn't belong to the school of macho who got off on that kind of thing—but there were plenty of men who did. Faithful husbands, family men, for whom the thrill of a naked girl gyrating between their legs proved too much of a temptation.

They were fools, thought Colin, to be taken in by the charade, to be seduced by the pouting lips and come-hither eyes. To him it was a sordid transaction. Why would you want to buy sexual promise? An empty encounter?

Worse than that, though, was the thought that Karen had been reduced to this, if what Chelsey was saying was true. And how appalling that she thought it was okay for her daughter to know.

'How long has she been working there?' he asked

Chelsey lightly. It was important not to show his shock. He wanted to get as much information out of her as possible.

'Ages,' said Chelsey. 'Her friend Sharanne is the manager there. She calls her when they're short. It's good money,' she assured him. 'She can get two hundred pounds in a night. And it's cash.'

She was eleven years old. She shouldn't know any of this. Sickened, Colin thought of Michelle at eleven. Her head had been filled with ponies and puppies and cupcakes, nothing more sinister. Okay, so eventually pop music and make-up and boys had filtered through, but in a controlled and healthy way.

Yet while in some ways Chelsey seemed so much younger than Michelle had at the same age, here she was talking about her mother effectively selling her body for cash in a matter-of-fact manner that chilled Colin's heart to the core.

'Have you been there?' he asked.

'A couple of times,' she told him. 'If she goes there in the day, I hang out in the changing rooms till she's finished her shift.'

'What do you do?'

Chelsey shrugged. 'Play on my DS. Watch the telly.'

Colin felt his fists clench. His daughter, his flesh and blood, subjected to that kind of immoral degradation. He couldn't bring himself to ask any more questions. He didn't want to know, not just yet. He wiped his forehead. It was coated with beads of sweat, oozing globules of shock and fear and disgust.

To him, the biggest surprise was that Karen had even got a job there. He would have thought her too old; well past her prime. But he supposed that with the right make-up, the right costume and subdued lighting, she would pass muster. She had the moves. She had the right look in her eye. He knew that well enough.

He had no idea what his next move should be. Karen doing a runner had been one thing, but this revelation raised the stakes even higher. He needed to keep his head; keep calm. Make some phone calls.

Alison. He couldn't think about Alison just yet.

And his priority was still Chelsey. This weekend had always been about her, and it still would be, if it killed him. Absolutely none of this was her fault. He took a quick glance at his phone to see if there was a message from Karen, either conciliatory or explanatory, but there was nothing.

'I think you should get dressed and we'll go down to breakfast,' he said, injecting a cheerfulness into his voice that he didn't feel. 'I don't know about you, but I'm starving.'

*   *   *

When she got back to their room, Claire was amazed to find that Luca was already up. She must have missed him on her way back. Maybe he was in the kitchen? Unusual, she thought, but actually she was relieved. She'd been dreading seeing him, having to fake enthusiasm for what had happened the night before. She felt drained, unable to muster so much as a smile.

His presence was everywhere in the room. Steam from his shower, wet towels and last night's clothes on the floor, a rumpled bed—okay, the chambermaids came and made it every morning, but did he have to leave it in quite such disarray?— and two empty coffee cups.

She picked up his shirt from the day before and breathed in its scent. The smell of him still affected her deeply—a mixture of excitement and uncertainty mixed with the desire for sex. The adrenalin he made her feel never seemed to fade. It was what had attracted her in the first place; the sense of danger he exuded. His unpredictability. The polar opposite of Nick. Maybe that was what had drawn her to him. Luca was so overpowering that he had wiped out the memories and given her something else to fill her head.

Only now, the two men in her life were jostling for pole position and she had no idea what she wanted. She looked at herself in the mirror. Who was she? Who was Claire Marlowe? She thought she had reinvented herself entirely and built a new persona—the strong, independent businesswoman, one half of a power couple intent on making their mark on the world. But no—the events of the last twenty-four hours showed her that the former Claire was still in there, the softer, more vulnerable girl who had once yearned to be part of the Barnes family unit; who had once thought she had found love and her future and the meaning of life, until fate had decided otherwise.

Yet even without the arrival of Nick to add to her confusion, everything was happening too quickly. With Trevor and Monique driving the project, and Luca a wildly enthusiastic passenger, she felt she was being swept along. No real consideration had been given to her opinion, she realised. They had praised her to the hilt, lauded her achievements, insisted they couldn't roll the project out without her, but they hadn't paused for a moment to ask if it was what she really wanted. She knew they considered it a no-brainer, but in truth her misgivings were many and deep. And that was without even taking Nick into consideration.

She sighed as she got dressed in some presentable clothes. She had to make her mind up one way or the other by the end of the weekend. No one else was going to do it for her.

As she pulled on her cardigan, her ring caught on the sleeve. She looked at it. She couldn't take it off yet—Luca would be crushed. She'd go and find him, she decided. She'd ask him if they could keep quiet about their engagement for the time being; tell him she was going to put the ring back in its box until they could make an official announcement. It was going to be impossible for her to make a decision if the happy news was broadcast all over Pennfleet. After all, if it was public knowledge, it would be even harder to walk away. If that was what she decided to do in the end.

*   *   *

When Chelsey presented herself, dressed and ready for breakfast, Colin felt profoundly depressed. The clothes she was wearing were cheap, too tight, garish. Her T-shirt, which bore the logo 'I love boys and shopping', strained across the puppy fat on her belly and yet again didn't meet the top of her leggings, which were trimmed with scratchy lace. He was, he realised, embarrassed to be seen with her dressed like this, in case anyone thought he considered what she was wearing attractive or

223

appropriate in any way. But what on earth could he say to her? He didn't know what else she had in her little case, but everything he had seen so far seemed to come from Primark and be two sizes too small.

He said nothing, of course, but led her down to the dining room. When she made a beeline for the table containing cereal, fresh fruit and baskets of morning goods, he predicted that she would reach for the box of Coco Pops, and she did.

'Do you know what?' he said to her gently. 'I think the people here have gone to a lot of trouble making this fresh fruit salad. Why don't we both try that? You can have boring old Coco Pops any day of the week.'

Chelsey looked uncertainly at the bowl of freshly prepared fruit, a colourful mélange of pineapple, melon, kiwi, strawberries and grapes.

'I'm not sure about that,' she said, pointing at the kiwi.

'Well,' said Colin, 'if you don't like it, I'll have it, because kiwi is my favourite.'

And he scooped them out two generous helpings into white bowls.

They sat at a table by the window.

'This is so nice. We never eat breakfast usually,' Chelsey told him. 'Mum always has black coffee and a cigarette.'

'Surely you don't go to school with no breakfast?'

'I get an Egg McMuffin on the way. From the drive-through.'

'You're kidding?' Colin was appalled. 'What about tea? Does she cook you your tea?'

'We have ping dinners.'

Colin frowned. 'What's a ping dinner?'

Chelsey mimed putting something into the

224

microwave. 'Ping!'

'Right.' It was, thought Colin, lucky for Karen that she wasn't here. What the hell was she playing at? He could already imagine her excuses. Hear her whining 'It's all right for you.'

And maybe it was all right for him. What did he know about the cold, hard reality of single motherhood? But then, he reminded himself, most single mothers didn't have over a thousand pounds a month paid into their account without question. They often had to fight for every penny they got from the fathers of their children. He had never missed a payment, never quibbled, never begrudged a penny of it. But he did resent the fact that clearly Karen wasn't spending the money on Chelsey, although she would no doubt argue otherwise. 'Have you any idea how much it costs?' He could already hear her shrill demand ringing in his ears. What the bloody hell was she spending it all on?

Definitely not Chelsey's wardrobe.

It was, he decided, time to make some changes.

'I thought we could go shopping this morning,' he suggested. 'I haven't really got any holiday clothes, and I know all girls love any opportunity for a new outfit.'

He smiled at her. She considered his suggestion, then shrugged.

'If you want,' she said. 'We need to take the DVDs back as well, don't forget,' she reminded him, anxious.

'So we do,' he said, and he loved her just a little bit more for worrying. 'Then what would you like to do? We could take a boat down the river. Or go to the beach. Or the Eden Project?'

Chelsey sprinkled sugar all over her fruit while

she thought about this. Colin had to sit on his hands to stop her. Then she gave him the most heartbreakingly sweet smile.

'I don't mind. It'll be fun whatever.' She looked out of the window. 'I love it here.'

Colin spooned up some pineapple. They were going to have the best day ever, he would make sure of it. He knew he was on borrowed time, that by this evening he would have to think seriously about Chelsey's future, but it wasn't going to spoil their time together. He was in limbo. He wasn't going to think about Karen. Or Alison. Or Ryan and Michelle.

Chelsey deserved to be the centre of someone's world for once.

*   *   *

Dressed and resolute, Claire took a deep breath and headed down the stairs. As she rounded the last flight, she stopped dead in her tracks at the sight that greeted her in the hall below.

On the table in the middle of the reception area was an enormous arrangement of flowers—a wild tangle of deep cream roses mixed with ivy and larkspur. Next to it was a tower of champagne coupes piled on top of each other, and several bottles of vintage Dom Perignon rested in a bucket of ice under the table. A bunch of pale-pink metallic balloons hovered overhead.

Claire frowned. Was there something she had forgotten about—a wedding party booked in? No way would she have overlooked something like that. Someone had clearly organised all this behind her back—but why? She'd only been gone half an

226

hour—it must have been a military operation. She looked around for further clues, and her heart sank as she realised that the only reason for organising this behind her back was to surprise . . . her.

She walked down the last few steps, her heart thumping, and her worst fears were realised as Trevor and Monique sneaked theatrically out of the dining room, smiling from ear to ear. Monique edged her way across the room looking coy, her arms spread wide.

'Luca told us over breakfast earlier. Amazing news. Congratulations. You must be so thrilled.'

'This is just a little gesture.' Trevor indicated the table. 'We thought your guests would like to share in your good news.'

Claire was speechless. This was a nightmare. Surely she was going to wake up in a moment and realise it was her imagination working overtime? But no—Trevor had grabbed a bottle and was opening it with ceremony, and Monique was grabbing her hand, demanding to look at the ring.

'Oh my goodness—that's just beautiful. And so *you*. He's so clever . . .'

Claire looked up to see Luca gazing proudly at her.

She dredged up a smile. With Monique holding her left hand, and Trevor pressing a glass of champagne into her right, she held out her cheek for a kiss. Luca must have been in on this. He didn't look in the least surprised to have had his reception area hijacked. What was he playing at? Grand gestures weren't really his thing.

By now Trevor had filled four glasses. And to make matters worse, here was the stag party coming down the stairs, dressed up for a day on the water,

Nick in their midst. Trevor beckoned them all over to the champagne tower with a flamboyant wave.

'Come on, everybody—there's plenty for everyone. You can't beat a glass of fizz to kick off the weekend . . .'

He busied himself filling more glasses and distributing them around. The stags fell on the offer with delight, not the types to turn down an offer of free booze. Except Nick, who hung back, looking slightly bemused. Claire didn't want to catch his eye. She turned away, and was grateful to see Angelica coming in through the door.

Angelica was looking round in astonishment. Trevor grabbed her and pulled her into the mêlée.

'You're just in time for the toast.'

'Toast?' Angelica looked at Claire for enlightenment, but before she could say anything, Monique brandished her hand in glee.

'Look! Isn't it just the most beautiful ring you've ever seen?' she gushed.

Angelica's eyes widened.

'You're engaged?'

Claire nodded.

'I think she's a bit overawed,' said Monique. 'She hasn't said a word!'

'To . . . Luca?' asked Angelica.

'Who else?' Monique looked more excited than Claire.

Trevor clapped his hands.

'Everyone, I want you all to raise your glasses and drink a toast to our wonderful host and hostess, who have just announced they are going to be married. I feel so proud and excited to be part of this happy day. It's what life is all about—true love. And I think you'll all agree they make a wonderful

228

couple.'

He held his glass aloft.

'To Claire and Luca.'

'To Claire and Luca,' chorused the assembled crowd.

As Claire held her glass to her lips, Luca slid his arm around her shoulder. Through the crowd she searched for Nick and met his eyes, trying to convey her desperation and convince him that she had been trapped. She wanted to explain how events had overtaken her, tell him she was going to find some way out of this mess if she could, at least until they could have a proper conversation, but Luca was holding her tight, laughing, kissing her neck, and she could do nothing but stand there with a frozen smile as Nick turned and walked away, striding across the hall towards the front door.

'We're taking the day off,' Luca was saying. 'Trevor has asked us out on his boat.'

'We can't have the day off!' she protested. 'The hotel's full . . .'

'It'll look after itself. Fred and Loz have got the kitchen under control; we'll be back by three so I can start to prep for tonight, and Angelica can keep on top of things—can't you, Angelica?'

He turned to Angelica, who wasn't sure what to say. She could see that Claire needed rescuing, but how could she refuse?

'Of course.' She gave a helpless shrug.

'I need to talk to you,' said Claire to Luca, desperate.

'We've got all day,' he told her. 'Go and get changed. I've got the kitchen to make us up a picnic basket. We deserve a day off.'

'I've even organised the weather for you.'

229

Trevor waved an airy hand at the glorious sunshine outside.

'We can top up our tans and talk soft furnishings.' Monique, who was a deep Cuprinol brown and didn't look as if her tan needed topping up at all, was bubbling with excitement. 'The men can talk figures.' She pressed her hands together, her fingers laden with the hallmarks of the Parfitts' marriage—engagement rings, wedding rings, eternity rings, all carefully chosen to complement each other and display their enormous wealth.

What on earth could she say?

'I'll be five minutes,' said Claire, wondering if she could squeeze out of the skylight and run away across the rooftops, and how long it would be before they noticed she had gone.

*　　　*　　　*

As Claire made her way towards the stairs, Angelica watched her thoughtfully. She didn't exactly look like a girl whose dream had just come true. As the reception area slowly emptied, with the stags rolling out into the street in high spirits, she turned to Luca, who was draining the last drops from a bottle of Dom Perignon into his glass.

'Congratulations,' she said. 'Claire's a very lucky girl.'

'Oh no,' said Luca, with a false modesty that didn't suit him. 'It's me who's the lucky one.' He knocked back the champagne with a gulp. 'You'll be all right here today, won't you?'

'Of course,' said Angelica.

'Where would we be without you?' Luca patted her on the shoulder.

230

He obviously had no recollection of their conversation yesterday, she thought. He didn't care one jot about her. His words of reassurance had been empty ones. All he was worried about was marrying Claire, and dashing off to London to open a glitzy new hotel, not whether Angelica was happy or not, or whether she had a future.

She had a future all right, thought Angelica, and it was pretty bleak. She was going to be left in boring Pennfleet, with her needy family and no chance of escape.

'Cheer up,' said Luca, noticing her gloomy countenance. 'It might never happen.'

Angelica looked at him.

'Maybe it already has,' she replied, but he'd walked away. She wondered just how much he knew about Nick, and whether that had anything to do with his impromptu proposal.

Then she realised that he must have had the ring all this time, and her heart sank a little further.

Of course Luca belonged to Claire. Of course he did.

*　　　*　　　*

Colin and Chelsey were the first customers in Au Bord de la Mer that morning. It was a children's boutique whose charming window displays winkled money out of the pockets of the stingiest of parents. And if there was one thing Colin wasn't, it was stingy.

'I want a complete wardrobe makeover,' he told the delighted assistant. 'She's grown out of everything recently. Could you take charge?'

Soon Chelsey was installed in the changing

room, which was done out like a mermaid's grotto, while the assistant brought her everything the shop had to offer in her size. Colin sat in the big leather armchair that had been thoughtfully provided for bored husbands and read the paper. From time to time he looked up as a new outfit was brought out for his approval. Gradually, the purchase pile grew higher and higher.

He bought her jeans with rolled-up cuffs, and a velour hoodie with stars all over it, and several cute T-shirts, a polka-dot mac; a pair of flowery wellingtons and some sneakers with velvet laces. A red-and-white striped dress, a swimsuit with an anchor on the front, and a softer-than-soft cardigan with candy-coloured buttons.

'Do you want to wear some of this now?' he asked her, and when she said yes eagerly, the assistant put the clothes she'd been wearing into a bag, and he had to resist the urge to ask her to put them in the bin. And then Chelsey stood in front of him, in the jeans and a T-shirt with a monkey on the front, and her sneakers, and she looked beautiful, he thought, not nearly so podgy. Like a proper little girl on holiday. She did need her hair cut, though; it was very long and straggly. But that could wait.

He paid in cash. He paid for everything in cash when he had his weekends with Karen and Chelsey. He didn't want to leave a paper trail.

He wouldn't have to worry about that for much longer.

*   *   *

The six stags made their way through the centre of

Pennfleet, their unexpected morning tipple filling them with *joie de vivre*. They stopped off at the bakery for pasties and doughnuts and the Spar shop for beer, bantering and laughing. The sun shone down on them, promising magic and fun. A glorious *Boys' Own* day spent on the water—who could ask for more? They earned admiring glances from girls and women passing them in the street—a bevy of attractive thirty-something men on a mission.

As they turned the corner to the harbour, Gus stopped in his tracks.

'Shit,' he said. 'I've left my mobile in the room.'

'Don't worry about it. You don't need your phone. We won't even have a signal,' Nick pointed out.

'No—I feel lost without it. I won't be a minute—catch up with you on the pontoon.'

He turned and jogged his way back to the hotel.

He had to do something about this situation. He could see that Nick's heart wasn't in today's adventure; that his mind was elsewhere. None of the others had noticed, because they were too wrapped up in the excitement, but Gus could sense that Nick was on edge.

He had seen Nick's face when Claire and Luca announced their engagement. He had also seen Claire and Nick exchange glances. Albeit for a fleeting moment, but there was no denying their complicity. Her unspoken message had been a plea for help. And then Nick had walked out of the hotel, unable to bear the tension, and Gus had gone after him.

'What am I supposed to do now?' Nick asked, his jaw clenched tighter than tight.

'Forget her,' Gus told him, and the look of

disgust Nick gave him made him shrivel inside.

'She doesn't want to marry that wanker. I know she doesn't,' he said.

He really was bewitched, thought Gus. He had to do something to break the spell.

So now here he was, hurrying back to the Townhouse with the mad idea of talking to Claire, even though he wasn't sure what he was going to say.

When he got to the hotel, it had quietened down considerably: the glasses had been cleared away, although the extravagant flowers and the helium balloons still denoted a celebration.

'I need to speak to Miss Marlowe,' Gus told the receptionist. 'It's rather urgent.'

'She's going out for the day,' Angelica replied. 'Is there anything I can help you with?'

'Not really. It doesn't matter.' Shit. He was too late. He backed away from the reception desk, smiling. 'Thanks anyway.'

And he turned and bumped straight into her. She was dressed in white shorts and a blue-and-white striped T-shirt and blue espadrilles, a straw basket over one arm.

'I know you're going out,' said Gus, 'but could I have a word?'

Claire hesitated. Luca was on his way down; they were meeting Trevor and Monique any moment.

'Of course,' she said, the consummate professional. 'Shall we pop into my office?'

She led the way. Gus followed. He flicked his eyes around the little room, with its flat-screen computer, neat files and wall charts. The centre of operations from where she controlled her empire. She really was terribly pretty, thought Gus, with that tumbling hair and those greeny-blue eyes and her Elizabeth Taylor eyebrows. Not chocolate-box pretty like Sophie, but compellingly pretty; a pretty that crept up on you. He could certainly see the attraction.

She looked at him quizzically, and he realised he was staring.

'I need to talk to you.'

'Of course.' Claire gave him her most professional smile. 'Is it about tonight's dinner? Luca's put together the most amazing menu, but obviously if there's anything you'd like us to organise . . .?' She laughed. 'I don't mean strippergrams or anything—we don't really have that sort of thing in Pennfleet.'

'It's not about the dinner.' Gus looked awkward. 'It's about Nick.'

Claire looked wary.

'This is very embarrassing.' Gus scratched at his curls, looking as if he would rather be anywhere else in the world. 'He told me. About the two of you.'

'I see.' Claire folded her arms.

'I know it's awfully bad timing. And I know that seeing you again has totally rocked him. Knocked him off his perch, to be honest. I've never seen him like this. Obviously, it's a hideous coincidence that we booked in here . . .'

'As coincidences go, it's up there,' agreed Claire. 'But it's happened.'

'I know,' said Gus. 'But you have to pretend it hasn't.'

Those Liz Taylor eyebrows went up.

'He's got to marry Sophie next weekend,' he went on fervently. 'If he calls the wedding off, he'll

235

break her heart. They're made for each other. Honestly, if you could see them together . . .'

Gus trailed off, distressed.

'I'm sure,' said Claire. 'Frankly, the whole thing's been a shock for both of us. Neither of us knows what to think.'

'*Nick* seems to think . . .'

'What?'

'That you're the love of his life. That now he's found you again, he can't let you go. That he can't go ahead with the wedding. I'm sorry. I'm not trying to interfere.'

'You're just doing your job,' said Claire. 'You're his best man. It's your duty to make sure he gets up the aisle.'

'I didn't think it was going to be this complicated.'

'No . . .'

Claire looked away, biting her lip, her body language still defensive. 'Look, I don't know what to think. We need to talk. But I don't know how we can. It's very difficult. What with . . .' She waved a hand in the air helplessly.

'What with you getting engaged and all?' suggested Gus.

Claire looked down at her ring.

'You couldn't make it up, could you?'

There was an awkward silence.

'There's over a hundred guests turning up on Saturday. And they're due to exchange on a flat later this week.' Gus paused, then went in for the kill. 'Sophie's giving up her job after the honeymoon. She wants to start a family. Did Nick tell you that?'

He hadn't. And the revelation eviscerated Claire

236

more than she had thought possible.

'Look.' Gus held out his iPhone. On it was displayed a picture of Nick and, presumably, Sophie, their arms around each other, beaming at the photographer. They were at a party—he was dishevelled, his black tie undone; she was still ravishingly perfect in a turquoise evening dress. That they were blissfully content was obvious. Claire could see they belonged to each other. Sophie was just the sort of girl who would marry into the Barnes family. The perfect, leggy, Sloaney blonde. The sort of girl who had featured recurrently in the Barnes photo montages. The sort of girl Claire never would be.

She felt a sudden burst of anger and pushed his hand away. She didn't want to look at their togetherness a moment longer.

'Look, I didn't ask you to barge into my hotel with his entourage. It's a complete nightmare, but we can't just pretend it hasn't happened. It's pretty momentous, for both of us. So bloody well leave us alone to sort it out for ourselves, will you?'

Christ, she was gorgeous when she was angry, those eyes flashing fire. Gus had got a real sense of her passion now. She had seemed like such a cool customer before. He realised he had to calm her down.

'I know, I know. And I'm sorry. I had no idea, obviously. And it's because I feel guilty that I was instrumental that I'm trying to sort it out.' Gus's tone was placatory. 'Can't you just . . . be happy for him? And be happy yourself? Leave things as they are? Like they would have been if I hadn't been dumb enough to book this place?'

'It's not that simple, is it?'

'Why not?' Gus gazed at her, his eyes wide. 'Surely that way nobody gets hurt?'

Claire turned to the window and looked out. He had no idea about hurt. She'd had more than her fair share of it—more than anyone deserved in one lifetime. And just as the pain was fading, the wounds had been opened again.

'Let him go, Claire.' Gus's voice was low and pleading. 'Just pretend he never walked in here. You've got your future, with Luca. How would *he* feel if you broke it off?'

'I don't know . . .' Claire realised she hadn't really thought beyond Luca's initial fury. His reaction would be explosive, volatile, because he was an alpha male filled with pride. How he would feel deep down, she didn't know. Did he really love her? A proper, profound, wholesome love that would endure? There were so many questions, questions she couldn't answer.

To her horror, she realised that there was a tear trickling down her cheek.

'Oh shit,' said Gus. 'I'm sorry . . .'

He stepped forward, not sure what to do, whether to console her by putting an arm round her. Her body language told him to stay away.

'Actually,' she said. 'I think you should mind your own business. Nick and I go back further than anyone—you or Sophie or Luca. So it's up to us to figure it out. Wouldn't you say?'

She tipped her chin up defiantly, her voice trembling, not feeling any of the assertiveness she was trying to put across.

'Okay,' said Gus. 'I'm sorry. You're right. I'm just making it more difficult. But Sophie isn't here to speak for herself—'

238

'I don't care about bloody Sophie!' Claire's voice was harsh. 'Because do you know what? Life isn't always fair. And she might have to learn that the hard way.'

Gus looked appalled.

'Fine,' he said. 'If that's how you feel. Forget I said anything.' He turned to walk out of the office. 'I just hope you think about what will happen if you fuck everything up. Because it's not just about you.'

Claire looked at him evenly.

'Sometimes,' she said, 'it has to be. Sometimes we have to be selfish. Don't you think?'

She stepped closer to him, and Gus could feel the force of her passion yet again.

'What if we do the "right thing"? What if Nick marries Sophie, and I marry Luca, but then we both spend the rest of our lives in love with someone else, wishing we'd had the courage of our convictions? What's the point of that? How is that the "right thing"?'

Gus very much wished he had kept his mouth shut. He wasn't really used to dealing with this level of emotion. Why had he gone steaming in?

Because he cared about Sophie, that was why. Because he couldn't bear to think of her broken heart if Nick cancelled the wedding. Because he believed in Sophie and Nick as a couple. Because they were the real deal. They were right together. Nick was being distracted by some teenage fantasy. He'd built Claire up into something more important than she was. And as long as he was able to feed himself on her, he would prolong the agony.

Maybe he should call Sophie? Get her to come down and talk some sense into Nick? No, that was crazy. That was dragging her into the mess when she should be enjoying her hen weekend. He needed to contain the situation, not compound it.

Claire was still staring at him, her eyes stormy, as dangerous as the sea in a force-ten gale. What could he say?

'Sorry,' he said. 'It's none of my business. Except they are my friends and I care about them. And the clock's ticking, Claire. If Nick's going to bail out, he needs to do it sooner rather than later. So we can tell the vicar. So we can tell the guests who are out there choosing outfits and buying presents not to bother. So we can tell the caterers to cancel the smoked salmon blinis and the bloody mini profiteroles—'

Claire didn't need to hear any more. She cut through him.

'I've arranged enough weddings here to understand the practical implications, thank you very much.' She was crisp. Businesslike. Unemotional. She had closed down completely. She gave Gus a bright, fixed smile. 'I hope you have a good day, and we look forward to seeing you at dinner.'

She strode across the room and pulled open the office door. Luca was standing outside, looking lean and tanned in faded jeans and a sea-green polo shirt.

It was anyone's guess how long he had been listening.

'Everything all right?' he asked with a dazzling smile. 'Are you ready, darling? The Parfitts are waiting.' He turned to Gus, the picture of charm. 'We'll see you tonight—we'll put you on the terrace if the weather holds.'

Gus managed a weak smile and a nod of thanks.

'Have a great day,' he said, and scarpered as quickly as he could.

Claire slumped back against the wall and looked up at the ceiling. She'd handled that really badly. Come across as a card-carrying bitch, in fact.

Luca came over and stroked her cheek.

'Are you all right? Was he having a moan about something? Those Hooray Henry types are never happy.'

'No.' Claire thought quickly. 'He just wanted to make sure we give the bill for dinner straight to him and not Nick.'

Luca nodded, his eyes raking across her face. She felt as if he was looking for clues. He was so close she could smell him; his scent always aroused her, made her blood heat. She shivered as he put his hand out to run his fingers through her hair. His mouth came down on hers, hard and hungry. She couldn't resist. She could never resist. Besides, it would look suspicious if she protested.

He broke off, gazing at her with a vulpine smile.

'Mrs Claire Bellamy. I'm liking it.'

'That's very presumptuous,' she murmured. 'How do you know I'm not going to keep my maiden name?'

'Because you're going to be my wife.' He nuzzled her neck and she felt her knees go weak. '*My* wife. And we're going to have it all,' he breathed. 'You and me. We've got the whole world at our feet.'

CHAPTER TWELVE

Laura stood for a moment at the bottom of the steps to Clarence House.

She'd kissed Dan goodbye ten minutes earlier. He'd hugged her tight, wished her luck; told her to call him on her mobile if she needed him.

She peered up at the front door, then realised that someone was waving at her from the ground-floor window.

Of course Tony Weston would be looking out for her. She raised a hand in reply, and began to climb the steep stone steps. He opened the door before she got to the top and stood in the doorway, barefoot, a mug of coffee in one hand, a smile of greeting on his face. He wore baggy blue linen shorts and a washed-out T-shirt; a plaited leather bracelet adorned one wrist, and he had no watch.

'Hey,' he said. 'I'm Tony. I'm guessing you're Emma?'

Emma? She was about to correct him, then remembered her alter ego for the day. She wondered what her friend Emma would think when she told her.

'Yes,' she said, and stood on the doorstep, waiting. Waiting for what, she wasn't sure. Some sort of recognition. From her. Or him. Some momentous sense of suddenly belonging. A wave of familiarity. But there was nothing.

Tony looked puzzled. His smile grew wider, as if he was suddenly worried he hadn't been welcoming enough.

'Well, come on in,' he urged, waving his mug

inwards. 'Wendy's making coffee. We saw you coming. You'd like a coffee, would you? Only we have tea, of course. About . . . seventeen different sorts, if that's what you'd prefer.'

'Coffee would be lovely,' Laura murmured.

'And how's your hotel? You're staying at the Townhouse? We go there for a glass of wine sometimes, but we can't afford the restaurant. Starving artists, you see . . .'

'Oh rubbish, don't listen to him.' A woman who was presumably Wendy came forward to greet her. 'We've been there at least three times this year already.'

'Only when friends take us,' pointed out Tony amiably. 'But I don't blame you for staying there. It's the only place, really.'

'I got a good deal,' said Laura, in case they thought she was the type of person who checked into that sort of hotel all the time without a second thought. 'It was really very reasonable. And we got an upgrade . . .'

She still hadn't quite got over the thrill of their sumptuous room.

'It's important to treat yourself every now and again,' Wendy told her, handing her a chunky mug filled with real coffee. 'Help yourself to milk and sugar.'

The room was large and light, open-plan, with a chaotic-looking kitchen at the back. Shelves were stuffed with spices and jars of pickles and bottles of oil, haphazardly arranged, with no thought to logic or order. It was the kitchen of people who loved to cook but weren't so enamoured of clearing up. The living area was full of artefacts and brightly coloured cushions and books, but was

243

clearly designed to focus on the stunning view of the harbour from the front window, which had no curtains—why would you ever want to block out the vista, either day or night?

'Wow,' said Laura. 'No need to ask why you bought this house.'

'You never tire of the view,' Tony told her. 'And it's never the same. In five minutes, it will have totally changed.'

Laura looked around the walls. There were a few paintings, some of which she suspected were by Tony, but no family photographs that she could discern. No pictures of offspring she could scrutinise for a family resemblance.

She sipped her coffee, not wanting to seem too nosy, but not sure what to say either. She was naturally quite shy, and felt further inhibited by the burden of the secret she was carrying, especially as Wendy was there. Laura examined her as discreetly as she could. She was older than Tony, she guessed, but that could have been because she was weathered by the sun, her skin nut-brown. She was tall and sinewy, dressed in a denim dress that ought to have been far too young for her, but because of her grace, she got away with it. Her hair was greying, cut short in a crop that should have been severe but somehow wasn't. She seemed like a woman who was very comfortable with who she was.

How long had Tony and Wendy been together? wondered Laura. Had they been together when she was conceived? She looked around the room for evidence of a long marriage. But there was nothing specific.

'I'm going to the farmers' market, then for a

swim,' said Wendy. 'I'll be back later. I've left soup and bread and cheese for your lunch.' She smiled at Laura. 'Enjoy your day.'

And she was gone, leaving Laura and Tony on their own.

'Well,' he said. 'Let's get started. You haven't paid me all this money to sit around drinking coffee.'

She followed him up the stairs to his studio—a large room on the first floor with the same outlook as the living room. Here he had set up two easels, with paper, and a table full of freshly sharpened pencils, oil paints and brushes.

'I thought the best thing to do,' he said, 'was to get you to have a go at drawing the view. So I can get an idea of your style. Then we can take it from there.'

'I don't think I've got a style,' said Laura, feeling a flutter of nerves. She couldn't remember the last time she'd picked up a pencil to draw. 'I'm pretty useless . . .'

'Everyone says that.' Tony gave her an easy smile. 'You wouldn't be here if you thought you were a genius, would you? Just don't feel self-conscious. I'm not here to judge you.'

Laura turned to face the easel, looking out to the view beyond. Her mouth felt dry; her hand was trembling. How long should she give it before broaching the subject? She needed to establish some sort of a relationship with Tony first, certainly. But the longer she left it, the harder it was going to be.

'I'm not sure where to begin . . .' she said.

*　　　*　　　*

245

The Parfitts' boat, *The Blonde Bombshell*, would have looked more at home in St Tropez or Sandbanks. She was far too grand for Pennfleet. She stood out, white and gleaming in her fibreglass splendour, amidst the scruffy yachts, dinghies and fishing vessels. Someone—a nameless, faceless underling—had brought her over to the little jetty by the Townhouse earlier that morning, and no doubt she would have been fuelled and stocked up with all the necessary goodies. The Parfitts were the sort of people who had underlings making things happen for them everywhere they went.

Claire stepped on board tentatively. Although she lived by the sea, she wasn't that much of a boat person. For a start, she didn't have time to go on the water. Luca, however, bounded on as if he had been born on a boat, and was soon prowling about the deck with Trevor, who took immense pride in showing him all the gizmos and gadgets he'd had installed.

In a trice, Monique had settled Claire on some white leather seating while the men fiddled about at the helm, Luca making all the right noises.

'It's just a little day boat, really,' Monique said. 'Though it does sleep four. We love pootling up and down the coast in it.'

She stretched herself out next to Claire and tipped her face up to the sky with a sigh of satisfaction. The engine started with a sexy, throaty purr. Trevor untied the ropes and the boat started to nudge forward. Luca was driving: even he was slightly awed by its size and power as he navigated his way amongst the rest of the boats in the harbour, which swung from side to side in their wake. Claire couldn't help feeling a little self-conscious. It was like driving a Ferrari through a supermarket car park. Everyone craned their neck to look, to see who was on board. She hoped no one recognised her. She didn't care for ostentation.

'I think it's time for a little drinkie,' said Monique. 'Gin and tonic do you?'

Claire nodded, hoping Monique would make it a strong one. Anything to numb the events of the past twenty-four hours. It had been almost a day since Nick had walked back into her life, and she still didn't have a clue what to do. She felt slightly sick, and wondered if it was her anxiety or the motion of the boat. She remembered someone telling her to look at the horizon if you felt seasick.

As she gazed out across the water, she caught sight of an old wooden boat just in front of them. It was a million miles from *The Blonde Bombshell*, dilapidated and cumbersome. To her horror, she saw that it was Nick and Gus and the rest of the crew setting out for the day. She shrank back in her seat, keeping her head low and praying that she wouldn't be recognised. But she hadn't taken into account Monique's eagle eyes.

'Oh look! Down there. Your stags.' She waved madly, then gave a sigh of longing. 'Oh, if only I was ten years younger.'

Try twenty, thought Claire, with uncharacteristic spite, then felt guilty. She could see Nick and Gus looking over at them and waving. She put her head down, burrowing in the picnic basket so it seemed as if she was otherwise occupied.

The Blonde Bombshell swept past, and Luca held up his hand in a regal gesture, his other hand on the wheel. Claire just caught sight of Nick's face. She could read what he was thinking quite clearly.

Tosser.

Luca wasn't a tosser. Not really. He just did a good impersonation of one a lot of the time. He had his positive side.

She had to believe that. After all, she was stuck with him now. She'd seen the picture of Nick with Sophie. How perfect they looked together. Gus was right. She couldn't destroy another woman's happiness in the hope of recapturing what she'd once had with Nick.

She should just be grateful for what she had now. Which by anyone's standards was a lot. Lolling about on a luxury yacht, whose owners were gagging for your input on the project of your dreams? Wake up, Claire, she told herself.

'Here you are, sweetheart.' Monique returned with two enormous glasses, tinkling with ice. 'This is the life, eh? You'd better get used to it.'

Claire took the gin and tonic eagerly. Monique raised hers with a dazzling smile.

'Here's to *The Blonde Bombshell*,' she said. 'And all who sail in her.'

'*The Blonde Bombshell*,' repeated Claire, and knocked back half the glass in one gulp.

*   *   *

Laura had become so absorbed in what she was doing, she had almost forgotten the purpose of her visit. She felt surprisingly relaxed. Tony's voice was low and gentle and reassuring as he talked her through the painting process. He was a natural teacher—he seemed to know exactly when to guide and when to let her get on with it. When to praise

248

and when to criticise, constructively.

'It's not about what you put in,' he told her. 'It's about what you leave out.'

It was great, getting messy and doing exactly what she wanted. As a social media consultant, she spent her whole working life trying to please other people and working to a brief, and at first she had found it hard to let go, but he'd given her some relaxation exercises to start with, to loosen her up, and before long she was splashing on the paint with confidence, mixing up the colours with a palette knife and experimenting with cadmium and crimson and cerulean, marvelling at how just the tiniest blob could change the intensity and alter the mood of what she was working on.

Eventually she had in front of her a painting of which she felt justifiably proud. It wouldn't score any points for originality, but it was bold and bright and looked like what it was: a jolly harbour scene, in turquoise and cobalt and emerald, with splashes of coral. Tony stood back and looked at it, arms folded. She realised it really mattered to her what he thought.

'You're talented,' he said at last. 'You've got quite a gift. A natural gift.'

And she couldn't quite tell him that of course she had; that it was in her genes. On both sides, possibly.

She looked at the painting and it became blurry through her tears.

Pennfleet in the Rain, she thought, then jumped as Tony put a hand on her shoulder.

'It's almost two o'clock,' he told her. 'We've been at it for four hours. Shall we have some lunch?'

Trevor moored *The Blonde Bombshell* just off Combesgate beach, a tiny cove that was only accessible by boat. They put the picnic hamper in the dinghy and rowed to shore. The beach wasn't sand, but tiny white pebbles. They spread out a double layer of rugs to sit on, then Luca unpacked the picnic with pride. There were individual salad Niçoises with quail eggs, and a fat potato and onion tortilla studded with chorizo, followed by feather-light blueberry friands, which they washed down with a very light English sparkling wine from a local vineyard Luca had discovered and was keen to support.

From a distance, it was the perfect scene. Four friends enjoying an idyllic al fresco lunch on what was effectively a private beach. The sun shone down on them; a light breeze stopped it from being too relentless. Before them the sea shimmered and on the horizon other boats glided past, but no one came to invade their privacy.

After lunch, Luca and Monique went off to explore the caves in the neighbouring cove while the tide was still out. Claire stripped down to her bikini and stretched out on the rug. Her eyes felt heavy. All she wanted to do was go to sleep, to stop the questions whirling around her head. Maybe when she woke everything would seem better.

She was just drifting off, enjoying the feeling of the sun on her face, when she sensed Trevor sitting down beside her.

'I'm glad to get you on your own, Claire,' he said. 'I want to talk to you.'

Claire struggled to open her eyes. She felt

exasperated. Why couldn't he just go away? She didn't want to hear any more facts and figures about the new hotel. She'd got the picture. She wanted to be on her own. But Trevor wasn't going to go away.

'I need to tell you something. About Monique and me. I think it's important. It might alter the way you look at our proposition.'

Claire sighed inwardly. Trevor wasn't going to let it drop. She rolled over on to one side, resting her head on her hand, and looked at him with a polite smile. What was he going to tell her? That they were swingers and were hoping to chuck in their car keys later that evening? Was that going to be the deal? She stifled a giggle: it wouldn't surprise her. They had that air about them.

But Trevor looked solemn. Not as if he was about to make a dodgy pass.

'We have a son. Jamie. He's coming up to twenty-two. This July.'

'Oh.' Claire was surprised. She'd never heard Jamie mentioned.

'You thought we were childless, I expect.' Trevor gave her a knowing smile.

'I don't know that I've ever really thought about it.' If anything, she'd assumed that Trevor and Monique might have grown-up children. They were both pushing fifty.

'We only had the one child. That's how it worked out. But we were happy. Jamie was the apple of our eye. He was a great kid. He adored his mum. They were like that.' Trevor crossed his fingers to show her. 'He was a good all-rounder. A smart kid. Good at footie. Played the trumpet. Popular. Then, when he was about sixteen, it all started to go wrong.'

251

He went quiet for a moment and looked down at the pebbles, picking up handfuls and letting them trickle through his fingers.

Claire wasn't sure what to say. 'It's a difficult age, I suppose.'

'He got in with the wrong crowd. We never stopped him from doing anything, but we didn't like his new friends. We were pretty sure he was smoking dope—his clothes used to smell funny, and he was . . . different. Moody and distant. Never opened his curtains. Sat in his room with his headphones on, playing on the computer. His grades went down. The school called us in and told us he was absent a lot of the time. We didn't know what to do. Our lovely son, who we'd been so proud of, seemed to have turned into a different person.'

'It must have been very hard.' Claire tried to look sympathetic.

'We tried to talk to him. We did our best. We tried to be supportive. But he didn't want to know. He told us we didn't understand. Understand what? He didn't want for anything. We were always there for him. We told him that whatever it took to make him happy, we would do it. We just wanted our old Jamie back, not this sullen, hostile, unhappy kid who didn't want anything to do with us.'

Claire could just imagine Trevor and Monique trying to deal with a recalcitrant teenager. They were both so full-on, so forceful. Even if their hearts were in the right place, she felt sure their overtures would have been unwelcome. She herself could remember being a moody teenager, and just wanting to be left alone. Part of her sympathised with Jamie.

'One day,' said Trevor, and Claire realised

that his voice had a quiver in it, 'one morning, we went to his room because he hadn't got up, and he wasn't there. He'd vanished. Disappeared.' It was a moment before he continued. 'We never saw him again.'

Claire sat up, shocked.

'Never?' she echoed.

Trevor shook his head. He was clearly finding it difficult to speak.

'We've no idea what happened. Where he went. Or why. There was no note. All he took was his phone, and his bank cards. Just the stuff he would have had with him on a normal day. He was only seventeen.'

His face creased up with the effort of sharing the memory.

'I'm so sorry,' Claire managed at last. What on earth was she supposed to say? 'That's terrible.'

Trevor nodded. 'I did everything I could. I got every copper I knew to pull strings. I hired the best private detectives I could find. I gave his friends money to help me find him.'

Claire could imagine Trevor swinging into action. A military operation oiled by large amounts of cash.

'And you never heard anything?'

'A month after he left, Monique got a text from him. It said, "Sorry Mum". That was it. We don't know whether he went abroad or . . . jumped off a bridge or . . . what. We have no idea where he is. He could have started a new life somewhere. Or be down and out. A druggie in some doorway . . .'

'How awful. Not knowing.'

'Yes.' Trevor looked her straight in the eye. 'It was a living hell. I've never felt so angry, or helpless, or desperate. And it totally broke Monique.'

'Well, yes, I can imagine.' Actually, she couldn't. Or didn't want to. 'But I had no idea. She seems so . . .' Claire sought for the words. Up, she thought. Monique was always so up, so bright and full of enthusiasm.

'She puts on a good act. Most people have no idea what she's gone through. She's learnt how to hide it. But it still torments her. She's never given up hoping. She still carries her phone round with her—the one she had when he went missing—in case he calls. She's got a new number for everyday, but she checks the old one constantly. Night and day. It's like an obsession. But then I suppose . . . she's never given up hope . . .'

He trailed off. Claire felt overwhelmed with pity.

'And you?' she asked softly. 'Have you given up hope?'

Trevor looked out to sea. His eyes were screwed up behind his sunglasses; whether to block out the sun or to hold back tears, she couldn't be sure. He wasn't an attractive man as such, she decided, but he had a diamond-geezer aura that drew you to him. And a sense of power that made you want him on your side. He would always look after you, Claire decided.

'They call it ambiguous loss,' he said. 'It's very difficult to deal with, because you don't have . . . what do they call it? Closure. And you never know the reason why. What went wrong. What you did wrong.' He paused for a moment. 'In the end, I learnt to focus on the present. I taught myself to come to terms with the fact that Jamie doesn't want to be found. And I decided I wasn't going to beat myself up about it. I did my best as his dad. The

254

best I knew how . . .'

'Of course you did.' Claire touched him on the arm.

'I knew if I carried on hoping, like Monique, that I'd drive myself crazy in the end. And she needs me to be strong.'

He picked up more pebbles, clawing at them urgently. Claire could feel the tension in him. The frustration that must still eat him up, all these years on.

'The reason I'm telling you all this,' he went on, 'is because this hotel project is the first thing that has really fired Monique up since Jamie disappeared. I think it could be the turning point. The thing that helps her move on. Which is why I so desperately want it to work. And why I want you both on board. Because you can make it happen. There's no way she could do it on her own— she's smart enough, but I don't think she's strong enough. And I've got too much else on to give it the attention it needs. Someone's got to finance it after all. But with you and Luca—it would be a great team.'

'I understand,' said Claire. She felt guilty that she'd thought it was just a vanity project to keep a silly woman with too much money happy. Poor Monique.

'I know Luca's committed.' Trevor pushed up his sunglasses and fixed her with a look that said the emotional stuff was over and now he meant business. 'But I can see you're not convinced.' He held a hand up as she started to speak. 'Which is absolutely right. You shouldn't be rushing in. As a woman, you're bound to have more reservations. It's okay for Luca to go charging ahead, but what about you? You've just got engaged. I expect you're thinking about your future. How it all fits in. How you'll cope if you want a family.'

'Well,' said Claire. 'There's a lot to think about, certainly.' Her heart was hammering. Trevor was getting too personal for her liking. Yet she admired him for his perspicacity. He knew something was amiss.

'All I'm saying,' replied Trevor, 'is that whatever it takes, whatever I can do to convince you, I'll do it. If you have concerns, or you want to make conditions, please talk to me. I don't want this project to fall through. I want to make it work for you. So I can make it work for Monique.'

Claire nodded. There wasn't much she could say, because she couldn't reveal the real source of her reluctance. Yet at the same time, she felt a sudden desire to take the project on. Trevor's story had moved her deeply. Of course, she knew that this was why he was so successful, because he was an expert in manipulating people, but he certainly hadn't been lying.

And she saw Monique in a different light now— underneath the make-up and the designer clothes and the flashy jewellery, she saw a woman, a mother, in constant pain.

'I've got some stuff I need to work out first,' she managed finally.

Trevor smiled. 'Whatever it takes. And remember—we haven't had this conversation. Monique doesn't like people to know about Jamie.'

He flipped his glasses back down to cover his eyes as Luca and Monique came into view. They were talking animatedly, Luca gesticulating, Monique nodding.

Claire didn't want to hear what they were saying. Now that she knew the stakes, she didn't want to be part of the conspiracy until she knew exactly where her future lay. And the only one who could figure that out was her.

She stood up. 'I'm going for a swim.'

She didn't wait for a reply. She ran down towards the water and straight into the sea, gasping at the coldness. But she didn't stop. She carried straight on until the water reached her waist, and then she plunged underneath the waves, down into the deep coolness, where there was no sound. She stayed there until her lungs nearly burst, wishing she could swim off into the silent green depths of the ocean where nothing and no one could reach her.

*   *   *

Laura and Tony sat on the terrace at the front of the house for lunch, an Indian parasol shielding them from the heat of the sun.

Tony brought out home-made watercress soup, served with a swirl of double cream and a sprinkling of chives from one of the pots of herbs that were ranged under the windows. With the soup were a chunky loaf of organic stoneground bread and a wedge of Sharpham Brie, ripened to gooey perfection.

They ate for a few minutes in silence. A gentle breeze came off the sea, bringing with it a tang of ozone that sharpened Laura's appetite: she was so nervous, she hadn't thought she could face food, but she was surprised to be hungry. Seagulls wheeled overhead, crying to each other.

'They're a bloody menace,' said Tony. 'They've

257

been known to come and take food off the table. You can't turn your back.'

'But they're part of the seaside, aren't they? You can't have sea without seagulls. They're iconic.'

'I suppose so.' He smiled at her as he sliced another couple of chunks of bread and passed her one on the end of the knife.

'So—how long have you lived here?' Laura busied herself with the butter.

'Fifteen years now. We decided we wanted to leave the rat race and have a simpler life. We've never regretted it. Okay, so we don't have a flash car and we don't stay at posh hotels if we go away, but I sleep at night now. I'm not very good at stress.'

Oh dear, thought Laura. You might not sleep tonight after what I'm about to tell you. She took a gulp of elderflower cordial. Her mouth felt so dry, she wasn't sure she was going to be able to form the next words. She had to confront him. Wendy might come back at any moment, and then it would be too late.

She cleared her throat before speaking.

'You used to teach at St Benedict's, didn't you?'

It came out as more of a statement than a question.

Or an accusation.

The fleeting look on Tony's face was a mixture of fear, surprise and guilt, which he managed to erase with admirable speed.

'St Benedict's?' He frowned, and shook his head.

'The girls' school? In Reading. I looked you up,' insisted Laura. 'You were head of art.'

'Oh!' A gleam of recollection came into his eye. Was she supposed to be taken in by his acting?

'Yes, I was there for a couple of terms. But it was an awfully long time ago. An awfully long time.' He put his hands on the table to push himself up, as if to accentuate how old he was. 'There's gooseberry fool if you'd like it . . .' He trailed off as he realised Laura was staring at him. 'Is something the matter?'

'Yes,' she said, looking down at the table. He sat back down.

'What?'

He knows, she thought. He knows.

She bent down and burrowed in her bag for the photocopy of the drawing she'd found in Marina's box file, then laid it out on the table.

'Did you draw this while you were there?'

He stared at the picture for what seemed like an eternity. Apart from the slightest crease between his brows, his face was expressionless. At long last, he spoke.

'Well,' he said. 'It *looks* like my signature, certainly. But I must have done hundreds of drawings like this during my life. I've no idea who it is, I'm afraid. I wouldn't remember anyone, really. My memory's dreadful these days.' He passed the drawing back to her with a smile. Was his hand shaking slightly, or was it the breeze ruffling the paper? 'Anyway, I'm hardly famous, so even if I did draw it, it won't be worth anything. Though I'm flattered that you might think so.'

He laughed, but it didn't fool her.

'I didn't bring it because I thought it was valuable,' she told him. 'And I know who it is. It's my mother. She was at the school. It must have been drawn not long before I was born.'

There wasn't a flicker of reaction.

'Really?' he asked, and a note of hostility had

259

crept into his tone.

'Yes,' said Laura, and she leant in towards him. 'And I brought it because I think you might be my father.'

He gazed at her in absolute astonishment, the horror on his face almost comical. Then he gave a splutter, something between a laugh and a cough.

'Oh, dear God. Oh, my dear girl.' He sat back and ran his hands through what was left of his hair. 'How on earth could I be your father? Wendy and I were already married when I was at St Benedict's. I'd have been old enough to be . . . your *mother's* father. Almost. Whatever made you think . . .?'

Laura snatched up the drawing and waved it at him.

'She kept this. With all her important stuff. And the dates add up. She was about to do her A-levels when she got pregnant. You were her teacher. Why else would she keep it a secret who my father was? If it had just been some random boy, she'd have told me. But she must have wanted to cover it up . . . Of course she could never tell anyone. An affair with a teacher—that's pretty scandalous.'

She realised she was ranting. She stopped. Tony nodded politely.

'It certainly would be,' he replied. 'If it were the case.'

Laura looked down at the picture, her only scrap of evidence. She took a deep breath and carried on.

'Look at this,' she said. 'It's not just a sketchy life drawing done in a school studio. Look at her face. Look at the way it's drawn. Whoever did this was in love with my mother. And she was in love with them. You can see that in her eyes.'

She was almost in tears, racked with the emotion.

The effort of wanting her theory to be proved right.

'Look,' said Tony. 'I understand how much you want to find out who your father is. It's a very powerful instinct, to want to know who we are and where we come from. But I'm very sorry. I'm not your man.' He spread his hands on the table in front of him, looking down at his long, tanned fingers. 'I can tell you this with absolute certainty because . . .' He looked up, squinting in the bright sun. 'This isn't easy. I don't speak about it often. But . . . Wendy and I were never able to have children. We tried for years. We had all the tests. I'm totally infertile. So you see . . . it can't be me. No matter how much you want it to be.'

'Oh.' The breath came out of Laura as if she'd been punched in the back.

'Quite apart from the fact that I didn't have a relationship with your mother. She was a pupil. It would have been a total abuse of my position.'

They sat in silence for a moment. The seagulls were still wheeling.

'Come on,' said Tony. 'Let's go inside and make a cup of tea.'

*   *   *

After Colin and Chelsey had finished their shopping spree, Chelsey had insisted she didn't want an all-singing, all-dancing excursion. All she wanted to do was go to the beach. And so when they went back to the Townhouse to drop off their purchases, Colin asked the kitchen if they could pack up a picnic, which Fred and Loz duly did—chicken sandwiches and mini quiche lorraines and tubs of fruit salad and the rest of Luca's blueberry friands—and together

261

they set off with buckets and spades and fishing nets for Neptune's Cove, a tiny crescent of golden sand at the mouth of the river, sheltered by cliffs on both sides.

Chelsey seemed quite content to just potter about, poking around in the tidal rock pools and splashing in the shallows. Such was her delight that Colin soon realised that she had rarely been given permission to behave like a child. He certainly couldn't imagine Karen packing up a picnic and sitting on the beach all day with her. But he was more than happy to. He rented a couple of deckchairs for them to make their camp, and watched her as she explored, going over when she waved to him to come and see what she had found, making sure she had enough sun cream on, traipsing over to the ice cream van for a 99 each when it got too hot.

By the middle of the afternoon, freckles had started to come out on her nose and her skin was already beginning to turn gold. She looked, he thought, like a healthy, happy kid on holiday, not the pallid, downtrodden creature he had picked up the day before. She had lost that horrible air of solemnity she seemed to carry with her and seemed a little more carefree. How much that had to do with Karen not being around, he couldn't be sure. But she had definitely come to life since her mother had left the scene. She was totally engrossed in gathering up shells, wiping the sand from them carefully and putting them in her bucket.

He couldn't help feeling that at eleven, she was a bit old for shell-gathering. But then she didn't seem to have had much of a childhood at all, so perhaps she was making up for lost time. Over the course of the day he'd managed to extricate as full a picture as he could of her life, and it seemed pretty grim.

Karen, it seemed, never helped her daughter with her homework or turned up to parents' evening. Chelsey's diet revolved around McDonald's, Subway and Domino's—she seemed proud that she knew how to phone for a pizza. And she seemed to spend a lot of time being dumped at other people's houses. Colin was furious. Furious with Karen and furious with himself. He should have taken control years ago. He should have taken more interest; he should have made the money he gave her conditional on certain things. He should have monitored Chelsey's school reports.

He should, in short, have been the father she so desperately needed. Was it too late? No, he thought. It was never too late. Chelsey still had a sweet nature and a desire to please. There was time to turn her life round. Get her a decent education and nurture her. Like Michelle and Ryan had been nurtured. He hadn't missed a single parents' evening for either of them, no matter how hard he had been working.

He pulled out his phone. He had twenty-four/ seven access to both his accountant and his solicitor. He paid them enough to be able to call them whenever he liked. Not that he often called them out of hours—Colin didn't operate like that— but he considered this an emergency. Martin Crane wouldn't mind. He'd drawn up the contract for every deal Colin had ever done since he started in business. Every year without fail, Colin sent him a Christmas cake laced with Courvoisier from the bakery.

Martin answered on the second ring.

'Colin,' he said crisply, fully alert. 'What can I do for you?'

'I need help,' Colin responded. 'It's probably not your line of work, but you should be able to find me the right man for the job. Or woman.'

'Do you want to put me in the picture?' Martin asked.

Colin hesitated. Then took the plunge. He'd spent enough time trying to sweep Chelsey under the carpet.

'I've got an illegitimate daughter. Eleven years old. I've been paying a grand a month maintenance her whole life. Her mum's done a bunk. Left me holding the baby, so to speak. And I want custody, as of . . . yesterday.'

'Is your name on the birth certificate?'

'I imagine so.' Colin felt sure Karen wouldn't have forgotten this trick in her quest to score money from him.

'And you're sure you are the father?'

Colin's stomach lurched. This thought hadn't occurred to him. But of course he couldn't be sure. Karen could have been stringing along any number of fools like him. For all he knew, she was claiming maintenance from half a dozen hapless idiots.

He looked over at Chelsey. She was lying on her towel now, iPod earphones in, knees bent, her feet tapping in time to the music.

Of course she was his. Karen was manipulative and opportunistic, but not that evil. And probably not even that clever.

'Positive,' he said, because he had to believe it.

'Okay. What you need is a shit-hot family lawyer. We're probably looking at getting a parental responsibility order, which might mean going to court. Depending on whether the mother cooperates. Be prepared for it to get messy—these things are never straightforward.'

'I'm ready for it.' Colin felt calm. Resolute. 'And by the way, Alison doesn't know anything. Yet.'

He heard Martin give a huff, as if to say, 'I don't envy you, mate'.

'I'm on it. It's a bank holiday weekend, so it might be a while before I get anyone, but I'll call you back as soon as,' said Martin, and rang off.

Colin knew that by Tuesday he would have the best man or woman for the job at his disposal. He would just have to hope that Karen didn't reappear on the scene before then, having had a change of heart. He wanted this to be a clean operation, and by staying away, Karen was giving him plenty of rope.

There was one more call he had to make. One he wasn't looking forward to in the least. He pressed 'Home' on his mobile, and waited for his wife to answer.

'Hello?' Alison always answered the phone with a querying tone, as if she was puzzled as to why anyone would want to call.

'Alison, love, it's me,' he said.

'Oh, hello.' She sounded pleased to hear him. 'You've just caught me. I was on my way into town.'

'Listen, I need you to get in the car. Drive down to the Townhouse by the Sea in Pennfleet.'

'What's happened?' Her pleasure turned to alarm. 'Are you okay?'

'Yes. Yes, I'm fine. There's just something I need to talk to you about.'

'Can't you come home?'

'No.' On this Colin was firm. 'No. I'll book us a

table for dinner. Be here as soon as you can.'

'Can't you tell me over the phone?'

'I need to see you. Face to face.'

'Okay.' She sounded perplexed and a little put out. 'The Townhouse in Pennfleet? Isn't that Cornwall? I thought you were in Bristol?'

'No.' His so-called conference did exist. He kept his alibi as watertight as he could. He'd even bought a three-day ticket. But he'd never darkened the door of the exhibition.

There was silence while Alison digested this information.

'Right.' She didn't sound too thrilled. 'Well, if you're not going to enlighten me, I'll be as quick as I can, I suppose.'

*   *   *

Laura sat inside at the breakfast bar while Tony made her a cup of tea.

She felt utterly mortified by her outburst. Her instinct was to run away and never come back, but Tony had been so calm and non-judgemental. A lot of people would have sent her away with a flea in her ear, she thought, but he seemed to take it in his stride, as if he was used to unhinged young women hurling accusations at him.

It was such a shame, she thought, that he wasn't her father. The house he and Wendy shared had such a calm and inviting feel to it. It was somewhere she would have loved to take refuge every now and again—long, sunny weekends by the sea to break up the monotony of working in London. Her job was such a treadmill, increasingly pressurised, and although of course she could book weekends away,

266

it involved too much effort and forward planning. But knowing she could slip down to Pennfleet for a much-deserved rest any time she liked would have been perfect . . .

She and Dan. She felt sure Tony would like Dan.

She told herself to stop fantasising. It wasn't going to happen. She was going to have to go back to the drawing board. Tony might not be her father, she mused, but he had been her mother's teacher, all those years ago. He might be able to provide her with a clue.

'There you go, Emma.' He put a large mug of tea in front of her, and reached for the biscuit tin.

'Actually,' Laura admitted sheepishly, 'my name's not Emma. I gave you a false name. Emma Stubbs is my best friend. My name's Laura Starling.' She leant forward with urgency. 'My mother was Marina. Marina Starling. Are you sure you don't remember her?'

Tony screwed up his face. 'I've got a vague recollection . . . it's an unusual name. But you have to make allowances.' He gave a self-deprecating grin. 'I am getting old, after all. Sometime I can't even remember what I had for breakfast this morning.'

'But you did do this drawing of her,' Laura persisted. 'It must have been you—it's got your signature on it.'

He shrugged.

'She probably did some modelling. Things were different in those days. And if we had a life-drawing class, of course I would draw the model as well. To show the students how it should be done.' Another self-deprecating grin. 'In theory.'

Laura looked down at the picture.

267

'I wonder why she kept it, then?'

Tony shrugged. 'Girls of that age love to keep things, don't they? They're magpies.'

'Maybe she had a crush on you?' Laura's eyes were wide with the possible scandal.

'I doubt it. I had a bit more hair in those days, but I wasn't exactly a heart-throb.' He pushed the tin of shortbread over to her. 'There you go. I always find a bit of sugar helps after an emotional outburst.'

'Oh God. I'm so sorry. You must think I'm a complete lunatic.' Laura laughed despite herself.

'Hey. No problem.' Tony took a sip of his tea. 'I'm rather flattered I was the chief suspect. It makes me feel more interesting than I really am.'

'And you don't remember anything about her class? It must have been your A-level class. You don't remember anything about who she hung out with? Anyone who might be able to give me a clue . . .?' Laura couldn't resist pressing him for more information.

Tony shook his head. 'It was a big school. I was only there a couple of terms. I didn't really get to know who was in and who was out.'

Disappointed, and feeling no further on with her investigation, Laura drank her tea as quickly as she could.

'Shall we go and finish your painting?' Tony asked her as she put down her cup.

'I think it's better if I just go,' she said.

'Are you sure? You were doing so well.'

Laura hesitated.

'Come on. No hard feelings,' Tony tried to persuade her. 'I don't want you to waste your money. And Wendy will think it strange if you

268

disappear.'

'No. I'm going to go back to the hotel. My boyfriend will be back soon. We haven't been away like this before. I want to make the most of the upgrade . . .'

She blushed, realising how this sounded.

'Well, I'm sorry I couldn't help you.'

'And I'm sorry about . . . bursting in here with wild accusations.'

Tony managed a laugh. 'Listen—it made a change from the usual middle-aged empty-nesters I get.'

Laura picked up her bag.

'Thank you. Again. Maybe you should tell your wife I was taken ill. Migraine. I get a lot of migraines. Especially when I'm stressed. And actually, I am feeling a bit headachey, so it wouldn't be a total lie.' Laura realised she was babbling.

'Don't worry,' said Tony. 'I'll think of something.'

Laura slid off the stool and stood up to go. On impulse, she went over to hug him. He'd been so sweet. Part of her did want to stay and finish her painting, but she'd rather be alone with her thoughts. She realised now that she had pinned all her hopes on him being her father. The disappointment was gutting.

Her father was out there somewhere. He had to be. She was just going to have to dig deeper into the past.

Or tie her mother up and put a gun to her head.

'Goodbye,' she said to Tony, who looked rather relieved that she was going. He must think she was completely bonkers. And maybe she was. How could she ever have thought that tiny little drawing was going to provide her with the answer she needed?

*   *   *

As soon as Laura had gone, Tony turned and went swiftly upstairs into his studio. He shut the door and crossed to the window, watching Laura as she walked back down the road until she finally disappeared around the corner and out of sight.

Then he bent double over the sill with his head in his hands.

A daughter. He had a daughter.

Of course she was his. As soon as she had revealed the true reason for her visit, the years had rolled away, bringing back every second of that insane, tempestuous, wonderful, terrible time. It had taken every ounce of his willpower, a strength he didn't know he had, to bring it all to an end. It was the only way. He'd had no choice.

Marina Starling. He could still see her face, as clearly as anything.

CHAPTER THIRTEEN

When Tony Weston had first got the job at St Benedict's, his friends had ribbed him mercilessly. It was the stuff of every male fantasy—head of art at a girls' school? He took the teasing good-naturedly on the surface, but actually it annoyed him. It made him feel as if he wasn't being taken seriously. As if they thought he was a dirty old man, even though he was only thirty-two. As if they didn't think he respected his wife, which he did. Wendy was his world. His rock. His soulmate. And the rise in salary that came with the post meant that when she got pregnant, she would be able to give up her job to look after their children. Wendy had no desire to be a working mother. It didn't make sense to her. If you could afford not to, why would you put yourself and your children through it? No, she would have her kiln in the garden, and when the children were old enough, she could spend any spare time doing her ceramics, and sell them.

So moving to Reading had been the perfect plan for the Westons. And although they weren't keen on the town itself, they found a big Victorian house in an area that wasn't too rundown, which they were going to do up gradually. Wendy found a job as a teaching assistant in a junior school and stopped taking the pill. They were totally on track.

But Tony hadn't accounted for Marina Starling.

He heard the name often enough, even before he met her. She was the subject of several staff meetings before term started. She was one of those tricky students who could go either way. Bright, but unmotivated. It was anyone's guess whether she would pull it out of the bag and leave with a decent clutch of qualifications, or be a spectacular failure and drift off into the world. The general consensus was that there was nothing you could do with a girl like that. She would choose her own destiny no matter who tried to intervene.

There was also a theory amongst the men in the staff room that it wouldn't matter if Marina left unqualified. A girl who looked like that would always go far. Tony had been sickened by their casually sexist judgement, but he could tell, by the way the women bristled, that what they said was true.

The day Marina walked into his art class, a canvas rucksack covered in badges slung over her shoulder, he thought his heart was going to stop.

She had raven-black hair teased into a wild nest that fell past her shoulders. Pale skin as smoothly perfect as the inside of a Wedgwood teacup. Kitten-round eyes ringed darkly with kohl. Her school jumper clung obscenely to her breasts; her legs were long and skinny beneath her skirt, clad in black tights and non-regulation Doc Martens with the laces undone.

He couldn't keep his eyes off her all the way through the lesson, though he tried desperately not to make it obvious. She was shrewd, and interested, which surprised him. She asked bold and insightful questions. When he did look at her she didn't blush, but smiled, a deep dimple appearing by her mouth.

'Don't you think,' she asked him in their first lesson, 'that Gaugin was actually a bit of a wanker?'

He was determined not to be fazed.

'He pleased himself, certainly,' he replied. 'Whether that makes him true to himself, or, as you so eloquently put it, a wanker, is for you to decide. Though he certainly got his comeuppance. Syphilis is not a pretty way to go.'

Touché, he thought. His reply seemed to please her.

For weeks they sparred in class. She challenged him constantly, and he retaliated. He didn't much care if the rest of the class noticed the spark between them. And he remembered only too clearly the day he walked into the life-drawing class and found her reclining in place of the usual lumpen model.

'Gretchen couldn't make it,' she told him. 'So I thought I'd sit in for her. It seems a shame to cancel the lesson.'

He should have protested. He should have sent her away to get dressed immediately. But doing so would have shown he was rattled. He knew that was what she intended. She spent every lesson playfully trying to provoke or shock him.

'Great idea,' he said, barely giving her a second glance, then sat down to sketch her. Once he was behind his easel, he could feast his eyes on her body. It was so exquisite that it made his throat ache. He knew it was wrong, but he would have to be superhuman not to want to look. He defied any man on earth not to take a prurient interest. Of course, he thought, these days a life-drawing situation like that would never be allowed, but things had been different then. Things had been possible. And, he told himself, she was seventeen. He knew, because he'd checked on her school record.

And why had he checked? he asked himself. Because he was bewitched, and it made him feel better to know she was well over the age of consent. Thoughts of her haunted him, day and night. Thoughts he tried desperately to keep at bay, because they were so dangerous, so wrong. He was being a bloody fool. Playing with Marina was playing with fire, because one day someone who mattered would notice and would say something.

One day he found her crying in the corner of the art room. She refused to tell him what was the matter, but continued to weep bitter tears. Even though a voice inside his head warned him not to, he stepped closer to her. He could smell her cheap,

273

sugary, teenage girl scent and it made his stomach turn over, not with revulsion but an overwhelming compulsion, a compulsion to touch her. He put a tentative arm around her, a gesture that could, just about, be construed as one designed to bring comfort. As soon as he made contact, she twisted round and pressed herself against him.

'Hold me,' she said.

Anything else, he could have resisted. If she'd asked him to fuck her, or kiss her, he would have pushed her away. But it was such a heartfelt plea. She was so tiny, so frail, but so ripe. As he pulled her in to him, he could feel the softness of her breasts against his chest, in sharp contrast to the bony shoulder blades he caressed with his hands.

And then suddenly they were tangled up in each other. Fingers and mouths and tongues entwined. Buttons came undone and clothes melted away. Not a word was spoken; their breath was synchronised. It was urgent but measured. Almost perfectly choreographed. He lifted her on to one of the wooden workbenches. She tilted her head back; he kissed the whiteness of her throat with tender savagery.

When it was over, she slid down him, on to the floor, stood in front of him with her head bowed, her breathing shallow.

'I've been thinking about that,' she said, 'since the day I first saw you.'

He brushed his fingertips slowly down her spine, touching her in wonder. This was the moment he would take to his grave. This was the most momentous thing that had ever happened to him. Jesus, he thought. He was a thirty-two-year-old teacher and he'd just screwed a pupil. A seventeen-year-old pupil.

And then he realised he didn't care. If he was hung, drawn and quartered for it, flayed alive, put in front of a firing squad, it would have been worth every glorious second. It had been like dying and being reborn in the same moment.

*   *   *

Their affair was passionate, intense, urgent, abandoned. He had to lay down some rules, because otherwise it would have spiralled out of control. No contact at school. No phone calls to his house. Nothing in writing, ever. They met in the lunch hour at her house, because her parents were never in. The neighbours wouldn't notice, she assured him. Sometimes he managed to get there at weekends, on the pretence of going to the DIY store, or the gym, or the library, then calling her from a phone box.

He knew it was irresponsible. He knew it was wrong. But their passion—not love; love didn't begin to express what they had between them—was more powerful than any moral sense either of them had. His should have been more developed than hers—he was the adult; he was the teacher, for heaven's sake—but every time he began to express a concern, she shushed him.

'People wait a lifetime for this,' she told him, 'and never experience it. We should be grateful for it while it lasts.'

It wasn't just sex. She intrigued him. Excited him. Stimulated him. Infuriated him. Surprised him—constantly. She was as skittish as a kitten but deeper than the stillest waters. She made him laugh.

275

And once, when they were having closer-than-close, desperate sex, she made him cry.

Of course, it had to come to an end. He'd known that all along.

On a school art trip to Paris, when half a dozen students got food poisoning from some dodgy coq au vin, they had both feigned illness too and stayed behind in the hotel, sacrificing the trip to Versailles. She had come to his room and they had spent the day in bed, losing themselves in each other, and Tony had looked up at her above him, her dark hair tousled and damp with sweat, and knew it had to stop.

'Wendy's pregnant,' he told her.

She rolled off him and on to the bed beside him, staring up at the ceiling.

'That's it, then,' she said.

'I'll always love you,' he told her, 'but we're having a baby. I have to put that first.'

'I know,' she said. 'I know you do.'

She gave him a look, and he suddenly understood the reason for her wordless anger, the anger he knew was there even though she wasn't expressing it.

'I never said I didn't have sex with her. I didn't want her to be suspicious. I couldn't just stop. You *knew* we wanted a family.' He defended himself as best he could.

Her green eyes were opaque with tears. She looked like the child she still was. She curled herself up into a tiny ball. She didn't say anything. It was worse than if she had ranted and railed at him. And when he tried to curl himself round her, she punched him, hard, in the stomach.

He bent double, gasping, winded, shocked by her

strength.

She pulled on her tights, laddering them in her haste, tugged on her paisley tea dress and her green baggy jumper.

'Marina . . .'

'Don't say anything,' she implored him through gritted teeth. 'I get it. I understand. Don't worry.'

'I'll always love you.'

She looked straight at him, as if searching for proof of this declaration. Then she gave a tense little nod, accompanied by a tight smile, and left the room.

He scarcely saw her for the rest of the trip, just glimpses of her wild nest of hair amongst the rest of the students as they visited the Louvre, the Jeu de Paume, the Musée d'Orsay. He felt bereft. He'd wanted to look at all the paintings with her, see her reaction, tell her his interpretations. He wanted to share everything with her for the rest of his life. But he couldn't.

The crossing back to England was wild. Tony spent the entire journey throwing up, not sure if it was *mal de mer* or *maladie d'amour* making him ill. Each wave tossed him nearer to Wendy.

When he got back, to his loyal and faithful wife with her tiny little bump, he realised something else. He couldn't stay on in Reading knowing that Marina was breathing the same air as him, knowing that he might bump into her at any time of the day or night, in the supermarket, or the post office, or a car park. He had to move himself away from the temptation. He had to put as many miles between them as possible. And so he applied for a job with an advertising agency in London, which, to his immense surprise, he got. He broke the terms of his contract with the school by not giving them a term's notice, but he made it clear to the head that for personal reasons he couldn't stay.

'It's very . . . delicate,' he told her. She *was* delicate, Marina, a fragile construction of blood and bone and breath.

The head recoiled slightly. No head of school wanted a teacher besmirched by personal problems. Delicate was a euphemism for messy scandal. She read the subtext.

'It's a tragedy that we're losing you,' she told him. 'You've been an inspiration to so many of our girls.'

And they left it at that.

When he phoned the school later that summer to ask what grades his pupils had got for their A-levels, Marina's name wasn't mentioned.

'What about Marina Starling?' he asked. 'I had her down for an A.'

'She didn't sit her exams in the end,' he was told. 'No one knows what happened to her. She just disappeared.'

*   *   *

They lost her, their baby girl.

A week before she was due to give birth, Wendy couldn't feel the baby kicking any more. The midwife's calm reassurance that it was quite common in the last stage of pregnancy did nothing to soothe her worry.

'The baby's probably resting,' Tony told her. 'Ready for the big journey.'

He could sense Wendy's disquiet. And when they finally went to the hospital, her worst fears were realised. They couldn't hear the heartbeat because there was no heartbeat. The baby inside her was dead. She still had to deliver her, though. A proper full-blown labour, with all the concomitant pain. Tony didn't understand why they couldn't deliver it by Caesarean—surely that was more humane?—but it wasn't hospital policy.

They held her for an hour afterwards, their baby daughter. She was unbelievably perfect. A rosebud mouth under a button nose. A shock of dark hair. Tiny fingers that Wendy curled round her thumb, before the midwife took her away in the yellow blanket they had chosen only the week before, together with her name, Rosalind.

Tony knew he had to be strong. If it was devastating for him, how much worse must it be for Wendy, who had felt the baby inside her for all those months; who had nurtured her. The tragedy made him realise how much he loved his wife, for her strength, her dignity, her quiet but contained grief. From that day on, he shut his mind to what Marina might be doing. He allowed himself no fantasy of a clandestine reunion. Wendy didn't deserve his treachery. She deserved his devotion.

Over the years, he wondered if he had paid for those few months of madness with Rosalind's death. He had never quite been able to scrub the shame from his mind. The grubbiness of it all crept up on him when he least expected it, making him squirm. He'd been reckless, self-indulgent, irresponsible. Wrong, wrong, wrong on so many levels. At the time, he had managed to persuade himself that it was a love story, but no—it was the sordid tale of a randy art teacher taking advantage of his star pupil. Classic tabloid fodder. In his

279

darkest moments he imagined the headlines if Marina ever decided to come clean, and the fear squeezed his guts. Would he be arrested, prosecuted, imprisoned?

Eventually, the fear faded. The trail went cold. There would be no evidence, only circumstantial. But now, as he stood at the window looking out on to the view that had given him and Wendy so much pleasure over the years, he realised that his ugly past had caught up with him. And there was evidence all right. DNA evidence. Living, breathing proof of every fuck he'd had with Marina. But he hadn't been able to acknowledge it to Laura. Of course he hadn't.

As he took in great gulps of fresh air to quell his nausea, he saw Wendy coming back along the road. He watched her climbing the steps with her long, easy strides. The striped bag containing her swimming costume and a towel was across her lean, athletic body, kept that way by the daily ritual of a swim in the sea. In her hand was the basket containing the things she had bought from the market: fresh olives, perhaps, a loaf of stoneground bread, coffee beans.

He stood back from the window, not wanting her to see him, not wanting her to raise her hand in greeting.

How could he tell her? How could he tell her that, in the same year their daughter had been stillborn, another girl had come into the world, a girl that he had fathered? It was unbearable to think of her grief, the grief she had thought she shared with him, but which she would now have to shoulder alone.

No. That part of his life had to stay in the

280

shadows. No matter how enticing it was to get to know his daughter, he had to keep the door firmly locked.

Thank God the girl had seemed convinced by his argument. He had longed for her to go, but he couldn't be seen to be hurrying her out in case he looked guilty. He had been so relieved when she decided to go back to the hotel. He wouldn't have been able to bear to spend the afternoon with her, or to see Wendy in the same room.

He heard the front door shut. With dread in his heart, he crossed the room and went down the stairs.

She was in the kitchen, filling the kettle.

'How's it going?' she asked him with a smile. 'Are you two ready for some more tea? I bought scones from the farmer's market, and some cream.'

'Emma had to go,' he told her. 'She's got a migraine. She was practically seeing double. She's gone back to the hotel to lie down.'

'Oh, what a shame.' Wendy busied herself taking her purchases from her bag. 'She seemed very nice.'

'Yes, very nice,' agreed Tony. 'And not a bad little painter either. But never mind. It means we've got the rest of the weekend to ourselves.'

Wendy looked at him. 'She's not coming back, then?'

Tony couldn't meet her eye. 'I don't think so.'

'I hope you didn't go giving her a refund. I know what a soft touch you are.'

'No, no, of course not.' The guilt was horrible. It was worse than the guilt he'd felt at the time. 'Tell you what, why don't we go out tonight? Nip up the river to the King's Arms for a crab supper?'

Wendy put her head to one side as she

considered his offer.

'Lovely,' she said. 'That would be really lovely.'

CHAPTER FOURTEEN

By six that evening, the Townhouse was absolutely buzzing. Half of Pennfleet seemed to have decided to pop in for a drink on the terrace. Mitch the barman was panicking that he might run out of ice, and sent a waiter down to the Spar shop for some spare bags for the freezer just in case. Everyone, it seemed, was in a holiday mood. The sun had brought out the best in them.

It had, however, brought out the worst in Claire. She'd had too much of it, on the deck of the boat and lying on the beach, and combined with unaccustomed daytime drinking she felt totally dehydrated. Two Nurofen and a bottle of water hadn't dented her headache. She should be smiling and buoyant for her customers. She should be congratulating herself. The Townhouse was at its best. This was when all her hard work came to fruition; when she was rewarded for the effort she put in behind the scenes. But tonight, instead of appreciating it, she was tense. Tense with waiting for the opportune moment. She had to do what she was going to do as soon as she could, but she had to time it right.

Perhaps it had been the coldness of the sea, but while she was under the water, she had seen everything so clearly. Trying to recapture her past was futile. There was absolutely no guarantee that she would find happiness with Nick, and it would

282

certainly cause distress to a lot of people. Staying with Luca was the right thing to do, and she had to make that clear to Nick as soon as she possibly could.

*　　*　　*

Laura was sitting at a table on the terrace, reading Stieg Larsson and nursing a Sea Urchin. The barman had talked her into it. It was his special cocktail for the bank holiday weekend, and he had wanted a guinea pig, so she had agreed. She was sipping it cautiously—she was a white wine girl usually—but she was enjoying the slightly heady sensation it gave her. It stopped her worrying about Dan. She was back earlier than expected, after all. She didn't want to phone him to find out where he was. She didn't want to seem needy. She'd sent him a text saying *Having a drink on the terrace. See you soon xx* but had heard nothing back. Every time someone wandered over to the railings to look at the view, she looked up to see if it was him. But it was gone six o'clock and still no sign.

And then suddenly he was there, strolling across the deck with a beer in his hand and a smile on his face.

She jumped up to hug him.

'How did it go?' he asked, dropping a kiss on to the top of her head.

She was going to play it down. She was just going to tell him the truth, that she'd got the wrong man, then ask him what he'd been up to. She'd wasted enough of Dan's time going on about it. He must have had a basinful of her banging on about her unknown father.

'It wasn't him. I got the wrong end of the stick totally.'

She just about managed a wobbly smile, but as soon as the words were out of her mouth, the emotion of the afternoon hit her and she burst into tears.

'Hey. Hey, it's okay . . .'

Dan pulled her to him and hugged her, soothing her as if she was a child. Laura was furious with herself. She'd meant to be so calm and mature about it. She'd meant to laugh it off, pick up her cocktail with a careless shrug, move on. And now everyone on the terrace was staring.

She didn't want to provide the early-evening entertainment. She brushed away her tears with a shaky laugh.

'I'm really sorry. I didn't mean to do that.'

'It's okay. It's cool.'

They sat back down at the wooden table she'd commandeered. Laura gulped some of her cocktail.

'What's in that?'

'Um . . . Campari, vodka, some blue liqueur thing, lime juice, wild hibiscus—it's called a Sea Urchin.'

'You be careful.' Dan looked at it askance. 'So come on—what happened?'

'Oh, it doesn't matter. You don't want to hear about it. It was just . . . embarrassing.'

'No, come on. Tell me. I want to know.'

And so, with reluctance, she told him. She found herself crying again when she got to the bit where Tony put her straight, but she was able to laugh at the same time.

'Oh God, I'm sorry. But I didn't realise how important it was to me. I felt as if I was going to

284

discover the missing piece of the jigsaw at last. Find the person who gave me all the bits of me that aren't Mum. But I'm no closer to knowing.' She wiped her tears away. 'It never used to bother me. But . . .' She was going to tell him. She was actually going to tell him. The Sea Urchin had loosened her tongue with its syrupy potency. 'Ever since I met you, I've felt the need to know exactly who I am. Because you're the first person who's ever really made me think about the future.' She looked down at her lap, her cheeks flaming. 'Babies, I mean. And where they come from. And where I came from. Sorry. That's too much information. Just tell me to shut up.'

She shut her eyes. She didn't open them, because for all she knew Dan would have done a runner. Men did, didn't they, if you started babbling about that sort of thing? She'd blown it. She'd totally blown it. She didn't have a father, and she wouldn't have a boyfriend now either. Six months, that was how long they'd been together. Not nearly long enough to start that kind of conversation . . .

She felt a hand on her shoulder. She opened her eyes and looked straight into his, their velvet greyness softer than ever.

'That's a lovely thing to say,' he told her. 'But you know—you don't have to worry. You're you. You're not two halves made up of two other people. You're Laura. You're yourself. And . . . that's the person I love.'

'What?' Laura stared at him, wide-eyed.

He repeated his words slowly. 'You're the person I love.'

'Oh.'

They blinked at each other, both equally

surprised. Dan gave a wry grin.

'I had no idea I was going to say that.'

'Nor did I.' Laura laughed shakily.

'It's true, though.'

She took another gulp of her Sea Urchin. Her head really was swimming now. She gazed at him in awe. Dan, with his über-fit body under his Nirvana T-shirt, his kindness, his incredible talent, loved her, ever-so-slightly-neurotic and lacking-in-confidence Laura, who had grown up in the shadow of her mother.

'You know what we should do now?' He gave her a cheeky grin and put down his beer. 'Let's forget this five-star nonsense. I mean, it looks great and all, but what I really fancy is fish and chips.'

*   *   *

At last Claire saw her chance. Luca was in the kitchen. The stags were gathering in the bar. She could see Gus chatting to Mitch, no doubt about the mysterious alchemy of the mixicologist—Mitch was shaking up his latest concoction, something lethal called a Sea Urchin. For a moment, she smiled. Mitch loved an opportunity to experiment with anything other than the predictable gin and tonics the typical Pennfleet visitor seemed to favour. He had a captive and appreciative audience in Gus.

Then she remembered the task in hand and the smile faded on her lips. This was it. This was her only chance.

She ran up the stairs as quickly as she could. Outside Nick's door she paused for a moment, remembering standing here less than twenty-four hours ago. She couldn't think about it. She knocked.

'Come in.' The sound of his voice made her heart beat a little faster. Nerves. It was nerves. She turned the handle and walked in.

He was standing by the window with his hands in his pockets. He was wearing jeans, and a pale-blue chambray shirt, untucked. The breeze from the open window brought a trace of Must de Cartier across the room, recently sprayed. It was still sharp. His skin hadn't yet warmed it; mellowed it, but the scent was so familiar. Claire remembered finding his jumper in her bedroom, just after they split. She'd borrowed it to walk home in one evening. The smell had made her cry. *Don't look back*, she reminded herself. *Look forward*.

'Hi.' She was as businesslike as possible. 'I just came to say . . . I hope you have a great evening tonight. Luca's put on a really special menu for you. And if there's anything you want—'

'Claire.' Nick cut straight across her as soon as he realised who it was. He walked towards her, his eyes bright with expectation. 'There's only one thing I want. You know that.'

'Yes. Well. About that too. Um . . .' She fixed a bright smile on to her face. 'I know we had a bit of a moment yesterday. I think we got slightly carried away. But as far as I'm concerned, it didn't happen.'

Nick stared at her.

'A bit of a moment?' He repeated her words back to her.

'Yeah. Just for old times' sake. It didn't actually mean anything.' Claire said it as if she did that kind of thing all the time.

'How can you say that?'

'Look, it was lovely and everything, and amazing

287

to see you, and great to . . . bury the hatchet after all this time . . .' Why couldn't he get the message? This was excruciating.

'Bury the hatchet?' Nick echoed her again. 'Is that what you call it? Claire, it was momentous. It was . . . the most important thing that's ever happened to me.'

'No,' said Claire. She had to be firm. 'No, it wasn't. You're investing too much into it. It was a quick bonk between two people who once meant a lot to each other.'

He looked at her in disbelief.

'But you still do. Mean a lot.'

'No, Nick. I'm a different person now. There can't be anything between us. You're getting married, and so am I. To the people who love who we are now. And that's the way it's got to be.'

'Is it?' His eyes bored into her. 'There's no law that says you have to marry the person you are engaged to. People break off their engagements all the time. And everyone survives. We could walk out of here, you and me. Together. Luca and Sophie would survive.'

Claire flinched at the sound of their names.

'Please. Don't make this difficult.' She tried to be brisk. 'You should be downstairs. Your friends are waiting. And I need to get back to work.'

Nick folded his arms. She wasn't going to fob him off that easily, she realised.

'Is it because I can't offer you all this?' he asked. 'Is it because I can't give you a five-star hotel and a white yacht and—'

'No!' cried Claire. 'You know me better than that.'

'Yes. I do. And I know this isn't the real you.

288

You're playing a part. That smarmy, jumped-up playboy isn't the man for you.'

'There's no need to bring Luca into this.' Claire's tone was harsh, but she had no choice. 'Please. I was hoping we could part friends. Unlike last time. You could have found me if you'd really wanted to, all those years ago.' She cringed as soon as the words left her mouth. It was a mistake, flinging that accusation at him. It made it seem as if she still cared.

'Your father made it very clear you didn't want to be found.'

She put up a hand.

'I don't want to rake it all up. Let's just move on, shall we?'

There was a silence that seemed to go on for ever. The two of them stood in the stillness of the room. From outside they could hear the excited chatter and babble of people enjoying themselves. It seemed like another world.

Finally Nick held out his hand.

'Fine,' he said. 'It was good to catch up with you, Claire. And I wish you every happiness in your new life.'

His tone was entirely neutral. Neither of them smiled as she took his hand and shook it.

'Me too,' she echoed. 'Every happiness . . .'

And she turned and left the room.

*　　　*　　　*

Dan and Laura sat on the harbour wall, scoffing scalding-hot chips and watching the last of the boats coming in for the evening.

'I want to show you something tomorrow,' said

Dan, squirting another sachet of ketchup over his chips. Laura had never met anyone who ate so much ketchup. Or anybody who ate so much and managed to stay so skinny.

'What?'

'Surprise,' he said with his mouth full.

'Something you found today?'

'Maybe.'

'Seals?' There were supposed to be seals further down the coast.

He shook his head, smiling.

'Puffins?'

'I'm not telling!'

She nudged him. 'Spoilsport.'

'You'll just have to wait and see.'

Laura frowned, wondering what on earth it could be.

Dan crumpled up his chip wrapper.

'Do you want to finish mine?' she asked. 'I'm stuffed.'

He took them off her and devoured them while she looked out to sea.

'It's perfect,' she sighed, as the fiery orange blob of the sun inched its way downwards.

'Perfect,' he agreed. 'I always forget how nice it is to get out of London.'

They both sat in silence, watching the light bounce off the water, a gentle breeze dancing round them. Laura felt calm. She didn't need to know who her father was. Of course she didn't. She had Dan. She slid her arm round his waist and rested her head on his shoulder. She loved him, she realised, with his down-to-earth attitude. He didn't need to impress anyone. He knew what he wanted. And that was why she felt so safe. She could trust him. She knew where she was with him. He didn't play games.

He picked up the last chip and smiled down at her.

'Last one?'

She opened her mouth and he fed it to her.

Dan was all she needed in the world.

*   *   *

Colin was sitting at the most discreet table in the dining room, waiting for Alison to arrive.

He couldn't for the life of him figure out the best way to have this conversation. Was it fair to drop his bombshell on her in public? Alison was a calm and measured woman, not likely to become hysterical, or slap him, or tip a jug of water over his head, but he was very aware that the dining room was going to be full of people. He couldn't talk to her in the privacy of his room, because Chelsey was there. He'd given her room service, and she seemed happy enough to be left while he went down to dinner. He swore this would be the last time she was fobbed off and left to fend for herself, but this was important. Nor could he leave the hotel. So the dining room it would have to be.

He clutched a tumbler of Laphroaig, his favourite malt whisky, in his right hand. He took a swig, enjoying its medicinal smokiness. And he definitely needed a slug for courage. Who knew what the forthcoming conversation would bring? By the end of it, would he have gained a daughter but lost a wife?

And then suddenly she was there, walking towards him with an uncertain smile. She was wearing a loose pink linen dress and ballet pumps, her dark-blonde hair blow-dried into a slightly tousled bob. Round her neck was the gold necklace he had given her for her last birthday. She looked . . . perfect. A confident woman in her prime who knew how to dress. He thought she had never looked better.

As he stood up to greet her, she leant in for a kiss and he smelled her perfume: Beautiful, by Estée Lauder. Father Christmas put a bottle in her stocking every year. It was so familiar. It made him afraid; afraid of everything he might be about to lose. But he had no choice.

'This is a lovely place,' she remarked, sitting down on the chair opposite him. 'You'd better tell me what you're doing here. I can't see any sign of a conference of any sort.'

She meant business, he could see that. With a wife's instinct, she knew she wasn't going to like the reason she'd been summoned here.

'Let's get you a drink.' Colin signalled to the waiter, who hurried over. 'A Bombay Sapphire with slimline tonic and a slice of lime, please.'

'Had we better make it a double?' Alison's tone was light, but Colin wasn't fooled. He was, however, comforted by her poise. She knew how to carry herself, did Alison. He felt a burst of pride, followed by another shard of fear. What he was about to tell her was either going to strengthen their marriage, or destroy it altogether.

But then he reminded himself she hadn't always been like this. There had been a time when she had pushed him away, when there had been nothing he could do for her, even though he had tried everything in the world he could think of to help.

Which was exactly why they were here now.

*   *   *

Claire focused on the paintings as she walked down the stairs. She might swap that seascape for the picture of the heron, she thought. She liked to move the paintings round every now and again, to refresh the walls. She didn't want returning visitors to get bored.

On the first-floor landing she bumped into Angelica.

'Oh, there you are! I've had someone on the phone about a booking for next week. They specifically wanted a room overlooking the harbour, so I swapped them with the person booked into Room Four, because they didn't specify.'

Claire nodded. She couldn't trust herself to speak.

Angelica peered at her.

'Claire? What's the matter?'

Claire shook her head to indicate nothing, but her face was crumpled with the effort of trying not to cry.

'Hey.' Angelica went to put her arms round her. Claire raised her hands to stop her.

'I'm fine,' she insisted. 'I'll be all right in a minute.'

It was obvious she wasn't. Her eyes were brimming with tears; her chin was wobbling. She was heading for a meltdown. Angelica looked round. No one should witness this. Not one of the guests; especially not any of the staff. She steered Claire towards the linen cupboard. It was huge, big enough for both of them. She pulled open the door and dragged her inside.

'It's okay. No one can see you in here.'

Claire fell against her and proceeded to cry her heart out. Angelica held her, feeling her whole body shudder. She stroked her gently, shushing her.

'Come on,' she said. 'We should take you to your room. You can't cry like this here.'

This seemed to alert Claire to the inappropriateness of the situation.

'I'll be fine. I'll be *fine*. Sorry.' She frantically brushed her tears away.

Angelica looked at her.

'Is it because of . . .?' She raised her eyes upstairs, to indicate Nick.

Claire gave a mixture of a nod and a shrug.

'If you really love him, you should follow your heart,' Angelica told her.

'How can I?' Claire demanded. 'There's Luca. And the hotel. And the bloody London thing. And anyway, he's getting married.' Fresh tears popped from her eyes, like bubbles from a bottle of Fairy Liquid. 'Oh God . . .' She pressed the heels of her hands under her eyes. 'I never cry. What's the matter with me?' She tried to laugh.

Angelica chewed her lip. It was plain that Claire was still besotted with her childhood sweetheart, but she obviously thought she couldn't go there. What if she knew the truth about Luca, though? Would that change how she felt? Should Angelica tell her about his lingering hands, the meaningful glances, the innuendo? She knew enough about men to know that if she'd given him half a chance, Luca would have taken things further. All the way . . .

Of course, she didn't have actual proof of

anything. Instinct was hardly concrete evidence. And it wasn't her place to interfere in Claire's life.

Besides, if she blew the whistle on Luca, it would get back to him, and she would probably be out of a job. And then she would have no chance of a future with him.

Not that she wanted a future with him, she reminded herself. Luca was bad news.

Oh God—why was life so difficult?

As Angelica wrestled with her conscience, Claire seemed to pull herself together. She straightened up, smoothed back her hair, patted under her eyes to make sure there was no trace of mascara.

'Sorry about that,' she told Angelica. 'I just had a bit of a wobble. Wrong time of the month. Too much pressure. You know how it is. Yes, that's fine about Room Four. Well done.'

And the next moment she had pulled open the door and vanished down the corridor. Angelica stared after her. That was no premenstrual wobble, she thought. That was a woman whose heart was broken. But if Claire didn't want to share with Angelica, there was nothing she could do to help.

She looked up as Nick came down the stairs, his face set and hard.

'Evening, sir,' said Angelica.

'Evening,' he managed, his accompanying smile as bleak as the nearby moors in the depths of winter.

She watched him as he made his way down the next staircase. No, she decided. She wasn't going to throw her penny's worth into the mix. She had enough problems of her own without stirring up trouble.

Colin couldn't delay the conversation any longer. They'd made polite chit-chat and ordered their drinks. Alison looked at him. There were two pink spots on her cheeks, the ones that always appeared the moment she drank alcohol, but otherwise she seemed calm.

'So?' she asked. 'What's this all about?'

Colin set his glass down.

'You know when we were going through that difficult patch? When Ryan was about five?'

Alison grimaced. 'Yes.' She paused. 'How could I forget? I totally lost the plot. It was awful.'

Colin nodded. 'I think in a funny kind of way I lost the plot too. It was a very stressful time.'

Alison took a sip of her drink. 'And . . .?'

'I . . . had an affair.'

There. That was it. He'd dropped his bombshell. But the walls hadn't come crashing down. Alison was sitting very still.

He supposed he'd better elaborate.

'I'm not going to sit here and defend it. It was a disgraceful thing to do. But at the time I felt very alone. Very unhappy. An opportunity presented itself, and for some reason it seemed the right thing to do. Of course, it wasn't . . .'

Alison stirred her drink with her swizzle stick.

'I suppose I'm not surprised,' she said quietly. 'I'm not happy about it, but I'm not surprised. Most men would have. I was a mess.'

For some reason, this made Colin feel worse than if she had reacted badly. To hear that he was no better than most men, when he had always prided himself on being the perfect husband and father, cut deep.

'Anyway,' she went on, 'that was then. Almost a lifetime ago. What's it got to do with now?'

She looked straight at him across the table. Alison was no fool. She knew there was more; that he hadn't just lured her down here to get his infidelity off his chest.

Colin steeled himself. He needn't think that her initial acceptance meant he was going to get an easy ride.

'You know I love you,' he told her. 'The affair was . . . a blip. I came to my senses and ended it, and it made me realise how much you mean to me.'

Alison raised her eyebrows. Colin ploughed on.

'By then you were . . . on the road to recovery, and things seemed to sort themselves out. You've made me very happy, Alison. I'm proud of our marriage. And our kids. And everything we've achieved.'

'But?' Her smile was only a half-smile. 'I'm guessing there is a but?'

Colin nodded. His guts were turning to water. This was the most difficult thing he had ever had to do in his life. For a moment he regretted choosing the restaurant for his confession, but he'd hoped it meant Alison wouldn't overreact. She wasn't one to cause a scene in public.

He chose the least emotive and most succinct words he could.

'There's a child.'

Alison recoiled.

'What?' Her voice was suddenly shrill. The next table looked over. She lowered her voice. She hated scenes, and unwanted attention. 'What do you mean—a child?'

'My . . .' What word could he use? Mistress? Lover? 'The woman I had the affair with became pregnant. She had a daughter.'

'A daughter?'

'Yes.' Colin glanced down at his plate. He felt as low as it was possible to feel. 'I'm sorry.'

Alison put her hands to her head and stared at the table. He couldn't see her expression, until she signalled to the waiter to bring her another drink, then looked at him. Her face was deadpan.

'I suppose the woman's turned up out of the blue, demanding money?'

'Not exactly.' He had to come clean. He had to tell her everything. It was only fair, given what he was going to ask. 'I've always . . . er . . . honoured my responsibility.'

'What do you mean?'

'I've been giving her money.'

Alison sat back in her chair. 'So . . . for all this time, without me knowing, you've been paying for your . . . your . . .'

She floundered for the right word. Colin put a hand on hers.

'Yes. I've been paying maintenance. And I see her once a year.'

Alison seemed to deflate before him, as if her bones had been pulled out of her like blocks from a Jenga tower.

'And the mother?'

'Yes. She comes too. But there's no . . . there's nothing between us.'

'Am I really supposed to believe that?'

'Alison, I'm being a hundred per cent honest with you here.'

'After years of sneaking off behind my back?'

298

He could hardly bear the look of hurt in her eyes.

'It wasn't something I wanted to happen.'

She looked away from him. She seemed baffled, a deep crease between her eyebrows.

'Why are you telling me all this now?'

He was silent for a moment. He wondered about bottling it altogether. Alison didn't need to know the full story. He could talk to Karen. More money would probably help. Karen was the sort of woman who saw things differently with a cheque in her hand.

But then he thought about the little girl upstairs. The fantastic day they'd had together. Simple pleasures, but they had been such huge ones to Chelsey. He didn't want to send her back to a life of fast food and a latch key.

He owed it to her. None of this was her fault.

'Her mother's . . . not well. She can't cope. Basically, she's done a runner and left me with Chelsey.'

'Chelsey.' Alison spoke the name with flat distaste. 'Is that what she's called? Did you choose the name together, you and . . .' She trailed off. 'You and . . . what is her name?'

'Karen.'

'Karen.' She spat the name out like an unwanted mouthful of food.

Colin couldn't read Alison's face. It was flat; expressionless. Her eyes seemed dead. At least she hadn't thrown her drink over him. At least she hadn't screamed at him. He had to take advantage of her momentary calm to limit the damage.

'The thing is, Alison, none of this is Chelsey's fault, and she needs me. She needs a good home. She needs someone who cares about her. She needs

. . . stability.'

'By which you mean her mother is unstable?'

'Yes. Yes, I think she is. I think she's probably depressed.'

Alison bit her lip. 'Like I was, all those years ago? Do you remember? When it was all I could do to get up and face the day, because I just wanted to fall into a black hole. Do you know how many times I thought about swallowing a bottle of tablets? Or driving into a brick wall?'

'Alison—'

'But I didn't, and you know why? The one thing that kept me going was you. You were so kind and caring and loving and supportive. You got me through it. But all the time—'

She broke off as the waiter approached with their drinks and put them down.

'Are you ready for me to take your order?

'Not yet,' Colin snapped. He never snapped at waiters usually.

The waiter melted away.

Alison looked up and took her fresh gin and tonic. She seemed to have composed herself.

'Look,' said Colin, 'we could rake it all up. We could spend all night throwing recriminations at each other. It wasn't easy for me either. And I made a mistake. A big mistake. But I've never been unfaithful to you since.'

'How do I know that?' She was becoming bitter now.

'You have to trust me.'

She stared right at him. He could imagine all the questions whirling round in her brain. Questions he had no idea how to answer for the best. The problem was, he had to make some sort of decision.

'Alison, I need to decide what to do. Chelsey's upstairs—'

'What?' Alison slammed her glass down. 'My God, Colin. How much more can you humiliate me?' Her voice was low as she spoke, but the venom in it was undeniable. 'You drag me down here to air your dirty linen in a full bloody restaurant—' Colin flinched; Alison rarely swore '—and then you tell me the child's upstairs? Do you think that's fair on me, to put me under that kind of pressure?'

'Of course I don't!' Colin was desperate to keep the nightmare under control. 'But I didn't have any choice. I had to tell you what was going on. I couldn't keep it a secret any longer. I've got to decide what to do with Chelsey, because her mother has made it clear that it's my turn.' He could feel the sweat breaking out under his arms.

Alison's tone was hostile. 'I hope you're not expecting me to welcome some little cuckoo into the nest?'

'She's not a cuckoo,' said Colin. 'She's my daughter. And I know you're angry. Of course you are. You have every right to be.'

'What about Michelle and Ryan? What are they supposed to think? What are you going to tell them?'

'Michelle and Ryan have got their own lives now.' Colin was firm. 'And I think, given time, they'd understand.'

'Do you?' The puzzlement in Alison's eyes had cleared. She could see everything all too clearly. 'By making me the enemy, I suppose? Telling them their mother wasn't fit for purpose so you had to play away?'

'Absolutely not!'

Alison spread her hands. 'That's effectively what you told me. I was a wreck, so you had to turn to Karen.'

'I was wrong,' said Colin. 'I'm not denying that. But I can't change what's happened, Alison, and there's a little girl involved. A little girl who's had a pretty tough time.'

He stopped. Alison was staring down at the table, tears in her eyes.

'Oh God,' he said. 'I'm so sorry.'

She bent down and picked up her handbag.

'I can't do this here,' she told him. 'I'm going home. You do whatever you think is right. She's obviously your priority. I can't argue with that. As you've pointed out, it's not *her* fault.'

'Alison—don't go. At least have dinner. Let's talk it over.'

She shook her head.

'You've had time to think about this. Nearly twelve years. I've had all of twelve minutes.'

She stood up. Her chair scraped against the slate floor, setting Colin's teeth on edge.

'Will you phone me?' he asked.

'I don't know,' she replied. 'I honestly don't know.'

'I am sorry. This isn't easy for me.'

Pain flickered over her face.

'No,' she said. 'I don't suppose it is.'

And she turned and walked back through the dining room, her head held high.

Colin picked up his malt. What now? he wondered. What did this mean? Was Alison going to leave him? Or, more to the point, kick him out? Which meant, he supposed, that it would be him and Chelsey against the world. He'd have to find them somewhere to live as soon as possible, just the two of them. Where, he had no idea. Near her school? God, no. That would be near Karen.

Bloody hell, thought Colin. What a mess. And all because he'd been a spineless fool looking for some attention. He wouldn't make that mistake again in a hurry.

                    *   *   *

Nick tensed as Luca came over and stood at the head of the table that had been laid for the stags' dinner out on the terrace. The table looked stunning, and suitably masculine, with pony-skin tablemats, black linen napkins and a phalanx of wine glasses at each place. Instead of flowers there were three squat glass vases each containing a globe artichoke. Storm lanterns held fat pillar candles, which flickered as the evening light began to fade.

The stags sat three each side of the table, which was perpendicular to the deck railings so they could all take advantage of the view. The air was still warm, but a patio heater stood to attention, ready to be turned on as the temperature dropped.

Luca held a piece of paper in his hand. Nick noted how he commanded everyone's attention just by a mere flicker of a smile. He had an enviable silent authority, thought Nick, that way of asserting that he was the most important person in the room without having to do or say anything.

And he was beautiful. Not feminine in any way, far from it. But the way his features were put together would make even the most macho of men have doubts about their sexuality, if only for a moment. And Nick had seen the eyes of all the women on the terrace drawn to him. No matter how hard they tried to hide it from their dining partners, there was a hunger there. It wasn't just Luca's food that was making their mouths water.

Nick didn't need Claire to explain herself at all. Why would she choose him over Luca, who was blessed with an incredible talent as well as charisma and beauty? Although Nick could sense that he was trouble too. It radiated off him. A man like Luca needed constant attention, adoration and stimulation. You could feel his restless energy; his quest for the next thrill.

He hoped Luca wouldn't hurt Claire, but he supposed he would never know.

Luca began to speak, his eyes raking up and down the table.

'Welcome to all of you. This is our first official stag night here at the Townhouse. We've always steered away from them, for obvious reasons, but I'm hoping that after tonight we can prove that there is a place for a civilised but sybaritic celebration in anticipation of forthcoming nuptials . . .'

And here his gaze came to rest lightly on Nick.

'We've chosen the menu carefully. We know there's probably going to be drinking involved, so we wanted to make it heavy enough to soak up the worst of your excesses—' he grinned round '—but without sacrificing the light touch for which we've become known. So . . .'

He looked down at his piece of paper.

'Tonight we're starting with potted shrimps from Morecambe, which is one of the few things on the menu tonight that won't be local, although I can promise you that the butter most certainly is.

304

For the main course I had to resist the temptation to serve venison—' here he paused for a moment, waiting for the penny to drop, and there was a resulting appreciative laugh '—but it's not really the season, so I've done my take on porchetta—loin of pork slow-cooked with fennel and rosemary, and served with crunchy garlic potatoes and wilted greens. We're going to finish up with whisky steamed pudding, which sounds stodgy but which is actually as light as a feather, studded with plump, juicy sultanas and cherries and served with a dollop of Cornish clotted cream laced with—of course—whisky. And if you're not stuffed to the gills by then, we have a board of local cheeses with quince jelly and a glass of delicious Maury, a French red dessert wine that I think you'll appreciate.'

He gave a little bow to indicate that he'd finished. Everyone applauded.

'We're starting tonight with a Tim Adams Riesling—one of my personal favourites as an aperitif, which will also set the shrimps off to perfection. And before you get stuck in, I'd just like to propose a toast . . .'

He raised his glass, his eyes glittering as he looked straight down the table to Nick.

'I want to take the opportunity to say thank you for choosing us for your special evening, and to wish you the very best in your new life—if you'd like to bring your wife back here on your first anniversary, there will be a bottle of champagne chilling in the bedroom.'

This announcement was greeted with roars of approval.

'So with no further ado, please raise your glasses to Nick and . . .?'

He looked enquiringly at Nick.

'Sophie,' replied Nick, through gritted teeth.

Luca smiled. 'To Nick and Sophie.'

'Nick and Sophie,' chorused the table, as they knocked back their wine with fervour.

Nick sat with his smile frozen to his face. Fury raged through his veins. That toast had been totally stage-managed by Luca. It was practically a gauntlet. For a moment he thought of turning the table over, grabbing Luca by the throat and throwing him into the middle of it. He'd be a bloody potted shrimp by the time he'd finished with him.

Bastard.

But of course he didn't. Instead he sat there forcing the food down, almost choking on every mouthful. And he didn't get drunk. He pretended to, of course, by filling everyone else's glasses up but missing his own.

He needed to stay sober. He was getting out of here as soon as it was polite. Back home, back to the Mill House, back to Sophie. As soon as he had her in his arms again, everything would be all right.

*   *   *

Under the same stars, a few streets away, Tony woke with a gasp. The moon slid past his window and peered in. He lay there with his heart pounding: the worry, the rich food at dinner, the wine . . . He could barely breathe. What if he was having a heart attack? He tried to relax and calm himself, but the more he tried to do so, the worse he felt.

Especially as a nasty little thought had popped into his head while he was sleeping, and was now flashing like a neon sign. What if Laura went back to Marina and told her she'd met him? He could just picture the scene. 'You won't believe what I did at the weekend, Mum. I went to see your old art teacher. I thought he might be my dad.'

He told himself over and over again that of course she wouldn't. Laura had seemed keen to keep the whole episode a secret. It had been a clandestine operation from the start. Marina had no idea what she was up to, and he didn't *think* she was going to go running back to tell her.

But she might do. The frustration of not discovering her father's identity might get the better of her. She might corner Marina and try and force a confession out of her.

And then what? Oh dear God, then what? If Marina cracked and confessed, Laura would be straight back down to confront him, not quite so enamoured any more, no longer trusting him. And he would have to admit to not wanting to know her. The thought of it made him groan out loud, and beside him, Wendy stirred.

'You all right?' she murmured.

'Too much chocolate mousse and cheese,' he told her, squeezing her hand. 'I'll be fine.'

He saw her smile in the moonlight and drift back off to sleep.

He lay awake, turning his conundrum over and over in his mind until dawn broke and he finally fell, exhausted, into a restless slumber.

*　　　*　　　*

Colin knew that his chances of sleeping were nil.

After Alison had left, he went back up to find

Chelsey. Together they sat and watched *Casualty*, because it was her favourite programme, even though he didn't think it was entirely suitable. But he had the rest of his life to have those arguments with her, he supposed, and he looked away at the gory bits, amazed that she seemed to enjoy them so much. Then he tucked her into bed, and went to his own room and started working out his finances.

He had to face up to the probability that his marriage was over. The house would have to be sold. There was no need to keep it on now that Michelle and Ryan were no longer at home full time. Unless Alison wanted to stay in it, of course. He didn't want to force her out, though surely it would be too large for her on her own.

All these questions would have to be addressed.

In the meantime, his pen flew across the pages: addition, subtraction, division, percentages. It kept his mind off the emotion. The fact that tonight, a twenty-year marriage had effectively ended. His naïve dream of a happy ending for everyone was in tatters. So now it was up to him to divide the spoils.

He was, Colin decided, much better at numbers than people.

*   *   *

After Alison fled the Townhouse, she went to find her car in the car park.

As she sat in the driver's seat, she realised that there was no way she should drive. Her head felt swimmy—whether from the drink or the shock, she couldn't be sure, but she was definitely over the limit. She couldn't possibly risk a three-hour drive on the motorway. Yet it was a bank holiday weekend in one of the most popular seaside resorts in England. Where on earth was she going to find somewhere to stay?

She climbed wearily out of her car, grabbing her handbag, and started to walk. She tramped around the streets, her eyes searching for a 'Vacancies' sign, pulling the cardigan she had brought round her as the heat of the day vanished and the damp sea air closed in. She was just starting to think that perhaps, after nearly an hour of brisk walking, she had sobered up sufficiently to drive when she saw a sign proclaiming 'B&B Rooms 2nite!' outside an unprepossessing thirties semi. She held out little hope for the standards of an establishment that wasn't fully booked on a night like this, but by now she was exhausted.

Ten minutes later she was installed in the most depressing room she had ever been in. She supposed it matched her mood as she sat gingerly on the bed surveying her surroundings. There were flouncy floral curtains in a bruised pink and purple. A matching counterpane was folded back to show the pillows and sheets underneath, a sickly green brushed nylon. The wardrobe was dark and heavy; the dressing table white with ornate gilt knobs, two of them missing. There was a travel kettle, a brown mug, a small jar of Tesco value coffee and a carton of UHT milk.

Alison remembered the week she and Colin had spent in Koh Samui last New Year. The infinity pool, the freshly prepared tropical fruit, the crisp white linen. The heavenly massages. She had been so content. Michelle and Ryan had been doing their own thing. It was the first time they hadn't come on holiday with their parents, and Alison had thought this was the start of a new phase in their life. A phase when they could please themselves, after years of worrying about what the children wanted. Not that she had ever minded or begrudged them, but it had been bliss for the two of them.

All that time she had been oblivious to the horrible secret Colin had been hiding.

The room smelled of cheap, harsh cleaning agents and some noxious air freshener. Together with the gin she had drunk on an empty stomach, it made her feel sick. She was overcome by a wave of tiredness, but she wasn't going to get into the bed. She shuddered at the thought of who might have been in it previously. Instead she lay down on top of it and curled her legs up, clutching the frilly yellow cushion that sat on top of the pillows to her stomach. She heard a noise, then realised that it was her; that she was groaning with pain.

Not the pain of what Colin had just told her, but the realisation that it was all her fault.

Of course it was.

She remembered how she had pushed him away in those dark, dark days. How the very touch of his hand on her had made her want to scream. How her teeth had gritted in bed every time he rolled near her. She had felt as if she was made of cardboard: grey, flat and lifeless.

When she had finally surfaced from the fug, she had been so relieved that Colin was still there and hadn't run off. She had been grateful for his loyalty. She'd known what a nightmare she'd been to live with, because she'd had to live with herself; with the loathing and hatred that built up to such a pitch inside her that she sometimes punched herself in the stomach, or pinched folds of skin and twisted them hard, or scratched herself till she bled.

What was she going to do now? What were people going to say? Whatever happened, the truth would come out in the end. With a start, she wondered if perhaps people knew already. Had she been the last to find out about Chelsey? Was she a laughing stock?

There was a sour taste in her mouth. The drink had dried it out. She thought she might vomit, and she heaved twice, great dry retches that came to nothing. Sleep was going to be her only refuge. It was the refuge she had taken during her depression; the only escape she'd had from the self-hatred. She shut her eyes against the harsh yellowy light of the bedside lamp—she didn't want to turn it off—and waited for the sweet relief of oblivion.

*   *   *

The stags crawled up the stairs of the Townhouse not long after midnight, kidding each other about what lightweights they had become, but aware of their promise that their party would not be a rowdy one. By half past, sedated by the sea air and the delicious food and wine they had consumed, they were all asleep,

All, that is, except Nick, who waited for the sound of Gus's gentle snores before quietly packing his bag, then picking up his shoes in one hand and his keys in the other. He'd text Gus when he got home: ask him to send his apologies to the other guys. He could tell them the truth if he liked. Nick didn't care. He just had to get out of there. He'd already settled the bill, so he had a clear conscience. The young receptionist had seemed

311

concerned that he was leaving, but Nick didn't give her any opportunity for conversation.

The little town was eerily silent as he made his way to the car park, in total contrast to the hustle and bustle of the day. He could hear the waves slapping against the harbour wall, the clanking of the buoys, but that was all. He imagined smugglers creeping about under cover of darkness, as stealthy as he was now. As he found his car and started the engine, he worried he was going to wake the whole town up, it sounded so loud.

He put his foot down as he went up the hill that led out of Pennfleet. He was on his way, away from the Townhouse. Away from his past. Away from Claire.

Home to his future wife.

CHAPTER FIFTEEN

He was gone.

Claire could feel it as soon as she woke up. She had no sense of Nick being near her at all. The hotel felt empty, as did she. It was strange, how someone's aura could affect you so deeply. How you could develop an instinct for their presence.

Her suspicions were confirmed when she saw Nick's conspicuous absence at the breakfast table. The stags were all tucking into the Townhouse's infamous Sunday brunch—it was quite the place for both tourists and locals to come and laze off their hangovers, and had become something of an institution. The restaurant and terrace were heaving, and a huge table groaned with piles of ricotta pancakes, kedgeree, devilled kidneys and jugs of spicy Bloody Mary.

'Nick had to go,' Gus told her awkwardly. 'They were short-staffed for an event.'

Claire knew, even from her short time working at Melchior Barnes, that it was highly unlikely they didn't have someone else to call on in an emergency. Gerald certainly wouldn't expect his son to come back from his stag weekend to hump a few boxes of wine around.

Gus could barely look at her. He knew he'd been instrumental in forcing them apart. But then that was his role as best man, thought Claire ruefully. To make sure the groom got up the aisle whatever happened.

She just smiled. 'Enjoy the rest of the weekend,' she told him, and moved swiftly on to talk to the couple at the next table, who were regulars.

'Look,' she said to them, and showed off her engagement ring. She tried her best to revel in their delight and congratulations. No, she didn't know when the wedding was going to be exactly, and yes, of course she was thrilled.

She hoped Gus was watching; that he would be convinced by her performance. She was trying to convince herself as much as anyone.

It's okay, she told herself. You can cope.

And then Luca came out of the kitchen, and started talking to some of the customers. The sun was shining, the hotel was buzzing; they were fully booked for lunch: this was everything they had worked their fingers to the bone to achieve, against the odds.

He caught her eye across the crowded dining room and smiled, and she felt a little green shoot

313

of hope in her heart. They *were* a team, she and Luca. Of course they were. And they were going to go on to greater things. She had to put what had happened behind her and think about the future.

She looked across the room and smiled back.

*   *   *

Alison slept for a full ten hours. When she woke up, she was surprised to feel calm. And incredibly focused. It was extraordinary, how your subconscious could work while you were asleep. Untangle the worries of the world and lay them out for you so you could see clearly. She had been exhausted last night, and in shock from Colin's bombshell, but now she felt rested and relaxed.

She left the hideous bed and breakfast as soon as she had been to the loo, washed her face and rinsed out her mouth, then run a comb through her hair. She didn't think she had ever slept in her clothes in her life. She freshened her breath with a Polo mint, and resolved to go and find a shop to buy a toothbrush and toothpaste. She'd paid for her room the night before, so she didn't have to speak to anyone before leaving, thank goodness. She wasn't in the mood to waste her words. She was saving them for Colin.

Outside the day was glorious, the sun burning bright with an infectious charm. She made her way to the centre of the town and found a Spar, where she bought some toiletries and a fresh croissant. She took it down to the harbour and ate it, wishing she had bought two, remembering she had eaten nothing since lunchtime the day before. Then she nipped into the public loo and brushed her teeth,

314

touched up her make-up and squirted Beautiful on to her wrists.

She knew exactly what she had to do. All the self-loathing and doubt of the night before had evaporated. She wasn't going to let some manipulative, scheming lowlife ruin everything. She wasn't going to blame herself either. She was simply going to rise to the occasion. The problem, after all, was not going to go away.

She knew she had to be strong and take control. That she would face criticism, and raised eyebrows. That there would be gossip; some idle, some malicious. It was going to be tough. She breathed in the salty tang of the air as it swept in from the sea. It invigorated her. She shook back her hair, smoothed down her dress and started walking briskly back towards the Townhouse.

*   *   *

Laura could barely keep up with Dan as he strode up one of the steep, narrow streets that typified Pennfleet. Stone cottages advertising holiday lets sat cheek by jowl with antique shops and tiny cafés. A cat stared out balefully from a window, while a small boy rolled down the centre of the street on a scooter, his nerves apparently made of steel.

Her calves were burning. She rarely encountered a hill in her part of London.

'Hey,' she panted. 'Wait for me.'

Dan turned and grinned. 'Lightweight.'

'Where are we going, anyway? Is it much further?'

'Nope,' he said. 'In fact, here we are.'

He stopped outside a whitewashed cottage.

Stone steps led up to the front door. The railings were peeling and the paintwork was a faded blue.

Dan produced a key from his pocket.

'You have no idea what I had to do to get this. The estate agent said it was more than her job was worth to let me have it, but I persuaded her.'

'Estate agent?' Laura ran her eye over the front of the building, then noticed the For Sale sign in one of the upstairs windows. 'Dan? What's going on?'

He ran up the steps. 'Come on. I want to show you.'

At the top, he unlocked the door and pushed it open. There was a strong smell of damp, and piles of unopened mail lay on the threadbare carpet.

'Is this what you were up to yesterday? Looking at houses?' Laura surveyed the interior doubtfully. There seemed to be just one large room downstairs, with a kitchen at the back and a staircase leading up to the first floor.

Dan stood in the middle of the room looking pleased with himself.

'I walked past it and it . . . spoke to me,' he told her.

'Spoke to you?'

He looked a bit sheepish. 'You know . . . how things do. There was just something about it. I went to the agent and got them to show it to me. It's been on the market a while.' He paused, as Laura looked around her. 'What do you think?'

'It's tiny. And poky. And it smells.'

'Just imagine it with all those rank units ripped out. And the wallpaper stripped off. And everything painted white.' He gesticulated around him. 'I bet there's wooden floorboards underneath that carpet.'

Laura still looked doubtful. 'You've really thought about this.'

Dan grinned.

'Come on. You haven't seen the best bit.'

He led her up the stairs. There was a tiny landing with two doors, one of which led to an outdated bathroom. He pushed open the other one. Inside, the room was flooded with a glorious light from a large picture window.

Laura walked over to it. The view was astonishing. She could see right over the pointy grey roofs of Pennfleet below her and straight out to an endless sea. She caught her breath in delight.

'Isn't it beautiful?' He stood behind her and wrapped his arms around her.

'Wow.' She looked up at him. 'But why are we even looking at it?'

'Do you want to hear my idea?'

'Go on.'

'We're both paying extortionate rents on flats in London. We see each other nearly every day. It would make total sense for one of us to move in with the other.'

'Yes . . . I can see your logic.' Laura didn't admit, at this point, that she had thought as much before. She probably spent at least fifty pounds a week on taxis, travelling backwards and forwards between Dan's flat and her own.

'And with the money we save on rent, we could take out a mortgage on this. I've got quite a bit put aside for a deposit—I was going to get somewhere in town. But if we bought this, we'd have somewhere to escape to at the weekends, plus we could rent it out when we weren't using it, which would help with the repayments.'

He put his hands on her shoulders and twizzled her round. 'What do you think?'

Laura didn't speak for a full ten seconds.

'I think . . . tongue-and-groove cabinets in the kitchen, painted pale blue, would go a long way to making it . . . liveable.' She looked up at him.

A big smile split his face. Her heart hammered. What on earth was she agreeing to? She gazed back out of the window in disbelief, trying to take in what this all meant. A fat seagull landed on the roof in front of her.

'I didn't know you felt like this,' she said. 'Enough to make such a big commitment.'

'Neither did I,' said Dan. 'Not till yesterday. But after you came back from your . . . your not-dad's, I realised how much I wanted to make things right for you. And how much you meant to me, I guess . . .'

He stopped, a bit embarrassed by his outpouring, and looked out of the window at the seagull. After a moment, he spoke again.

'I'll put in an offer then, shall I?'

*   *   *

Tony was supposedly on the croissant and newspaper run. Which he estimated should give him at least half an hour, because he could pretend to have stopped for a chat with someone, or even been sucked into having a coffee. Of course, he would also have to factor in time to actually buy croissants and the *Sunday Times*, otherwise Wendy would think it strange if he came home empty-handed.

He wasn't wearing the most attractive outfit for

318

his mission either, he observed, but Wendy would also have thought it strange if he had gone out looking groomed and suave instead of in his usual scruffy T-shirt and shorts.

As he walked in through the front door of the Townhouse, the delicious smell of fresh coffee hit him. Their Sunday brunches had become something of a fixture in Pennfleet. With chagrin, he thought how much Wendy would enjoy coming here. He'd bring her here next week, perhaps.

Guilt, he thought. Was he now set fair for endless atonement?

He hurried over to the reception. He knew the receptionist slightly. Angelina? Angelica—that was it. Some movie star name, anyway. Her mum had cleaned for them once, in the days when they'd had more cash going spare. Wendy had been convinced she was stealing, so they had tactfully let her go, claiming poverty, which wasn't so far from the truth.

He'd have to be careful. He didn't want Angelica overhearing anything and spreading it around town. It didn't take long for rumours to spread like wildfire in Pennfleet, though gossip tended to flourish more in the winter, when the locals had time on their hands.

He'd brought his cover story. The painting that Laura had done the day before, carefully rolled up.

'Hi. I wondered if I could speak to Laura Starling? I've got a painting she did with me yesterday. It's dry now—I thought she might like to take it home with her.'

Angelica turned to look at the keys behind her.

'I'm sorry. I'm afraid they've gone out. I don't know when they'll be back.'

'Oh.' Tony's face clouded. What was he supposed to do now? 'Well, thanks anyway.'

Angelica held out her hand. 'Do you want me to take it for you? I can have it put in the room.'

No. That would get rid of his alibi.

'No. It's fine, thanks.'

He turned to go. He had Laura's mobile number. He could ring her, he supposed. But it would be a very difficult conversation to have on the phone.

But if he didn't contact her and put his mind at rest . . . His stomach roiled with the uncertainty. How had he got himself into this predicament?

And then he saw her. She was coming in through the front door, arm in arm with a tall guy who must be her boyfriend. They looked totally loved up, and he remembered with a pang just how that felt. Not that he didn't love Wendy, but there was nothing like young love.

Passion.

'Laura.' He stepped into her path, and she looked up in surprise. 'I brought your painting for you. In case you wanted to keep it.'

'Oh.' She looked nonplussed. 'Thank you. I didn't think it was worth saving, really.'

There was an awkward silence. Tony couldn't be sure how much she had told her boyfriend, so he had to be careful.

'And . . . there's something I need to talk to you about. What we were discussing yesterday?'

Her eyes were wide as she looked at him. 'You've remembered something?'

He nodded. She turned to Dan.

'Do you mind? We won't be long.'

Dan spread his hands. 'No problem. I'll drop the key back in to the estate agent's. They're open until midday.'

She turned back to Tony.

'Let's go on to the terrace.'

As they made their way outside, Tony glanced over his shoulder to see if Angelica had noticed anything, but of course she hadn't. Why would she? It was the last thing anyone in their right mind would imagine, that Tony Weston was about to claim paternity of one of the hotel's guests.

*   *   *

Chelsey had looked suspiciously at the kedgeree and the kidneys when she and Colin came down for breakfast, so they decided to go for the full English.

'If we have a big breakfast,' he told her, 'we won't need much for lunch.'

Then he remembered, from experience, that that rule never worked on holiday. Michelle and Ryan had always been ravenous by midday even if they went for the full works. But what the hell?

'Can we go to the beach again?' asked Chelsey.

'Of course.'

She frowned. 'Is Mum actually coming back? Or are you taking me home?'

'Well,' said Colin. 'I'm not quite sure yet. There's a few things we need to sort out.'

A breeze came in through the open French windows and ruffled Chelsey's hair.

'I tell you what,' he went on, 'how would you like to stay here for a bit?'

'Oh yeah!' Chelsey beamed. 'I'd love it.'

Colin smiled. Why not? Where else would he go? The factory and the bakeries would run themselves—he was on the end of a phone if they

321

needed him. And it wouldn't matter if Chelsey missed a few days of school.

He looked up at the waiter, about to ask for his coffee to be topped up.

But it wasn't a waiter. It was Alison.

She seemed very calm. She looked at Chelsey, gave her the briefest of smiles.

'I need a little word with your daddy,' she said.

Colin put down his coffee, pulled a five-pound note out of his pocket and handed it to Chelsey.

'Sweetheart, go along to the shop where we got the DVDs, would you?' he asked. 'And buy me a newspaper. Get yourself a magazine as well, if you like.'

'Can I have some sweets?'

'No.' He was going to start as he meant to go on. 'You've just finished breakfast, and we don't want to spoil your lunch.'

'Okay.'

She didn't protest, and he was proud of her for it. She was far more sweet-natured and biddable than her mother.

As soon as Chelsey had left the dining room, Alison slid into the chair next to hers.

'Coffee?' he asked.

'Please.'

He signalled to the waiter to bring another cup.

'I'm glad you came back,' he told Alison. 'I was worried.'

'I ended up in a real dump. I'd had too much to drink to drive home.'

'That's what I thought.' He reached out his hand to touch hers. She looked strained, with mauve shadows under her eyes, and he felt the guilt tighten his chest yet again. 'I'm sorry. You know that, don't you?'

'I'm sure you are.'

'I never meant to hurt you.'

'No. No, of course not. But you never meant to get caught out either, I don't suppose.'

'I was stupid.'

She didn't contradict him. Colin picked up a sugar lump and lobbed it into his coffee.

'The thing is,' she said, 'it's not as if we can make Chelsey disappear, can we? She's here on this earth whether we like it or not. So we've got to find a way out of this that causes the least damage to everyone.'

'Right.' Colin was surprised. He'd expected an emotional diatribe.

'I've thought about it,' she told him, 'and I don't see why my whole life should fall apart because of this. Yes, I've got every right to throw you out and take you to the cleaners. That's what all my friends would tell me to do. But it would mean sacrificing the home I love, and my social life, and our family life. I don't want to argue over who gets the silver. I don't want to be the divorcee who no one invites for dinner. I don't want the kids to be in a dilemma about who they spend Christmas with. I've seen too many people living that life and I know it's not for me.'

'So . . . what are you saying?'

The waiter arrived with her cup. Alison smiled her thanks. Colin filled it from the cafetière, then passed her the milk.

'Chelsey should come and live with us. And we should be totally upfront about her background. I can't live with gossip and speculation either. It's always worse than the truth, so we'll tell the truth.'

'You mean—tell everyone that I had an affair?'

Alison met his eyes with a steady gaze.

'Yes. People will make that assumption anyway.' She shrugged. 'So we don't give them the pleasure of spreading rumours.'

Colin sat back in his chair, rather shell-shocked by Alison's businesslike demeanour.

'Wow.' He couldn't hide his relief. 'Are you sure? I mean . . . it's a pretty big thing, to expect you to take her on.'

'What's the alternative? She's your responsibility, Colin. Either I take her on or I lose you.'

Colin stirred his coffee again. Shit, he thought. He was going to cry.

'I can't tell you how grateful I am.'

'You needn't think you've got away with it totally.' Alison's tone was dry. 'I don't suppose I'm going to be sweetness and light. I'm going to find it tough. I expect there'll be days when I want to kill you for what you've done.' Her fingers tightened around her coffee cup, her knuckles white. Maybe she wasn't as calm and in control as she looked. 'And there's one condition.'

'Yes?'

'I never want to meet the mother. I never want to come face to face with her. That would be a humiliation too far.'

Colin shuddered at the thought.

'Of course not,' he promised. 'You are a far, far better person than I am. Or ever will be.'

'I wasn't once,' she replied. 'I know that. I know I'm partly to blame for this.'

'No. What I did was unforgivable. And inexcusable.'

Alison shrugged. 'We're all human.'

Yes, thought Colin. He'd been human all right.

*   *   *

On the terrace, Tony waited for the waiter to bring him and Laura a Bloody Mary each before he began his confession. He took a gulp, relishing the bite of the horseradish and the kick of the vodka.

Laura sipped hers more cautiously. She was wary, wondering what was to come.

Tony put down his glass and leant forward. Their table was right by the water, away from other customers, but he didn't want to take any risks. He spoke in a low voice.

'Obviously I don't know if I am your father. Not for sure. But I want you to know . . . I did have an affair with your mother.'

She looked at him with mistrust.

'So you lied to me?'

'I panicked,' he defended himself. 'It's pretty momentous, when someone appears out of the blue saying they might be your daughter.'

'I know. I realise that. But you totally denied it. You said you barely remembered her!' Her voice was high with indignation.

'Can I explain?' Tony wanted to keep things calm. 'Please? Just listen.'

Laura put her head in one hand, then nodded her acquiescence. Tony looked out across the water for a moment. It was the same scene he saw from his own living room, but from a different perspective. From here, everything was brighter, sharper, less subtle.

'We fell in love, your mother and I,' he told Laura. 'It was very wrong, but there's not much you

325

can do when it happens. When it hits you like an express train. We were powerless.'

'You were married.' Her tone was accusing. 'She was a *pupil*.'

'I know.' Tony sighed. 'But neither of those things could stop us. It was a very strange and wonderful time. Borrowed time. We both knew it couldn't last. It was incredibly intense. Don't worry—' he managed a smile as he saw the expression on Laura's face '—I'm not going to go into details.'

'Please don't,' she said.

'It finally came to an end when my wife became pregnant. Wendy.' He winced. Saying Wendy's name out loud brought her into the frame, and he was desperate to keep her out. 'Wendy was expecting a baby, and so I finished the relationship. It was the right thing to do.'

'You told me you were infertile,' Laura remembered. 'That's a wicked lie.'

Bloody hell. The young could be so judgemental. He sighed. 'I know.'

Laura was frowning, working things out.

'So you mean your wife was pregnant? And then my mum must have found out she was pregnant with me?'

'I guess so.'

'So . . . do I have a brother? Or a sister?' She seemed very excited by this prospect. 'It would only be a half, but—'

'No.' This was the difficult bit. The bit he didn't really want to discuss, but the bit that was key to what happened next. 'Our baby died.'

She stared at him for a moment.

'Oh my God.' There was genuine remorse in her

326

voice. 'Oh my God—I'm so sorry.'

'So you see, the one innocent person in all of this was Wendy. She had no idea what went on. And then . . . to lose her firstborn child. It was terrible, Laura.'

'Didn't you have another?'

'No. She couldn't. Wendy couldn't . . .'

'That's so unbelievably sad.'

'Yes.' Tony took another fortifying slurp of vodka. He didn't think he had ever told anyone about this part of his life before. 'That's why I didn't want to acknowledge you. Because if Wendy ever found out that I had a child by someone else, it would break her heart all over again. And she doesn't deserve that.'

'No,' agreed Laura. 'No, I can understand that.'

She was turning everything over in her mind.

'But . . . the fact remains. You must be my dad.'

'I guess so.'

They looked across the table at each other.

'I'd love to get to know you, Laura. You're my daughter—let's assume so, at least—and I treasure that. I want to know everything about you. But it's very difficult. I can't let you into my life. I just can't.'

Laura looked down at the table. Tony feasted his eyes on her features, searching for signs of Marina, signs of himself, and couldn't help wondering how much she would have shared with the baby girl he lost all those years ago. They'd be almost the same age.

He knew Wendy still did the calculations. That she would know, exactly, if he asked her, how old her daughter would have been today. Maybe she had even looked at Laura and thought *that's about how old Rosalind would have been*. The notion almost took his breath away.

'I want to know about you too.' She looked up, squinting in the glare of the sun. 'I want to know about the other half of me. But of course I understand. I don't want Wendy to get hurt.' She stirred her drink with the celery stick. 'Dan and I might be buying a cottage here . . .'

'Really?'

'Well, it's early days . . . but we thought that instead of buying a flat in London, we'd get somewhere to escape to. Rent it out as a holiday let to make some money.'

They looked at each other for a moment, scanning for similarities.

I've got a daughter, thought Tony. Someone is going to carry on my genes.

I've got a dad, thought Laura. At last I can find out who I am.

'We'd be able to see each other if you do buy a house here,' he said finally. 'As long as we're careful.'

Laura looked across the terrace to see Dan walking towards them. She held out her hand, drew him to her.

'Tony, this is Dan. Dan—this is my dad.' Her heart gave a little jump. She had never said those words before in her life.

Dan grinned easily and sat down. 'How's it going?'

It was a rhetorical question. Dan never invaded anyone's privacy. But Tony replied nevertheless.

'Good,' he said. 'Really . . . good.'

Dan looked at Laura. 'I put an offer in on the cottage. Told them we'd need some time to get the money together. They're going to let us know.'

Tony finished his Bloody Mary. 'I feel like I should order champagne,' he said. 'It's not every day I meet my daughter. But . . .'

He gave a shrug. Someone would see. Someone would mention it to Wendy.

'It's okay,' said Laura. 'I understand.'

Tony stood up. 'And I need to go. I was only supposed to be popping out for the paper.'

Laura stood up too. They looked at each other, awkward for a moment, then she gave him a quick hug.

'I'll email you,' she said.

And then he left, turning and raising his hand in a gesture of farewell that to any onlooker said everything, but nothing.

*   *   *

Colin watched as Chelsey walked back through the dining room, arms laden with a Sunday paper and magazine. His pulse rate rose. He felt strangely proud of her, and he was flooded with hope for her future. She was such a vulnerable little thing. He prayed that everything was going to work out.

'Alison, this is Chelsey,' he said as she plonked the newspaper on the table in front of him.

Alison smiled and leant towards her. 'Hello, Chelsey.'

Chelsey didn't miss a beat. She gave Alison a cursory glance, followed by a bright smile.

'Hi,' she said, before sliding on to the banquette next to Colin. She flipped a pink and sparkly magazine on to the table in front of her, tucked her hair behind her ears and began to read.

Colin looked around the dining room. He supposed everyone thought they were a normal family unit. Although perhaps not, if they'd seen him in the dining room with Karen the night before. Maybe they were all wondering what the story was. Trying to figure out which of the women was his wife. Either way, he didn't care. Everyone had secrets. Some darker than others.

He turned to Alison.

'Chelsey and I were planning to go to the beach today, if you want to come.'

Alison nodded. 'That sounds lovely.'

'And we also thought we'd stay on here for another couple of days.'

It might be easier, he thought, if Chelsey and Alison got to know each other on neutral territory, while he sorted out the legal side of things

Alison looked doubtful. 'I haven't brought anything with me. No change of clothes or toiletries. I even had to buy a toothbrush from the Spar.'

Colin shrugged her objection away.

'We can pick some stuff up in town. There's some nice shops.'

Chelsey glanced up from her magazine. She looked puzzled.

'Are you his wife, then?'

She'd obviously been turning things over in her mind.

Colin looked awkward.

'Yes,' said Alison. 'I'm Mrs Turner. But you can call me Alison, if you like.'

Chelsey considered this offer, then shrugged. 'Okay,' she replied, and went back to her magazine.

Colin and Alison looked at each other.

'I'll have to phone and cancel my tennis match for tomorrow,' she said. 'I won't be very popular, I don't suppose . . .'

*   *   *

Trevor and Monique had set off on *The Blonde Bombshell* after an early breakfast. They wanted to take the boat further round the bay and explore some of the other towns on the Cornish coast. They'd moored in a tiny little harbour and got out the Sunday papers and a bottle of wine. The boat rocked gently in the water as they sat in peaceful companionship. In an hour or so they would head for shore and find somewhere for lunch.

After a while, Trevor looked up to see Monique standing on the port side of the boat. She was looking at her bloody phone again. He put down his paper and came over to her.

'There's no signal here, love.'

'I know.' She looked down at the phone. It was positively prehistoric by today's standards, clumsy and big. 'But I've been thinking . . .'

'What is it?'

'I think we've come to a turning point in our lives. We've got exciting times ahead. I can feel it in my bones.'

'Definitely,' Trevor agreed.

'If I'm going to make something of this, I've got to accept . . .' She paused, struggling to find the right words. 'I've got to accept that Jamie isn't going to come back. I've got to stop hoping.'

Trevor could hardly bear to look at the pain that came into her eyes; the way her mouth drooped with grief, just as it had the day they had discovered

Jamie had gone. He put an arm around her.

'You should stop torturing yourself,' he agreed. 'You check that thing ten, twenty, a hundred times a day, just in case.'

The phone was symbolic. A talisman. But its hold over Monique had become disproportionate.

'I just want him to know I'm here.' Her anguish cut through him. 'I'm his mum. I just want him to know . . .'

'He knows, love. He knows that you're always here for him.'

Trevor had no way of knowing this was true. He had no more idea than she did what Jamie's state of mind was, but it didn't cost him anything to reassure her.

Monique was running her fingers over the screen.

'It's the first thing I think about when I wake up in the morning. The last thing I look at before I go to sleep. I know there's never going to be a message. But I can't help looking. Just in case.'

Trevor wanted to rip the phone out of her hands and throw it over the edge of the boat. But it had to come from her. Intervention wouldn't help. It was a step she had to take on her own.

'He'll always be able to find us if he wants to,' he told her. 'But you should stop torturing yourself.'

'I know . . .'

'This is your life, Monique,' he told her. 'We don't get another chance. You need to start living it again. We've got so much we can do. I'm so proud of you, and I know you can do great things. But you can't live like this any more. You have to move on. I know it's tough, babe.'

Tears glistened on her cheeks. He wanted to

wipe them away. He never wanted her to cry again. He couldn't believe a human being could have so many tears inside them.

The sea stretched endlessly before them, nothing else between them and the horizon. The phone barely made a splash as she dropped it in. Who knew how deep the water was here? Hundreds of feet. How long, Trevor wondered, before it finally settled on the sea bed, burying itself in the sand, where it would stay silent for ever?

He held Monique tight, her slight body shaking with sobs. He wanted to squeeze all his love into her, enough love to fill the gaping hole he knew was still there.

'It's okay,' he whispered. 'It's okay . . .'

CHAPTER SIXTEEN

Brunch morphed seamlessly into Sunday lunch, with barely any time to make the transition. Guests lingering over their pancakes were urged out as politely as possible so the dining room could be laid up again. The chalkboard went up with Sunday's special: roast rib of beef. They could have booked the restaurant three times over, as optimistic passers-by flooded in to see if there was a table available.

By three o'clock, Claire was exhausted. She wasn't officially supposed to be working in the restaurant, but she liked to oversee it when they were at full capacity. That was the difference between a well-run place and a bad one, how they coped when they were stretched, and an extra pair of eyes could mean a happy customer rather than a disgruntled one.

Things were calmer now. Guests were drinking coffee or finishing their wine. Claire came back out to the reception area, worried that it had been somewhat neglected. There was a young mum fast asleep on the sofa. Claire had seen her and her husband at lunch doing battle with their young baby. Little Plum, at nine months, had the entire restaurant in the palm of her tiny, shrimp-like hand as soon as she arrived. A vision of pink loveliness with a riot of white-blonde curls, dressed in a broderie anglaise blouse and OshKosh dungarees, she had the staff at her beck and call. Her exhausted parents were nevertheless doting. Now her mother was in a postprandial slumber, a copy of *Country Life* open on her lap.

Plum looked up at Claire from her place on the floor, surrounded by toys and a beaker of juice. She wrinkled her nose and raised her arms. Claire bent down to scoop her up, and as she lifted the warm, soft bundle, something moved deep inside her.

She stood stock still, gazing into Plum's solemn eyes with awe, confounded.

'Oh my goodness,' she laughed, jiggling her up and down. 'What have you started, you little dollop?'

Plum giggled in response, waking her mother, who jumped to her feet with profuse apologies, mortified to have fallen asleep on her watch.

'Don't worry,' said Claire, handing Plum back to her. 'You're supposed to be on holiday.'

'There's no such thing as a holiday with babies. Honestly, running a bank was a picnic compared to this.' The woman's reply was heartfelt as she rolled Plum on to her back on the sofa and waggled her feet until she shrieked with laughter. The joy her daughter brought her clearly outweighed her exhaustion and the fact that her life had been turned upside down.

As Claire walked away, she tried to ignore the seismic wave that had shaken her to the core. It was too terrifying to confront alone. It hadn't come from her mind, but from somewhere unknown inside her. A primal urge that she did her best to bury. It was echoing something Trevor had said to her yesterday, about starting a family.

She couldn't hide it from herself any longer. It was time to face up to the fact that this should be her next priority. As she stood there, the realisation hit her, almost taking her breath away. Was this how it happened to everyone? One day you were going about your business, and the next the urge to procreate swept all other considerations aside. Bloody hell, as if she wasn't confused enough already, Mother Nature had decided to stick her oar in. How was she supposed to throw motherhood into the equation?

There had been another clue lately, when she'd had a late period. Normally this would have thrown her into a state of panic, and she would have rushed off to the doctor or the chemist for something to allay her fears. Only this time she had felt a sense of calm, even intrigue, and was surprised to find herself disappointed when she finally came on a week late. She hadn't dwelled on it at the time, but now she pulled it out of her mental filing cabinet as evidence of her train of thought.

She hurried back through the dining room and straight through the double doors into the kitchen.

Fred and Loz were winding down with a beer while they did the last of the clearing up.

Luca was writing up the evening menu. He looked up as Claire approached.

'We need to talk.'

He put down his pen. 'Sure.' He stood up. 'Let's take a bottle of wine out on to the terrace.'

She shook her head. 'Not here,' she said. 'In private.'

* * *

As soon as they walked into their bedroom, more pieces of the puzzle fell into place. Claire felt claustrophobic. As she looked round, she realised that her whole life was effectively contained in here: although she and Luca had the run of the hotel and all the benefits that brought, this twelve-by-twelve room was the only bit of space she could call her own, and even then she couldn't be sure she wasn't going to be interrupted by a chambermaid or a night porter at any time. A constant supply of fresh, fluffy white towels was no replacement for privacy. If she wanted to gossip with a girlfriend, yes, of course she had staff to bring her any variety of coffee she fancied, with home-made shortbread, but the chances of her confidences being overheard were high. She could never have an off day, or look any other than her efficient best. It didn't seem to bother Luca, who behaved exactly as he liked and didn't care a jot what anyone else thought. But Claire found it wearing she realised now.

'So . . . what is it?' Luca demanded. 'What do you want to talk about?'

'I want a home,' she told him. 'If we're going

336

to get married, and we've got all these grandiose plans, I want us to have a house of our own, filled with our own things; a place where I can be myself.'

Luca shrugged. 'Okay,' he said. 'That's perfectly reasonable.'

'I can't even have a snarly PMT moment here without raised eyebrows; I can't come down to breakfast in my pyjamas, turn my music up loud, sing along if I want to, dance if I feel like it. Even leaving a banana skin on the table and having it still there two hours later would be a luxury!' As she spoke, Claire realised that any trace that she existed was wiped up after her by a crack team of staff eager to prove their housekeeping skills. She had trained them well. So well that a forensic team would find it hard to prove that Claire had even set foot inside the Townhouse.

'Hey, calm down.' Luca put his hands on her shoulders, laughing. 'Where's all this coming from?'

'I don't know!' She did know. Of course she did. And more important than the house was the other thing. If that didn't fit into Luca's life plan, then there was no point. 'Yes, I do,' she finished. 'I want . . . a baby.'

The silence that followed seemed endless. Luca's face was totally blank.

That was it. She'd thrown down the gauntlet. He was going to run a mile. Of course he wouldn't want a baby. He was sniffy about having them in the hotel, let alone letting one invade their life.

And then suddenly, he smiled.

'That's amazing,' he said.

'What?'

'That's wonderful,' he reiterated.

'But . . . how can we?' she blurted. 'With

everything that's going on? A hotel in London . . . running this place . . . And how are we going to afford a house of our own?'

'For heaven's sake, Claire.' Luca picked up her hand. 'Stop thinking so much about things. Of course you should have a baby. We'll manage. People do it all the time. It'll be tough, but anything worthwhile always is.'

He drew her towards him and held her in his arms. 'We've never talked about it properly, but I've always just assumed we'd have a family. It's the natural thing to do. And if now's the right time, then . . . so be it.'

He stroked her hair. Claire melted into him.

'I didn't know I felt like this. It just came over me. I suddenly realised what it was I wanted. I mean, I love the hotel, and of course I'm excited about the London thing, but—'

'Claire, you don't have to explain. I get it. A baby. A gorgeous, laughing baby who looks just like you. It's perfect. We'll sort all the other stuff out as we go along. It'll all fall into place.'

He kissed the corner of her mouth, moving his hands over her shoulders, entwining his fingers in her hair. She felt the familiar warmth spreading inside her, and slid her hands round his waist, pushing them up under his shirt, feeling the velvet skin underneath.

'Maybe we should start practising now,' he murmured, dropping hot kisses on her neck. They walked backwards towards the bed, falling on to it in a tangle of limbs.

'What about the hotel?' she gasped. 'We should be getting ready for afternoon tea . . .'

'Bugger the hotel,' he replied, undoing the

338

buttons on her blouse. 'Let them eat cake. There's plenty of it . . .'

CHAPTER SEVENTEEN

Bank Holiday Monday dawned as bright and optimistic as Sunday had been, and the village of Pennfleet unfurled itself with enthusiasm. The sea seemed to glitter more invitingly than ever; boats bobbed in impatience as they awaited their passengers and the smell of coffee and frying bacon wound its way through the streets. Cars started arriving even earlier than usual as eager visitors claimed their pitch, wanting to make the most of their day of freedom.

Angelica, however, woke with a sense of dread, ready for confrontation. She'd been steeling herself for it all night. She rolled out of bed and padded through the house in her pyjamas. Everyone was still asleep, of course. She was the only mug who had to work.

She opened the door to her mother's bedroom. Inside, it was pitch black. Trudy never opened the heavy dark-purple curtains. Angelica picked her way over the discarded boots and clothes. There was a brimming ashtray next to the bed; empty glasses and cups everywhere. A large-screen telly on the wall shone green in the darkness.

'Mum,' she called. 'Come on. You've got to get up. Dill's football thing is at ten. You've got to drive him there. And make him a packed lunch.'

There was no response.

'Mum! Come on.'

'For God's sake. It's a bloody bank holiday. Leave me alone.'

'You've got to get Dill ready. He has to get his kit on.'

'Forget it. I don't want to get up.'

Angelica reached out a hand and pulled back the duvet. Trudy screamed and sat up. She was wearing a shorter than short purple satin nightdress, the spaghetti straps digging into her flesh.

'Are you seriously going to let him down?' Angelica demanded.

'It's only a game of football.'

'Not to him it isn't.'

The school had organised a special training day, with a player from Plymouth Argyle. Dill had been looking forward to it for weeks. Jeff had promised to take him, but of course Jeff wasn't here any more.

Trudy lay down again and pulled the pillow over her head.

Angelica dropped the duvet back on her in disgust. She could rant and rave and scream, but she knew it would make no difference. What a waste of space her mother was.

Maybe she should phone in sick? But no—she needed the money. It was double time on a bank holiday. Besides, someone would be bound to see her and dump her in it. That was how life worked.

She clenched her fists in an effort to keep down her anger, then left the room to go and break the bad news to Dill.

*   *   *

In leafy Berkshire, Nick woke to the sound of the

340

mower buzzing up and down the lawn outside. He and his father had agreed that this was the best day to cut the grass before the wedding. They didn't want it to be too short, like a squaddie's haircut. If they cut it today, it would have enough time to recover before the tent people came on Thursday.

The thought of the marquee waiting to welcome all those guests made Nick groan. He pulled the duvet over his head, but he could still see it there in his mind's eye, white and majestic. He could even see the table with the cake—three tiers, fruit, chocolate and plain sponge, he seemed to remember from the discussions they'd had.

He hadn't said much to Gerald about his impromptu return in the small hours of Sunday morning. His father had the tact not to probe, but had understood with fatherly intuition that Nick had undergone some sort of crisis he didn't want to discuss. He probably thought he'd got drunk and snogged a girl at Pennfleet Yacht Club and was riddled with shame.

If only that had been his crime. He would swap a hundred stag-night snogs for what had really happened.

It was stifling under the duvet, so he threw it back and stared up at the ceiling. He really should get up and help his father. It wasn't fair to let Gerald do all the donkey work, although he was always quite happy preparing for a social occasion. It was what Gerald did best.

It was what Isobel had done best, too. It was when the Barnes family really came into their own, when they were preparing to welcome guests. Nick thought about how much she would have adored getting ready for his wedding. Sophie had done

341

a fantastic job, of course, but his mother would have made it extra special, with those little touches that only she could bring, the ones that had always made their parties so much more memorable than anyone else's. Where had Isobel got it, that magic? he wondered. Or had it simply been her presence that had made the difference? Her warmth, her magnetism, her generosity, her *joie de vivre* . . .

Today he was meeting Sophie for lunch, to go through all her endless lists again. To be fair, she had been remarkably unhysterical about the whole wedding—he had heard serious horror stories from friends who had been married recently—but still he found the thought of discussing the photographer's brief and who was going to collect the bridesmaids' presents stultifying.

He walked over to the window and drew back the curtains, blinking at the brightness of the sun. He could smell the scent of freshly mown grass. He wondered if the weather would hold until Saturday, then wondered bleakly how many times he would have to have that conversation over the next few days.

He didn't care about the weather. Not one jot. In fact, he couldn't bear the thought of the sun shining next Saturday, and all the guests running round bleating about fairy-tale weddings and how lucky they were . . .

He could see his father carrying yet another load of grass clippings to the compost heap behind the shed. He'd go out and do a few rows up and down the lawn while Gerald made them a cup of tea. Then he'd better have a shower and drive over to Sophie's.

It was going to be the last time they would meet

before they saw each other at the altar.

*   *   *

At the Townhouse, Angelica sat at reception staring into space, unable to shake off an uncharacteristic feeling of resentment.

It had taken her nearly half an hour to pacify Dill. He had kicked and screamed and cried when she'd told him he couldn't go to the training day. It had taken all her strength to stop him from hurting himself. Eventually he had calmed down when she had promised to take him to a real, proper football match as soon as she could.

She knew he would be stuck inside all day watching DVDs while her mother slept. Maybe if she got away early she could take him to the beach this evening, but she was due to work until seven, and by the time she got home she'd be knackered and would just want a shower and something to eat, not to have to get his swimming things together and walk all the way to Neptune's Cove, which was his favourite . . .

When it should be bloody Trudy who was doing it.

It wasn't right. It wasn't fair. She was used to being let down by her mother, but it wasn't fair on Dill. He had enough to contend with.

To compound her dark mood, Claire seemed very chirpy. She was checking out the young couple Angelica had upgraded.

'I hope you enjoyed your stay,' she said, as they paid their bill.

'We loved it,' the girl said. 'We're hoping to be back soon. We've put an offer in on a house.'

'That's fantastic,' Claire replied as she folded up their receipt and put it in an envelope. 'Good luck.'

The couple gathered up their bags and walked off arm in arm. Two more satisfied customers, thought Angelica. Well, they would be, wouldn't they? They'd got twice the room for half the price. She wished she could snap out of her sour mood. She didn't begrudge the couple their upgrade—of course she didn't . . .

'Go and wake that lazy lump for me, would you?' Claire asked.

Angelica got off her chair and made her way over to the stairs. She should have phoned in sick. She was tired of putting a brave face on it. Good old Angelica, who everyone relied on but didn't give a toss about. It was all right for Claire to be all perky, with her sparkly diamond ring and her glittering future. It had been Angelica's shoulder she'd cried on, though, hadn't it? When everything hadn't seemed so rosy?

She stomped up the stairs. She hated feeling like this. Where was she supposed to find a shoulder to cry on when she needed it? Could somebody tell her that?

*　　　　*　　　　*

While they packed up the last of their things, Alison was showing Chelsey photographs of her dog, Monty, on her phone. They'd decided not to stay on, but to take Chelsey back home while arrangements were made.

'He's a springer spaniel,' Alison told her. 'And he's very naughty. I have to take him to special classes.'

'I've always wanted a dog,' said Chelsey. 'But Mum wouldn't let me.'

Colin had to turn away. The emotion kept getting to him. He imagined Chelsey with Monty in the garden, running around like his kids once had. Was it going to work?

It had to, he thought.

And even if it didn't, even if their marriage buckled under the strain, at least he didn't have to live with the guilt any more. The secret was out. He could do his best for Chelsey from now on; do everything in his power to give her a happy life and whatever she wanted.

The two of them were giggling over the photos. For a moment he felt like the outsider. Alison had always been wonderful with children.

Alison had always been wonderful full stop, he reflected.

'Come on, you two,' he said. 'Let's make the most of that weather.'

They were hiring a boat. Colin wasn't sure how good he was going to be at skippering, but at least it would give him something to focus on while the two of them bonded.

He picked up his phone and checked it, nervous that there might be a text from Karen saying she'd made a mistake, saying she was coming to collect Chelsey.

Nothing. Colin felt relief. Every hour of silence from Karen was another nail in her coffin. He'd be able to get a court order, hopefully custody in the long run. He didn't want things to get nasty, but he thought he had enough evidence to prove she was unfit. Of course, it would be so much better if they could do things in a civilised manner. Karen was

Chelsey's mother, after all, and she should stay in contact with her.

And it wasn't all going to be plain sailing. Another year and Chelsey would be hitting the troublesome teenage years. He might well regret taking her on.

No, thought Colin. He was never going to regret taking her on, whatever happened. Chelsey was his flesh and blood. She deserved every opportunity, every chance that his other children had been given.

Now that he'd got her, he wasn't going to let her go.

He zipped up her little case and picked it up.

'Come on then. Let's check out. We can leave our cases and pick them up later.'

'Can we come back one day?' asked Chelsey. 'I love it here.'

Colin looked around the room. It had been a strange weekend. Traumatic, emotional, difficult . . . but there was no doubt that Pennfleet was special. The Townhouse was special. A good find, he thought.

'Of course,' he told her, because he was never going to be able to say no to her. He could see that from the wry smile Alison gave him.

There was nothing wrong with that, was there?

*   *   *

Luca was still fast asleep in bed.

'Oi,' said Angelica, prodding him. 'Some of us have got work to do. Get up.'

He opened his eyes and looked up at her.

'You're full of charm this morning,' he told her.

'Fuck off,' she said, and burst into tears.

He sat up, alarmed. 'What's the matter?' he asked. He didn't like crying women. It was one of the things he valued Claire for, the fact that she didn't turn the taps on at any given opportunity.

'Like you care,' Angelica sobbed. 'Like you give a toss about anyone except yourself.'

'That's not fair.'

He put out a hand to stroke her. She shut her eyes.

'Don't,' she said, but she didn't move.

He ran his fingers through her hair. 'Poor Angelica,' he soothed. 'What's the matter? This isn't like you.'

She shut her eyes even tighter, to keep the tears in. 'You don't know how much you mean to me, do you?' she asked eventually, her voice taut with the effort of not crying.

'Mean to you?' he laughed. 'No, of course I don't.'

'Don't laugh at me.'

'I'm not laughing at you.' He patted the bed next to him. 'Sit down. Tell me what this is all about.'

She hesitated, then sat down, against her better judgement. Luca was leaning back against the wooden headboard. His hair was wild, and he needed a shave. His chest was golden against the white of the bed linen. She breathed him in and thought she would faint as his familiar scent curdled her insides.

He was staring at her, puzzled. 'Come on,' he said.

Angelica wasn't at all sure how to proceed. Whether to treat this as an informal staff meeting, or unburden herself to him as a friend. Or to tell him the truth.

He lifted his hand and stroked her bare arm with the back of his fingers.

'What?' he asked softly.

His touch made her crumble. She couldn't treat him as a boss or a friend.

'You're all I think about,' she told him. 'Day and night. Awake or asleep, you're always there. On the edge of my dreams . . .'

'Bloody hell,' said Luca. And as her tears started to fall again, he put his arms round her and pulled her towards him. 'Come here. You shouldn't cry.'

She was leaning against his chest. His arms were around her.

Oh God, thought Angelica. What on earth had she said? It had just seemed so unfair. Poor Dill. Her bloody mother. The loved-up couple. Everyone walking around in the bank holiday sunshine, happy with their lot. When all she could see unfolding in front of her was a lifetime of frustration.

And now, the moment she had fantasised about so many times was here. His warm hands were sliding up her legs, under her skirt, into her knickers. She squirmed.

'No,' she said, but she felt helpless. This was everything she had ever longed for. She had fought it for so long, and now, when she was at her most vulnerable, she didn't think she could resist. Even though she knew it was wrong. Even though it would only bring her more heartache.

But at least she would know how it felt. At least she would know what she was missing. His hands were inside her shirt, running over her skin. It was everything she had ever imagined. Everything she had ever allowed herself to dream about. And Angelica thought that if she died today, she would die happy, as the feelings built up inside her, growing in force until she could hardly bear it.

'Don't stop,' she begged, and tears rolled down her face.

'I won't.' Luca's breathing was ragged. 'I won't . . .'

*   *   *

Claire ran up the stairs, two at a time. Where on earth *was* everybody? Didn't they know how busy they were going to be today? The hotel seemed to be full of people wanting coffee on the terrace, or a table for lunch, or cocktails, and she wasn't a bloody magician. She needed Angelica on reception and Luca in the kitchen, but neither of them was to be found. She reached the bedroom door. Angelica must have gone to wake Luca, who'd probably ignored her and gone straight back to sleep again.

As she opened the door and surveyed the scene inside, she felt . . .

Nothing.

Not anger. Not jealousy. Not shock. Or outrage.

Nothing.

She turned and shut the door gently. She stood on the landing for a moment. All she could hear was her heart thudding inside her. Adrenalin. The fight-or-flight impulse.

She wasn't going to fight. There was nothing to fight for, she realised. Nothing that she wanted. He could have it all, as far as she was concerned. And good luck to him. They would be fine, Luca and Angelica. She wasn't going to hang around and fight over the spoils. She had more dignity than that.

349

Besides, there wasn't much time. She knew that. If she was going to get what she did want, she would have to move fast.

She set off down the stairs, thinking as she went. She didn't need to take anything with her. Her bag and keys were downstairs in the office. She could send for everything else later, if need be.

As she reached the first-floor landing, she paused for a moment. She was outside Trevor and Monique's room, and for a split second she felt a pang of guilt at what she was about to do. She remembered everything Trevor had told her, and it occurred to her that by leaving, she was jeopardising their dream. She owed them if not an apology then at least an explanation.

She stood outside their room, about to knock. They'd be disappointed, she knew that. And then a further thought occurred to her. Why should she just walk away and leave Luca with the fruits of her hard labour, not to mention her initial investment?

She looked at her watch, took a deep breath and tapped on the door.

Trevor opened it with a beaming smile.

'Claire!' He stepped aside to let her in. 'What can I do for you?' He looked at her hopefully. 'Have you come to sign on the dotted line?'

Inside, Monique was sitting at the dressing table applying the last of her maquillage. Beside her the French windows were open to the balcony, showing a glimpse of the glorious day outside. Claire felt a lump rise in her throat. She would be giving up all of this.

'No,' she said. 'In fact, I've got a totally different proposition.'

Trevor and Monique looked at her expectantly.

'I've come to ask if you'll buy my share of the Townhouse.'

There was a moment's silence while the two of them took in what she was saying.

'What do you mean?' said Trevor.

'Luca and I own forty per cent each,' Claire explained. 'But . . . I don't want to carry on. We're finished, Luca and I.'

'Oh my God!' Monique got to her feet. She was still clad in a white satin nightdress with matching negligee. 'What's happened? The engagement . . . it was only yesterday . . . You seemed so happy!'

Claire looked down at her ring. She'd totally forgotten about it. She tugged it off and rolled it round in her fingers, nervous.

'I'm not going to go into details,' she replied. 'But I thought I would give you first refusal. And obviously . . . I can't go ahead with the London deal. I'm so sorry. I know how much it means to you. I hope you'll find another way of pulling it together.'

Trevor and Monique looked at each other.

'What do you think?' Trevor asked.

Monique spread her hands out, holding them palms upwards.

'Trev—babe—you don't even need to ask, surely. I mean, we love this place. We're a part of it. It's a part of us.'

Trevor looked out of the window into the distance, turning Claire's proposition over in his mind.

'Well,' he said finally. 'I can't pretend we're not disappointed. About London. It was going to be a dream come true for us. But we can't hold you back from what you want to do. And yes, in theory, we'll

351

buy you out.'

'Thank you,' Claire held out her hand for him to shake. 'I've got to go now, but I'll be in touch. To work out the details.'

'A handshake from me is as good as a contract,' Trevor told her.

Claire turned to shake Monique's hand too, but was surprised to find herself engulfed in a white satin, Envy-drenched hug.

'If you want to talk, chick,' said Monique, 'then I'm here. I'm a woman of the world. If you want any advice . . .'

For one wild moment Claire felt tempted to unburden herself. But time wasn't on her side. She extricated herself carefully.

'Thank you both so much,' she said, and left the room before the lump that had risen in her throat choked her. She didn't want to think about what she was leaving behind. She had to look forward. And hope that she wasn't too late.

Moments later, she was at the reception desk. There were people milling around, looking for attention, but she didn't care. She found an envelope, put the ring inside it, and scrawled a few words on a compliment slip: *Hopefully you kept the receipt.* Then she sealed the envelope and wrote Luca's name on the front.

A customer came up to the desk and complained about the service being slow.

'We just want coffee. We've been waiting for ages.'

'The receptionist will be back in a moment,' she told him. 'She's just . . . seeing to the boss. So to speak.'

She dropped the envelope into the in-tray,

smiled her sweetest smile, picked up her bag and keys and walked out of the door.

*   *   *

In the grand suite, Trevor's heart was heavy as he turned to his wife.

He dreaded her reaction to Claire's news. She'd put a brave face on it while Claire was there, but he hoped that now she'd gone, Monique wasn't going to fall apart. The hotel in London had been the thing that had kept her going.

To his surprise, she seemed unfazed.

'Are you okay?' he asked.

'Absolutely,' she said. 'In fact, I think this is the best thing that could have happened.'

Trevor was astonished.

'How?'

'If we buy into here, I can run the place. I can cut my teeth on it. Learn the ropes. It's already up and running, so it's ideal. Then, when I know what I'm doing, we can look at London again. I reckon I could do it on my own.'

She smiled at him. There was a light in her eyes that hadn't been there for years. The darkness seemed to have gone. Trevor thought his heart was going to burst. She was so much stronger than he had thought. He walked over and took her in his arms.

'I'm so proud of you,' he said.

*   *   *

Luca was raging through the hotel. Where the bloody hell was Claire? She'd totally vanished.

Her bag and her car keys were gone. She wouldn't answer her phone.

'What does she think she's doing?' he roared. 'She can't just walk out of here.'

Angelica came back from the car park. He'd sent her to see if Claire's car was still there.

'It's gone,' she told him.

He stepped towards her, his face dark with fury, and grabbed her arms.

'This is all your fault,' he shouted. 'She must have seen us.'

His fingers were digging into her.

'My fault?' she said calmly. 'I don't think so.'

'What the hell am I supposed to do now?' he demanded.

He was shaking Angelica. She struggled to pull away. Behind Luca, she could see Trevor coming down the stairs.

'Let her go at once.' Trevor strode across the room. 'I don't ever want to see you lay another finger on that girl.'

Luca scowled. 'It's none of your business,' he snarled.

'Yes it is,' replied Trevor. 'In fact, that's exactly what it is.'

'What are you talking about?' Luca released Angelica and turned to face Trevor.

'Claire's offered me and Monique her share of the business,' Trevor told him.

'What do you mean? She can't just do that. What the bloody hell's she playing at? And where's she gone?'

'I've no idea. She didn't say.'

Luca stood stock still, trying to take it all in.

'You might as well have the whole lot then,' he

354

managed finally, and walked out of the door.

Trevor looked at Angelica. 'Are you all right, love?'

She shook her head. 'What are we supposed to do now?'

'Don't worry. He'll come back when he's calmed down.' Trevor was assured. Confident. 'I'll get Monique to come down and give you a hand.'

Angelica's eyes welled up. 'This *is* all my fault,' she said.

Trevor patted her on the shoulder. 'I don't think so. Whatever's gone on today, I think it all started a long time ago . . .'

*   *   *

It took Claire just under three hours to drive to Mimsbury. No doubt she would have a raft of speeding tickets in the post the following week. And although she had all the time in the world to debate what she was doing as she drove, not once did she feel the urge to turn around, or have any doubt that what she was doing was the right thing.

In her heart of hearts, she belonged to Nick. And if he didn't feel the same way, well . . . Claire was ready to make her own way in the world. Start again on her terms.

She didn't want to think about Luca and Angelica. They were irrelevant now. She certainly wasn't going to give them the satisfaction of a showdown, or a chance to defend themselves. Although if she really thought about it, she felt more betrayed by Angelica than Luca. She shivered to think how she had trusted the girl with her secrets. It had reminded her of something she already knew—that secrets were trouble; that they made you vulnerable.

The only way to get through life from now on, she decided, was not to have any.

She turned off the main road and down the narrow lane that led to Mimsbury. She hadn't been back since she had left for Sausalito—her parents had moved again not long after she had gone—but it was still achingly familiar even after all this time. The hedgerows and verges were full to bursting, and every now and then she passed an exquisite red-brick cottage swathed in roses. She drove across the hump-backed bridge, the canal cool and silent beneath, then over the level crossing next to the little station, which had been the scene of that fateful meeting so many years ago, then through a dark tunnel of overhanging oak trees before they thinned out and Mimsbury appeared in all its glory, as perfect as ever, as if it was waiting for the arrival of the Best Kept Village judges any minute. She slowed down on instinct, even before she passed the twenty-miles-an-hour sign.

The Mimsbury Arms looked just the same. If she breathed in, she would be able to smell it— the woodsmoke from the fire, the hoppy scent of beer, Mel's musky perfume, chips from the kitchen. A wave of nostalgia slid through her, making her feel slightly nauseous, and just for a moment she wondered about the wisdom of coming back.

And then, as she turned the corner, there was the Mill House. It still took her breath away, as if she was seeing it for the first time. It stood, quiet and still in the summer sun, waiting for her, the mellow red bricks hazy in the heat, the river snaking its sinuous way alongside. She pulled on to the gravel chippings at the side of the house and pulled on the handbrake. Stepping out of the car, she felt as if a camera crew should be following her; as if her every move and every reaction should be remarked upon by a commentator speaking in a suitably hushed tone.

She crunched towards the front door. She couldn't stop to think about what she was doing. She had to move forward. On to the next phase of her life, whatever it might bring. She rang the bell. It drilled into the heart of the house, an intrusive sound on such a peaceful afternoon. There followed a long silence. No one was in.

For some reason, that eventuality hadn't occurred to her. Disappointment nipped at her. She stepped back, chewing her thumbnail, unsure what to do. Should she go to the pub and wait? Somehow that took the urgency out of the situation. Her mission would lose its momentum. She was about to turn and go back to the car when she heard the handle rattle and the door opened slowly.

It was Gerald. He'd obviously just woken up. He looked bewildered and dishevelled, blinking at the light flooding into the cool dark of the hall.

'So sorry. I was having a snooze in the garden ...' He peered at her, not recognising her as yet.

'Gerald,' she said, not sure how much enthusiasm to inject into her voice, as she had no idea how he was going to react. 'It's me. Claire.'

He looked smaller than she remembered. Frail almost. And quite grey. But it had been more than ten years, and at Gerald's time of life, she supposed, ten years made all the difference. And he'd lost a lot of weight, which was always ageing.

Then he suddenly smiled, and his face lit up, and

the Gerald she remembered was there, the bon viveur, the party-thrower, the charmer.

'Claire!' he cried, and there was no doubting the genuine joy in his voice. He stepped forward, and she let him put his arms around her, and stood very still as he hugged her. 'My darling girl!' She remembered how theatrical he always sounded when he was overexcited. 'This is such a surprise. Such a shock. But such a pleasure.' He stepped back and held her at arm's length, surveying her. 'You'd better come in. I'm so glad to see you. You have no idea . . .'

Claire stepped into the hall, and felt the familiar walls embrace her. It hadn't changed. The grandfather clock was still there, the hands pointing now at ten past two, in the same place it had been when she had last seen it; its tick as loud and relentlessly steady. The air smelled of beeswax, and the coir matting on the floor. And still—or was she imagining it?—the faint scent of violets. She could almost—almost—imagine Isobel bounding down the stairs, greeting her with delight, hugging her . . .

'Come on, come through.' Gerald urged her into the kitchen.

As she walked in, the past jumped up and grabbed her. She faltered in the doorway, overwhelmed by nostalgia. Again, nothing had changed. The table smothered in paperwork, empty Emma Bridgewater mugs and the remains of someone's toast and Marmite; the photographs on the wall, the view through the French windows. The smell. Of the oil that fired the Aga, the garden outside, the lingering scent of toast from lunch, freshly ground coffee beans . . .

It was marginally messier than it would have

358

been during Isobel's reign. There were no fresh flowers in the old enamel jug. The milk bottle was out on the side, and the sugar was in a bag, not a bowl, a teaspoon sticking out of it, which would have horrified her.

'What can I get you?' asked Gerald, ever the host. 'No—don't answer. If ever there was an excuse for champagne, this must surely be it . . .'

He looked at her, smiling, his eyes shining with genuine pleasure.

Claire found it hard to speak. There were so many emotions jostling for position inside her. Memories of the past mixed with her hopes for the future, all combined with a certain awkwardness. What should she say to Gerald? How could she explain her presence here?

Although he didn't seem to want to know. He just appeared to accept that she was here, as he made his way to the fridge and pulled out a bottle, just as she had seen him do so many times. He hadn't even waited for her agreement. He turned and looked at her, one hand expertly removing the foil and then easing the cork from its neck. He poured two glasses and handed her one.

'I am so delighted to see you,' he said. 'I've thought about you a great deal over the years. Wondered how you are. You look well.'

Claire nodded. 'I am . . .' Her voice was little more than a whisper.

They clinked glasses and drank, and she found the courage to speak up.

'I thought about you too. A lot.' It was too much. The memory was too much. She felt her face crumple. 'I'm sorry . . . I'm so sorry. About everything.'

359

'My dear girl, you have no reason to be sorry. You never did have. But we never had the chance to tell you. None of us blamed you.' He stopped and reached for one of her hands. She looked down, and noticed again how old he had become. His hands were gnarled and spotted. 'None of us blamed you. How could we? You did what you thought was right. I'm just desperately sorry it had to end the way it did. It grieved me almost more than Isobel's dying, because I'd known for a long time that was inevitable, and I'd come to terms with it. Although we never spoke about it, which was perhaps the problem. It's a Barnes failing, pretending everything is all right when it isn't . . .'

He looked deep into her eyes and smiled. 'I'm glad you're here,' he went on. 'Because I've never had the chance to thank you. You gave me those last precious few weeks with Isobel. That Christmas was magical. I would never have had that if it weren't for you. She needed you, to give her the strength to do what she did.'

At last Claire felt the guilt and the grief of twelve years work its way free from her heart. Tears were streaming down her face as she let Gerald fold her in his arms, and the comfort and relief that his embrace brought was the sweetest feeling. Eventually her sobs subsided, and she pulled herself free, wiping away the tears, laughing shakily, sipping her champagne to give her fortitude.

'That's better,' said Gerald. 'That's much better.'

He pulled out a chair at the table for her, and then one for himself. They both sat. 'Now, are you going to tell me why you're here?'

'Didn't Nick mention that he'd seen me?'

'No.' Gerald's eyes were troubled. 'He's played

360

his cards very close to his chest. He came back from his stag weekend early. I know something's the matter.' He looked at Claire. 'You know about the wedding?'

She gave a rueful smile.

'Yes.'

Gerald gestured outside. 'I've spent the past two months getting that garden into shape. I'd let it run rather wild over the past few years. It was always more Isobel's thing than mine. I was lawn monitor, but she dealt with the beds and the roses. I like to think she'd have approved of what I've managed . . .'

Claire looked out. It was an English garden at its best: soft, blowsy, drooping blooms nodding in the breeze, pale pinks and yellows mixed in with a thousand shades of green. And the river winding through its tranquil midst.

'It looks stunning,' she told him. Now that she was more aware of her surroundings, she could see evidence of wedding preparations. There were boxes of wine glasses piled up in the corner of the kitchen. A guest list pinned to the wall. A pile of CDs where someone was compiling a playlist on the Mac—probably Shrimp; he had always been the music guru.

The Mac was, she realised, the only new thing in the kitchen since she had last been here. Otherwise it was just as it ever had been.

Gerald was standing in the doorway, looking out at the garden. He must be imagining all the parties they'd ever had, thought Claire, the ghosts of the guests dancing across the lawn.

'I want it to be perfect for him,' he said. 'As perfect as Isobel would have made it.'

Claire felt a rushing in her ears. What on earth

was she doing here? She must have been mad to think she could come waltzing in and cancel someone else's wedding, just because she once happened to have been in love with the groom. Nick was her past, not her future. She couldn't change the course of what was going to happen. She had no right whatsoever.

She got to her feet.

'Listen, I ought to go. I'm on my way somewhere. I was just passing, and thought I'd call in to say hello. I hope it all goes well . . .'

Gerald turned, frowning. 'No, don't go. Nick will be sorry to have missed you. Stay a bit longer.'

'No, honestly.' Claire was fumbling for her keys in her bag. 'It was lovely to see you . . .'

She could see that Gerald was puzzled by her hasty departure. She had to go before he started asking questions. She went over and kissed him on the cheek. As she pulled away, he took her elbow.

'Claire—why did you come?'

She shook her head, not trusting herself to speak. The sooner she got to the car the better. Although where she was going to go, she had no idea. Maybe her parents? They'd be glad to see her; wouldn't ask awkward questions . . . She pulled away with a tight smile and turned to go.

Nick was standing in the doorway.

For a moment they stared at each other.

'I was just going,' said Claire. 'I came to say . . . good luck. For the wedding . . .'

Gerald was looking between the two of them.

'What's going on?' he asked.

Nobody answered him as Nick stepped into the room towards Claire, not taking his eyes off her face.

362

'It's been cancelled.'

Claire's heart was thumping.

'The wedding's been cancelled. I've just been to tell Sophie I can't go through with it.'

Claire put a hand to her mouth.

'Oh my God,' she whispered.

Nick looked tired, as if he hadn't slept.

'I woke up this morning and realised . . . you're the only person I've ever loved. Sophie is . . . wonderful, but we never had that special . . .' He waved his hands helplessly in the air, unable to explain. 'That whatever-it-is. The thing. The thing Dad and Mum had. The meant-to-be-together thing. Some couples have it and some don't.'

He stared at her.

'I told her I couldn't marry her,' he said. 'I told her I couldn't marry her if I was in love with someone else. Even if that someone else didn't want me.'

'But I do want you,' said Claire. 'Luca and I . . . it's all over. I came to tell you . . . just in case there was a chance . . .'

They each took a step forward. They were only a foot apart.

'I was coming back down,' he told her. 'I was going to get straight back in the car. Beg you to think again. But you beat me to it.'

He grabbed her, pulled her to him.

As they embraced, Gerald gave an awkward cough.

'Excuse me. I'd better . . . go and put the mower away.'

They didn't notice him as he slipped through the French windows. They hugged each other tightly, not speaking, not even kissing, just holding on as if

363

they were never going to let go again.

*   *   *

Trevor was right. As predicted, Luca walked back into the Townhouse later that afternoon. He looked drawn, grim-faced. He walked straight past Angelica and into the office.

Angelica brought him a brandy. He was sitting at Claire's desk, staring into space. He knocked it back in a single gulp.

'Thank you,' he said. 'And I apologise. My behaviour was inexcusable.'

His tone was stiff—Luca wasn't the sort who apologised easily—but Angelica recognised an olive branch.

'It's okay.'

'And I suppose you'd better consider yourself acting manageress.'

He'd obviously come up with a game plan during his absence. And realised he couldn't manage without her.

'In that case,' she replied, 'you're going to have to give me a rise.'

He looked at her sharply. 'You'll be lucky.'

She shrugged. 'Fine. Find someone else then. Just don't expect me to show them the ropes.'

She looked down at him. Somehow, the spell had been broken. The hold he'd had over her was gone. He was no longer the stuff of her fantasies. She'd taken what she wanted from him; she'd fulfilled her dream. And now he just seemed ordinary. Less than ordinary: a weak, foolish, not very nice man, albeit wrapped up in a beguiling package that she had been stupid enough to fall for.

Did she feel guilty? About betraying Claire? No, she thought. Claire had known all along that Luca wasn't the man for her. She hadn't needed proof, but Angelica had given it to her anyway.

If it hadn't been her, she reasoned, it would have been someone else.

She'd done Claire a favour. Given her the courage to follow her heart.

She took the glass off Luca.

'Come on,' she said briskly. 'You need to get back in the kitchen. You can't wallow round here feeling sorry for yourself.'

She walked out of the office. She wasn't going to let him use her. If she had a raise in salary, maybe she could afford to move out of home. Get a flat for her and Dill. Give him the life he deserved. It would be tough, but with the extra money she was earning, she'd be able to manage.

They didn't need anyone else, her and Dill.

*   *   *

Claire and Nick were walking hand in hand through Mimsbury. It was, thought Claire, as if she had never been away. She could be eighteen again.

Eventually they reached the church. Nick opened the gate and led her up the path through the perfect English graveyard. The oldest and most precarious stones had been carefully repositioned and laid flat. The grass was kept just the right length: not too manicured, but not so long that it looked unkempt, and just enough to let any wild flowers peep through. Birds sang in the nearby trees and the air was filled with the scent of blossom. It was the perfect place to be laid to rest because it looked

365

just that: restful.

Isobel's stone was in plain white marble with hand-cut lettering, and simply bore her name and the dates of her birth and death, with no unnecessary adornment or sentiment.

'She wouldn't have wanted anything tacky or over the top,' said Nick.

'Of course not.' Claire stood in front of the stone, her head bowed. She didn't want to speak, or pray. She just wanted to remember, without any guilt, the vibrant and beautiful wife and mother that Isobel had been. At last, in the quiet of the graveyard, with no sound but the birds and the wind rustling the trees, she felt a calmness and tranquillity she hadn't felt for years. And she hoped that wherever she was, Isobel felt the same, because although what she had done might not have been right, she deserved to rest in peace.

'I still miss her.' Nick broke the silence. 'I still miss her every day. I'm never going to stop wishing she was still here . . .'

'Hey.' Claire turned and put her arms round him, pulling him in close, trying to absorb some of his pain. She knew how close Isobel had been to her boys, how strong the bond had been between them, and she hoped that one day, if it ever happened, she would share the same connection with her own children.

'It would have meant a lot to her, you coming here today.' Nick's voice was muffled, still buried in her shoulder. 'She adored you, you know.'

'I just hope I can live up to her,' replied Claire. 'Be as good a mother as she was.'

'You will be,' said Nick. 'I know you will . . .'

Afterwards, they wandered back to the Mill House. They didn't speak much—they didn't want to break the spell with mere words. Instead, they went into the garden, and Claire sat down under the weeping willow next to the river. Nick went inside to make a cup of tea.

While he was waiting for the kettle to boil on the Aga, he went up to his bedroom and opened his dressing table drawer. In there was a small box. Inside it was a ring. Isobel's engagement ring. She had left it to him, again with a note.

I hope this ring brings as much happiness to the girl you love as it did to me.

He looked at it, as the light from the window glanced off the white diamonds. He remembered it on Isobel's hand. She never took it off.

He hadn't given it to Sophie. When he had proposed, he had taken her to a small jeweller in Sandleford and they had chosen a ring together. For some reason, it had never felt the right thing to do, to give her Isobel's ring. It had stayed in the back of his dressing table drawer all this time.

Isobel had meant it for Claire. He knew that. Today wasn't the day to give it to her, though. They needed some time to get over the momentous decisions they had both made in walking away from Luca and Sophie. A proposal today would be inauspicious. Indecently hasty. The ring had been there for twelve years. It could wait a while longer. And he thought how happy Isobel would have been to know it was going to find its way to its rightful owner at last.

He snapped the lid shut and put the box

back in the drawer, then went back down to the kitchen, finding the teapot, making the tea, putting chocolate digestives on a plate.

When he came back out, ten minutes later, he found Claire curled up on the blanket, fast asleep in the sunshine. He put the tray on the grass and sat down next to her. A few minutes later, he too was fast asleep.

It had been a long weekend.